FIREBORN

FIREBORN SERIES BOOK THREE

VANESSA RICCI-THODE

THODESTOOL FICTION

Copyright © 2023 Vanessa Ricci-Thode
Published by Thodestool Fiction
Waterloo ON

All rights reserved. No part of this publication may be reproduced, stored in a retrieval system or transmitted, in any form or by any means, electronic, mechanical, recording or otherwise (except brief passages for purposes of review) without the prior permission of the author or a licence from The Canadian Copyright Licensing Agency (Access Copyright).

Without in any way limiting the author's exclusive rights under copyright, any use of this publication to "train" generative artificial intelligence (AI) technologies to generate text is expressly prohibited. The author reserves all rights to license uses of this work for generative AI training and development of machine learning language models.

Publisher: Vanessa Ricci-Thode
Editors: Kristopher Mielke, Una Verdandi
Cover Designed by GetCovers

Library and Archives Canada Cataloguing in Publication

Print ISBN 978-1-7388450-4-0
Ebook ISBN 978-1-7388450-5-7

www.thodestool.ca

This is a first edition of *Fireborn*.

For all the good dogs (they're all good dogs).

AUTHOR'S NOTE

Hello reader! This is the third book of the Fireborn series. If you're skipping book one and/or two or it's been a while, below is a spoiler-filled synopsis to get you caught up or to act as a refresher! Also note that Canadian spelling is being used throughout the book.

Previously in the Fireborn Series

Dragon Whisperer

Dionelle was born immune to fire. After moving to her new husband's farm, she catches the attention of the ruling nobles in the city. Forced into the position of dragon whisperer by the cruel Lord Draxli and Lady Karth Dunham, Dionelle is torn between keeping the peace in her kingdom and keeping her husband, Reiser's, desire to keep her safe from controlling her. Tension mounts between the newlyweds as Dionelle grows to love her job and the dragons she works with, exacerbated by her sister's jealous rage.

Then Dionelle fails to come home from her final apprenticing lesson. Discovering her mentor has been murdered, Reiser is pulled into the mystery of her disappearance and the snare of politics surrounding Pasdale's corrupt ruling nobles.

Reiser has no choice but to work with the dragons to find his wife, going against the Dunhams' wishes as they try to write Dionelle off for dead so they can select a new dragon whisperer. The dragons, however, will not be lied to—particularly the black dragoness who leads the local blaze and has grown fond of Dionelle. Enlisting Dionelle's best friend, a dragon scholar named Ondias, and finding allyship from two court wizards, Zev and Nandara, Reiser discovers that Dionelle's sister has manipulated a powerful wizard into murdering her mentor and banishing Dionelle to the fire realm. Dionelle's unique pyromantic nature is due to being part fire demon, allowing her to survive the fire realm. Taken by fire demons, Dionelle is trapped in their realm behind a wall of deceit exploiting the troubles in her life.

Meanwhile, the presence of a human in the fire realm is throwing all of the elements off balance, and the world is slowly tearing itself apart with wild weather swings and dangerous earthquakes.

In a desperate bid to save Dionelle and the world, Reiser becomes the first human to visit the dragon city—a towering structure of diamond and obsidian suspended over a valley—where he is enchanted to be fireproof and sent to the fire realm. He discovers Dionelle is alive and well—and pregnant. He uses the tenuous bond the pair forged before their separation to bring her home again. The elements stabilize, and Dionelle and Ondias are treated with a trip to the dragon city when Reiser is brought back there to remove the enchantment.

The story ends with the Dunhams removed from power: Draxli exiled and Karth executed. Dionelle's sister is imprisoned in a distant sanitorium. The king's cousin, Lady Zyx, is installed as the new ruler of Pasdale and peace returns to the land.

Trueflame

Neesha, Dionelle's nearly adult daughter, is determined to be as unlike her mother as possible, despite also being part fire demon. She's a talented pyromancer intent on gaining entrance to the Wizards Guild and shunning every attempt to bridle her with marriage. An unplanned pregnancy throws a wrench in her plans, leaving her with an impossible deadline to pass her Guild exams before motherhood sidelines her.

And still her parents are desperately trying to get her married, with their most recent attempts concentrated on a recently widowed farmer named Stone.

Neesha bristles against the new attempts to control her life, even as she alienates herself from her family. But Dionelle needs Neesha to tame her wild ways because Draxli Dunham has allied himself with a powerful aquamancer named Loch and a handful of traitor dragons, and he is coming to reclaim Pasdale and satisfy his vendetta against the Joasera family.

Terrified, Neesha works with Dionelle and the dragons to mount a defense against Draxli's attack. Neesha is permitted temporary entrance into the Guild in order to use her magic to defend Pasdale. She uses her power and the help of demons to open a portal to the fire realm and wield trueflame against the flood Loch has made for Draxli. She vaporizes the waters, saving Pasdale.

But her allies quickly learn that Draxli's real target has been the dragon city. They race to defend it, but do not get there in time, staging only the beginning of a defense before the waters wash away one of the support columns and the dragon city falls.

In the depths of mourning, Neesha convinces her mother and the other wizards that the only way to win is for her to go to the fire realm so they can capitalize on the destabilized elements and use any demons and trueflame she can send back. The plan works, but Neesha is unable to control the fire demons, who run wild while Neesha goes into labour in the dragon chamber of the Wizards Guild. Her daughter, who she names Mita, is fireborn like Neesha and Dionelle.

Now that Neesha's risks no longer endanger Mita directly, she uses the fire realm again to rush to Pasdale, commanding dragons, demons, and trueflame until she and the black dragoness finally push back Draxli's forces and end him for good. But Neesha's spirit is lost to the flame. She is preserved in a magical coma in the remnants of the dragon city, while Dionelle has gone silent in her mourning.

Content warnings for Fireborn: burns, death by dragon, death by fire, death of a child, demon possession, imprisonment, kidnapping, the dog lives

Heat level: low

CHAPTER ONE

Spark Joasera had less than an hour to find a present for her cousin's birthday, and every shiny thing in the market called out to her. Most were inaccessible, either because of price or vendors who refused to serve her family. Spark eyed the tables strewn with bright fabric or glittering baubles, jars of spices, delicate herbs hanging from poles, fine cuts of meat, the baskets of fresh produce—both basic staples and rarities grown under glass domes—and the very best baked goods, piles of cakes, breads, buns, and pastries, the rich scents making her wish they weren't rushing to pick up a few last-minute items before heading home to make Bren's birthday dinner. But she didn't look at the merchants. She trudged along behind her grandmother, who knew all the most delicate intricacies of local politics.

She knew who was safe.

Nanny Di led her deeper into the maze of tables and tents, passed a blacksmith with blades Spark dearly wanted to linger over, to admire the workmanship and wonder how she'd improve it. But even the tiniest dagger, little more than a decoration, was far beyond her means.

Spark paused beyond the blacksmith's corner and opened up her coin purse. She sighed and rushed to catch up with Nanny, who hadn't noticed her stop.

"Nanny, do you think any of the blacksmiths would take me as an apprentice—"

Nanny jerked to a halt and gave Spark a wide-eyed look over her shoulder.

"Come on, there's got to be one of them who will see the benefit of a fireproof assistant."

Nanny blinked once, her jaw tight. She shook her head and kept going, Spark hurrying to keep up.

"Not one? There's got to be one! Nanny, we need the money."

Nanny shook her head again but wouldn't even look at Spark now. It was always like this when Spark brought up finding something outside of their homestead for her to do. Not that she really needed an apprenticeship, the quality of her work was already outstanding. Didn't matter how brilliant she was if everyone would rather see her wares reduced to slag than buy them.

And she already had an apprenticeship with Nanny's friend Nandara, learning more about magic so she could become a full member of the Wizards Guild. She'd been a member under the specialist tiers for pyromancy since she was twelve, the earliest they'd let her take the exam—making her the youngest member to date—but full membership would allow her greater options.

Well, it would if anyone would so much as look at her, let alone talk to her or work with her.

She was sixteen, and recently done school, and she needed *something* to do with herself other than study magic. Her grandfather insisted they didn't need the money and that she was more help out in the fields with him, but she didn't want to be a farmer. She needed more.

But it took all of them to keep the farm running, now that they didn't get outside help. She couldn't bear the thought of letting them down, so she sighed and continued trudging through the market behind Nanny.

Nanny gathered a few quick supplies from locals before heading to the travelling caravans. Unlike locals, these people talked with them, were friendly, and gave them fair prices without any haggling. Of course, Nanny haggled anyway, which was a delight for Spark to watch.

This time, it was with an academic Nanny knew. She found a book she wanted, something out of the dragon city judging by the way it was quickly wrapped up and tucked out of sight. Nanny always looked for new information about the dragons, things from far flung places, or the scholars studying them in the dragon city itself. Information untainted by Magistrate Loch's twisted words.

The academic gave Nanny the price: ten pennies. Nanny raised an eyebrow and didn't move, scrutinizing the man. He smiled shrewdly and offered her nine pennies. The corners of Nanny's lips flickered up, and she counted out six pennies in front of him. He offered her eight. Nanny remained silent as the hills. And so it went until the man chuckled, rolled his eyes, and took the six pennies.

While he spoke to Nanny, Spark heard familiar derisive laughter from a few tables over. She tried to ignore it but her traitor gaze landed on the group of whispering girls watching her and Nanny. Sight of their ringleader nearly made Spark's heart stop.

Janny with the glossy black hair that swayed down to her waist. Janny who more floated than walked. Janny who had always stayed out of the gossip, who had been almost kind to Spark, right up until a few weeks before school ended. Spark's stomach twisted. Janny used to make her stomach fizzy, but now it felt like the fizz was on fire.

"And this is Mita, is it?" The man glanced at Spark, and she refocused on the conversation.

The nickname had been well earned, but Spark's mother had named her Mita after the patron saint of dragons.

"Hello, sir."

"You look so much like your mother." He smiled.

"Um, thanks."

Having never seen an image of Neesha as an adult, she had no idea if this was a compliment or not. But Nanny smiled, even if her eyes were sad. Spark got one side of her mouth to curl up.

Spark had seen an old portrait of Nanny from the days before she married Pappy, when Nanny's power had been different, and she'd been almost as white as Spark. Spark was like snow in the moonlight, her skin and hair so white it nearly shone. Her eyes were rich liquid fire, amber through and through. Nanny was still thin as a whip, but her hair—shot through with silver—was rich and dark like coffee, pulled into a tight braid. Nanny's blue eyes held a flash of fire now and then, but the physical manifestation of her power had faded.

Nanny's smile drooped at the corners. She ran her fingers through the tangle of short hair that Spark kept shorn down like a little sheep then wrapped one arm around Spark in a side-hug, upset as she often was at the mention of Neesha.

Nanny Di got a face full of chest when she hugged Spark, not that Spark was particularly well endowed in that regard. She was broad like her grandfather but lean like her grandmother, and the tallness, well maybe that came from her father. Spark didn't know anything about him. None of them did. But her height together with the fireborn complexion she'd inherited from her mother left Spark looking like a long piece of parchment.

The man slid out from behind his table to give Nanny a hug, but Spark noticed him slipping a scroll to Nanny as he did. She wondered who it was from. Someone in the dragon city, likely Nanny's best friend, Ondias. From what Spark overheard from the adults, Nanny sometimes got messages from actual dragons. She didn't know why, but it made her uncomfortable.

Spark had met dragons, long ago before she'd started school, and had only the vaguest remembrance of it. Fuzzy portraits of memory, like scenes from long ago dreams. They didn't seem real—no one saw dragons anymore. Not in Pasdale. Not wild dragons. Rarely captive ones, either.

Nanny slipped the message into her pocket so quickly Spark wouldn't have noticed if she didn't already know about the practice. It was no danger to Nanny—at least no more than she already faced—for her to receive the banned messages from her friends in the dragon city, but any merchants found passing her the scrolls would face sanctions.

When there were enough wizards out in the dragon city, they magicked their messages to Nanny and saved the merchants the trouble.

Nanny smiled at the man, a hand over her heart. She gave him a quick wave, and then motioned with her head for Spark to follow her. They continued on, Nanny collecting another book at another vendor, this one not someone she knew.

And then Spark saw it. A whole cart full of rubbish metal scraps. It was perfect. She snagged Nanny's cloak to stop her before she bustled on past.

It was a tinker's cart, of course. He had all manner of wonderful things that weren't broken trash that other people were more interested in. But Spark wanted to take his entire junk pile with her. Just give him her soul for the cart. She had only a few pennies, whatever Uncle Breen had been able to spare. She hoped it would do.

Nanny's hand fell on Spark's shoulder, breaking her reverie. Nanny had her head tilted to one side, a half smile as she appraised Spark. She raised one eyebrow.

"Yes, for Bren, I know. But I can make him something." Spark buzzed with an even better idea. "I can *show him* how to make something. We can make it together. Nanny, it's perfect!"

Nanny's smile grew and her hand moved from Spark's shoulder to her face. She gestured toward the cart, and Spark bounced over and started poking through the pieces. Couldn't take it all, so she had to find something *just right*.

The tinker chatted idly with Spark while she looked through his supplies.

"Anything I can help you with?" he asked.

"I'll know when I see it." She smiled politely, hoping it would signal to him that she knew what she was doing. Sometimes they didn't trust her. She wasn't the only girl who could handle a forge, but it was rare enough she usually had to explain herself.

This tinker, thankfully, held out his hands in a placating gesture and let her look. Bent utensils, half a pitchfork, the corner of a plow, a dull axe blade. And then she found two matching scrap iron rods. Despite bartering, they cost all her pennies, and she was certain the tinker gave them to her out of pity. She hadn't been able to hide the grin when she found them.

She tucked them into Nanny Di's pack and they continued on.

"Di! Spark! Wait."

They'd reached the edge of the city, but Spark recognized the voice and stopped immediately. Nandara, a powerful elemental wizard and Spark's mentor, rushed toward them. Spark had a lesson with her yesterday and was surprised to see her again so soon. Nandara's greying blonde hair flared out behind her as she strode forward, green eyes flashing. Her grey wizarding robes billowed around her medium build, and she stopped in front of them, a bit taller than Nanny but nowhere near as tall as Spark.

"What a relief to catch you. I thought I'd have to make the trip out to you." Her pale cheeks flushed pink from the rush to catch up with them. She touched Nanny's shoulder, then smiled at Spark. "How are you today?"

"It's just always the same."

This response usually drew a smile from Nandara, but the smile already on her face froze and her eyes scrunched.

"I haven't got a lot of time right now, but I'd like you to come by tomorrow so we can finish up with your apprenticeship."

"Finish?" Spark's mouth fell open. She should have at least two more years of intense study. Nandara couldn't possibly be thinking of putting her through her full Guild exams already. She'd never pass.

"I'm sorry, Spark. We'll need to go through some things so I can get you set to finish your studies on your own. With Dionelle's oversight of course."

"But..." Spark shook her head and appealed to Nanny, who stared at Nandara, her head tilted, with an expectant look on her face.

"I know this is sudden, but Riz finally agrees that it's time to go."

Riz was Nandara's husband, recently retired from Loch's court. Nandara was a court wizard but had been slowly reducing her role for years. She had been teaching Spark almost as long as Nanny had, though the family couldn't pay her.

Spark helped Nandara with chores as much as she could to try to make it even. Nandara had mentored Spark's mother, too, and Pappy said she'd have mentored Spark for nothing even if they had the money to pay her. Not just out of loyalty, but because she felt guilty that she hadn't fully prepared Neesha for the battles that eventually consumed her.

"We're packing now," Nandara said. "We plan to leave first thing in the morning come week's end. We leave for the Guild first. I've got some business there. We want to visit Sharanda, but we'll eventually make our way to the dragon city to be with Jatten. We want to get there while the mountains are still passable. It's a little late for that, of course, but Riz thinks the new king will have some ridiculous travel taxes. He wants to be beyond the reach of Golden Hill before that happens."

Spark shook her head through the explanation, not liking any of it for an instant. Nandara was their connection to the world outside. The only friend they had left. So many of their friends had left Pasdale ages ago to be closer to the dragons or farther from Magistrate Loch—or both.

Nanny was far too still and her face was pinched, her jaw clenched, like she'd stepped on a sharp rock and was stifling a cry. She nodded so slowly and shallowly it was nearly imperceptible.

Spark tried to parse what Nandara said, trying to find what had Nanny so troubled. The adults often spoke in code. The words themselves weren't alarming, but the concern in each woman's face and the intensity of Nandara's quiet voice said more than Spark would ever know.

The new king in Golden Hill had been there for nearly a moon, she'd heard, but the news travelled to Pasdale slowly and they'd only known for a week. But the adults spoke about it plenty. Always with these looks and strange undertones.

Lost in thought and watching wagons clatter past, Spark missed some of what Nandara said until a hushed warning caught her attention.

"—will be dangerous. We can't wait. I'm so sorry. You really should make plans too."

Nandara noticed Spark watching them and forced a smile, turning her attention.

"Why don't you come with me? I can continue your lessons, and you can see the Guild. They'd be delighted to have you back."

Spark started to correct her, that she'd never been to the Wizards Guild, before she remembered. It had been a long time since anyone had mentioned, but Spark was born there. In the dragon chamber, if Pappy's wine-fuelled evening tales were to be believed.

"Then you don't have to cut your studies short," Nandara continued. "You can meet some other wizards, learn things that books and Di's kitchen can never teach you. See the dragon city. There are plenty of other apprentices there, from all sorts of trades, some of them your age or nearly so, like my grandson. Do you remember the dragon city?"

Spark shook her head. Like the dragons themselves, it was merely a vague notion. One that made little sense. She couldn't tell what was real memory and what was pure fancy wrought by story and imagination.

This wasn't the first time Nandara had tried, with Nanny's acquiescence, to convince Spark to come with her on her travels. Sometimes they talked about Spark going to live with Nanny's extended family to the south beyond Pasdale. This felt different. Spark wasn't sure if it was because Nandara was leaving for good. If Spark went, how would she get back? The dragon city was half the world away. And even if she knew the things Loch said about dragons were lies, the uncertainty and fear were hard to let go of. Especially when she couldn't properly remember dragons.

The two iron rods poked out of Nanny's bag, and Spark's stomach felt like it was full of ice. The thought of leaving filled her with dread. She didn't want Nandara to go. Nothing about this seemed right. But this was something different, something more. Maybe something she needed?

"Do I have to decide right now?"

"Of course not, dear. You've got a few days until I go. We can talk about it more tomorrow."

Nandara smiled, but it didn't reach her eyes. Spark had never seen her look so sad, not even the one time Nandara had spoken of Neesha. Nandara folded Spark into her arms and hugged her so tightly Spark thought she might try to carry her off with her to the Red Mountains. She embraced Nanny for even longer.

"I won't keep you. Give Bren my wishes."

The crowds on the streets swallowed Nandara, and Nanny continued walking out into the plains, Spark trailing her. They passed by one of the smoke-belching mills on the edge of the city, and Spark glared at it the whole way. The mills were a new addition, sprung up like squat ugly toadstools, a blight on the farmland in the valley. Spark always wanted to blast the fires out of those great furnaces and bring the buildings to ruin. She couldn't account for why. Nanny hated them too. It was in the way her jaw tightened when they went by. But eventually, Nanny slumped, her head bowed and gaze focused on the ground ahead of them.

Spark couldn't stop watching her grandmother. She couldn't remember ever seeing her so sad, not even when people brought up Neesha. The tragic loss of her daughter distressed her beyond words, but the loss of the dragons that followed so swiftly afterward compounded her grief. They still lived out in the mountains but didn't come anywhere near Pasdale anymore, not when so many of them had been captured and forced into the mills.

Spark's attention was divided between concern for Nanny and trying to work out how she would finish her studies with Nandara and still find time to get the forge ready to make something with Bren. She didn't think she could do anything to make Nanny feel better since the dragons couldn't be helped. And it was safer not to let her thoughts stray down that path. She had her family and that had to be enough. They had a birthday party to prepare for.

Spark's boots slapped the cold ground as she barrelled toward the family farm at the northern end of the valley, trying to outwalk her thoughts. Spark half wanted to run, sometimes wished she could fly like Nanny's dragons.

Would Spark be able to work if she left? There'd be more lessons, but that wouldn't be her whole day. Could she put her blacksmithing to good use? Could she sneak money home to Nanny through the merchants the way Ondias snuck messages? This brought a smile to her face, however fleeting.

She was mentally composing a list of questions to ask Nandara tomorrow, all the while telling herself leaving was madness. There was nothing for her in Pasdale. And there was everything.

There was her family. Her cousin Bren and Uncle Breen and Nanny Di and Pappy. Like there had always been.

The homestead came into view—the two family homes, the barn, the little outbuildings. The old wooden house was falling into disrepair without the money to fix it, but it held solid against the elements. Bren and Uncle Breen lived there while Spark lived in the newer stone house with her grandparents and—until six seasons ago—her great-grandmother.

Spark sighed. Her insides felt heavy at the thought of Granny Sharice, who had been bright and joyous as always at dinner one night and then hadn't woken up the next day. Spark had already gone to school. Granny was shrouded and brought to the temple for her pyre by the time Spark got home. And now Nandara was leaving.

With every loss, her world contracted.

She looked again to the farm and the pair of houses, of everything she had. She smiled when she spotted her dog, Shadow, sitting sentinel on the porch, watching their approach. He was a white and black fireswift shepherd, not that they had any sheep left for him to herd, only the cart-horses who paid him no mind and the chickens who scattered at the first hint of him.

She whistled and he barked in response, launching himself off the porch, clearing the stairs in a leap, and racing down the dusty lane toward her and Nanny. Shadow ran a few circles around the two of them, Nanny grinning as he did, before he stopped and leaned against Spark's legs for scritches. She knelt and buried her face in his thick, soft fur until her worries melted and she followed Nanny into the house.

Through years of practiced grace, Spark and Nanny moved around each other, wordlessly preparing dinner while Shadow wove his way between them, waiting to catch any scraps that fell.

The back door clattered when Bren burst into the house, his boyish enthusiasm filling the room. He and Uncle Breen and Pappy all looked so much alike with their easy grins, olive complexions and barrel-chested builds, but Bren's youth shone through the mischief in his brown eyes. Shadow darted over to greet him, licking his hands.

"Hi Spark! Guess what—I picked twelve bushels of apples today!"

Spark smiled. "New record! You'll get the whole orchard done in a day before you know it."

It was too bad Spark and Bren weren't closer in age. They were lucky as it was that only five years separated them. Uncle Breen's betrothal to a noblewoman fell apart months after Spark was born. He'd found another match, this one a lovely milkmaid who didn't care about the rumours swirling around the fireborn Joasera women. Spark barely remembered her, only the vaguest notion of golden hair and warm kindness.

Spark sat with Bren, and Shadow curled up at her feet.

"How was the market? Anything good?"

"Oh, you know, the same." She leaned in conspiratorially. "Nanny got a secret message."

Spark wanted to keep her tinker prize a secret until after dinner, but remembered Nandara's news. Something must have bled through in her expression because Bren pounced on it.

"What else? Was someone mean? If it was that girl again I'm going to find where she lives and throw—"

"No, no. Just some news from Nandara. She's travelling soon."

"Oh! That's fun." Bren grinned and leaned forward. "Is she going somewhere warm for the winter? That would be neat! Do you think we can go south to see Nanny's family?"

He meant Uncle Bly and Great Uncle Cusec, who had moved their families after things started going poorly for them in Pasdale. Far enough south that people didn't mind dragons or people who liked dragons. But also far enough south that they hadn't been to visit since Bren was maybe five years old.

"What's it like?" He bounced in his seat, hands tapping against his knees.

Spark sank deeper into her chair and told him what she could remember, grateful for a distraction from Nandara and the choices laid at Spark's feet.

"That sounds amazing!" Bren said upon hearing how lushly green everything was. And hot. "No winter at all? I'd love that."

Spark was pretty sure he mostly loved that it was so close to more family and people who didn't give a heap of dragon dung who they were. She expected he'd leave and join them as soon as he was old enough to go on his own.

A knock on the door jamb caused Shadow to yip, and Spark turned to see Nanny watching them. She gestured to the kitchen.

"Why don't you sit with Bren and rest? I can manage dinner." Spark ushered Nanny into the parlour.

Nanny smiled encouragingly at the boy, and he spilled out everything he'd done that day, every last ear of corn he'd brought in and every last bushel of apples he'd helped store. Pappy was out feeding the horses and sent Bren in early, letting him have a break for his birthday.

Spark occasionally got up to stir the boiling corn and the spare soup Nanny had made. Spark preferred a good thick stew, but Bren loved the notion of a hearty meal made from whatever was left in the icebox and the spare bits in the pantry. They'd humour him today. There was candy too, hidden in the cupboard.

It was another hour until sundown, but Spark hoped Uncle Breen wouldn't be too long. He worked in the city, shovelling filth for pennies. His employers weren't necessarily cruel—he was far enough removed from his fireborn kin, especially in appearance and power, that he was spared harsher treatment. But they were not as kind as they could be.

When Spark returned to the parlour, Bren was telling Nanny about what he planned to do after dinner, depending, of course, on what his gifts were.

"Oh, maybe if I get a slingshot I can practice in the front lane for a bit. Spark can make me a fire to see by?" He glanced hopefully in Spark's direction. "Oh, or maybe I'll get some swords?" He blinked. "But there's no one to play with. So maybe I can teach Shadow to hold a sword in his mouth?"

Heavy boots thudded on the porch, Shadow barked in earnest, and both Pappy and Uncle Breen pushed in the front door, chatting idly.

"Pa!" Bren hurled himself across the room at his father. And the story of his day started again. Spark shared a grin with Nanny.

"I'll go finish dinner."

Spark cradled the roasting pan in her hands and focused. She was getting good at this kind of control, having practiced first on toolmaking in Pappy's forge. Now she was refining it in the kitchen. Her hands glowed. She shook the pan to make sure its contents heated evenly.

She barely noticed Nanny come in to observe until she was certain the potatoes were cooked and let her attention wander. Nanny stood to the side, nodding slowly. Shadow sat next to her, rapt, rooting for her to drop the whole pan. Nanny took the lid off using a tea towel. She was impervious to the flame itself, but felt the pain of heat all the same. Nanny jabbed at the potatoes and smiled.

Spark grinned. She had to keep her skills fresh. And when she could cook meals in seconds, she could make things easier for all of them.

While Pappy set out plates and cutlery, Spark and Nanny carried food out to the table. Uncle Breen was still hearing about Bren's day.

"And what about you?" Uncle asked as Spark sat down.

"It was the same as always," Spark said with a wan smile.

"And ain't that a blessing," he said.

Bren quietly stared down at the tabletop, but the adults nodded in agreement. Nothing changed and that kept them all safe.

"This is the best soup you've ever done!" Bren said between mouthfuls.

Nanny's eyes twinkled, a flicker of amber chasing itself around her irises. Spark wondered how many bowls Bren would eat today. Four maybe. Often it was five, but he'd want to save room for all the treats after dinner.

Spark dug into her bowl and the fresh warm bread, pleased with the potatoes she'd managed to get perfect. She slipped some bread crust to Shadow under the table, let a chunk of meat fall to him. Then she sat and absorbed the comfortable silence, letting it shroud her like her favourite blanket. The sound of five souls at peace.

Did she really want to leave this behind?

Bren's spoon dropped into his bowl, still half full. The clatter startled her. Shadow trotted out from under the table with his ears pointing up, looking at the boy. Bren stared forward, his lip trembling and a bright sheen of tears glistening in his dark eyes.

"Son, is everything okay?"

"Why is it always just us? Why does this have to be it?"

A hot lump fell into Spark's stomach, congealing around her meal. Family was enough for Spark, but Bren liked people and didn't understand why they couldn't like him because of something his aunt may have done so many years ago. Something his nanny used to do, ages ago. As if dragons were really so bad!

Uncle tried convincing Bren that their small family was enough. Bren shook his head, tears streaking down his cheeks. He wiped them on his sleeve, sniffling.

"But it's not! No one plays with me. I don't like the fields, even if it's better than school. And school was fine anyway, it was everyone else there that was the problem. I just want some friends."

He flopped forward, resting his head in his arms. Great sobs shuddered through his body. The weight of his sadness pressed Spark deeper into her chair. The adults all sagged with her, Pappy rubbing Bren's back.

"You've got friends in us," Pappy said. "What do friends have that we can't provide?"

"I want someone to play swords with me," Bren whimpered.

Spark glanced to Nanny, who had always been the one to play with Spark when she was a girl. But Nanny's head was bowed, her eyes not seeing. Uncle and Pappy had to work long hours. Uncle's job outside of the house was the only source of income now that no one paid Nanny for her magic.

"I can play swords with you," Spark said.

Bren looked up with an expression of such pathetic hope that Spark knew she couldn't break this promise.

"But I don't even have swords."

"Well, you have sticks, they're good enough for now." Spark was already out of her seat and rummaging through Nanny's pack by the door. She laid the two lengths of iron next to Bren's abandoned bowl of soup. "And if your skill proves worthy and you don't burn down the whole forge, we'll have real swords to play with before you know it."

She'd made a battle-axe over the summer. It was in the style of the Eastern invaders, an ancient but sturdy design, and she'd loved their swords since first laying eyes on one in a textbook. Like dragons, the Easterners' society had been ruled by women, but she'd never been able to get Bren to take an interest in it. Maybe making an Eastern sword, albeit a blunted one, was the key. They could play swords with real weapons.

Spark's heart was warmed by her cousin's happy tears as he ran his fingers over the metal, and thoughts of leaving evaporated. Bren needed her. Her family needed her. Nandara's troubling news would have to wait.

CHAPTER TWO

Spark stood in the middle of an empty stone room not much bigger than a closet, spinning a little fire in the middle of the floor until it grew into a monster funnelling up to the ceiling.

"Good," Nandara called from the other room, watching through a panel of tempered glass. "Now two."

Spark scowled at the flame, concentrating on the warm feeling rushing out her hands and trying to pull all the power sideways into two funnels. But the funnel followed the command of her right hand and nothing happened on the left side. When Spark focused on her left hand, the flame nearly vanished entirely. She flared out her power to try to catch it.

"Gah!" The entire room filled with a fireball. It devoured the oxygen, leaving Spark gasping as she pushed all that flame out of existence, like stuffing a blanket into a small box.

She'd collapsed to one knee by the time Nandara slid the stone panel aside and cool fresh air poured into the room.

Spark pounded on the floor with the side of her fist.

"It shouldn't be this difficult!" she growled and stood.

"Don't be so hard on yourself."

"Everyone hates me enough even without my lack of control. And soon you'll be gone..." Spark took a breath and scowled into a corner. "Was it this hard for my mother?"

"Not like this, no. But then again, Neesha didn't have the raw power you do. It will come. Let's work on your splicing."

Spark stood at the far edge of the room while Nandara moved beyond the threshold. She'd suggested a lesson Spark was good at to make her feel better. But it remained good practice, and this exercise was fun.

Nandara retrieved a candle and set it on the floor next to her. She reached for her flint, but Spark grinned and snapped her fingers, the candle flame leaping to life. Nandara smiled, pulled fire from the candle and gestured to make it bigger, about the size of a child's ball, floating between her hands.

She thrust it straight at Spark's face.

Spark didn't have to put a hand up anymore to split the fireball in two and shunt the halves around her. They extinguished against the wall behind her.

Nandara threw little fireballs of varying sizes at her, some of them bigger than a washtub, some of them small as marbles. Spark divided them all. When she got bored with halving them, she split them into more and more pieces until it seemed like they were exploding in front of her.

Nandara sent another large one at her, and she stuffed it away into nothing, like the funnel gone wrong earlier.

Nandara grinned. "Well done! You manage to get even better at that every time."

She snuffed out the candle and indicated with her head for Spark to follow her into the study room. The lesson was almost over and there were piles of books for Spark to take home. Spark looked at the stack Nandara set aside, trying to focus on the descriptions of them all.

"Doesn't Nanny know this?"

"Spark, you know you can't rely on her to get you all the information you need."

"She'll write it out if I need her to."

Nandara nodded slowly. "It makes me feel better to give it to you."

Spark watched her, how she sagged like Nanny did.

"You still want me to come with you."

"You'd learn so much."

"That's not just it."

Nandara tilted her head. "What do you mean?"

"I'm not a little girl anymore, and I see how upset you both are. Nanny was never this upset about Ondias leaving for the dragon city for good."

Nandara folded her arms around her middle.

"No, this is different." She sighed and closed her eyes.

Spark had a glimmer of hope that she could get the truth out of Nandara. But then someone hammered on the front door, and both of them startled. Nandara barely had time to start toward it before it swung inward and nearly a dozen city guards flooded into the house, all wearing brightly polished armour, cloaks in the pale blue of the magistrate.

"What do you think you're doing?" Nandara snapped, more anger pouring out of the woman than Spark thought possible.

"Apologies, m'lady, but we've orders from Magistrate Loch to collect your apprentice." Even though Nanny Di was just as powerful a wizard as Nandara, Spark had never heard so much respect as the guard directed at Nandara.

"On what grounds?"

"He is the magistrate, m'lady."

"Yes, he's certainly not the king. I demand to know his purposes or I will not release this girl."

But then a calm shape walked in behind the guards. It was Nanny, her head held high. Defiant. She nodded once to Nandara, and Nandara took a step away from the guards.

Spark stayed in the doorway, fighting the urge to run out the back and hide. She could find a good hearth to climb into, let the blaze conceal her until they gave up looking. But those men had Nanny with them, and she couldn't just leave her. And Nanny didn't look worried.

Spark swallowed and took a step forward into the room. A guard moved toward her but Nandara stormed into his path. She gestured behind her for Spark to come forward. Moving slowly, Spark joined Nandara at her side.

"Go with them," Nandara whispered, barely audible, "but stay with your grandmother. No matter what. If word reaches me that you're in danger, I will bring the full force of the Guild down on Loch."

Spark gave Nandara a wide-eyed look, trembling on wobbly legs as she staggered across the room to join Nanny Di, who reached out an arm and linked elbows with Spark. Together they marched through the city, surrounded by armed guards.

Spark was certain they'd spent the entire day in the hallway outside of the magistrate's court. In fact, she was certain they'd spend the rest of their lives there. She couldn't tell how much time had passed, but her feet hurt from pacing across the stone floor. Her stomach was tight, simultaneously empty and full of ice.

The doors flung open, startling her, and some pompous blowhard with a feathered plume in his helmet came to fetch them. There were more guards in the court room, which was more like a throne room with the raised dais where Magistrate Loch loomed in a gilded chair. Large as the chair was, it was dwarfed by the pale stork of a man with long blond hair and beard probably meant to be majestic, but stringy and lank instead. The room itself felt the way the magistrate looked—clammy and damp like it had recently rained.

Spark shivered. It was worse than the humiliating little parade through the city.

Nanny was infamous enough as the city's former dragon whisperer that she was just as recognizable as Spark. The whole city knew exactly who'd been brought by armed guard before the magistrate. Like criminals.

"You will kneel before His Lordship," the plume barked, giving Nanny a shove forward.

Spark immediately bent to comply, but Nanny grabbed her arm, glaring at the magistrate in his silly chair. Nanny stood as tall as Spark had ever seen her. A tiny mountain. One that held more power than they knew. As the plume loomed over them, likely to make them kneel whether they wanted to or not, Nanny's power flared and all the torches in the room flared with it. The air warmed and the dampness sizzled away.

Wizards positioned throughout the room aimed suppression spells at Spark and Nanny both—like heavy, stifling curtains. These were no Guild wizards, though; Nandara had been the last Guild-sanctioned wizard to work for this court. Their combined power was not enough to completely stifle Nanny, but the lights dimmed, Nanny's power fading.

Red hot rage pulsed through Spark's veins, and she stepped closer to her grandmother. Spark directed that heat back out into the room, torchlight erupting. The magistrate and his dogs had no idea what to expect from Spark. She was an unknown quantity, even to herself.

There were some clues in the things her mother had been able to do, but those secrets died with her. Nandara and Nanny had seen mere glimpses of the truth with Neesha. But Spark was not her mother. It was clear straight from her birth that she was stronger. And different. So much so that while the guards' suppression spells almost incapacitated Nanny's magic, they could not contain Spark. They were a mere inconvenience. Snowflakes in an inferno.

"Stand down," Magistrate Loch barked out, and the suppression spells rolled back, giving Nanny some breathing room. "Do not needlessly escalate. We do not know what we're dealing with with this little monster."

Nanny tensed, grinding her teeth, and Spark whirled around to look up at the dais. She clenched her jaw to hide the way her lip trembled. There were gasps from the assembled courtiers and guards, and Spark had half a second to wonder if they finally thought the magistrate had gone too far. But no, there was no empathy there. Nanny gripped her shoulder, not looking at her but a steadying reassurance all the same.

Spark lived up to her nickname. Her fury was manifest, a glittering shower raining down around her feet to bounce harmlessly to nothing on the tiled floor. It would be nothing for her to pull up a conflagration like none of them had ever seen. And she'd heard about the fire her mother had unleashed to stem the floods Loch had a hand in creating.

She could just breathe in—she saw it in her mind—just breathe in, open herself to the anger and the full force of the power inside of her and breathe it out. A dragon unlike any of them had ever known before. She could bathe this whole city in amber death. It would not touch her. It would not touch Nanny.

But she couldn't control it either. Just like her mother hadn't been able to.

Spark took a deep breath and held it all in, pulling all her fury down into her core, stomping it down like errant embers escaping a hearth.

"Keep that little beast of yours on a leash." Magistrate Loch's lip curled as he glared at Nanny.

The lights in the room flashed, a warning from Nanny, who stood tall, chin jutting. Spark stood next to her, staring forward at an empty spot in the middle of the room, breathing quick and shallow through her nose, her heart pounding. She put all of her focus into holding still, hoping it would be enough to distract her from the anger that would shower them in more embarrassment.

The silence stretched out and thickened, growing heavy, trying to press Spark down into the stone floor. But Nanny stood tall and steady, defiant but relaxed. Her gaze didn't leave the magistrate for an instant.

"Tell me, Dionelle, when are you going to see reason?" he asked.

Nanny blinked slowly. She stood firm.

"You will answer me!"

At that, Nanny's eyebrows twitched up, just a touch, but she kept her lips pressed shut. Her expression shifted, looking at the magistrate the way she sometimes did when a bit of dung got encrusted to her good boots and she was pondering the best way to scrub them clean.

Magistrate Dung. It was fitting, really. But Spark couldn't get the image out of her mind, a soggy, fetid turd up there on that gleaming chair. She clenched her jaw tighter and focused on Nanny. She could not afford to giggle.

"So you're going to keep up this charade, are you?" the magistrate said, trying to match Nanny's expression, but not quite achieving it. "Or perhaps it's not an act and you've simply lost the good sense to speak, it would explain so much. You don't have to agree with the industrial progress we have made here, but your life could be so much easier if you would cease attempting to thwart it. Enough with the petitions to the Wizards Guild. End your foolish communication with the dragon city and stand down. Your life could be so much simpler."

Nanny looked away slowly, not quite rolling her eyes as she did so, and crossed her arms. She huffed out a deep, bored sigh. Spark couldn't stop watching her but gripped her hands in front of herself to hide the trembling. Her heart beat so fast she felt lightheaded.

Why is Nanny provoking him like this?

"Have it your way." The magistrate's tone was soft, almost bored.

Nanny blinked and looked at him.

"But I see you've still got your little beastie under apprenticeship. That's an encouraging start. Is she actually going to finish? Or is Nandara going to usher the undeserving monster into the Guild like she did with Neesha? Seems you fireborn women don't think the rules apply to you."

Spark swallowed. She'd heard about how her mother, her apprenticeship incomplete, had been given temporary membership to the Guild so she could help defend Pasdale against the onslaught Loch had been a part of.

Of course, no one outside the Guild knew that part anymore. He'd reversed their roles in that battle, with Neesha as the monster and himself as the hero. When Neesha had died in the conflagration that saved the city, when she wasn't around to tell her side of the story, Loch had swept in, the hero aquamancer to push back the last of the floodwater. Champion of the people. They'd let him take over as magistrate because of it.

Spark wanted to puke.

But then she remembered something else. That Magistrate Loch, despite being a deeply talented and powerful aquamancer, had never been admitted to the Guild. The new Guild entrance rules were because of him, to keep from isolating powerful elementals and other wizards with singular focus. She wondered how badly it would sting him when she did gain full entrance. Did it burn him that she had specialist membership? She'd be sure to get her full membership the right way—just to rub it in.

Nanny stared impassively, her arms crossed.

"Seems the only reasonable thing you've done in your entire life is rescind your demon power. What about your little beast?"

"I have a n—"

"Silence!" The word came out like a slap in the face. As the magistrate shouted, the plume took a menacing step forward.

"You will speak to His Lordship only when addressed, ye ungodly beast."

"I'm not a—"

The plume advanced on her again and Spark silenced, recoiling and bumping into her grandmother. Nanny put a comforting hand on her shoulder. She glared at the magistrate.

"You denounce those flaming monsters of yours and have that little beastie recant her power, and you will see your former glory restored."

"What does he mean about my power?" Spark whispered, her words barely audible and yet somehow echoing in this horrible cavernous chamber.

Nanny looked at her askance, her jaw tight, and gave the briefest shake of her head. *Later*, that look said. Maybe Nandara would tell her what the magistrate meant. Nanny resumed glaring at him.

"Exorcise your demons, little beast, and join the rest of us in being human. No more embarrassing yourself with power you can't control. No more maimed classmates on your conscience. And no more threat to the rest of us. I think your witch of a mother did us enough damage to last several lifetimes."

Spark balled her hands into fists. He wanted her to get rid of her power? That was possible? She shook with rage, as much at the suggestion as at the notion her mother had somehow caused the city's woes since Lady Zyx was killed. Killed by Loch's flood, no less. Of course, the believed version these days was that the flood was Draxli's and that Loch had pulled it back. That Neesha's fire killed Lady Zyx, and never mind the woman had drowned.

The death of Lady Zyx had marked the end of a peaceful golden age in Pasdale, and as blame was cemented through rumour and lies, Spark's entire family had fallen into disrepute. The fire and the demons had been blamed on Neesha and the dragons. No one wanted to believe that a pyromancer could be strong enough to burn away a deluge like the one that had besieged the valley. Loch's stupid story that he'd been the one to pull back the water was easier to swallow, and no one wanted to listen to the Guild with all its evidence that Loch had been the one to actually *cause* the flood in the first place.

And so Lady Zyx's death was blamed on Neesha and the dragons who had been trying to help her. With Neesha dead, the dragons were left to bear the brunt of it. It was an easy step from there to capturing and enslaving them to drive industry. Anywhere there was opposition to this, Nanny was right in the middle of it, powerless but not voiceless as she demanded freedom for those enslaved and pardon for the remaining society of wild dragons.

Spark wanted to strangle the truth out of the magistrate. She wished her mother was alive to tell her side of that day, to display her power for all to see and set the record straight. And now Magistrate Turd wanted Spark to give up all that power, all she had left of her mother.

Borrowing Nanny's courage, Spark stood up straighter and snapped, "No," emphatically before falling defiantly silent.

"Fools, the lot of you."

Nanny raised an eyebrow, the rest of her expression unchanging. She let out another long breath. Was she bored? Spark almost wanted to get her to talk, just so they could leave. But of course nothing Nanny said would appease the magistrate. Nanny would never betray the dragons, and Spark would never give up her power.

Spark worried the silence would stretch on for eternity, that they would stand there glaring at the magistrate until they died on their feet. But Nanny whirled around and marched toward the doors.

"You will not leave until His Lordship releases you!" The plume shouted as Spark hurried to fall in stride beside Nanny. Every muscle in her back tensed, waiting for a spear to jab through her.

"How long do you think your Guild can protect you, Dionelle?" the magistrate asked, his voice glacial.

Spark shuddered. Nanny paused, breaking her stride for a fraction of a second. The flames in the room flared. The crowd parted, letting Nanny pass. Spark wished she could see Nanny's expression, expecting to see murder there, but kept her gaze trained forward as Nanny bullied through the crowd and pushed out the court room doors.

Even on the long road back to their farm, the city walls well behind them, Spark kept turning back, always surprised to find no palace guards chasing after them. There was no mob, no Magistrate Loch riding one of those horrible water serpents Spark heard about from the attack on the city that cost her mother her life.

She kept pondering his final threat, wondering what it meant. How was the Guild protecting them? Spark hadn't heard of anything from the Guild, hadn't overheard Pappy or Nandara speaking of it. Nandara was the only Guild wizard they ever saw.

More than that, what exactly was the Guild protecting them from? And what would happen when the Guild couldn't protect them anymore? How could it possibly get any worse for them—would the magistrate lock them up? If he did, what grounds could he possibly have?

Nanny's face was set in that same mask of defiance, but her pace slowed and she slumped. Spark wondered how much the confrontation and the spells she'd used had worn her down. Spark could wield fire for eternity without the barest hint of a yawn, but working other elements or other kinds of magic drained her quickly. Was pyromancy so tiring for Nanny?

"Nanny, will it be all right? What was he talking about?"

Nanny straightened and smiled at Spark. It set her at ease. Nanny was small and her power wasn't what it used to be; she was getting older, but she remained a force of nature. Spark smiled back, confident in their ability to weather the worst of it, the five them together on their little farm, as they always had.

The confidence on Nanny's face evaporated into unmitigated rage when they passed the mills. Nanny glared, her hands balled to white-knuckle fists. She stopped abruptly, her body rigid. Spark peeked around her, the textile mill drawing Nanny's ire. A dragon was being led around the side of the building.

It had been so long since Spark saw wild dragons she didn't fully remember what they looked like. The ones at the mills were such pathetic beasts, like the one drawing Nanny's attention. It was brown and dull, had been declawed, its teeth yanked out. It still had wings, but those were tightly chained at its sides.

It was unusual to see them at all. They were usually kept in the mills, never let out, there only to drive the machines with their flames. When Spark glanced to her grandmother, a block of ice dropped into her stomach. Nanny was crying.

"Nanny!" Spark put a hand on her shoulder and Nanny looked around at her, tears shining on her cheeks.

"Oh, Mita," she said, her voice soft and clear.

The cold from Spark's stomach buzzed through her body, making her fingers tingle and her scalp itch. Swifter than she should have been able to, Nanny reached out and pulled Spark into a tight hug. She held Spark by the shoulders, making her stoop so she could look Spark in the eye.

"Trust the dragons," Nanny said. Her voice was firm, like there wasn't anything more important in the whole world. Amber flickered through Nanny's blue eyes, a mirror of the fires in Spark's own strange gaze. "Their intentions are always pure. Misguided sometimes, but pure. Trust them." She gestured to the west, away from the mill. West, toward the dragon city.

Then she smiled sadly like she did when friends spoke of the great things Neesha had done in the days before she died. Nanny glanced at the mill once more and then resumed the walk home, like the whole thing never happened.

Spark blinked and shook herself, trotting to catch up.

Part of her mind tried processing what Nanny said while the other was far too distracted by the fact Nanny said anything at all. Shaking her head, Spark could only wonder if she had imagined it. And to tell her to trust the dragons? She couldn't possibly mean the beasts in the mills, but Spark couldn't fathom befriending any of the wild ones.

Sure, they'd once come to talk to Nanny all the time, according to Pappy. The same dragons who had been there when Spark was born. That was back when Nanny used to talk. When the dragons had voices too. But they'd all gone silent.

Since her mother died.

Spark linked arms with Nanny and tried to keep her head higher while they walked. Even if Nanny had said what she did, there were no dragons around. There was Nanny and Pappy, Bren and Uncle Breen. They were all that mattered.

CHAPTER THREE

As Spark finished cleaning up breakfast, Bren burst through the door, tracking filth halfway into the kitchen before a glare from Spark stopped him dead. He'd been out mucking the stables, his last chore for the day.

"Now you've got to wait while I clean that up," Spark teased.

"Aw no! C'mon, Spark, can't you clean it up after?"

"Your gift isn't going anywhere. Next time don't track your chores across mine."

Spark mopped up far slower than she had to, just to watch Bren squirm. She should have been hurrying, barely having time for chores and her studies as it was. Nandara had left for good first thing that morning, and the sheer fact of it carried all the weight of a dragon. If Spark had questions, Nanny would have to answer them. And Nanny wasn't nearly so adventurous in what she was willing to teach Spark as Nandara was.

If someone would teach her more, could she help Nanny in whatever she was doing to help the dragons? Could Spark succeed where her mother had failed?

Pushing those thoughts from her mind, Spark finished cleaning. The rest of the day was about Bren. As he waited for her, his grin threatened to split his face. Spark made a show of slowly putting her things away. Bren bounced on the balls of his feet in the doorway.

"All right," she said.

He dashed out the door, charging straight to the forge behind the barn. Spark sauntered out while Bren called to her from the door, trying to get her to move faster. Shadow came trotting over to see what all the fuss was about, but tottered off when Spark reached Bren. The dog had no use for the heat and noise of the place.

It was all cool and quiet, but it wouldn't take Spark long to change that. She laid her tools out on the anvil, quizzing him on the use of each.

"And that's the hammer for smashing things."

Spark gave him sideways look. "Less smashing than you think. You're probably going to have to use two hands on the hammer, but if you do, I'll hold the metal. You can take a turn holding, just to get a feel for it, if that's what it comes to."

"Holy wow! This is the best birthday gift ever!"

Bren hopped around the room, pumping his fists into the air and whooping. Spark caught hold of him and stuffed him into the apron and gloves. Neither were hers and both were comically large on the boy, as they belonged to Pappy who was a full head and shoulders taller than Bren.

"I'm going to light the fire, so you've got to stay back and take care."

Bren bounced in one spot and that was the best she'd get out of him until they started work and he had more to focus his attention on. She quizzed him on how to properly start the fire and how to use the bellows. They were old and in disrepair, but it was important for him to understand the concept. While he recited what he knew, Spark crouched in front of the forge.

With her outstretched hands beginning to tingle, she called up her power and released it into the cold coal, a familiar *whoosh* wafting them with heat. Then it was only a matter of focusing her will to make it hotter. She reached her hand in, increased the heat, and then stood back. It wasn't much pyromancy, but enough to cool the room noticeably, like a sudden breeze.

Spark didn't use excessive pyromancy in the house, worried she'd freeze everyone. Nandara told her once about how Neesha's pyromancy hadn't cooled the air when she'd drawn power directly from the fire realm. But Spark shoved those thoughts away, unwilling to consider the fire realm right along with the growing list of absentee adults.

"Now, if I weren't here, how would you know when the fire is ready?"

Bren opened his mouth, blinked, shut it. "Ask Pappy?"

Spark laughed and grabbed her metal rod, driving it into the fire. She nodded to Bren, who picked up the tongs to do the same with his. She let him tell her when the metal was ready, giving him a couple of hints.

He was focused, his childish exuberance channelled into the work, making him look older. She envisioned the man he would be some day, handsome and intense. He was so still she barely recognized him. He pulled his piece out a fraction before Spark did hers and set it on the anvil. She corrected his grip on the hammer and let him go. She worked at her metal, and he mirrored her actions. A season ago she doubted he'd be able to wield the hammer with enough power, but the summer out in the field with Pappy had toughened him.

And so they worked side by side for the whole morning, Bren shadowing everything Spark did, but only to start. Once he had a feel for it, he shaped the metal on his own. The end result was that his blade was longer and narrower than hers.

She took him over to the work table to get the pommel ready. Once they finished, he looked longingly to the sharpening stone.

"Not a chance," Spark said through merry laughter. "You can have a sharp sword when you can prove you're not going to skewer someone with it, least of all yourself."

He pretended to pout, but then drew his blade, forcing Spark to parry with hers. She reined him in long enough to help her tidy up, and then they were slashing at each other in the yard between buildings. Shadow ran over, running a circle around them, barking all the while. He'd dart into a gap between them only to leap away again, joining in their poorly choreographed battle.

By the time Nanny whistled them in for dinner, Spark's sides hurt so much from laughing, she kept checking to make sure Bren hadn't managed to get her with his sword. It was only once her attention turned back to the house that she remembered all the work left inside for her.

She sighed.

The stone house, she had learned, was necessary when her mother was younger, when tempers flared and fires followed. There hadn't been any of that when Spark was growing up. Fires ran rampant, sure, but not from anger. Nanny had been a patient mentor, breezily putting out Spark's little blazes with a wave of her hand. As the only other soul in their family able to withstand fire, Nanny Di had been Spark's most dedicated companion as she learned to control her magic.

Despite Nanny's decades of service to Pasdale, the court never called on her anymore, even out of desperation. An entire outlying neighbourhood burned to the ground in the summer's drought, and Nanny could have stopped the fire before it claimed a second house. But everyone would rather watch their lives burn than trust in the power of any fireborn.

Nanny and Pappy had never said anything about it, but Spark had heard rumours that the unique power she, her mother, and grandmother wielded had come from demons. She couldn't see how, had never seen an elemental demon in her life, but that didn't stop the rumours or the hate that followed them.

Spark had no shortage of power, but she didn't get much opportunity to put it to good use. No one in the valley was interested in Spark's power. She shook her head and went into the house. Today, she would just enjoy time with her family.

The evening was rich and warm, and the family took their chairs out on the porch to enjoy the lingering traces of summer as they ate. Spark took a moment to roast the rabbit and vegetables Nanny had set out earlier in the day. That done, she heaped it onto plates, which she brought out, two at a time, serving Nanny and Pappy first, then Bren and Uncle. She brought her own plate out last and leaned on the railing, watching out into the mountains in the west, wondering if there was any adventure out there, wondering where Nandara was.

She'd barely got a start on her meal when Bren left his empty plate in his seat and darted out into the front lane, sword in hand. He slayed imaginary demons, and Spark was happy to watch him. The adults had goofy smiles on their faces.

His form with the sword was terrible, but what he lacked in grace he made up for in enthusiasm. It made Spark wonder if he'd ever had a single lesson in his life. She had no use for weapons at all but could wield her sword with infinitely more poise. And she'd gotten good at handling her axe. She had it out, resting near the front door, so she could see how it fared against Bren's sword once she finished eating.

"You kids get some play in while you can," Pappy called. "We'll need to head out into the orchard and use up the last of the daylight on those apples."

The weather was fine this evening but that meant it would be all the worse if there was a sudden cold snap. The trees in their orchard were young, all of them planted since Nanny moved to Pasdale, but they'd give the family a season's worth of apples.

Spark finished up her meal and brought her dish and Bren's into the kitchen. She passed Uncle in the doorway with a stack of dishes as well. Pappy was already halfway to the orchard.

Nanny smiled after him, her eyes shining. She nodded toward Bren when Spark came out.

"Yeah, just a few minutes. Lots to be done."

Nanny shrugged, watching Spark pick up the axe. Spark reached the bottom of the stairs when a shrill cry split the air from the direction of the city. Her shoulders came up around her ears, and she nearly dropped the axe. Nanny was on her feet in an instant, running down the stairs and out around the side of the house. Her eyes widened with shock but her mouth curled up in what could have been joy.

Shadow, who had been napping on the porch, started squealing out a high-pitched whine Spark wouldn't have thought possible for a dog. The cry came again, louder this time, and Spark winced against it. Shadow leapt down the stairs and disappeared into the crop fields.

Nanny was around the house, visible in profile. She stilled entirely for a beat. Her mouth fell open and her hands balled into fists. Back stiff, eyes fixed on the distance, she spun her hands, calling up a summoning spell, a swirling column of light that vanished skyward.

Before Spark wondered who she could possibly summon, Nanny ran to the house, her face twisted in horror.

"Nanny? What's going on?"

Nanny caught hold of Bren's arm on her way past and dragged him up the stairs with her as she went.

"Nanny!" he shouted. "You're hurting me."

"Dragons—hide!" Nanny said.

Spark and Bren both stopped. The sound of her voice shocked Spark, even if she'd heard it recently. But Bren's mouth fell open and he stared, not heeding the words.

"Ma? What is it?" Uncle asked, coming out to the porch.

"She said there's dragons," Spark said.

"May the spirits save us," he whispered, face blanching. "Get Pa," he said to Nanny. "I'll get these two into the cellar."

Uncle grabbed Bren by the shoulders and motioned for Spark to follow.

"She's talking," Bren said.

"Uncle, why are dragons bad?" Spark asked.

"If she's this upset, they're not her friends," Uncle Breen said. "Now downstairs, quickly."

"But Pa, why is she talking?"

Uncle held firm to Bren and dragged him down to the cellar.

With shaking hands, Spark grabbed her firecloak from near the door and saw that Nanny's firecloak was gone. She ran outside to join Nanny, snatching up her axe as she went, but when she got out into the yard, the screeching dragons were so loud it shook her body and drove a spike of sound straight through her mind. She stumbled under the onslaught of it but caught sight of Nanny in the middle of the yard.

Spark froze. Overhead, dragons loomed large enough to eclipse the twilit sky. Spark's heart hammered in her ears. She sucked in a quick breath, unable to let it out.

The dragons were too close.

Great fiery gusts came from Nanny. Her spells were the only thing keeping the dragons from dropping straight onto the buildings. They spewed fire at the homestead and at Nanny, but she repelled it all, channelling their flame into bursts that threatened to knock them from the air.

They were all in chains, all dull brown. Covered in dirt and filth, Pappy once said. Dragons were brightly coloured and diligently neat by nature. Chains or no chains, it was clear that these were captive dragons.

Spark suspected she could see people riding them, up on their shoulders and in between the great horns of the largest leading the onslaught. But with the assault of fire and ash, it was impossible to be certain of much.

"Nanny!"

Heart pounding, Spark pulled fire from the abundantly hot air, not really certain what to do. It swirled through her like an angry wildfire. She weaved it into a funnel of flame, driving it into the dragons nearest the barn and scattering them.

No sooner than she'd released it, she conjured another, feeling the magic like a rush of hot wind coursing through her, up her legs and out her hands. Like her bones had turned to flame. The air directly around her was a cool bubble.

Nanny glanced her way and Spark expected her to be angry. But Nanny nodded, a tight smile on her face. Then she froze, her eyes widening as her gaze shifted over Spark's shoulder. Nanny ran. Spark turned as one of Nanny's spells shot overhead. Spark followed its trajectory and instantly went numb.

Another half dozen dragons had circled behind Spark and Nanny. Spark could barely breathe. Nanny's spell succeeded in scattering two dragons. Spark hurled another blazing funnel at them and blew one out of the air, flinging it to the ground near the house. The walls shuddered and the ground beneath Spark's feet trembled.

But three dragons closed in on the house, with more near the barn.

Spark turned and shot a lance of fire, blasting one of those little shapes off a dragon's back. She flung another funnel at the cluster of dragons, knocking another from the air and scattering the rest.

Heat drove out the numbness.

She took a deep breath, trying not to cough on the bitter taste of smoke and ash. Maybe they could drive away the dragons and salvage the homestead.

Nanny screamed in wordless anguish, turning Spark's blood to ice. The old wooden house was ablaze and two dragons dived toward the stone house where Bren and Uncle Breen hid.

"No." At first the word fell from Spark's lips in a whisper. She screamed. "No!"

With shaky hands, Spark hurled a fire tornado in one direction. Nanny pushed gusts of wind in another. Spark moved next to her grandmother. Nanny, who knew how to control all the elements, threw vast clumps of earth at the attackers, knocking a rider off one of the dragons and yet another beast out of the air.

Three of the dragons writhed on the ground, tangled in their chains. Some of their masters were dark, unmoving heaps on the ground.

Spark hadn't yet learned much about any elements other than fire. She had so much power when it came to pyromancy it could take her years to gain proper mastery of it and move on to other elements. But fire wasn't much use in a fight with a dragon. The best she could do was blow them off course.

The air cooled despite the raging fires around them. Nanny's earth and wind spells softened the ground beneath them to the consistency of mud and stilled the air, making it harder to breathe. Nanny trembled from the effort of magic. How much longer could she keep it up?

Spark's skin buzzed and her body felt heavy. She cast out, looking for farther flung sources of fuel.

Some of the dragons were close enough that Spark pulled the fire straight out of one and flung it at the rest. More of their riders fell off. Spark had a moment to wonder exactly who these people were until a dragon burst through Nanny's defenses.

Spark stopped trying to protect the barn and whirled around to see a dragon careening toward the house. She pulled fire from a nearby dragon and drove it at this new threat, but she was too late. The dragon sideswiped the house and kept going.

It was like watching a child crush an anthill, the house toppling in the dragon's wake. Spark thought she might collapse.

Nanny screamed, worse than the last time, her voice breaking. But she kept throwing magic—wind, fire and earth—at the dragons and their masters. If there had been a stream nearby, Spark had no doubt Nanny would have used it to somehow drown them all.

Spark couldn't take her eyes away from the house. She couldn't think, couldn't remember any spells. She held her breath and trembled, wondering if Bren and Uncle Breen could be okay. They were in the cellar—maybe the worst missed them. She and Nanny could dig, get them out.

But fire burned the rubble.

Spark's insides turned to ice and her legs wobbled. The growing buzz in her ears dampened the sound of battle around her, like she heard it from down a long hallway.

Through the din, one sound stood out. Pappy's voice behind her, screaming for Bren and Uncle Breen. Spark staggered around to find him running toward them from the barn where he must have been hiding all this time. He stared at the house, eyes shining with grief and panic, oblivious to everything else. Nanny screamed too, gesturing for him to turn back.

He didn't see the dragons.

The air around Nanny changed, still cold but feeling hollow, desperate. She even tried knocking Pappy back with a gust of wind, but he pushed through it toward the house. To Bren and Uncle Breen. Nanny's efforts couldn't get through.

There were too many dragons.

When Pappy was halfway between the barn and the house, a dragon swooped through Nanny's defenses.

Transfixed in helpless terror, Spark couldn't look away. Numb legs held her in place, eyes wide, jaw clenched, breath trapped in her throat. Then Nanny was in front of her, her firm but gentle arms around Spark, pulling her face down to Nanny's shoulder, holding her. Sparing her.

Spark still heard it.

Spark didn't hear the sound of the dragon colliding with her grandfather in the din of battle. But she heard the way Pappy's screams for Bren and Breen were abruptly cut short.

She clung to Nanny. Nanny sobbed once, choking on a scream. Still pressing Spark's head against her shoulder, Nanny turned, looking behind her. Spark tried to look too, but Nanny pushed her away.

"Run, Mita."

Nanny pushed Spark again, away from the dragons, away from the house and death. Spark resisted, trying to call her power, meaning to stay with Nanny and fight to the last. She couldn't possibly abandon the family, even if Nanny was all that was left of it.

Especially if Nanny was all that was left.

The tears streaking down Nanny's cheeks glistened orange in the firelight as Nanny pushed hard, much harder than a woman her size should have been able to. Fire sprang up around them like none Spark had ever seen in her life. But it wasn't from the dragons. This flame was Nanny's doing.

"Run!" she shouted one last time, with that soft lovely voice Spark wasn't used to hearing but could listen to forever.

Flames obscured Spark's vision, and she couldn't tell where Nanny was or where the homestead had been. It was all flame licking up around her.

Spark staggered in the direction Nanny had pushed her. She stumbled but gained momentum, driven by the sound of Pappy's death and the vision of the house crumbling. Cold numbness flooded through her, driving fire away. Part of her mind wondered if she'd ever call on her pyromancy again. But those thoughts were distant as she ran, breaking through the wall of flame and out into the night.

Blackness surrounded Spark when she cleared the last of the fields and made it into the cool forest at the edge of the valley. Only then did she stop running and turn back, only once.

Even from this distance she saw the conflagration that had once been her home. The dragons were leaving.

Overtaken once again by images of death, Spark turned and ran deeper into the forest. The whole world was nothing but darkness and running, stumbling over roots and fallen branches. A painful stitch stabbed in her side, each desperate gasp for air seared. But it was distant, something happening to another girl.

She didn't stop until sometime in the night, unsure of the real time because she'd never learned to read the stars and moons. She stopped only because it had become impossible to go further. There was nowhere to go but straight up. Spark had made it all the way to the western mountains with nothing but a cliff face in front of her.

From the elevated height, the lights of Pasdale spread out behind her. A distant dot of fire in the north marked where her home had been. Her family.

Those dragons had come with a purpose. Someone sent them. If they didn't realize already, it wouldn't take them long to figure out that Spark wasn't there. Not in the cellar with Uncle and Bren. Not in the yard with Nanny and Pappy.

Her mind skittered away from the destruction, from the fate of her family. It urged her to keep moving. She climbed, going carefully, searching for ways around and over obstacles. Spark was careful, not sure how she'd made it through the forest and the rocks in the darkness. She tried not to think, but one thought dominated her mind.

They would look for her. She had to keep going.

43

CHAPTER FOUR

I t was the cold that woke Spark before dawn, rousing her from broken sleep filled with nightmares. She shivered so hard her body ached, but at least she had Shadow curled at her back, providing enough warmth for her to asleep at all. The dog had miraculously survived and found her in the night. She'd assumed he'd been killed, but after cresting a hill in the night—letting gravity help her down the other side, and relieved to have a hill between herself, Pasdale, and that hellish fire—she'd heard barking. She'd initially feared wolves but soon recognized Shadow's bark.

So she'd hunkered down at the base of a large pine, calling into the night for Shadow until he found her. The familiar comfort of him at her side was such a stark contrast to the waking nightmare she lived. With someone to share her grief, she'd finally cried.

But now, with daylight approaching, there was no time to mourn. She blinked in the gloom as enough light crept over the mountains for her to see.

When she lifted her head, searing pain stabbed down her spine. She'd fallen asleep curled up with her head on rocks. There wasn't a part of her that didn't hurt. She worked her strong fingers into her knotted muscles, trying to loosen them, but she couldn't linger.

She slunk out of her hiding place, sheltered by spires of rock and gnarled roots under wide pine boughs, with Shadow creeping along beside her.

Still clinging to the battle-axe she didn't remember picking up the night before, Spark ran. It was hard to ignore the pain jolting her feet with every step or how parched her mouth was, like her tongue was made of sand.

Shadow loped at her side, making it look easy, and they scrabbled up the mountainside. Spark hoped to reach the pass before anyone thought to look that way. She didn't stop for rest until the sun cleared the horizon and the morning heat baked up out of the rocks. The world spun around her. She slowed her pace, sinking into the shade under a mountain ash, panting and trying to produce enough spit to wet her cracked lips.

Shadow sat on his haunches next to her, his ears flattened, head lowered. Mournful.

There were low-hanging branches with dewy leaves that Spark pulled to her face and licked. The bitter green taste was hard to stomach, but she needed the water, no matter how insignificant the amount. It was enough to get the sandy feeling out of her mouth, but not quite enough to stop how woozy she felt when she stood on leaden legs. She staggered westward anyway. She couldn't let them find her.

Snow capped some of the highest mountains, still distant, but there had to be water somewhere. There'd be a stream or a pond, maybe a bog. Anything would do. Anything would help her survive a bit longer. Finding water was her only hope.

If she slowed too much and let *them* find her, there'd be no hope at all. They'd tear her to pieces.

Spark scowled at the rock in front of her and focused on moving forward, keeping her thoughts away from last night. If she kept going west, and managed not to die, she would reach the Great Sea. If she got that far, she had no idea what she'd do.

Turn south?

She could go south to her uncles, Cusec and Bly and their families. They were far to the south, beyond this kingdom. Spark thought about turning south anyway, as going west didn't make any sense. There were only small, scattered tribes that Spark knew nothing about in the wilderness between Pasdale and the sea. There were bigger communities to the north, and far enough south was more family. The only family she had now.

But Nanny sent her west. Regardless, she had to get further away from Pasdale before she changed direction.

Shadow whimpered, but he matched her pace. The axe grew heavier, made of the moon, but she couldn't stand the thought of leaving it. It was all she had left. The clothes she wore and the axe she barely knew how to use. And Shadow.

"Good boy. Do you know where there's water? Aren't you thirsty?"

The dog watched her, his ears perked attentively, but it was unlikely he understood what she said.

As she neared the crest of the latest hill, Shadow halted and flattened his ears, growling a warning from deep in his chest. Spark paused to watch him. He focused on the summit. As Spark turned her head, the night sky erupted over her, blackening everything.

Spark slid along the rocks, having lost her footing without realizing. She came to a stop, lying on her back staring up at a massive black dragon flying overhead, skimming the hilltops. Shadow barked furiously beside her, his feet planted firmly, hackles raised. Trembling, heart pounding, Spark tried to shush him.

The dragon heard him and spotted the pair.

It dipped its wing, circling around to land nearby. The ground shook under the impact of its landing. Spark stood barely as tall as the dragon's claws. It made Spark feel small, like staring out into the vastness of the night sky.

Spark had read a bit in Nanny's books about the dragons and their ways. The females were the biggest ones, so this was a dragoness. Like that massive one leading the attack last night.

Spark grew cold, her legs wobbling. She doubted running would do any good. This dragon didn't seem a threat, no more than a dragon ever was, at least. It hadn't tried to crush her or eat her or hit her with flame, not that the latter would do any good.

Trust the dragons.

Nanny's words surprised her all over again. Nanny had told her three things about dragons. Run and hide had been the last. Before that...

This gleaming black dragoness was wild. Not one sent from Pasdale. How long had it been since Spark had seen a wild dragon? *Wild* wasn't quite the right word. This dragoness was calm, sharp intelligence glittering in her black eyes.

Of course, there were rules to talking to dragons.

Spark got an arm around Shadow, wrestling him to silence, and then she bowed her head to the dragoness. Be polite! Rule number one, the first thing Nanny taught her about dragons. They valued manners above all else.

"Mistress," Spark croaked with a throat made of sand. "Your presence honours me."

Did it? Spark pushed aside the wayward thought and focused on the beast, squeezing Shadow to hide how she trembled. The dragoness snorted at Spark's words. It sounded sarcastic.

The dragoness moved forward and lay her chin on the ground. Her teeth gleamed against her impossible black scales, and Spark tried not to notice that those teeth were almost as tall as her. It hurt to look at the dragoness. She was so black Spark could barely discern her features. It made Spark dizzy. Even dizzier than the lack of water.

She'll go for fire first. That was Nanny's voice. Another thing Nanny taught her early on, even if she'd never actually spoken the lesson.

Spark didn't fear the dragon's fire, but Shadow wouldn't survive it. Could she shield him? Maybe she could get him under the firecloak?

"We mean you no harm." Spark squeezed her eyes shut and huddled against Shadow, who was shaking, teeth bared. Spark buried her face in his fur and clung to him, trying to keep him still and stop her spinning head.

But Shadow yipped and thrashed and squirmed free of her grasp. She reached to catch him, commanding him to stop, but he bolted. Spark looked up in time to see why.

The dragoness was up, reaching for Spark. She startled but her fingers found the grip on her axe. As she raised it, she realized it wouldn't do her a bit of good. The axe was designed for battling people, not dragons. Her little axe would be no more than a mosquito bite to this dragoness. Not that it could pierce dragon skin.

Spark scrabbled backward, but the dragoness's clawed hand closed around her and lifted her off the ground. Her grip was firm but gentle. But then she turned her attention toward Shadow, who was retreating and barking. Spark gripped the axe tighter.

"Please, don't hurt him! He's just a dog and he's all I've got left."

The dragoness held Spark up to her face, black head tilted and dark eyes widening. The recognizable expression on the dragoness's face stilled Spark. She held her breath. First sarcasm, now this. Nanny's books insisted the dragons had personalities, this was just the first Spark had actually seen of it. The dragons in Pasdale certainly didn't show signs of being any different than sheep. Dangerous sheep. And so many people in Pasdale insisted dragons were nothing more than hungry, fiery monsters.

Spark would have loved for those fools to see this dragoness, with her surprise and her concern and her sense of humour.

The dragoness looked toward Pasdale, every part of her utterly still like she'd turned to stone, a mountain of obsidian holding Spark in its grip. She sighed, a hot gale rushing past Spark. And though the dragoness hadn't moved, Spark swore she drooped.

"You were on your way to Pasdale, weren't you? Why?"

The dragoness swung her great head toward Spark, narrowing her eyes and baring her teeth.

"I don't mean to question your intentions," Spark said quickly, stumbling over her own words in her haste. "But there's nothing there but death. You don't want to go there. It's awful."

A sob hitched on Spark's words, but she held her breath and forced it back.

The dragoness looked toward Pasdale, clearly sagging this time, her dark features darkening even more.

Spark couldn't stop watching her, wondering. Had someone sent her? Nandara? Had Nanny called for her—was that what the summoning was about? Could this be one of the dragons from Pappy's stories? He'd spoken of a dragoness Nanny was especially close to, one who'd been there when Spark's mother died.

"Will you speak?" Spark asked softly.

The dragoness bared her teeth, growling like thunder rolling over the mountains.

Tread carefully. Spark's thoughts seized on the fact she was talking to a *dragon*. One large enough to hold her in her hand like Spark was a bug.

"I know you can," Spark said, tone softer. "If you want to. Just like Nanny."

The dragoness held Spark's eye for a moment. She grunted and spread her wings, beating them like great sails, drowning out all sound of Shadow barking. The force of her wings was enough to blow the dog across the rocks. The force of the lift made Spark feel like her brain was about to exit her backside. Spark pressed her face to the gaps between the dragoness's claws and called the dog, but quickly lost sight of him as the dragoness brought Spark over the hill toward the pass.

Spark tried to feel relief at moving farther from Pasdale and at greater speed than she imagined possible. She tried to enjoy the wind in her face and the heat of the dragoness all around her. But she couldn't stop thinking about Shadow, about whether she was safe with the dragoness, about the connection this dragoness may have had to her family. Which of course led to thoughts of her family. Bittersweet ones.

Memories were all she had left.

Spark thought she was done with tears, but a fresh force of them marched over her cheeks, being dried by the wind and the dragoness's heat. Being carried off by a dragon should worry her more than it did. But she didn't sense any malice in this dragoness. Nanny's words, haunting now, echoed back to her.

They didn't go to the pass. After only a moment, the dragoness landed, this time next to a clear stream burbling through the granite, all of it covered by moss, soft and cool and lushly green.

Spark collapsed next to it, sticking her hot, puffy face directly into the cold water, letting it wash away her tears as she drank deep, washing away the sticky sand feeling and the hot tight feeling of grief. The cold helped clarify some questions in her mind. She sat back and looked up at the dragoness looming over her like some big black living house. Bigger than a house. Spark could barely fathom the sheer size of this creature.

The dragoness looked skyward, not paying any attention to Spark at all, her head held high, vigilant.

"Mistress?"

The dragoness swung her carriage-sized head around to watch Spark.

"You don't have to talk, but if I ask you questions, will you nod yes or no? Please?"

She watched Spark, still as the surrounding mountains. Then she drew in a deep breath and nodded.

"Are you Nanny's friend?"

She nodded immediately.

"Were you trying to help her?"

Another nod.

"Do you know why those dragons killed my family?"

Another nod. Spark's throat tightened.

"I'm still in danger." The words hurt to say, and weren't any sort of question. Spark swallowed against the growing lump when the dragoness nodded.

"Can you help me get to my Uncle Bly in the south?"

After a pause, the dragoness shook her head.

"But he's the only family I have left! Please. I can't stay out here by myself."

The dragoness stilled, looking toward Pasdale. All at once she turned to Spark, reaching for her. Spark held up her axe and backed away.

"Are you taking me somewhere—somewhere safe?"

The dragoness nodded and held out a massive, clawed hand, waiting. The dragoness would take her or not, but it was for Spark to decide.

"Thank you, Mistress." Spark bowed low, bending over the axe. "I can't leave without Shadow. He's all I've got."

The dragoness narrowed her eyes and looked at the hill behind them. Spark followed her gaze and spotted the little black shape of Shadow coming down the hillside through the scrub and slabs of granite. The dragoness huffed at Spark, a gentle gesture by dragon standards, but enough to blow Spark off balance. She stretched languidly along the rock beside Spark, taking up half the hillside to wait.

Spark couldn't tear her gaze away from the gleaming black shape, how even with her wings folded up, the dragoness was larger than Spark could properly comprehend. One of Pappy's stories came back to her, about the same dragoness as always, but mentioning how dark she was. How she gave him a fright one night, blending in with the midnight around him. It had to be the same dragon.

With one of Pappy's stories came a flood of them, rushing in to fill Spark's mind with lore. These stories always came back to a specific dragoness.

"Are you the one who was there when I was born? The one who helped Mamma before she died? Nanny's friend."

The dragoness was in the midst of shaking out her wings when Spark found the courage to ask. The great beast drew her wings in and stared, still as stone. Then she bared her teeth, this time in a massive, ghastly grin.

There was no malice in it, but seeing that many huge teeth at once made Spark recoil.

But it was still a smile, a show of encouragement, this dragoness suddenly taking on an air of comfort. Hot tears prickled Spark's eyes, and she took a few slow breaths until the emotion subsided. When it did, the heavy sense of loneliness eased. She remembered more and more of Pappy's stories about this dragoness. She became a familiar element, serving as a link to the family Spark missed so desperately.

The dragoness surprised Spark by gently nuzzling her with a shockingly soft snout. Nandara commented once on how soft dragon skin was, but Spark hadn't really believed her. It was so odd to her that a creature so large, one that could kill her thoughtlessly like squashing beetles underfoot, could be so gentle. And not merely gentle, but affectionate.

Pappy had said that the dragoness comforted Neesha through Spark's birth. She hadn't believed that at the time. But now?

The dragoness lay with her chin on the ground next to Spark so they were eye level with each other. Her spiralling horns towered over Spark, double Spark's height. She didn't look at Spark though, instead watching the little shape of Shadow drawing closer. Spark reached out her hand to stroke the dragoness's soft nose, but she shifted suddenly, a fractional shift, and narrowed her eyes.

"May I touch you?"

Another unmoving pause from the dragoness. Then she snorted and shifted toward Spark. Spark was tentative, remembering exactly what sort of beast she approached, but lay her hand on the side of her nose. She was surprised by how warm the dragoness was. Spark had always run hot, like Nanny and likely her mother, and most living things always felt cool to her. The dragoness's heat was pleasant, reassuring. Like Nanny's embrace.

Spark's breath caught, hot tears stung her eyes.

The dragoness tilted her head, moving fractionally, to nestle at Spark's side.

Spark nodded off again, nearly fell off the dragoness, and startled herself upright, nearly dropping the axe out of her lap. She looked around blearily, her backside aching, and noted the mountains hadn't changed much. At least the shadows around them lengthened with the encroaching eventide. The dragoness loped along at a slow steady pace. She'd been going slower when Spark had trudged along beside her.

Shadow caught up to them earlier, but had been far too afraid of the dragoness for her to pick him up. So it seemed they were walking to wherever they were going. Spark assumed it was the dragon city. It was in the west. But she hadn't had the energy to ask.

They'd walked until Spark nearly collapsed, and then the dragoness set Spark down between a pair of spikes at the base of her tail, facing back the way they'd come. She was wedged in, but could take a spill if she wasn't careful. It would be like falling off a palace.

Spark felt the dragoness's impatience, knew she wanted to take to the skies. The danger increased the longer it took them to get away from Pasdale. But Spark already had to leave everyone else, she wouldn't leave Shadow too. So they walked, the dog barely visible, trailing along behind.

The journey from Pasdale stretched out before Spark. She was ashamed of the way she kept dozing off. She wanted to be vigilant, to warn the dragoness if danger approached. They would walk, but only as long as there wasn't obvious peril. If it came down to it, she hoped Shadow would let the dragoness pick him up. For now, they were safe.

Spark had nightmares every time she tried to sleep. Closing her eyes meant hearing the sound of Nanny's screams and the way Pappy's had abruptly ended.

Spark jolted. She opened her eyes and steadied herself on the dragon, weeping again, a river of sorrow squeezing her dry. Now that she only had to put enough thought into not falling off the dragoness, she had plenty of time to ruminate. Gripping her axe reminded her of sparring with Bren, of helping him make that foolish sword. She half wanted to pitch her axe out into the desolate mountains, empty of woodland creatures as far as Spark could see—downside to a dragon companion, everything had the good sense to be scared away.

It seemed unwise to throw away one of the few possessions she had. So she held the axe and let it remind her of better times.

Spark kept her empty gaze on the landscape around them as the night deepened until everything was as black as the dragoness. The stars glittered above, but the contrast of the bright night sky to the shadowy black land only made the mountains so much more desolate.

By the time the dragoness stopped, Spark lost all track of time, but it felt like it had been nighttime forever.

The dragoness plucked Spark from her tail—Spark flinched every time she reached for her—and set her in a sheltered area somewhere in a mountainside. The dragoness's eyes glittered in the starlight, intent on Spark. Then, in a midnight whirlwind, she was gone.

Spark was too shocked to call out, momentarily panicking out of fear that the dragoness was leaving her. But if she was leaving Spark, it wouldn't matter how much Spark screamed for her to come back.

So she waited, watching out into the night, a slice of stars visible beyond whatever rocky outcropping protected her. But the dragoness could be anywhere, and Spark had no way of knowing. The dragoness was perfectly camouflaged against the night.

Spark let her axe clatter to the stone beside her, her hands stiff from gripping it so long. It wouldn't do her anymore good tonight. Not that it had done her any good up to this point. She hugged her legs to her chest and rested her head on her knees, sobbing. Shadow's barks echoed from somewhere far below, leaving her to wonder where the dragoness had left her. But everything beneath her was lost in darkness. The horizon glowed faintly, likely the moons beginning to rise. She hoped their light would give her some answers.

Spark shrank into her hiding place, appreciating it for what it was. If the dragoness had truly left her, at least she was somewhere safe, away from the threat of any wildlife. Weeping silently with her head on her knees, she dozed, pulled to the edge of sleep with only Shadow's barking to keep her awake.

When the dog stopped abruptly, Spark sat alert. The whoosh of wings filled the night air, followed by a scrape on the rocks. A pair of black eyes glittered in the starlight. Something clattered against the stones in front of Spark before it was all lit with a soft red glow.

The dragoness had her face pressed near the opening with her large jaw hanging open, fire gurgling in her throat. It gave Spark enough light to see.

There was a pile of tinder in front of her, wood that looked suspiciously like a single branch that had been shredded. There was also a hare, or what looked like a hare, but it had been skinned. Spark shuddered when she noticed a bit of gore on the dragoness's claws gripping at the edge of her little hiding spot.

"How did you even catch this?" Spark blurted. She blushed in the dim light and remembered herself. "But thank you. Is a fire safe here?"

The dragoness nodded and left, climbing up the face of the mountainside. Spark assumed she was standing watch or finding a place to sleep.

Spark's belly growled with a hollow ache that some water and a few berries hadn't been able to quell. With her stomach gurgling, Spark quickly arranged the pile of sticks and thrust a hand into the centre. Tired as she was, it was easy to pull fire out of the air and get a proper blaze going.

She huddled closer to the flames, trying to drive away the chill. In her haste, she forgot to leave a spit to roast the meat. So she rolled up her sleeves and held the carcass into the fire. She ate without really tasting it, eating until her stomach was so full it ached. She pushed the rest over the ledge and into the darkness below, hoping it made it down to Shadow. He could likely forage, but there was no harm in sharing.

With a full belly, Spark lay down but something dug into her hip. No matter how she moved, it was still there. Something in her pocket. She sat up and fished out the smooth, hard object. Even without the dwindling firelight, she could clearly see what it was.

Nanny's pendant, a deep blue stone that glowed gently with love's silver light. How had it got there? Had Nanny somehow managed to slip it in her pocket before sending her away?

But of course, Nanny knew what was happening. It was why she'd run Spark off. It had saved her life.

Spark curled in on herself, bitter tears and soul-wracking sobs her only company until she drifted to sleep. She dreamed of fire all night long, like she'd fallen asleep with her eyes open, watching the little campfire next to her. But the fire of her dream was deeper and menacing. She shivered all night long.

Spark woke to rumbling, like thunder, but darkness surrounded her. Her fire was nothing but cold ashes. Every inch of her ached. When she sat up, the quality of the darkness shifted, resolving into the shape of the dragoness hanging onto the ledge. She watched Spark, rumbling deep in her chest. Beyond her, Spark noticed the faintest traces of light to the east.

The dragoness held out her huge hand and Spark had to clench her whole body to keep from recoiling. But she understood: it was time to go. The dragoness put Spark onto her tail and resumed walking. Spark was happy to be against the dragoness's warm skin, even if she would have liked hours more sleep.

The journey was quiet, loneliness pressing down on Spark with the weight of the mountains.

The dragoness's silence was much like Nanny's, a gentle comfort. But Spark had never gone whole days like this without hearing someone's voice. There had always been Bren chattering constantly, and Uncle Breen and Pappy to help fill the silence. Their absence was a yawning ache inside of her.

And no matter how deep her grief, she nodded off, catching herself as soon as she tilted. Startling herself awake yet again, she rubbed her face and stared blearily at the mountains the way they'd come. A blot in the sky had her sitting up straight, her limbs tingling.

"Mistress, what is that?"

The dragoness stopped and looked back only briefly before grabbing Spark and diving between trees. She'd been walking the gravel riverbed but nestled among the towering pines covering the slope. She went still, staring at the horizon with her teeth bared.

"Shouldn't we go?"

The dragoness scowled and glanced at the trees overhead.

"Oh, right." Camouflage in the shadows. It would be better if she were a green or grey dragon, but this was better than nothing.

The blot on the horizon got close enough to clearly identify as a dragon. Tightness spread across Spark's chest and she shook. Even once the dragon disappeared and didn't return, fear coiled around Spark's heart.

Why are we just sitting here?

Spark remained crouched at the dragoness's side, but the heat and the relative softness of the forest floor lulled her and she fell asleep, more out of exhaustion than anything. When she woke, she thought it was night, but realized after a moment that it was dusk and it was the dragoness's great wing spread above Spark, creating a living tent.

She woke only because the dragoness stood up, but there was a warm ball curled next to Spark. Shadow had joined her. She buried her face in his soft fur, sobbing.

Despite the dragoness standing over them, looming like a vast black mountain on legs, Shadow didn't try to run off.

The dragoness crouched slightly, enough to lay her hand flat on the ground near them. Spark crawled over to it, one hand gripping Shadow's scruff. The dog put a tentative paw in the dragoness's palm and pulled it back immediately. Spark held her breath. Then he put it back, paused to sniff, and hopped into her hand. Spark sat with her arms around him to keep him from changing his mind.

The dragoness slowly curled her claws up, cupping Spark and Shadow in her massive hand. She was equally slow when she capped the other hand over them, making them a little cave, with gaps between her fingers where they could look out. The gaps were small, but Shadow would be able to slip through them if he put his mind to it. Spark gripped him tightly.

Not moving any faster, the dragoness lifted her hands closer to her body and stood on her hind legs, stretching to an impressive, mountainous height. Shadow pressed into Spark and whimpered, his gaze bouncing between Spark and the treetops below.

"It's okay."

The dragoness's mighty wings beat against the air, and her incredible power vibrated through Spark as she lifted off the ground. And then the forest and the mountaintops were below them, sinking away at an alarming speed. They rose so high that Spark thought they might bump into a moon.

Spark wished she could see the way they'd come. If it were daytime, she was certain she'd be able to see to Pasdale, maybe even all the way to Golden Hill. She looked for the dragon city, but she saw nothing but sky and mountains. The whole world was nothing but mountains, endless in all directions, disappearing in a line of haze on the horizon. The Great Sea was out there somewhere, but there was no sign of it yet.

As the dragoness built up her speed, the wind streamed past with incredible power, taking Spark's breath away if she tried facing directly into it. And it was so cold it burned. Shadow was lying down, his ears flat and his nose facing the dragoness. Spark couldn't hear him over the great roar of air but felt the tension of it in his body as he whimpered. The dragoness was warm enough to keep them comfortable so long as they kept pressed against her.

The dragoness only stopped flying during the day, before the sun rose. And she always started the journey in the evening, just before full dark, when the dragons from Pasdale couldn't see her. Out of the days of travel, the only time Spark felt in danger was when they stopped at the shore of the Great Sea. The dragoness stopped only long enough for them to catch some fish before heading back up into the mountains.

Spark had heard the stories of the battle that took her mother, how Loch and other powerful aquamancers had called forth a legion of water demons to do their bidding, to collapse the dragon city and nearly drown all of Pasdale. Neesha had saved Pasdale by opening a portal directly to the fire realm, something no one had ever done before. She'd unleashed a legion of fire demons and used trueflame from the fire realm to evaporate the floods.

It was told that the aquamancers and the water demons bore a grudge not just to the fireborn women, but to the dragons as well. There had been stories of great waterspouts pulling dragons out of the air to watery deaths.

The journey across the Great Sea took a full night, but the crossing confirmed Spark's belief—they were headed for the dragon city. She barely sat still the whole way. It had been far too long since she'd been there to remember, but she'd heard plenty about the journey from Pappy, the first human to ever make the trek.

She wished he was there with her to see it again.

CHAPTER FIVE

S park was asleep against the dragoness's thumb, the cold air buffeting her face, when she was jolted awake by the dragoness's thunderous cries, echoing Spark's nightmares. Her chest tightened and her limbs buzzed. The cry was deafening in such close proximity, vibrating through Spark's body until she thought it would cleave her head. Spark saw Shadow barking but couldn't hear him over the noise.

The dragoness called out at regular intervals, letting out a long screech every minute or two. Were they under attack? Was it some kind of greeting or warning? Spark wished she knew more about their vocalizations.

Spark tried peeking through the dragoness's fingers, but she couldn't see much of anything around the dragoness's hands. Squinting into the wind, she saw glittering red mountains below. Those hadn't been there when she fell asleep that morning, but the long shadows told her she'd been asleep most of the day. The Red Mountains meant they were close to the dragon city, but Spark was worried about another attack.

The city wasn't indestructible. There'd only been one successful attack against it, the assault led by the aquamancers. Her mother and Nanny had both been there, but it was Nandara who had given Spark the account.

Now that they were so close, Spark's mind raced. Most of her dragon knowledge had been absorbed through Pappy's tales and was decades old. The dragons valued manners, but she didn't really know what they considered rude. A misstep could be deadly.

Something glittered in the distance and caught Spark's attention, interrupting her fear. She leaned forward into the wind, squinting to see better. They'd passed sparkling glaciers and high glacial lakes on the journey, but nothing like this. Nothing quite so brilliant.

The approach was something Pappy had talked about the most. He'd only ever been minimally involved with the dragons, but Spark had smiled every time she saw the faraway look in his eyes when he spoke of the city.

Even now, if Spark were to close her eyes, she'd see how it used to capture his imagination. And the thing he'd talked about the most was the way it glittered. Seeing it without him made her heart ache and her lungs seize. But she focused on the city, wanting to savour the approach as he had. For the first time that trip, she allowed herself to enjoy the feel of the wind on her face and the spectacular view of the world far below.

It took longer than Spark expected for the glitter on the horizon to materialize into anything discernable. The massive spires Pappy had spoken of were gone, the dragons only recently beginning to rebuild after years of restoring one of the mountains that supported the city. It was still stunning. The sheer size of it took Spark's breath away.

She'd seen hasty sketches of the city, both before and after it fell, but even that combined with Pappy's stories hadn't prepared her for it.

The city was made of diamond and obsidian and held aloft by colossal arched supports braced into four opposing mountains and stretched over the width of a vast valley. The valley was a little smaller than the valley of Pasdale. The city supports sat at the four points of the compass, the diamond columns ran east-west and obsidian north-south. According to Nandara, the northern one had been destroyed when an aquamantic deluge washed away the mountainside, but it appeared that the mountainside had since been restored and the column rebuilt. Where the columns met in the centre, they swirled together to form the core of the city, a dazzling sphere that sparkled with refracted light. The size of the city alone was mind-boggling. It didn't look real. And the city had been many times larger, reaching far above the cloud tops at its pinnacle.

The spires of the dragon city were beginning to spiral up from the core, the rebuilding efforts making good progress. Now that she could see the whole valley, shimmering clan towers dotted the mountainsides in a rainbow of colours, all dappled with points of light reflected off the city above.

With the city in sight, dragons answered the dragoness's call, and she called out more frequently. Dragons every colour of the rainbow circled around the valley. None of them approached.

As the dragoness brought them closer, Spark saw the little blot of the human settlement on the valley floor. It had once been directly below the dragon city, but was in the southern part of the valley now. The valley floor, particularly right under the city and to the north, was littered with massive shards of obsidian and diamond.

Eventually a stunning blue dragon, this one smaller, a male, broke from the mass of dragons swirling around the valley and approached the dragoness. He flew so close that Spark went rigid. But he nuzzled the dragoness, growling out something far gentler than the cries Spark heard through the whole approach. He dropped away from her and flew along beneath her until she angled toward the ground and the human settlement. He glided sideways and remained hovering above, disappearing from Spark's view.

Now the ground came up quickly, patches of grass and mud and ramshackle buildings of shoddy stone, some nothing more than tarpaulin tents. There were vast open patches between the buildings. The settlement wasn't particularly large, but it sprawled out along the southern tip of the valley a cautious distance from the banks of the river.

The dragoness settled into one of the open spaces between buildings.

"Mistress!" a woman's voice called. Spark heard running footsteps but couldn't see anyone from between the dragoness's fingers.

"It pleases me so much that you have returned," the woman said. She wasn't merely being polite, either. Spark heard her sincerity. "What news do you bring?"

The dragoness was silent, Spark felt the heaviness of it, heard the woman draw in a breath, waiting. The dragoness lowered her hands to the ground and set Spark and Shadow into the grass. Shadow leaned against Spark.

"Mita! Oh my stars!"

Spark looked blearily around at the sound of her name and found the concerned pale face of a plump woman, her long red hair pulled into a braid and threaded with grey.

"Ondias?"

Ondias looked up at the dragoness, her hazel eyes wide with concern, waiting for answers. The dragoness remained silent.

"You made it to Pasdale?" Ondias asked.

The dragoness moved her head in that fractional way of hers. No, the dragoness had not made it to Pasdale.

"So she *was* coming to help us," Spark said, her voice catching on the words. She bunched her hands into fists, gripping Shadow's fur.

"We got a message from Nandara and the Guild that things were looking bad in Pasdale," Ondias said. "The dragoness left immediately. Mita, what's happened?"

"She didn't make it in time." Spark pushed the words through her tight throat as tears rolled unbidden down her cheeks.

In three swift steps, Ondias reached Spark, kneeling down to wrap her arms around Spark's shoulders.

Spark let go of Shadow and collapsed against her grandmother's best friend, sobbing out her grief, the wound opened anew. And she wept not only with grief, but with the gratitude of finally being somewhere safe, of hearing another voice, one she trusted, after a week of silence. Ondias held her tight and let her cry, stroking her short tangle of hair so much like Nanny once did.

And never will again.

Spark sobbed harder against the thought, barely able to draw air. Every part of her body was rigid with grief.

"Oh, Mita. Please, what's happened? Have our fears been fulfilled? Nandara's final message was dire. Did Loch reach his limits? Can you tell me?"

Spark rubbed tears from her face with the palms of her hands. She took a deep breath, tried sticking with facts. The tears returned as she spoke.

"Dragons. So many dragons, the captive ones, still in chains... They're gone, all of them. Pappy—" Spark sobbed, unable to speak the words, hearing it all over again.

"Oh, weeping moons," Ondias whispered, gripping Spark tighter, her tears dripping onto Spark's shoulder. "Everyone?"

"The dragons killed everyone."

"How did you...?"

"Nanny. Used fire to conceal me, made me run."

"And you ran far enough for our mistress to find you before Loch could. There's a lucky thing." Ondias released her and looked up at the dragoness. "You'll take care of this with them?" She nodded up toward the city. "I know it was the right thing to do, but bringing her here is still your responsibility. The consequences are yours."

"Consequences?" Spark asked, her voice rising.

"Yes, dear." Ondias turned away from the dragoness. "You don't need to concern yourself with that. The mistress will sort it. You are safe here, safe as you can ever be. And you've got to be exhausted, that journey from Pasdale isn't an easy one even when you're prepared."

Ondias had an arm around Spark's waist, easing the axe from her grip and leading her into the jumble of buildings.

"Just come with me. Let's get you cleaned up and fed. I'll make up a bed for you."

After a week in the wilderness sleeping on dirt and stones, the thought of a real bed and comforts of home brought fresh tears. Spark leaned against Ondias, appreciating the woman's support.

They hadn't gone far when some of the dragons above screeched, like when they came for Spark's family. The sound drove her to her knees, wrenching her axe from Ondias as she did.

Three dragons, an indigo and grey female and two males, one teal and one yellow-orange, bore down. Spark went numb. Shadow bolted, disappearing between two crumbling stone buildings. But the black dragoness beat her massive wings, taking to the air, the force of the gale blowing Spark onto her side and causing Ondias to stumble.

The dragoness flew straight at the attackers, jaws open, claws extended, her spiny tail thrashing.

The males swooped aside immediately, but the indigo dragoness continued to dive. Spark lay on her back, trembling, as the dragonesses collided in the air, gnashing and slashing at each other, tumbling over and over but staying aloft. The black dragoness threw the other aside and spiralled away after the yellowy male. When the teal male dived at her from above, she whipped her tail out to connect with the side of his head.

He fell nearly all the way into the settlement, before drunkenly flying off, disappearing up toward the city. Chased by the indigo dragoness, the black dragoness caught up with the other male. She grabbed his wings in her claws and yanked him out of the air, sending him flailing toward the ground. Spark was transfixed, holding her breath.

Ondias pulled on her arm, trying to get her to stand.

"They've seen you. We need to get inside."

Spark didn't care if they'd seen her. She couldn't help the black dragoness, but it seemed wrong not to bear witness to whatever this was. Ondias wasn't much bigger than Nanny, and she lived the soft life of an academic; she had little chance of budging Spark.

The second male rebounded, heading back to where the dragonesses wrestled in midair. Spark couldn't be sure if the black dragoness was winning. It was all teeth and claws and whipping tails. But when the male reached them, the black dragoness somersaulted away from the indigo one and caught the male by the throat with her teeth. She flung him away like Shadow flinging field mice in the yard. The male scarcely avoided crashing into the settlement. He didn't rejoin the combat, instead fleeing the way the first one had.

The blue dragon who had come to greet them on their descent into the valley circled the battling dragonesses, crying out as the black dragoness clawed at the face of her opponent.

Outmatched and outnumbered, the indigo dragoness relented and flew off, screeching over her shoulder as she did. The black dragoness, with her blue mate not far behind, chased her retreating foe up toward the city.

"There, it's over. Now let's get inside."

Spark went with Ondias, but her sense of terror from watching the dragons fight was not eased by the look of the settlement. It was supposed to have been a temporary camp until something permanent could be built, but there were only a few stone buildings. It made Spark ache for the home she'd lost, the stability of it, the warmth and safety. She'd been brought to a godsdamn mucky hell.

"Why are they fighting?" Spark asked.

"The dragons have a process for letting new humans into the settlement. It's been in place since you were still in nappies. Our mistress has breached it by bringing you here without consulting them first."

"But I've been here before. Since I was in nappies. Black moons, they've got to know who I am. Who else looks like this?"

"Your heritage might be part of the problem. The dragons became more involved with humans than they ever have because of Dionelle, but it's also brought them more misery than they've ever known. It's over for now. She'll sort it with the Superiors, remind them you've been here before, as you say."

Spark bit her lips and kept following Ondias, wishing that she'd gone south to her uncles. Maybe she could still get there and away from this madness.

Much to Spark's relief, Ondias led her into one of the sturdier looking stone buildings. It was crammed full of decades' worth of living, but it was secure and homey, if desperately cluttered. Old thick rugs overlapping in many layers covered the floor, with heavy drapes at the windows, worn but soft furniture, all oversized. It was a mismatch of things, Spark supposed because everyone in the settlement was at the mercy of traders and what the dragons would fly in for them. There were no roads to the dragon city.

"She said she was bringing me somewhere safe," Spark said, embarrassed at the whimper.

"You are safe. No safer place for you. The danger is for the dragoness right now, but she won't let the others harm you. I won't let them."

"What can you do?"

"They're not monsters." Ondias was terse. Scowling. "I know you're used to those brutish thugs they keep in Pasdale, but those are not true dragons. Those ones have been debased, they're mindless."

Her voice rose, but Spark wasn't sure exactly what part of it all made Ondias so angry.

"I have rapport with these dragons. You are my guest and it would be rude of them to harm my guest. Really, Mita, do try to remember who taught your grandmother most of what she knows about dragons."

"Knew," Spark whispered.

The anger fizzled out of Ondias entirely and she nodded, looking at a spot next to her on the floor.

"If it was such a risk for her to bring me here, then why did she? I wanted to go south to my uncles."

Ondias gave her another sharp look. "She brought you here because it was the right thing to do. She doesn't care about the risk. She loves your family like her own."

Spark nodded wearily. The idea of dragons as friend or family was foreign to her, but the dragoness's actions stood out. It didn't change Spark's desire to find her uncles, to join the last bit of family she had left, even if she had been too young to remember them when they'd moved away.

"You can have the back room." Ondias's voice was gentle, but stiff. "It was Lina's at one point, but she built a place of her own when she came back."

Spark knew better than to poke the hornet's nest of Ondias's family life, having heard plenty from Nandara. She glanced at the pair of diagonal, nullifying slashes through the marriage tattoo on Ondias's wrist and kept silent, following her into the little cluttered room.

Stacks of books and crates, half-finished tapestries, piles of clothes, battered cookware, bits of furniture in need of repair. While Ondias hastily pulled things off the bed, stacking things even more precariously around the room, Spark leaned her axe against the door and pulled off the filthy firecloak, draping it over a low stack of crates. At last, Ondias shook out the blankets and turned them down, ushering Spark into the bed.

"You can stay in this room as long as you like. We can get you something of your own, if you want, once we get your affairs sorted out."

Spark sank down into the straw mattress like it was a feather bed. Ondias swaddled her in the blankets, then quietly cleared a few more things, reorganizing some of the piles to take up less space. Then she promised to bring Spark a meal and left the girl to silence.

Watching out the window, hoping to get a glimpse of the black dragoness, Spark tried to make sense of her situation, of how to go on without her family. She fell asleep before Ondias returned.

An untold period of days blurred past with Spark scarcely moving from that bed, either sleeping or clutching Nanny's pendant while watching the dragon city through the stained window. Ondias and her daughter Lina, who was the village healer, had been doing an annoying amount of checking in on her across all those days. During that time, Ondias's kindness gained a hard edge while Lina only softened more.

The dragons, in all their bright colours, came and went. Sometimes the dragoness would peek in on her, her eye taking up the whole window in what was likely supposed to be a comforting gesture but nearly gave Spark a heart attack every time. Other times, Spark heard her great feet thudding along the ground as she circled Ondias's creaky old house.

After that first battle, Spark had noticed a bright red gash on the side of the dragoness's neck during one of her rounds past the window. It had since healed and there were no fresh wounds. Spark hoped that was a good sign.

This rhythm was interrupted when Ondias barged in with steel in her voice. "You have a visitor. Get cleaned up and come to the kitchen."

Ondias left as quickly as she'd arrived, not bothering to check on Spark at all.

Not ready to get out of bed yet, Spark went back to watching out the window. Shadow lay on her feet, and Spark was content to be with his warmth. He was largely an outdoor animal, but stuck close to Spark since Ondias found him cowering under a long-collapsed shed after they'd first arrived. He probably couldn't tell these dragons were different from the ones who destroyed their family.

The dragons screeched day and night, a dreadful, deafening cacophony that made Spark's mind ache. But the cries she regularly heard were different from the attack. She assumed one day she'd learn to parse what they all meant. For now, she only wanted her bed.

But curiosity picked at her thoughts. A guest. She didn't know anyone here. Hadn't known Ondias until the dragoness dropped Spark in her lap. There was Lina, but she practically lived here and didn't need her presence announced.

Spark strained to listen. Voices came from the front of the house where the kitchen and parlour were crammed together inside the main door. At least one of them was a woman, but that was likely Ondias. They spoke too softly for Spark to pick anything out.

Grumbling to herself, Spark pushed back the blankets and went to the basin of water Ondias left for her. She hated how primitive everything was, how there wasn't even running water. And this place was supposed to be her home? The thought of living here was so heavy it stole the air from her lungs. She gripped the sides of the basin with both hands and leaned over it, gasping.

It took all her energy not to collapse back into bed and lie there until she ceased to exist.

She shuffled down the hallway, past the privy and two other bedrooms crammed with stuff and stopped short when she reached the main room. A familiar woman with a greying blonde braid sat at the kitchen table with her back to Spark.

"Nandara! You made it!"

Spark rushed to her, and Nandara sprang up and out of her seat, sweeping Spark into a fierce embrace. Spark thought she was out of tears but wept with relief at seeing Nandara safe.

"You knew!" Spark gripped the fabric of Nandara's sleeves in tight fists.

"I had concerns," Nandara said. "But I never thought for an instant that Loch would do something so bold and devastating."

"It was the magistrate that sent those dragons to kill us?"

"I have only suspicions. Especially after he dragged you before him in such a foolish spectacle right before I left."

"Nanny and Pappy knew the dangers, didn't they?"

"Yes. And I tried to get them to tell you. I've been trying for over a year to get them to leave. But they were so stubborn, especially Dionelle. I think, in her mind, she thought if she stayed she could change Loch's mind somehow, that if she just endured it long enough they'd all see the truth."

Nandara shook her head and gave Spark's arm a squeeze.

"Have you heard any news?" Spark asked. "You must still have friends in Pasdale."

"Yes." She glanced sideways at Ondias. "But I haven't heard anything. The Guild is trying to get to the bottom of what happened, but even they must tread carefully. Magistrate Loch has a strong ally in the new king in Golden Hill, one who hates dragons almost as much as Loch does."

"So my family was murdered, and he's just going to get away with it?"

Nandara held her eye but was silent for longer than Spark could stand.

"The Guild will do what it can. It could take some time."

"The new king. That's why you left? Because the Guild was protecting you and us... but they couldn't anymore?"

"Yes. The new king complicates the situation."

Spark spun away from Nandara with her hands balled into fists, sparks showering down around her. Ondias gasped. They bounced harmlessly off the carpet beneath her feet, and Spark looked over her shoulder to see Nandara working some magic to keep fires suppressed.

Spark turned away, letting the anger flow through her, hot and fast, her heart pounding to keep pace. The thought of Magistrate Loch getting away with destroying her family made her stomach fill with fire until she shook.

Part of her wanted to run and never stop. Part of her desperately wanted to go back to bed. What she didn't want was to stand there and listen to these two women tell her this was all there was. This terrible reality, devoid of justice, was her life now.

"I'm so sorry, Spark, I can only guess at how hard this is for you," Nandara said. "I know they were your whole world. I know I was only a small part of that, but I'm here now."

"How long are you staying?"

"At least as long as my grandson is apprenticing here," Nandara said. "And it looks as though he's got some years left."

Spark collapsed into the chair next to Nandara.

"You're really going to stay?"

"I've always loved it here. I'll need to go back to the Guild for business now and then, but I expect I'll stay here as long as I can keep up with this kind of life."

"Why is it such a dump here?" Spark blurted, too weary to skirt the issue. "I thought there'd be a proper city full of people."

Ondias bristled at the comment. "It's not that bad. But the population is fairly transient, with scholars, artists and apprentices coming and going. They keep tents, not invested enough to build permanent structures, especially when so few of them remain through the winter."

"But you don't plan to leave and that's why you've got a real house?"

"Yes. A few people have made this place home. Those are the stone structures you've seen."

"But how can the population be so transient? I thought the dragons don't let new people in."

"Oh, they still do," Nandara said. "But not as many new ones as they used to. Mostly, it's the same people coming back for a short time and then leaving again—mostly through the winter—to teach others what they've learned, to bring their art or knowledge to new corners of the world, and then they come back. Those people who don't spread their knowledge leave for the winter and stay in the cities south of here."

"I've got family in the south. Why can't I go there?"

"Perhaps in time. I don't think you're quite safe anywhere just yet."

"You think Loch realizes I got away?"

"It's possible. What he did was about you and Dionelle, about your connection to the dragons and to the fire realm. Loch knows exactly what your mother did. He fears you have the same kind of power."

"And that's why he wanted me to... do whatever Nanny did? She didn't look fireborn anymore."

"No, she left much of her power in the fire realm before your mother was ever born. Loch would like nothing better than for you to renounce your power."

"He can rot."

This made Nandara smile.

"The only way you can be safe from him is to renounce your power or learn to control it," Ondias said. "Now that Nandara is here, you need to resume your apprenticeship. Full Guild entrance will go further to protect you."

"Oh yes?" Spark's stomach filled with fire. "Like it protected Nanny?"

Ondias scowled.

"The Guild was trying to protect her, but I've told you how stubborn she was," Nandara said. "She wasn't taking any precautions that would have helped the Guild ensure her safety."

"By running away? Like I had to in the end? Where would she have gone?"

"She could have come here," Ondias said. "She could have gone south to be with your uncles, as you want to now."

"Then why can't I?"

"If she'd left years ago," Nandara said gently, "it would have de-escalated things, put you all out of Loch's mind. But he's obsessed. Especially after you entered the Guild through the new tiers. If he knows you survived that attack, he won't stop hunting you until one of you is dead."

"And you think I'm safer here because there are dragons? Nandara, you were *here* when the city fell."

"Yes. But that attack took us by surprise. And Loch does not have the same contingent of aquamancers behind him anymore. The Guild is monitoring him and any sorcerer who goes near him to ensure this never happens again. With you here now, if you learn more control, you could thwart that kind of attack. Your mother tried, but we didn't have the time to prepare before the water came."

Nandara looked down at her hands folded on the table, her voice growing quieter as she spoke.

"But I still have no one here," Spark said softly.

"You have the dragoness. She's outside in a field, watching this house as we speak," Nandara said. "Do you understand the bond she has with your family? With you?"

Spark nodded. "But dragons aren't a family."

"You can build a new family, Spark. Dragons aren't a family by themselves, but the dragoness is part of your family as much as I am or Shadow is. Most of the apprentices here are your age. My grandson isn't much older than you."

Nandara and Ondias glanced at each other. It happened so fast Spark nearly missed it.

"You can have friends again. Or at all. No one here cares that you're fireborn. The people here are wise enough to value it. They remember your mother's sacrifice. It's different here."

"So get on with your apprenticeship," Ondias said. "Let Nandara teach you magic and let me teach you the ways of the dragons so you're not so godsdamn afraid of everything. Make it a home."

Spark took a shuddering breath and let it out slowly. What choice did she really have? She suspected the only way out of the city was by grace of a dragon, and the black dragoness had already indicated she wouldn't take Spark to her uncles. The choice wasn't whether or not she should make this place a home. She had no choice at all in that matter. All she could choose was how.

Spark shook her head. "I'm really tired."

All she could think about was her family. About going back to Pasdale and the safe bubble of life with Nanny and Pappy, Bren and Uncle Breen.

The pain of losing them was suffocating. She hadn't fully accepted yet that her old life was gone, that her uncles in the south weren't the answer.

But if family wasn't the answer, she feared there wasn't one. Part of her resented having survived. She doubted her ability to keep going. She knew, deep inside where her thoughts were ephemeral, she had to get past that first.

CHAPTER SIX

S park only spent another day in bed before Ondias was back, relentless about getting her up for good.

"I need you to come with me to the market."

Spark wanted to argue, but knew that tone, even if Nanny never had the voice to use it, the expression was there, the no-nonsense air about her. Spark dragged her heels, summoning the energy not only to leave the bed but to leave the house. It took a lot more scrubbing at the basin than going to greet Nandara had. Curiosity was all that pulled Spark forward. She'd only seen of the settlement what lay beyond her bedroom window and what she'd noticed from the descent the first day.

She was curious about the people, knowing there were scholars and artists to learn from. She left her axe by the door, but pulled her firecloak around her. It wasn't a particularly cold day, but she needed it all the same.

Following Ondias through the muddy streets, Spark felt eyes on her, heard the whispering behind hands. She ducked her head, trying to press it down into her rib cage, and wished she had a hood on the cloak. Seemingly oblivious to the attention, Ondias brought her to a little market square with no stone on any of the streets but planks of wood under the tables.

It was a miniature version of the market in Pasdale and the familiarity set Spark at ease. There were supplies all around but not many people behind tables.

"We get by mostly on bartering," Ondias said. "Those who frequently travel beyond the valley to earn a living bring back supplies and trade them for the food grown here or for help in the upkeep of their homes."

"I didn't even notice farms."

Ondias smiled. "They're not exactly the first thing you see when you come to this place."

Spark glanced up at the sparkling city. She was certain she could make a hundred descents into the valley and not notice farmlands even when she looked for them.

"Even now, it's still something to see, after all the years I've been here. Even though it's a fraction of the splendour it was before, it's still something that stuns me every time I let my thoughts linger on it."

Ondias pressed deeper into the market. Spark trailed her, trying to disappear behind the small woman, but everyone Ondias stopped to talk to stared at Spark. Spark was horrified at first, until people started grinning and introducing themselves. The whispers didn't cease, but it lacked the malice she was used to. She stood taller but her gaze darted from face to face.

Ondias introduced Spark to a rapid-fire succession of artists and scholars, wizards and dragon admirers, all of them grinning like fools. Spark instantly forgot everyone's names, too busy watching the dragon city to really pay attention. She scrutinized the support arches and followed the circling paths of the dragons flying overhead.

"She's out hunting," Ondias said.

Spark didn't realize she'd been looking for the black dragoness until Ondias pointed it out.

"They go in groups, eat their fill and come back with as much as they can carry. When they're especially successful, they share with us. We've got some chickens and a couple goats and one stubborn and oblivious mule, but we're still working on cultivating our own livestock. It's difficult, as I'm sure you can imagine."

Spark tried not to giggle at the thought of a cow or horse being flown in by dragon.

"Someone could cultivate some herds in the plains south of the mountains," Spark said.

"Someone could. I wish someone would."

"You've tried?"

"Some. I try not to meddle in the affairs of dragons anymore. They don't seem as interested in bargaining with humans."

Ondias picked up only a couple of things in the market before moving on. She stopped at one of the most derelict buildings Spark had seen. It was made out of stone, but one wall had crumbled away entirely. The door was gone. It wasn't entirely open to the elements as someone had done a decent job of covering it with a large tarp, though that had grown frayed.

Ondias pushed back a corner of the tarp and Spark's mouth fell open.

It was a forge.

Ancient and derelict as everything else, but still a forge. Some rusted tools hung on the wall and to one side stood a wooden workbench that had had the good fortune not to rot away. The anvil was dusty and spotted with rust, but in working condition. Spark stepped over the pile of rubble and gave the workbench a shake, pleased by how sturdy it was. She plucked the rusted-shut tongs off the wall, turning them over in her hands to see if they were salvageable or good scrap. As she did, she ducked her head down into the forge.

She found coal older than the hills and colder than the arctics piled inside. A quick test blast of flame revealed the chimney wasn't clogged. Spark cleared away some debris and set the tongs on the workbench, deciding they'd need to be melted down. Tall order for other blacksmiths when there were no useable tools around. Well, there was a hammer that looked like it would do the trick. Spark could probably use a stone if she had to. And of course, she didn't need tongs to make tongs. She didn't need tongs at all and wondered if she should leave them as scrap and form them into something more useful later.

Ondias cleared her throat and startled Spark. She'd forgotten Ondias was there, that they were on any sort of errand.

"Oh, sorry. You probably want to finish your chores."

"This was my chore." Ondias looked at her pointedly. "We haven't had a blacksmith in a decade."

"No wonder this place is such a dump then. Well, you've got me now. And you've got me out of bed."

Spark gave the woman an appreciative look. She picked up stray bricks that had fallen from the wall and stacked them neatly off to one side.

"So bartering is how you get everything done around here?" Spark looked thoughtfully at the brick she held. "Well, you need a new roof, and

I'll need some supplies in here to get started. And we should start turning some of those awful tents into real homes."

Ondias smiled.

"Nandara knows terramancy. Couldn't she pull walls up out of the ground for us?"

"I believe she could."

"Well then. You want a blacksmith again? She's not living in a rickety dump. Are there men who can spare some strength? Or a dragon who might be bartered with?"

Ondias narrowed her eyes at the mention of bartering with dragons, but she didn't seem completely against the idea.

"I'm sure you can manage something," she said. "You'll get to know everyone here before long—there are only five hundred of us. Five hundred and fourteen now with you, Nandara and Riz."

"You know them all, don't you?"

"Quite well. I know everyone who's come and gone from this place. I've been here since the start, since it was just me and your grandmother sleeping under a wagon, worrying about your grandfather."

Spark stopped piling bricks and looked at Ondias. She'd known Ondias started the place, invited to do so by the dragons. Ondias and Nanny were the reason people started seeing dragons as more than beasts. Or enormous nuisances. Spark hadn't heard a story about them sleeping under a wagon. How would they get a wagon out here?

Ondias frowned, looking at the forge with her gaze focused inward.

"I travelled a lot then," Ondias said, her voice thick with remembering. "I was learning a lot, teaching a lot. Those were the good days. When Lady Zyx was around to support us. When Draxli and Loch hadn't come in with their meddling and their tangled words and their floods."

"I don't know much about it. I know what Mamma did, but no one ever talked about the city."

"Ah, well, Reiser wouldn't have had first-hand knowledge, and I suppose Dionelle never wrote it down. What a pity."

Spark wanted to hear more about sleeping under wagons, but Ondias's mood had turned.

"Did you keep the letters Nanny sent you? Is there anything in them I could learn from?"

Ondias looked at her sideways. "You've seen that room where you sleep." She headed out of the ruin. "I'll go through my letters and see what's appropriate for your eyes. I don't know if that tale will be in there though."

Spark slumped and followed Ondias out into the wide lane lined with old tents.

"We'll get dinner started and talk a little more about what you'll need. Maybe there'll be some wine in the back of the pantry, and I'll even tell you about my first time out here."

Passing through the market on the way back, Spark stopped when a large man called her name and waved her over.

"Mita! Can it be?"

Ondias stiffened as he started toward them, but Spark watched him curiously. He was older, not as old as Ondias, maybe forty, mountainous with tawny skin and a bushy black beard streaked with grey. Spark wasn't surprised to be recognized by a stranger, not even in the middle of nowhere. Especially not here.

"It's her, Stone." Ondias's tone was colder than midwinter. "She's had a rough trip here."

He stopped a cautious distance from the pair of them, giving Spark a good look.

"Here on her own?" His tone was careful.

"My family is dead." It left her hollowed out, breathless.

Stone's expression twisted, pained, and his big frame sagged.

"She needs rest," Ondias said.

"And I made a promise to Neesha, whether any of you want to believe it or not." He stood straighter.

"It's all right," Spark said to Ondias. "I've had enough rest to last me to the end of my days. You can start dinner without me if you don't want to stay here."

Ondias grew colder, giving Spark a sharp look. She huffed and marched away. Spark blinked and watched her go.

"Why doesn't she like you?" Spark asked the man Ondias called Stone.

"Oh, now there's a tale."

"I'm getting tired of people telling me there are tales and then not telling them."

Stone grinned at her, but his brown eyes held a touch of sadness.

"You were a tiny thing the last time I saw you," he said. "Amazing how much time has passed. I lose track of it out here."

"You know my family?" Spark really wanted this story. She couldn't ever remember anyone talking about a man named Stone.

"Aye. And you have no idea who I am, do you?"

"Should I?"

He furrowed his brow, his mouth pinched in a line. "No, I suppose not. It was a long time ago. I was almost someone to you, before it all went wrong."

He glanced out into the mountains and then at her. "Come sit with me for a spell, and I'll give you a story."

Spark shrugged and followed him across the market. He sat behind one of the produce tables and pulled over a crate for Spark to sit on.

"What's this promise you made to my mother?"

"Well, now, that has everything to do with why Ondias don't like me. It started, when it comes down to it, when Di and Reiser tried to match me with your ma."

Spark's eyebrows shot up. "You mean you were almost someone to me because you were almost my stepfather?"

"In a manner." Stone smiled and folded Spark into his massive arms. A fatherly hug, like the ones she used to get from Pappy. It set her at ease, despite Ondias's clear dislike of the man.

"It weren't that easy. Nothing was with your ma." He sighed and everything about him sagged. "I'd lost my wife not long before and loved your ma the moment I met her. Didn't care she was already working on bringing you into the world and loved her anyway. But your ma, she was still a girl in a lot of ways, especially at the start of it. She had airs, thought I was beneath her, rejected me outright to start. Then Draxli brought Loch, looking for the three of you, twisting the truth and people's opinions against dragons and fireborn the same. She got some perspective right quick."

He'd been staring out into the square while he spoke, but now he looked out into the hills.

"Pappy said Mamma was going to do anything to keep me safe."

"Aye, it's true. She fought against the reality of motherhood right up until there was a threat against it. Then she was fierce as any dragon. Changed her mind about me, all at once. One day she's cutting the long way through the market so she doesn't have to talk to me, next she's giving me the terms of our betrothal. But that was your ma. She ran hot or cold. Mostly hot, if we're being honest." He chuckled.

"So she changed her mind about your betrothal and it still didn't happen?"

"That's right. She agreed to be my wife right before you were born."

He sighed and looked out at a point in the mountains. Spark followed his gaze to one of the city's diamond support columns. It was sparkling, dazzling. She wondered if it reminded him of something or if he just liked the way it shone.

"When it came time to confront Draxli and his army, it was down to your ma. She'd saved the city once already, in an effort with your nan and some other Guild wizards. Took a frightful toll on her though. She wouldn't do it again until after you were born. Well, you came into the world and she was hell-bent on ending Draxli. I was lucky to see her before that last battle."

When he looked at Spark this time, she saw the lost future in his eyes and half expected to see tears on his face. He gazed off into the hills once more.

"I saw her, she was on her way to call that final blaze that ended it all. I was lucky to find her when I did. She told me what was happening, what she planned to do. I told her not to hold back, despite the risks. We both knew she was doing what she did to protect you."

He glared in the direction Ondias went.

"Zev was with her, he gave us some distance, but must have heard what we said. When the fire took your ma, Ondias blamed me. Like *I* made her do what she did."

"Ondias thinks it's your fault my mamma died?"

"Ridiculous, isn't it? Not a soul in the world, except maybe you, could make your ma do anything she didn't want to. She'd have done it no matter what, no one wants to see that. Maybe your nan did, but of course she'd never say."

"I'm surprised she's still holding it against you, based on something Zev said, even if he was telling the truth. I haven't heard that whole story, but I know she'd be happy enough to see him devoured by dragons."

Stone chuckled. "Well now, Ondias and your nan are friends for a lot of reasons, and I believe shared stubbornness is one of them."

"But you didn't do anything wrong."

"I gave Nee some peace of mind going into that end, but no one wants to see that. I let her go. She needed someone to give her permission to do whatever it took. To not come back. I promised her I would treat you as my own."

He looked long at her before he continued.

"I haven't, of course. You didn't need me to. Whatever Ondias thinks, she's shared it with Dionelle. They all turned cold toward me after we lost your ma. So I came here, hoping she'd return to us. I want to be here for her if she does."

Spark replayed his last words in her mind, staring as she tried to put it all together.

"There's no coming back," she said, uncertain.

"Ah, they've not told you."

"Another tale, is there?"

He paused, thoughtful. "We've got some daylight left. Will you come for a walk with me?"

Spark sat still, her thoughts chasing each other around her mind like rabbits in the spring. She'd learned more from Stone in a few minutes than from years of family stories. Those stories always left out some key things. But his words troubled her too. There was darkness there.

It was far too strange that Spark hadn't known he existed when he'd clearly meant so much to her mother. Were a few twisted words really enough to cut the man from their lives entirely?

"You've got more to tell me about Mamma?"

"More than you can imagine."

Spark got to her feet and followed him out of the settlement toward the slope supporting the glittering diamond column he kept watching. A series of switchbacks led up the long trail. Without Stone's guidance, Spark wouldn't have noticed the narrow little path.

"Took me a long time to find an easy way up," he said. "Your nan would get one of the dragons to bring her here. They've never trusted me that much. I don't know their ways, and it's harder now that they don't talk. But I found a way up. I had to."

Spark expected a story, but he didn't say anything else as they steadily climbed to the base of the support. Spark worried about how much daylight they had left. Sunset neared and even if gravity made the way back easier, she didn't think they'd have light left to guide their way out of the mountains.

Stone hadn't broken a sweat, but Spark's legs ached, and she huffed along like she'd run all day. He was from sturdy farm stock, but so was Spark. She wondered how often he came up here.

A dozen yards from the support, Stone stepped aside and gestured Spark forward. Ahead of her stood a large white gem embedded in an oval outcropping at the base of the unbroken diamond support. Spark realized all at once that it wasn't a stone she was looking at. It was human. A woman.

And only three women in the world had ever looked so startlingly, unnaturally white. Like snow come alive.

Spark shook her head.

"There are other fireborn? I don't..."

Stone came closer, his large hand falling on her shoulder. "It's your ma," he said softly.

"What?" Spark shook. Out of confusion at first, but then anger. Why hadn't she been pyred? Why had they built this bizarre, forgotten shrine? Before Spark could hurl the words at Stone, he gave her more of the story.

"The power of the dragons courses through the whole of these mountains. Their power is much weaker since she opened the fire portal, but it's still far more than enough to sustain her."

"She's *alive*?"

Spark felt empty and cold at first, but her fury blazed into a hot white point in her mind. Her chest was hot and buzzing. Stone moved back. Spark stepped forward, right up to the column containing her mother, peering in on her with one hand against the cold diamond. It thrummed.

Neesha had the same unruly hair as Spark. Hers was half-tamed in a braid, something Spark gave up on as a child. If Neesha's eyes had been open, Spark expected they would be amber. She wondered if there'd be any other colour, like Nanny's blue-amber eyes. But the resemblances between Spark and her mother, other than obvious fireborn traits, were sparse. From what Spark knew, even their personalities were different, with Spark being far more even tempered.

"Did she ever tell you who my father is?"

"No, she didn't," he said, carefully. "I don't think she was sure, not really."

Spark face grew hot, even if Stone's admission wasn't news. Pappy never stopped feeling betrayed by what Neesha did—the disgrace she brought their family—even if he loved Spark fiercely. It didn't matter that Neesha gave her life to save them all.

Spark's anger grew so hot she was numb.

"What happened to her?" Spark bit off the words, spitting them out like an accusation.

Stone's voice softened, like he was trying to tame a dragon. "I wasn't there to see first-hand. Your nan was the one to pull her out of the flames. But the fire portal was open for a long time after the battle ended, and your ma never woke up. There were demons involved—she could take them into her and control them—but I think they were controlling her right back."

"Could she be in their realm? Do you think if I went there I could find her?"

"If you went there it would damn us all. Do you know what happened when your nan was there?"

"It nearly tore the world apart."

That story Spark heard the most. Even tempered or not, no one would let her repeat the ignorant mistake of her grandmother or the reckless mistakes of her mother. Spark was strong enough to open a fire portal, though she'd never tried. Neesha had needed the help of a fire demon to do it, but Spark needed no such aid. So every scrap of pyromancy she'd ever learned came heaped with warnings.

"Mita..." Stone's voice was full of caution. "Neesha had your nan to get her out of that realm. Your nan had Reiser to get her out, but he needed the dragons to help. They wouldn't help again. That means you've got no one to help you if you get stuck there. I don't like this, you can be sure of that, but we can't risk the world to bring your ma back. There's no guarantee that's where she is."

"So you just stand around waiting for her to wake up?" Spark was disgusted by the cowardice.

He held up his hands. "There's nothing I can do. I'm no wizard, no scholar. I have no influence. All I can do is hope."

"I'll get her back."

"Mita, you need to think careful on this."

Stone moved closer to her, and she realized then how far away he'd been. She wasn't surprised by the shower of sparks warming the ground at her feet to a soft glow. He came closer anyway.

"Mita, your ma did this to keep you safe. Could be she's staying wherever she is to keep protecting you. No one really understands what makes you the way you are. There's no way of knowing what she meant to happen. You can decide to help her, I grant you that. But she would want you to stay safe, no matter what you do. It's best you leave it be, let Neesha find her own way home."

"You don't know what you're talking about!"

Spark spun on her heel and propelled herself down the mountain, no regard for the path they'd taken on the trek up. She wasn't sure what was worse, that her mother was alive and no one ever told her, or that there was nothing anyone could do to help Neesha. Through her anger, Spark felt profoundly tired.

No family left but distant uncles and this husk of a mother. It was so tempting to let the blackness open up before her and tip right into it.

Ondias and Nandara and now Stone all wanted her to move on. Like a family was nothing, just something you gave up on. Start over? With what?

She had herself, and now she had her mother. The two of them together would be an unstoppable force. They could swoop down on Pasdale and reduce Loch to ashes and then power on south to her uncles.

There was plenty for her, if she could manage it. If she restored her mother, the whole future would open up, full of possibility and stability. Devoid of loneliness. She didn't like that Stone and everyone else was right about the danger. It meant she'd have to be careful. She needed to learn as much as she could about her mother's power, about pyromancy and the fire realm.

Then she could put her family back together.

CHAPTER SEVEN

Spark shoved the front door open hard enough as she barged into Ondias's that it banged against the wall before rebounding closed behind her. Ondias and Lina were sitting down to dinner and it startled them both.

"Are you all right?" Lina asked.

"No." Spark grabbed the plate they'd left out for her and zipped straight to her room. She didn't mind Lina, but aside from being tall like Zev and having his black hair, Lina looked too much like Ondias, who Spark currently wanted to incinerate.

Spark sat on the bed and crammed food into her mouth, not because she was hungry but because she needed something to keep her from screaming. With her back to the rest of the house, she stared out the window, watching a bright glow from inside the dragon city. One section of it was always aflame. She couldn't see her mother from this room, but the glow in the city gave her comfort.

Lina was gone when Spark brought her dirty plate to the kitchen. Ondias was at the table, trying to cut Spark with her gaze. Spark wasn't having any of it. She didn't acknowledge the woman as she washed and dried the plate and stuffed it back into the cupboard. She thought of going back to her room, but still felt like screaming and didn't have anything left to stuff down on top of the urge.

"Do you really hate Stone because my mother did something foolish no one could stop her from doing anyway?" Spark blurted. "Seems foolish things were her way of life."

"Is that what he told you?"

"I had to hear it from a stranger that she was even still alive!"

Ondias kept glaring.

"All this time trying to get me out here for my own good, to keep me safe, and none of you bloody well thought to tell me she was here? And now you want me to trust you?"

"Nandara wanted to tell you, but your grandparents wouldn't let her."

"She could have anyway. If any of them had told me anything, I'd have come here. Maybe Nanny would have too and the others would still be alive. Is it really that hard to tell someone the truth?"

"You don't know what you're talking about."

"Oh, yes. I'm just a little girl, can't possibly be trusted with information that could save my life."

Spark was close to spouting fire and tried to calm herself down. Much as she wanted to scream, she wanted more strongly to learn about her mother.

"Everyone's always so quick to tell me what I shouldn't do with my pyromancy, but no one wants to teach me what I *should* do with it. If I knew more, I could have helped Nanny, maybe stopped those dragons. If I'd known the truth about what happened to Mamma, I could have avoided that mess altogether. So when's it going to stop? I'm on my own now—when are you going to start treating me like an adult?"

Ondias's hazel eyes flashed and she opened her mouth but snapped it shut and sucked air through flared nostrils.

"You're laying blame in the wrong place," Ondias said. "We did what we thought was best to help you and your family. In the end, it was Dionelle's stubbornness that did the worst damage. Even so, Loch is the real threat here."

"I could have done something."

"What, like your mother did?"

"She stopped them, didn't she?"

"And what good did it do her?"

"She still saved everyone, even without full training. And I'm far stronger than she ever was."

"Is that a fact?"

"It's what Nandara says."

Ondias stood in front of Spark, arms crossed, glaring up. "Then maybe you should take this up with her."

"I will, next time I see her. But I'm tired of people withholding information I need to know. You're here, she's not."

Ondias shook her head and sighed. "Fine, what is it you want to know?"

"For starters, you could answer me about Stone."

"That man is trouble. He was no good for your ma in the end, and clearly still doesn't have the sense when to shut his fool mouth."

"So he shouldn't have told me the truth? Shouldn't have told Mamma the truth? You really think he could have stopped her?"

"I know there was no stopping her, but he should have tried anyway. It would have been the right thing to do."

Spark snorted rudely. "Stopping Draxli was the right thing to do. That's exactly what she did! Do you think it would have helped her at all to have Stone turning against her like everyone else?"

"Letting her run wild never helped."

"So she should have let Draxli and Loch flood the city and take it all over? Let them drown the dragons, and me, her, and Nanny right along with them? What exactly is it you think she should have done? Do you really think you could have made the decision she did? Would you really have sacrificed your life with Zev and your children to save Pasdale? Oh sure, you'd do it in a heartbeat now, but then?"

Ondias's expression blackened at mention of Zev. When she spoke, her voice was low. "Don't you pretend to know me, girl."

"Don't pretend to know my mother! You knew her through the filter of your friendship with Nanny and Pappy. You knew her from the outside looking in. You didn't know her any better than you know me."

Spark had been treading on thin ice all along, but mention of Zev snuffed out any chance she had of learning more from Ondias. Ondias's expression only got darker, and Spark was thinking clearly enough to see things would only continue to devolve. She shoved out the door as fiercely as she'd come in.

She stormed through the night, swerving around buildings at random, not paying attention to where she went, only that she kept moving. When she wound up in the market square, she stopped and looked around. She wanted to find Nandara, though whether to shout at her or seek comfort

Spark wasn't certain. She wanted to find Stone and see what else he knew. But Spark didn't know where to find either of them and the market was empty. Spark didn't see anyone else out at all. And she was bone tired of relying on the kindness of strangers.

A familiar weight pressed in on her, so much like the night the dragons took her family. Loneliness yawned before her, darker than the darkest night. Spark struggled to resist the urge to lie down in the middle of the cold lane. But if nothing else, Ondias had at least shown her the one place that was hers, one place she could feel like she belonged. It was the only place she remembered how to find.

Spark pulled back the tarp on the old blacksmith's shop and called a small fire to the palm of her hand. The one remaining window, devoid of glass, had been boarded up, but there were patches of roof missing. Spark saw the stars and a shining section of the city's arches. She had light enough.

In a moment, she'd have warmth enough too. She went to the forge and drove her hands up to the wrists into the coals, igniting them instantly. After she fanned them to a full blaze, she went back to picking up pieces of brick and stacking them in a neat pile. Exhausted as she was, she was too wound up for anything and needed to keep moving, so she cleaned up the space well into the night until her mind was as weary as her body.

Shadow eventually joined her, and his quiet companionship and reliable familiarity helped set her at ease. Spark curled up with her dog in a mossy patch under the worktable and pulled Nanny's pendant out from under her shirt. A moon ago she'd had a warm bed and loving family. This new reality was a hot coal to swallow. Learning about her mother hadn't helped. She let flow a lifetime of pent up tears, weeping for Neesha now that she had the truth.

It was a truth she was resistant to. There had to be a way to help Neesha. Spark was in a place full of dragons and dragon scholars and pyromancers. The information she sought would be in this valley or nowhere at all. And after a decade, this little village that ran on bartering had a new blacksmith.

CHAPTER EIGHT

S park stood at the workbench begrudgingly eating the bowl of porridge Ondias brought her that morning. The sting of last night's argument was fresh for them both, Ondias scowling and not saying much more than Spark. Spark had stayed under that work table all night, managed some sleep out of pure contrariness, but the old blacksmith's place remained unlivable.

"Dionelle said that if anything ever happened to her, she wanted me and Nandara to watch over you."

Ondias's words tore at her like shattered glass. Spark finished shovelling the food into her mouth and pushed the bowl away.

"I've gone sixteen years without hearing Di talk, don't think giving me the silent treatment now is going to have any effect."

Spark's silence had nothing to do with having any sort of effect on Ondias and everything to do with not wanting to talk to the woman. There was nothing to say. Spark hadn't forgiven any of them for hiding the truth about her mother, and she definitely didn't want to hear anymore about Nanny. Her chest constricted at the merest mention of family. Hot tears stung her eyes.

Spark picked up a rusty old spade and started heaving dirt from the floor back out the crumbled wall it had blown in through. She'd seen a patch of stone floor in the morning light, and she was determined to find it all.

"It's time for you to learn properly about dragons. Not the sorts of things you can learn in books. Not even the ones I wrote myself."

This made Spark look up, a fresh spade of dirt hefted and ready to pitch. She watched Ondias for a beat, then tossed the dirt through the hole in the wall and shovelled a new spadeful. Spark would let her talk, but it wasn't going to stop her from cleaning this place up. Making it hers.

"There are some things you can only learn through living them. There are some secrets the dragons won't share, some things they won't allow us to commit to paper."

Spark kept working, wishing the woman would get on with it or leave. It made sense to learn as much about the dragons as she could. The black dragoness seemed willing to overlook Spark's missteps and was maybe shielding the others from her blunders, but she certainly wasn't teaching Spark anything. If she was going to live here, she had to learn to deal with the dragons. As fireborn, she needed to work alongside them.

"Nandara will continue your mentorship. But you are absolutely not opening a fire portal to look for your mother's spirit."

Spark drove the point of the spade into the dirt, feeling it *thunk* against the stone below, and leaned on it while she looked at Ondias.

"Ah, so you don't hate Stone that much do you?" Spark said.

"He came to speak to me this morning, worried about you."

"He can save his worry."

Ondias leaned against the workbench.

"You're really not considering that foolishness?" Ondias asked.

"Can't consider anything until I've learned all I can. Could be there's an even better way to do it than opening a fire portal. Something safe. Won't know till I learn."

Ondias scowled. Spark resumed shovelling. The tension between them electrified the air so that every move Spark made prickled. Spark had no idea what Ondias was so angry about but hoped she'd get over it soon. She'd never lived with such hostile company before, so used to the gentle way her family wove their days together, the way their actions were always informed by kindness, even when they were cross with each other. This? It was hell.

"Nandara can worry about keeping you from blowing us all up," Ondias muttered. "I'm going to worry about keeping you from being eaten by a dragon with your manners."

"Nothing wrong with my dragon manners. The dragoness likes me just fine."

"And for that reason she overlooks how rude you are."

"I'm not rude! To dragons."

Ondias snorted derisively.

"Dionelle was the best dragon whisperer Pasdale ever had and yet you can't even manage basic interaction."

Spark shrugged, shovelled more dirt, wanted to hit Ondias with the spade every time she mentioned Nanny.

"You have to treat their presence like a gift," Ondias continued. "Like you're indebted to them just because they didn't eat you. You need to remember that, that they're dreadfully self-important, and it will inform all of your interactions with them."

"That sounds terrible."

"It can be trying, like dealing with hyper-intelligent toddlers. Some of the younger dragons, like our mistress, enjoy the company of humans and don't require as much coddling. I can only assume it's why she hasn't eaten you yet."

"Or maybe she's just got a better temperament than you."

"Mita, you're not the only one who lost someone in that attack." Ondias's voice broke.

Spark's stomach clenched and she swallowed.

"Your family was like my family, like the dragoness's family," Ondias said gently. "That we were too afraid of the dangers in Pasdale to visit you doesn't make that less true."

The abrupt end to Pappy's screams echoed through Spark's mind. Ondias could talk about what she'd all lost all she wanted, the damned woman hadn't *watched them all die*. Spark gritted her teeth and heaved some dirt harder than necessary.

"Whoa now," a woman's voice called from beyond the hole in the wall.

Spark looked up, startled as the voice's owner stepped sprightly through the hole and held her hand out in greeting. This woman was like an princess out of a dream, with a thick, curvy body, a cascade of dark mahogany hair down to her waist, smooth, dark ochre skin and playful brown eyes set into a wide, round face. Realizing she stood slack-jawed, Spark snapped her mouth shut and held out her hand as well.

"I'm Spark."

"Not Mita?"

"Um. Well, yes. But most people call me Spark."

"As you'll have it. I'm Ember."

As Spark's lips curled in a smile that she hoped wasn't too dopey, she had to fight to keep the sheen of tears from filming over her eyes. Ember was so forward and had an energy so much like Bren.

"We're in the middle of something," Ondias said, a sharp edge in her voice.

Spark's brain caught up with what was going on, wondered why Ondias would be so rude to this woman who was really not far past girlhood, not more than a couple of years Spark's senior. But then Spark saw the resemblance, not only in her dark complexion, but in the shape of her mouth and the line of her brow. She must be Stone's daughter. So Ondias hated the whole family?

"It's all right, Ondias. I don't mind meeting some new people. Got to get to know everyone, might as well start now."

Ondias sniffed, collected the empty porridge bowl, and left.

"Has she always been this awful?" Spark asked Ember once Ondias was gone.

"Not usually this bad. You mention Zev or something?"

Spark sighed. "Not today."

"If it was this week she'll be ornery for a week yet. She's sweet but prickly and can turn into a dragon if you say the wrong thing. Pa says she used to be cheerful, before the thing with Zev."

"Does she blame the whole world for it or something?"

"Pa says she's jealous of anyone with a family keeping it together. You know her kids took Zev's side at first? They always disagreed with what he did—no one could hide the fact he tore the rift in their marriage—but their kids stayed with him because he went back to civilization."

"Oh." Spark had heard little about what happened. She caught snatches of it now and then, vague hints overheard in conversations between Pappy and Nandara.

"But Lina's here," Spark said.

"Oh, aye, she came back because she realized what a bumpkin she really is. And the place needed a healer. And she's always been close to her ma."

"She doesn't seem like a miserable cow."

Ember laughed, a hearty, mirthful sound. "I think Ondias has hoarded all the misery forever. None left for anyone else."

Spark chuckled, wishing it were true, and set the spade aside.

"You're really cleaning this place up? I saw the smoke out the chimney, knew it must be you after Pa commented talking to you last night. Sorry about your ma."

"Sorry about yours."

Ember shrugged. "I never really had one, same as you, but at least I always knew the truth about mine."

Spark scowled. "It's weird because I never missed her when I thought she was dead. There was no mother-shaped hole in my life. Nanny raised me like any mother would have. But now I can't stop thinking about what if."

Spark looked at her feet. Ember came closer, standing right next to her.

"You look a lot like her," Ember said. "And not just your colouring. Pa said he'd have recognized you even if you were purple or normal coloured."

Spark looked up, giving Ember side-eye.

"You don't see it? Pa says you walk like her. But it's also in the shape of your jaw and that hair. My word! No wonder you keep yours short."

"I don't suppose your pa has mentioned much about my mamma's power?"

"He said you can pull flame out of the air. That true? You don't need even a spark already lit?"

"It's true."

"Now there's something!" Ember looked over at the forge and then the bit of floor Spark had already cleaned. "You a blacksmith then?"

Spark nodded. "Don't want to live with Ondias a moment longer than I have to, even if she is nice sometimes. This space is big enough to be a home. It's just me."

Ember put her hand on Spark's shoulder and gave her a pitying look.

"I heard about your family. I'm really sorry. I don't know what I'd do if I didn't have Pa and River. Even if River is... well, he's ornery. But still, family is everything. I hope you find some peace here. It's a beautiful place, at the very least. And beauty is good for the soul."

Spark watched Ember's full lips as she spoke and nodded absently, hoping she didn't have her mouth gaping open. Ember was right about beauty. Spark felt better in the few minutes Ember had been there. Between Ember and the dragon city, Spark didn't think she'd ever need to look at anything else again.

"If you need help getting this place going, you let us know. Pa is eager to help you get settled. And I'll do what I can, but I doubt I've got any skills that would be useful to you."

"Oh, I don't know about that."

Ember gave her a sideways look. Her grin was crooked, but her eyes twinkled with amusement. Spark realized what she'd said and winced.

"I mean you're good company. I haven't had good company since... Since Pasdale."

Ember gave her a full smile. "Well, I'm the best seamstress in town, so I might be able to help you with some finishing touches in here. Later. Once you've got anything to finish."

"I can't sew worth a cow pie, so that sounds like a good deal. I'm happy to barter, if there's anything you need repaired."

"That sounds—"

"So this is where you've flounced off to this time."

Spark startled but Ember barely noticed when a large young man pushed in through the tarp, shouting at her. In an instant, Spark knew this must be Ember's brother; he was a younger, ugly version of Stone. And maybe it wasn't completely fair to call him ugly. It was the scowl on his face. It fit too easily into his features, like he'd been built to be in a permanently foul mood.

"Couldn't leave it alone, could ya?" He grabbed his sister by the arm.

"What difference does it make?" Ember said lightly, shrugging out of his grip.

"Pa told you to stay out of it."

"I'm not bothering anything. I just came to say hello. You don't think it's great we've got a blacksmith again?"

River glared at their surroundings.

"I'll get excited when we've got a real smithy and not some pretender hiding out in a dump."

Spark blinked, less hurt or offended and more flat out surprised by the rudeness coming out of a complete stranger.

"Honestly, that's uncalled for." Ember's cheery tone held a touch of reproach.

"One freak in this place was bad enough, but now we've got a second, this one walking around and talking."

Spark's anger washed over her so quickly she had no hope of stymying it. The coals in the forge roared to life in a monster blaze, but she squeezed her hands into fists and reined it all in. Ember jumped back from the blaze, but River only grinned at it.

"There, you see? She's nothing but a freak and a menace."

"Honestly, do you wonder why no one wants to be around you?" Ember pushed his shoulder and drove him toward the hole in the wall they'd both come through.

"There's a door," Spark managed, her voice soft and her cheeks hot.

Ember gave her another pitying look. "Yes, I'll use the door next time. Good luck with all of this." She turned to River. "Let's just go. You've done enough damage for one day."

The place felt colder once Ember was gone, and Spark looked to the forge to make sure she hadn't put the fire all the way out. A gentle flame still burned. Spark's spade leaned against the work table, but she didn't pick it up right away. Instead, she climbed up onto the table and sat with her back against the wall, knees drawn up to her chest.

Between Ondias's sudden hostility as testament to all Spark had lost and Ember reminding her of her cousin and best friend gone forever, Spark could scarcely draw a breath. A vast gulf opened inside her, yawning to devour her. She tried focusing on the present, but there was so much grief.

Was River an outlier or did they all think she was a freak? There'd been plenty of whispering when she'd gone through the market. They were friendly enough to her face, but this wasn't Pasdale. They didn't have to hate her to think she was a freak.

Spark let out a long slow breath and climbed down from the table to resume shovelling. Once she had proper walls and a door—with a lock—she'd have to see if Ember would tell her more.

With a worn-down broom nicked from Ondias's junk piles, Spark swept the stone floor. Her back and shoulders ached, and she was hungry enough that the broom started to look appetizing. She wasn't going back to Ondias's if she didn't have to. But she'd either have to swallow her pride or figure out some basic repairs to trade for food.

Spark didn't need to clean things up or gather more tools to do simple things, but she was reluctant to let people see the full extent of her power. Without a wall, she would have to work metal more traditionally. The hammer she'd tested needed to be melted down, but she'd need a bucket for quenching and a decent stone she could use to form the hammer first.

She'd kept the fire burning in the forge, though she didn't need the heat. She hoped it would attract attention, like it had with Ember, so she could meet more people without Ondias around like some sort of chaperone. No one had come since Ember left.

She wondered if she should slink back to Ondias's and wait for the end of the day. People were probably busy with work.

"Um."

Spark turned to the door to see a young man, tall and skinny like a rake, or maybe a mop with his shaggy black corkscrew hair. Even his long face was sharp and angular with high cheek bones and a prominent nose. He looked to be the same age as Ember, and he had a bundle tucked under one spidery dark umber arm.

"You'd have more luck kicking the dirt out the door than using that thing," he said. "Why don't you use a proper broom?"

"I haven't got a proper broom."

He shrugged, his bony shoulders stabbing the air. "Have it your way." He came into the room and set his package down on the work table.

"What's this?" Spark asked.

"Open it and you'll find out." He was already on his way out.

"That's it? You're not going to introduce yourself? I'm Spark."

The young man stopped in the doorway. "I know who you are. You think there's anybody here doesn't know who you are?"

"Fine, but I don't know a damn one of you. Just bloody Ondias."

"And Nandara. I hear you met Ember and River this morning, Stone last night. That must have been a riot."

"Oh, yes. And did you hear what I had for breakfast?"

"That slop Ondias calls porridge."

Spark stared openly. "Actually? Steal the moons, is there nothing I've done that everyone in town doesn't already know about?"

He stabbed the air with his shoulders again. "Bet half them already know I'm in here talking to you. So what?"

"Look, I'm just trying to be friendly. You're the one making it into something."

"I don't care why you came here or who your mother and grandmother are, and I definitely don't give an arse that my gran loves you like one of the family. That damn thing's from her." He gestured to the package on the table. "She damn-near got killed because of you. Stupid stubborn fireborn like the rest of your family. Go ahead and get yourself killed over your pride, leave the rest of us out of it."

"What even...?"

He glared at her, his eyes a shock of emerald against his dark skin and black locks falling over his forehead. She'd seen those eyes before.

"Wait, you're Jatten!"

"Everyone calls me Jatt. And so what?"

"Nandara didn't stay because of me, she stayed because of Nanny! That's got nothing to do with me."

"It's got everything to do with you!" He threw his arms up in frustration. "Your gran wouldn't leave because *you* wouldn't leave. Meanwhile I'm stuck here and my mum is way out in Greenveil and all we can do is worry about Gran and Gramps while Pasdale got crazier. Every message to us from the Guild was worse and worse."

"You think I knew any of that?"

"You knew Gran was trying to get you to leave."

"There wasn't any sense of urgency to it until there was that new king. I had no idea."

"If you'd just left, even for a season, Gran could have convinced the rest of your family to go. She damn-near got herself killed to save the lot of you."

"Fat lot of good it did!"

Spark ground her teeth and gripped the broom handle, ready to swat Jatt in the head. Her pulse throbbed in her temples. She didn't care at all how much the forge flared behind her. Did he really think his grandmother being in a bit of danger compared at all to her losing everyone she'd ever loved?

But Nandara always intended to come to the dragon city to be with him. It wouldn't do her any favours to insult her mentor's grandson. But it wouldn't do her any favours to let him stomp all over her either. *He* wasn't her mentor.

"Nandara's a grown woman and she stayed because she wanted to," Spark snapped. "You're selling yourself a lie if you think there's any more to it than that. Same goes for my Nanny. She could have moved the whole family south like my uncles already did."

"Your whole family is insane."

"My whole family is *dead*!"

This time, the forge flared so much that flames licked at Spark as she stood in the middle of the room. She tossed the broom aside to swat the flames from her shirt. That was all she needed, to burn away her last items of clothing in a fit of rage.

When she turned, Jatt stood there with his mouth open. She advanced on him, shaking a fist.

"Don't stand here and act like a victim when your family is safe, no matter how close it was, when my whole family is ashes in the wind! If your nan, or anyone else, had bothered to tell me the truth about my mother, I'd have come here in a heartbeat to see her. So go ahead and plant your blame firmly up your bony arse."

"Whatever." He waved dismissively. "You're a fool. I haven't got time for this, my master's waiting for me."

She noticed the paint staining his hands and clothes as he stomped out her door. Nandara said something about him being an artist. She hoped a dragon ate all his paintings and shat on his studio.

Shaking and trying not to cry, she went to the work table and unwrapped the cloth to find a small round of bread, a portion of hard cheese, and a water skin.

Too bad Jatt's words had taken her appetite.

CHAPTER NINE

Spark pushed into the building and lit the forge, not caring that it only attracted people intent on picking fights with her. A particularly loud racket from the dragons woke her earlier than normal that morning—not that she slept well given the dark thoughts that plagued her—and she half wanted a fight to go with her foul mood. Ondias had been in bed when Spark rushed out of the house that morning with Shadow at her heels and some pilfered items in tow.

She had a little bundle wrapped up in a shabby old blanket that had been cushioning two pieces of furniture stacked on top of each other. Spark took one of the pieces of furniture, too. It was a wobbly old stool, but it would give her something other than the floor or table to sit on. She unwrapped it all, refolding the blanket and leaving it under the table, where she hadn't yet shovelled away the moss-covered dirt.

She'd taken some old nubs from candle sticks too, which she could draw out to last her a week. The last thing she'd stuffed into her bundle before running off that morning had been some food. A round of bread and a jar of preserves. She hadn't thought to grab a spoon or knife, but she reckoned she could dip chunks of bread straight into the preserves. Maybe Nandara would send her lunch again, hopefully with a friendlier messenger this time.

"Now what do I do?" she asked Shadow. The dog tilted his head, ears perked up. "I should have stolen some books, too. Nothing for it, I'm not going back there until dinner."

It wasn't so much that Spark had stolen anything, aside from the food. She planned to return it all as soon as she got the old smithy properly functioning and had enough of her own stuff accumulated that she didn't need to resort to thievery. Besides, it was all stuff she'd have been using if living with Ondias.

There was a tap near the door and Spark jumped up to answer it, hoping it was Ember. She threw the tarp back and cried out, jumping back. Glittering blackness filled the doorway.

"Skin me alive, mistress, give me some warning, would you?"

The dragoness hit her with a thin line of fire, slamming it into her face.

"Right, fine, that was a terrible greeting on both our parts—let's start again?"

The dragoness snorted, blowing Spark farther across the room. Shadow leapt out the hole in the wall and darted away.

"All right, from the top. Maybe you can do something less human than knock? Then I'll know it's you."

Another line of fire exploded in Spark's face. Then the dragoness scraped one monstrous claw down the wall. Spark shuddered and winced, but there was no mistaking the sound. Spark ran to the threshold, pretending to throw it open.

"Greetings, mistress! How excellent to see you again. I trust your hunt went well?"

The dragoness narrowed her eyes.

"What? I thought I got it right that time." Spark ran through the interaction and couldn't think of where she could do better. She gave a mental shrug and moved out into the lane, where the dragoness lay with her chin on the ground, looking through Spark's door.

"I'm going to make this old ruin my home. What do you think?"

The dragoness snorted and stood up.

"You're right. It's not much, but what else can I do? A forge is the perfect place for me." She paused. "Thank you for bringing me here. I realize I haven't really seen you since we got here. Did things go well with your superiors? You had quite the gash. Are you better?"

The dragoness leaned down, her great head coming a long way to reach the ground, the skin on her neck was black and gleaming, not so much as a trace of a scar.

"Good. I'm glad you're all right. I'd hate to think you suffered on my part."

The dragoness snorted and stood up straight.

"What brought you by this morning?" She thought about what Ondias said. Could winning over a dragon go any worse than trying to befriend any of the blasted people in this village? "Er, what has made you honour my humble door with your presence?"

The dragoness lifted one massive hand and lightly flicked Spark over. Well, it was light for a dragon, but took all the wind out of Spark and sent her careening across the lane.

"Blasted moons, you dragons are impossible!" Spark wheezed, rubbing her ribs.

The dragoness's eyes glittered even more. She gave Spark another of her ghastly, toothy grins.

"Ah, yes, nearly tear the human apart for a joke. Excellent. Really, though? Did you just come to knock me around?"

This time the dragoness set her hand on the ground, palm up, and waited. As soon as Spark climbed onto her hand, she closed her talons around the girl and sprang up into the air.

"You're going to knock my house down doing that!" Spark called, wondering if the dragoness heard her over the sound of the wind whistling past. The rush of air made Spark grin.

Spark's eyes widened as the dragoness climbed into the sky, heading for the dragon city. Her mother and both of her grandparents had been inside the city, although there hadn't been any humans going up there since Spark arrived, so she'd thought it was off limits. But if the dragoness was bringing her it must be okay. It wasn't like humans could get to it on their own. Still, things had changed, and she didn't want to see the dragoness in another fight because of this.

The outside of the city was dotted with wide oval openings, and the dragoness swooped into one of them, sliding down a short tunnel into a vast space. She set Spark down on the glossy floor, swirled diamond and obsidian stretching across the cavernous room. There were other dragons in there—seven of them—at the opposite end of the space. They looked up as the dragoness dropped in but went back to their business.

"Are they the Superiors?"

She nodded.

"Is it a good idea for me to be here?"

She shook her head.

Spark's eyes widened and she flexed her hands. "Mistress, aren't you in enough trouble?"

The dragoness tilted her head to the side and narrowed her eyes, but then she started walking along the wide, rounded edge of the room.

"Why don't you have names?"

Spark was tired of calling her "mistress" all the time. It wasn't bad when it was only the two of them, but there were more than a dozen dragonesses in the valley and giving them all the same title was tedious and bound to lead to confusion.

"I mean, I know you have names for each other in your language, names people can't say. But there must be some kind of translation into our language. Why don't you tell me what the other dragons call you?"

The dragoness glared.

"Fine. I'll make up a name then."

Spark watched her walking past an obsidian panel that streaked across the floor to swirl in the middle with the diamonds. Spark could call her that, but Obsidian seemed too obvious. Midnight seemed trite. Spark remembered how looking at the dragoness often made her dizzy.

"I'm going to call you Abyss."

The dragoness flicked out her tail and swatted Spark with it, knocking her down. Not hard enough to hurt, but hard enough to get her point across.

"You can call me whatever you want in your own language. I'm sure your kind must have a word for 'little white freak.' If not, you can make one up."

The dragoness snarled.

"Is that my new dragon name?"

Abyss kept walking. They approached a bright section of the vast room, a spot against a diamond wall. A brilliant light shone there, the one Spark had noticed from the valley floor. It was visible on overcast days, like a star just out of reach.

A fire roared, one that burned hotter than anything Spark had ever seen outside of pyromancy. As Abyss walked closer to it, Spark noticed large, brightly coloured boulders amidst the flames, each one taller than Spark.

Abyss stopped at the edge of the fire and looked down at Spark. Waiting. Spark couldn't fathom what for. Abyss snorted and tapped carefully at Spark's boots. Then she walked into the fire.

Spark slipped out of her boots and rolled up her pants, but it was so hot she worried about her clothing igniting. A bit of warning would have allowed her to strip out of anything flammable. She could have worn her firecloak. But she curiously trotted after Abyss. The floor here was covered in coals, but the flames themselves flared up only around the boulders.

The boulders were all smooth, each a different colour but uniform in shape. All oval.

"Steal the moons, these are dragon eggs!"

Abyss gave her a quick, confirming glance and picked her way to some of the biggest eggs in there—two nestled against the wall. One of them was jet black with a single thread of cerulean shot through it. It was a curious contrast to its sibling, which was the purest of white, and Spark half expected a frizzy-haired, amber-eyed dragon to spring out. The first egg made more sense, considering its parentage. Had Abyss adopted a different dragon's egg?

Spark wanted to ask. She had so many questions. But she also sensed the solemnity of the moment and was certain Abyss would crush her where she stood if she asked anything rude. She had no idea what was and wasn't rude to these dragons. Especially to Abyss, who had her own code.

Abyss inspected the eggs, turning them over, running her claws along their surfaces. Spark waited for her to breathe fire onto them, but instead she vomited out a strange yellow gel, coating the eggs in it and letting it puddle beneath them. The surrounding flames took to this gel immediately, burning slowly but brighter than before.

At last, Abyss turned and made her way back out between the egg clusters. Spark dutifully followed her. Tendrils of smoke began curling up Spark's pant legs, so she was grateful for the timing of their departure. Much longer and her clothing would combust.

"Mistress, can I ask you something? Some*things*. About the eggs?"

Abyss stopped and looked at her.

"Are both of them yours?"

She narrowed her eyes and nodded.

"Always both yours? You didn't adopt one?"

Eyes stayed narrowed. Otherwise, Abyss didn't move.

"It's just that the one is white. Is that normal? I mean, the black and blue, that makes sense. Same colours as you and your mate. I'm not asking to be rude, I just don't know anything about your kind. Nanny never conveyed much. I think she missed you too much and talking about it hurt her. Does that make sense?"

Abyss hunched down to rest her chin on the floor, at Spark's eye level.

"Okay, so why a white one?"

Abyss waggled her eyebrows.

"Really. You don't know?"

Abyss swung her great head around, pointing her chin at the Superiors who openly glared in their direction. Spark lowered her voice.

"They don't know either?"

Abyss moved her head fractionally, a subtle shake.

"All right. Is two eggs the normal amount? Is there a normal amount?"

Abyss abruptly stood up and kept walking.

"What? Did I say something wrong?"

Abyss glared.

"Would Ondias know if I asked her?"

Abyss kept walking.

"Fine, I'll ask Ondias."

Abyss ignored her until they reached the tunnel they'd original come in.

"Thank you for bringing me up here. Its beauty is beyond measure or words. And it was an honour to meet your young."

Abyss picked her up and flew out of the wide tunnel. She glided down to the settlement below, filling Spark with disappointment that she didn't do a lap around the valley so Spark could feel the wind through her short hair. Abyss landed not far from Ondias's house. Spark felt like she'd done something wrong, like she hadn't reacted properly to what she assumed was a momentous occasion.

"I wasn't having one over on you, I'm shocked you'd bring me up to your eggs. It was... Look, I'm not a poet. But I do appreciate you sharing them with me. They're both beautiful. I hope they're healthy."

Abyss watched Spark.

"Right. I'll talk to Ondias about it."

Abyss nodded fractionally.

"I haven't upset you?"

A fractional shake of her head.

"Good. I know Nanny loved you. I know all you went through with Mamma. I'd like it if we could be friends like that too." Spark glanced up toward the city. "Even if the other dragons give you a hard time for it. And I really won't call you Abyss if you don't want me to. But you see how it's easier, don't you?"

Abyss leaned forward and Spark braced for another swat or explosion of fire, but this time the dragoness nuzzled Spark with her great soft snout.

"All right. I'm going to rebuild that forge. Will you help me?"

She glanced over at the building, then huffed and took off into the air. Spark managed not to get knocked down by her wing force this time. By the time Abyss was gone, Ondias stood in her doorway.

"What's that all about?" Ondias asked.

"I'd like another dragon lesson."

"Oh, you want them on demand?" She crossed her arms.

"So you're not going to tell me about those dragon eggs up in the city?"

Ondias's eyebrows shot up. "You saw them?"

"Abyss brought me up there."

Ondias pressed her fingertips into her closed eyes. "The stars weep, are you giving them names? They're not pets, Mita. They have their own names."

"Until she tells me what hers is, I'm calling her Abyss."

"Not if she hasn't consented to it."

"Well she didn't eat me. That's consent, isn't it?"

Ondias growled in frustration and rubbed her hands over her face.

"What's there to tell about the eggs?"

"Everything." Spark couldn't quite keep the incredulous tone from her voice. There had been no mention at all of what dragons did with their eggs in any of Nanny's books. Ondias must have known that—the two women read all the same books. Ondias even wrote some of them.

Ondias ushered Spark inside and into one of the large soft chairs amongst the clutter near the hearth.

"The largest ones are nearest to hatching. And the colour of the eggshell is the colour of the dragon inside."

"Why do a black and a blue dragon have a white egg?"

Ondias rested her chin on tented fingers and stared into the hearth. "That's a mystery we'll have to wait quite some time to have answered."

"So those eggs aren't ready to hatch? They were some of the bigger ones in there."

"Yes, but even the biggest won't hatch before spring."

"So they get bigger? And that's how you can tell when they'll hatch?"

"That's part of it. It usually takes around five years, and our mistress's eggs are not quite four years old. Sometimes it can take even longer than that."

"So she's in the city and not in the mountains near Pasdale because she's waiting here for her eggs to hatch?"

"Yes, they bring their clutches to the city, but that's new, that started only a few years ago." Ondias went silent, clenching her jaw. This anger, though, wasn't directed at Spark. "She's really got three eggs."

Spark winced, realizing why her questions had been so upsetting for Abyss.

"Where's the third?"

"It's in Pasdale, as best we can tell. It was stolen from her home in the mountains. A few other dragonesses had eggs stolen and now they come here to the city until the eggs hatch and the hatchlings are big enough to defend themselves. It's the safest place they've got."

"Stolen? How the devil could someone steal something that big?"

"They used slave dragons, for a start, ones wounded right after the war when they were at their weakest. And the eggs aren't that big at first. No bigger than a pony to start."

"Why steal a dragon egg?"

Ondias looked at Spark askance. "Raising them into slavery makes for a far more obedient beast than one taken from the wild. They breed the dragons they've already got, but it's a slow process. A dragoness can only produce a single clutch of eggs in her lifespan and is the most difficult dragon to catch and force to submit. And a determined dragoness without hope can self-immolate."

"I can't imagine fire harming a dragon."

"You need air to breathe, but under the right circumstances, it can kill you all the same."

"So it's mostly males they have in the mills in Pasdale."

"There are mills like that growing all across the kingdom." Her voice was heavy with sadness. "It would probably be less work to convince the dragons to help us freely with that kind of industry, but people have become set in their ways. I tried to make them see, but there's only so much one woman can achieve."

Spark glared into the hearth for a while, wondering if she really wanted to learn that much more. Since Ondias was being reasonable, she asked one more question.

"What's that yellow goo Abyss put on her eggs?"

"Dragon venom. One of their best-kept secrets. I don't think even the captive ones in Pasdale have given that one up."

Spark blinked and looked squarely at Ondias. "Venom? It does more than catch fire?"

"It's a slow burning gel, but yes, it will numb flesh on contact and can be paralyzing. They use it in battle or when their dinner is swift or puts up a fight."

"But it's not poisonous?"

"Not exactly. It doesn't do well to eat it, if that's what you're asking."

Spark had no idea what she was asking anymore.

"Thanks." She stood up. "You're friends with her, aren't you?"

Ondias nodded slowly. "All of them, really—all of them who will call a human a friend. But friends with her the most. She saved my life once. More than once, but that first time really stands out."

"A tale for another time, right?"

Ondias gave her a shrewd look.

"Right," Spark said. "Next time you're bored and want to tell me about it, or about you and Nanny sleeping under a wagon, bring some wine to the forge. I've got work to do."

CHAPTER TEN

Every time Spark stopped to refill her hand-wagon, she'd glance up to Abyss circling overhead. She was certain the dragoness was smirking. She was certainly paying attention, at any rate. Spark wished she'd come down and help.

With the wagon full of rubble—bits of the red mountain rock as big as Spark could carry—she set off across the valley floor. It was her second day hauling rock from the ruins and dumping them at the forge. She'd cleaned it up the best she could, rebuilding the old wall, but not in its original location. She was expanding the building, making it something easier to live in. With all the brick used up, she needed something to finish the walls and extend the floor, and then she could repair and extend the roof.

She still slept at Ondias's and ate from there, mostly things she swiped from the larder on her way out the door every morning. She worked late into the night by the light of borrowed candles and lanterns. Spark was no mason, but she could pull fire out of the air as hot as she needed, hot enough to fuse stone. And so she was slowly building a home.

It was completely open on one side, the tarp doing an inadequate job of keeping the elements and onlookers out. But only for now. Using red stone from the crumbled mountainside had an interesting effect. Three walls of the building were made of valley bedrock, which was charcoal coloured instead of red. And the fourth wall going up was a patchwork of fused crimson pieces.

Spark collected more than rock from the north end of the valley. Before bringing back rubble, she'd spent a day searching through the wreckage of the original settlement, looking for bits of metal to melt down or anything that might work. She'd come back with a full load of scraps and an old skillet that hadn't rusted all the way through. The skillet she cleaned up and cured so she could use it, if she needed to. She tried not to show off with pyromancy.

Too many people peeked in on her, either standing in the open doorway or at the edges of the tarp billowing in the wind. Hardly anyone ever actually spoke to her, but she frequently had an audience. And now that she'd built up a red section of wall nearly to her waist, people really took notice. The shoddy repair work on the old tents and rickety buildings had ceased. Now the people who had been in the valley the longest were out in the north end with Spark, filling their own wagons with blocks of ruby-rock.

Old buildings were being given new life. People in tents were putting down foundations. With harvest over and winter weeks away, more people were building and rebuilding. Some of the men, including Stone, smashed down the larger boulders into blocks that everyone else could manage.

They had a proper quarry started.

Spark stared wistfully at one scholar passing by with a cartload of blocks being hauled by a pack mule. She didn't have anything to trade yet or she'd have bartered for a cartload or two. She had enough scrap to make a few repairs, but she didn't want metalwork to slow her down. Her priority was making the space hers.

She'd wanted to ask Nandara for a bit of terramancy for a wall, but she hadn't actually seen the woman in days and didn't want to wait. The sooner she had a place of her own, the better. Spark wasn't too sure why things remained strained between them—Spark had been careful about what she said.

Ondias always came by when Spark was building the wall or unloading the cart. She'd natter about dragons while Spark worked. And once the wagon was empty, she'd watch Spark head out for a fresh load, always back when Spark returned. Spark wished she'd come haul stones while she nattered.

Every time Spark felt exhausted and was tempted to slow down, she reminded herself of the turning season. There were bound to be things she couldn't barter for. She needed the building complete and the forge up and running, necessities bartered for well before winter. It wouldn't be much longer before the passes were snowed in and the trading camp to the south emptied out until spring. It was her last chance to get the supplies she'd need to make it through the winter without relying on Ondias.

Spark needed glass for windows and a proper door with a lock. She could always use the tarp to cover the windows once the wall and roof were finished. Making glass would be tricky—she doubted there was any spare glass to barter for, but she could always build a door. She had what she needed, even if she had to use the brittle scrap wood of the old camp to start.

It was a big job to consider, and it would be a close thing to get it all done before the snows came. The days were already getting cooler, though today Spark worked with her sleeves rolled up.

Abyss circled around to land behind Spark, walking next to her and watching the other humans work.

"You could help, you know. Use the trading wagon and fill it with stones and in one trip I'd have everything I needed to finish. I could be done by tomorrow."

Ondias would have been aghast to hear Spark talk to Abyss so frankly. According to Ondias's lessons, Spark was being rude. Yet Abyss wasn't objecting at all, not even to the name. Of course, she wasn't helping either. But Spark thought it would be insincere to switch tactics.

"I could use the time I save to help you." Spark pointed up to the city. "I don't know if I can work with the diamond, but I've already fused some obsidian."

Spark kept walking, making conversation with the dragon more than actually expecting any aid. But then Abyss nudged her back. She watched Spark, her head tilted slightly to one side.

"You want to see me do it?"

Abyss narrowed her eyes and gave Spark one of those fractional nods of hers. Spark let go of the wagon's handles and hunted out a couple of obsidian shards left over from the original city and too small for the dragons to bother with. The valley floor was littered with fragments of obsidian and diamond, though most of the diamond had been scavenged long ago.

Spark still had the good fortune of finding a few bits. Those she'd stashed away under the coals in her forge so she could trade them later for the monumental amount of supplies she'd need.

Spark held up two pieces of obsidian and fused them, much as she'd done with the crimson blocks for her walls. She held it up in the palm of her hand for Abyss to inspect. As far as Spark could tell, it looked like one unbroken piece. It took some time to learn to fuse it with a smooth edge, but the forge wall had been good practice.

Abyss stared at it, her eyes glittering with calculation. She picked up the little wagon and glided away. Spark chased after her, only reaching the edge of the settlement before Abyss came back her way, the empty wagon grasped in her hand. She left it in the market, a loaner from Stone, but scooped Spark up in its place.

From the edge of the settlement, Abyss picked up the wheel-less supply wagon they used to haul goods from traders to the settlement. It had been designed to be pulled by horses but now had a handle attached over the top for dragons to grasp, like a shed-sized basket. If not this wagon then one like it was how Ondias and Nanny first came to the city.

Spark still hadn't heard the story about the two of them sleeping under it, though.

As a toddler, Spark had likely first come to the dragon city by a similar wagon. It was rarely used to ferry humans anymore, but was useful for supplies.

Abyss landed in the quarry, setting Spark and the large wagon down next to the fresh pile of blocks. She watched Spark select them before carefully plucking them from Spark's arms, using her talons like tongs, and dropping them into the wagon. It took a staggeringly short amount of time to fill the wagon and fly it to the forge.

Spark stared stupidly at the massive pile in the wide lane outside what would soon be her home. Abyss had saved her at least a day's worth of work, maybe two. And Spark probably had more than she would need. That meant she could trade the rest. A nice bonus. And it would save someone else the trouble of having to haul it in. Spark wouldn't get that much for the extra blocks, but hoped it would be enough to get her some fabric to make clothing for the winter.

Of course, Spark still had to learn how to make clothing. She could mend clothing but hadn't the faintest clue how to actually make it. Maybe she could find something to barter with Ember.

But if Spark could trade help from Abyss now and then, it would give her so much more time for everything she needed to do. Even if she spent a chunk of time helping with the dragon city.

Maybe the other dragons wouldn't want her up there, but she'd do what she could to help. She owed Abyss that much.

Spark was out in the market before dawn, her firecloak pulled tight around her to keep out the grey morning chill while mist roiled around her boots. Shadow's paws pattered softly beside her. Not many people were out this early, but Stone was there.

"Morning, Mita. You're up mighty early. And pleased with yourself over something."

Spark bit her lips to hide the grin.

"I'm ready. Forge is ready. I'm heading over there now to get it all set up for the day. You mind passing word around? I finished my hammer last night. Had to bring the bucket back to Ondias though." She frowned. "I guess that's the first thing I should trade for." She grinned again.

Stone grinned too.

"What else do you think you'll be needing?"

"Everything, Stone. Just everything." She went through her mental catalogue. "Food, some warm clothing, a bed would be nice. That's just to start."

She rattled off the whole list, including her most wishful items, glass and a door, or things she could use to make glass and a door. Her stomach churned thinking of all her needs, never mind comforts, and she had to focus on Stone to keep her mind off how deep her losses ran. How much couldn't be replaced.

Stone chuckled. "I'll spread word there's a blacksmith, and she needs everything but walls and a roof."

Spark smiled and waved as she headed off. She lit the pitiful few coals she had left in the forge, enough to get her through a few jobs, and hopefully more coal would come in the bargain. Then she picked up the two eggs she'd lifted from Ondias's icebox and held them in loose fists. With a quick glance at the tarps over her windows and door, she heated her breakfast. She nibbled at it, stomach churning with resentment.

Only weeks ago she'd shared a large, hearty breakfast, at a full and boisterous table with a loving family. While she forced down each bite of egg, her mind replayed the way she and Nanny Di used to glide around each other through their morning chores in wordless warmth as they prepared breakfast each day. How Bren always burst through the door after completing his morning chores to see if there was a pan-biscuit treat.

Spark couldn't remember the last time she and Nanny had made pan biscuits. She used the back of her hand to wipe away tears. Crammed the last egg into her mouth and washed it down.

She pulled back the tarps and sat on the anvil to wait.

After only a few minutes, Stone was the first one through her door with Ember and River. River sullenly set an armload of worn and broken tools on the worktable but didn't utter a word. He didn't linger, disappearing toward the market as soon as his part of the chore was done. Spark liked him much better when Stone was around.

Ember set a notebook stuffed with sketches of clothing on the worktable as well.

"What do you need?" Ember asked. "Shirts? Some new trousers? Something a little more exciting?" She shimmied at that last one.

Spark swallowed and tried to keep her expression neutral. "Everything."

Ember laughed and stepped closer, squaring her hands in front of Spark, measuring quickly. She turned Spark around, lifting her arms and inspecting her.

"You have bizarre dimensions." Ember grinned. "I love a challenge."

She picked up the notebook and disappeared out the door while Spark blinked silently in her wake.

"She's like her mother, that one," Stone said, a hint of apology in his voice. "And I've got some old timbers I've been saving for no particular reason. I can put them together into bedframe for you."

"I can't barter—"

"I promised Neesha." He waved a hand, good natured but solemn. "I'll trade with you, because I think that's what you need, but no one said it has to be a balanced trade. Let me do that for you, at least."

It was on Spark's lips to refuse, but she was in no position to turn away help, especially when the help came from a source other than Ondias. Her intentions were good ones, but her home was not somewhere Spark could thrive. Ondias's bitter grief pricked at Spark, dredging up memories she wasn't ready for, so that she constantly felt like a walking toothache.

"Thank you, Stone. I appreciate all you've done."

"How long will you need to get everything back in working order for me?"

Spark examined the tools on the table, running her hands along each and doing the calculations with unconscious ease.

"Come back tomorrow morning."

She expected to have it done sooner than that, but needed more time to get back into it. And if she didn't get the privacy she needed to work pyromancy to its fullest, it would take longer than usual. Morning would be plenty of time either way.

Stone left her to it, and she pulled the simplest fixes off the table and laid them on the anvil. She kept her back between the door and her work, glanced at the windows to make sure no one was watching, and used her hands to quickly fuse together a few of the pieces and repair one crack.

She set the repaired items down at the far end of the work table, keeping what needed work closest to the forge. After finishing one more repair, she heard footsteps in the lane and put the newest pieces into the fire.

"No need to put on a show for me," Nandara said. "I can feel your pyromancy from here."

"Is it that cold?" Spark took a quick look around.

"Spark, I've been doing this since before your mother was born," Nandara said, her tone teasing.

Spark pulled the broken spade from the fire, barely a dull orange, and used her hands to fuse it. The air around the anvil was cooler than it had been, even for the chill of morning, but it wasn't anything Spark was concerned about.

"I'm glad you're here," Spark said. "I was starting to wonder if you'd left."

"Just been getting settled in, same as you. Trying to convince Jatt not to be quite such a child."

"Oh. Did he tell you...?"

"That you had an argument? He didn't have to. Spark, this place is quite small. I'm sure half the settlement heard you shouting."

Spark's cheeks grew hot.

"He's a young man with a young man's ego, but he'll get over it."

Spark nodded. "Do you have repairs for me?"

"I'm afraid we haven't been here long enough to break anything." Nandara smiled. "I wanted to see it for myself all that you've done. I'm glad you're finding your way here."

"Thanks."

"Now that we're both settled, we should resume your apprenticeship."

Nandara didn't stay long, but Spark felt all the better for her visit. She planned to come back in the evenings to mentor Spark. With little else to keep her busy, she could teach Spark most days as opposed to her spare once or twice a week when they'd been in Pasdale. Spark looked forward to the familiar routine, to a bit of familiar company in a strange place.

Anything for another taste of the way things used to be.

She liked Stone and Ember well enough, but they were strangers. Nandara was the known quantity Spark needed for any hope of stability.

And there were other apprentices, other people her age or nearly so, with their master scholars or artists or wizards. Young people like Jatt. They travelled in intimidating droves in their spare time, but Spark hoped to find some camaraderie among them.

And of course there was Abyss, who was around far more than Spark ever expected. Ondias commented how frequently she saw the dragoness now that Spark was there. Her blue mate spent most of his time in other parts of the mountains, but Abyss didn't stray far unless she was out with a hunting party. Spark looked forward to seeing more of her.

Spark wedged the two pieces of the wagon axle together and held her hands over the break, super-heating the metal in a few seconds. Wearing her firecloak to protect her clothes, she used her body to keep the heated pieces wedged together and pulled the heat out carefully so the mend would set.

There'd been a steady stream of people, some bringing her things to be repaired or requests for entirely new items. Some brought her scrap metal to repurpose. The owner of the axle brought her a swatch of cured dragon skin. Sanctioned, he'd insisted. It had been a forge apron at one point. Spark didn't have a need for that, but she could put the skin to use.

She inspected the axle, wouldn't have been able to tell there was a break if she hadn't just seen it. She hefted the piece under the table on the finished side and picked up one of a dozen broken hooks.

Someone cleared his throat from the doorway and an instant later the little bell rang. That had also been one of yesterday's trades, since she didn't have a door for people to knock on. Her previous day's visitors brought her plenty, some of it stacked at the back of the worktable. She had a new chair and another stool. The woman whose hooks she was repairing brought her a small shelving unit.

Spark turned to the door where a portly, middle-aged man with pink skin, squinty brown eyes, and silvery blond hair stood. He smiled and pulled his wizarding robes tighter around him.

"Been busy with the pyromancy, have you?"

This again.

"Yes, sir. Still haven't got as much coal as I'd like. Need to rely on magic for some of the bigger projects."

She pointed to the axle under the table.

"Remarkable. You must be exhausted."

"Yes, sir." This, of course, was a baldfaced lie. Spark could use enough pyromancy to turn the whole valley into a leagues-deep glacier without exhausting herself. That part she was absolutely keeping to herself. If Nanny and her mother hadn't let that bit slip, then it was unlikely that anyone else knew that pyromancy didn't tire a fireborn. Spark hadn't done much other kinds of magic, but she'd felt the pull of it, felt it depleting her resources.

"Please, call me Tueben."

"Sure. I'm Spark. Nice to meet you."

"Ah, Spark. Is that what everyone calls you? I never had the pleasure of meeting your mother, but I worked with your grandmother a few times through the Guild."

"Is that so?" Spark tried to sound interested. She'd had this conversation nearly a dozen times in the last day.

"It was after her power changed, mind you, so she didn't have the same, erm, colouring as you, but..."

Spark wondered sometimes what she would look like if her power faded in the same way. Not that she knew what had happened to Nanny—she had denounced her power somehow, whatever that meant. Spark leaned against the anvil and let him talk, nodding along and trying to keep her gaze focused in his general direction. They all knew her grandmother hadn't spoken since Spark was born, that her mother had died—or whatever her condition was—when Spark had been mere hours old. And yet they expected her to know so much.

But the way they all acted like her family was still alive, like Nanny was off in Pasdale, like Neesha was too busy to talk to anyone, that was what needled Spark the most. They acted like they weren't poking a raw nerve every time they brought up her family.

Tueben came up for air, smiling breezily at her.

"So, what are you working on?" he asked.

"Repairing hooks for Miss Praxin. She said she's running out of places to dry herbs."

"Ah, yes. I think she's responsible for most of Lina's supplies."

Spark really took note of the man. He didn't have anything with him at all, for trade or repair or even a gift to bring her. There had been a few of those, mostly people like Tueben who came in to talk about the good ol' days when Nanny used to talk and Neesha had been properly alive. Those ones were the worst, as much as Spark needed the supplies some of them gifted.

"If that's the case, I really shouldn't delay with her repairs," Spark said. "Have you got any metalwork you need done?"

"Eh? Oh, no. I just wanted to stop in and meet you. It's been so long since I'd seen you or your grandmother."

Spark nodded. He wasn't taking the hint. They never did.

"Okay, it's great to have some company," she said. "But I do need to get back to work. You're welcome to have a seat. I'm still listening, but I'll need to focus on the metalwork. I don't want you to think I'm being rude."

"Of course! Don't let me keep you."

He settled in on the stool she'd indicated, and she picked up one of the broken hooks. With an audience, she'd have to bang it flat and make joints for the scarf weld, attach the pieces without magic, and then hook the end again. Using pyromancy would have taken a fraction of the time. She hoped he didn't linger too long.

He kept talking about a particular dragon Spark didn't know anything about, one from the Pasdale blaze so long ago. She didn't know anything about any of the dragons. Did they think she was some kind of dragon whisperer? There were hardly any of those anymore.

Spark fanned the flames with her hand, a quick wave to get the temperature in the forge up. She tossed the first hook's pieces in. Tueben wasn't paying too much attention at this point, but when she thrust her hands in to retrieve the glowing pieces, he gasped and the stool clattered as he quickly rose to his feet.

"What?" Spark stood and spun away from the forge, wondering if she'd knocked some coals out. But the whole place was stone, so what was the danger?

He stared at her hands, at the glowing pieces of metal she held.

"Ah. Been a while since you've seen a fireborn at work?"

He blustered an apology and righted the stool to sit. Spark banged out the hook and hammered the two pieces together. He wasn't saying anything now, watching her handle the nearly molten iron with her bare hands.

"It really is something to see," he said. "Well, I've monopolized enough of your time. I was supposed to be taking a quick lunch break, and I'm sure my students will be waiting for me."

"It was nice meeting you," Spark said.

She was relieved he left and took his awkward questions and commentary with him, but at the same time, she felt so much more alone. Every question made her ache. These wizards seemed to think they could reach back and touch some long-gone past through her, talked like she wasn't even there.

She lightly hammered the hook around the horn of the anvil to get the shape back before setting it aside. Most of a dozen hooks still waited. Spark wanted to return them, return all the broken pieces, close up the forge and just quit. Or put some kind of snippy disclaimer on the door to remind them she was not her mother, not Nanny.

Spark took down the bell and pushed the tarp across the door. There were enough supplies to last her a few days and enough work to get her through to the evening. She eased back on pyromancy, mostly so the work would last the day and give her an excuse to turn people away.

Everyone either had their curiosity slaked or got the hint with the closed door, such as it was. No one else came in to see her until evening when Nandara came for her lesson.

"Everything okay?" Nandara asked.

Spark let the words pour out, telling Nandara exactly how alone she was. Nandara frowned and came closer, putting a comforting arm around Spark's shoulders.

"I'm sorry, Spark. That sounds awful for you." Nandara gave her one of those sad smiles adults sometimes did. "I know it's a huge change from Pasdale, but you need to remember this place is different. Your mother was a hero, and people here know it. Everyone is here because they love dragons. You fascinate them because of your closeness to the dragons, to their element, and because of your family's role in helping to shape this city. You were tucked away in Ondias's back room so you didn't see it, but most of this settlement was mourning right alongside you at the news of what happened to your family, to Dionelle."

"I'm not Nanny. But no one really sees that."

"You're the only connection they have to her or to your mother."

"Is that why Ondias is so... prickly?"

Nandara sighed. "It's especially hard for Ondias because she was so close to Dionelle. Ondias couldn't talk to anyone about dragons like she could with Di. The two of them fed off each other when it came to dragons. And she watched your mother grow up, knew your whole family like her own. I think she expects you to be more like Di or Neesha and forgets you're your own person. You're someone new."

"So just by being myself I keep disappointing her?"

Nandara tried not to smile. "In a way. She'll adjust."

"It still hurts, the way everyone has all these questions about Nanny. I'm just not ready for that. It just makes me miss her so much more."

"I know there's a lot you don't know about her and about your family's entwined history with this city. Would it help you to learn some of it?"

"You're not going to hoard your information the way Ondias does?"

Nandara gave her a reproachful look, but smiled through it all the same.

"It would be nice to know more about this place and about Nanny. I heard Pappy's stories, but there were some things he didn't know, some things he hadn't seen first-hand. You were there through it all, weren't you?"

"In a lot of ways I was. I helped Reiser with the Dunhams when Dionelle was missing, in the fire realm. I taught Di so much. And then your mother. I was with her, with both of them, when she took back the city from the water. From what Loch had helped do."

Nandara sighed and her shoulders drooped.

"I'd like to hear it. Whatever you'd like to share. I know some of it is hard for you, even now."

"Not that hard," Nandara said. "Not in the face of your losses. If learning about the past will help you feel more settled here, then it's no great burden."

Nandara set Spark to some spellwork. She stood back to watch Spark's form while she recounted what she knew of the first time Ondias and Dionelle spent in the valley, sleeping under the wagon. They'd come with Abyss because Pappy had been unwell. The dragons treated him with their spellcraft so he could survive the fire realm, but they hadn't thought to give the spell any kind of expiration. It had worn him down, and the dragons rushed him back to the city to undo what they'd done. It sounded like he'd been near death by the time the dragons set him to right.

"It was a hard week, travelling all the way here with Reiser so sick and Di pregnant with Neesha. And then they all had to sleep out in the wilderness, nothing but that overturned wagon against the elements, until the dragoness was strong enough to bring them all back to Pasdale. She'd flown herself ragged to help your grandparents."

"If Abyss travelled through the fire realm with Mamma, why couldn't she do it for Nanny?"

"Only fire demons or a great collection of dragons can open the way to the fire realm. It's not something Abyss can do on her own."

"But Mamma opened one on her own. So I probably could too."

Nandara gave her a severe look. "I'm certain you could. You understand why, don't you?"

"Because I'm fireborn."

"Do you know what that really means?"

Spark blinked.

"Spark, you're possibly more fire demon than girl. It's fire demons that made you and Neesha and Dionelle what you are. Dionelle didn't talk about it. I think she internalized some of her sister's awful words on the subject. But it started with her, she was the first fireborn, something none of us knew until she ended up in the fire realm. She spent half her pregnancy with Neesha in the fire realm, surrounded by demons and being sustained by that realm's energy. Your mother spent some time there while pregnant with you, and she also let demons possess her while pregnant. It's all added up so that each fireborn in your family has been stronger than the last. You have more demon than your mother or grandmother."

Spark sank onto the anvil and stared into the fire. "Demons...? So all the gossip in Pasdale was true?"

Nandara gave her a sad smile. "I don't know about that, but they were correct that you get at least some of your power from demons and the fire realm."

"Does that make me dangerous?"

Nandara sat next to her, an arm around her shoulders. "No more dangerous than any pyromancer before you. But it does mean you need to take great care with your power. It's why we work so hard on your lessons."

"Are there others like us? Elementals with demons in them?"

"Only one I've heard of—an aquamancer far to the south who joined the Guild through the specialist tiers. But the Guild only recently began looking in earnest. There are some elementals who are deeply but narrowly powerful within their element, like Loch, but they have no direct connection to the elemental realms the way you have."

Spark nodded slowly but didn't look up.

"I'm sorry, I wanted to cheer you up with a bit of knowledge." Nandara patted Spark's arm and stood. "I hope you can use what I say to understand everyone else here a little better. Maybe you can bring their stories and questions back around to you, how you're different. Make them see *you*, Mita."

"Tueben saw the truth watching me work metal," Spark said. "It scared him."

"I suspect it startled him, is all. I wouldn't be surprised if he's back in a day or two full of questions. Maybe ones just for you this time."

Spark nodded but wasn't convinced.

"There's a home here for you, I promise there is. It's not like Pasdale. It will take some time for you to find your place, but you will."

It was late when Nandara left. Shadow was back in for the night and curled up next to the anvil, waiting for Spark to go to bed. Spark lingered, wondering if she should stay at the forge or get some proper rest at Ondias's.

This place would be a home sooner if she let Stone help her like he wanted. Everyone seemed to like him, and he was always at the market, the centre of gossip in the village. Stone was trying to fulfill whatever promises he'd made to her mother, but Spark was already indebted to him for his kindnesses. Could she ever repay him?

Maybe it was time to stop keeping score and build the best life she could.

CHAPTER ELEVEN

S park inspected her repair to a split plow. Fusing metal was as easy as fusing rock, and she felt guilty that the plow's owner had traded the work—which put frost on her walls but hadn't taken long—for a good straw mattress to fit the bedframe Stone recently brought her.

Spark still had only stolen blankets from Ondias's house to sleep under, but this newest acquisition meant Spark could finally call this place home. Stone kept her in any food items she lacked, though the work she did for townspeople was enough to keep her fed.

It was barely midday when Spark finished the last of her work. She looked guiltily at the new bed pushed off to one side and then back to the plow. Its owner had been insistent on the trade. The plow was a valuable piece of equipment, and this farmer had winter crops to prepare. Spark tried looking at the value in the pieces she repaired and less at the time she spent fixing them. It had been easier when she made small tools or repaired Miss Praxin's hooks.

The bell at the door jingled, surprising Spark. She'd pulled the tarp closed and everyone knew by now it meant she was working and they should come back later. But Ember came in with some new clothing for Spark. She'd been by the day before to do a fitting and had whisked it all away to put on the final touches.

"Has winter come early in here?" Ember joked.

Spark fanned the forge flames, hoping the outside warmth would seep in and help with the frost.

"What are you going to do when proper winter comes?" Ember asked.

"Dress warmer."

Ember smiled and set the clothing down on a corner of the mattress.

"Well, at least you've got more shirts to layer on! The bed looks good. You've got a real home now."

"Going to need some blankets of my own, but it's a start."

"Oh, come now, Ondias isn't going to miss anything. How can she, with that mountain of trash she lives in?"

"She's categorized the whole thing, knows where every last speck of dust is."

Ember grinned.

Spark gave the plow a final inspection, whacking it with her hammer to make sure it wouldn't just crumble. It was sound. She struggled out of her firecloak.

"It's so bulky," Ember said, running her hands along the strange fabric. "Why don't we craft you something else out of it? There's enough fabric to make yourself a full suit. And then you'd have enough left over you could make an apron—say for an apprentice someday? It'd be easy."

Ember had been dropping subtle hints about learning to work metal. Spark wasn't sure what to make of this yet but always changed the subject as quickly as she could. Showing someone how to work metal had been the last thing she'd done before losing everyone she loved. The thought of doing it again squeezed her chest.

"Maybe some day," Spark said. "This is good enough for now, and I've got plenty else I need to work on."

Ember traced her fingers along the plow Spark was pushing off to the side. Spark heard a faint call on the wind and stopped. It sounded like a dragon, but distant and weak, unlike anything Spark had heard before. Ember stopped too and cocked her head.

"Is that—" Spark began, but Ember hushed her.

There was another faint cry.

"It's a distress call," Ember said.

"What should we do?"

"Nothing we can do, really. They'll come for you if they need you."

But Spark was only half paying attention to her.

The cry came again and Ember darted out the door. When Spark joined her in the lane, she was looking west, but Spark saw no sign of anything in that direction. Overhead, the afternoon sky filled with dragons. Spark had never seen them do this before, seemingly every single dragon in the city circling above.

"Is an attack likely to come from the west?" Spark asked. "What's beyond here?"

"Another ocean, I think." Ember blinked. "You know, I've never actually looked at the maps to see."

The pair clambered up the woodpile stacked neatly beside Spark's home, a recent thing she'd been working for, and they stood on the roof to get a better view of the horizon. The dragon cries grew closer, and Spark had never heard one take so long to reach the city after the first vocalizations.

"I know what this is," Ember said. "It's a death cry."

"A death cry?" Spark looked at her sharply.

"We'd probably hear it more often, but a lot of the dragons don't make it all the way to the city before they lose their ability to cry out." She looked out to the west. "Sounds like this one's going to make it all the way home."

"Has one of ours been wounded?" Spark looked up at the massive blaze of dragons overhead, trying to see if anyone was missing.

"Hard to tell. Could be an old dragon that's reached the end of its days. They come here to die. Didn't you know?"

Spark shook her head and looked to the horizon. Finally, two dragonesses from the city appeared over the mountaintop, coming in next to the support column. They each held the arms of a lemony little male dragon, whose head drooped and wings barely flapped. He vocalized one last time before he was pulled up into the city and all of the dragons funnelled down into it.

"I don't remember reading of this before. Is it another of their secrets?"

"No, this is a new custom," Ember said. "They started it maybe ten years ago, I was just a girl. They won't die any place humans can find them. They make a point of dying where other dragons can protect their remains. Most of them make the pilgrimage here."

"To preserve secrets?"

"To keep their skins from our use."

"Fresh skins? Or will they be upset about that old hide I have?"

"I think you're going to have to ask them if you want to be sure."

"It must take ages for a dragon's body to break down," Spark said. "If most of them come here to die, isn't that going to work out to a couple or more a year?"

"It doesn't always. A lot of them, especially the ones coming from farther, don't always make it here and try to die over the deepest depths of the ocean, falling from the air mid-flight to sink beyond reach."

"Even still, there should be a few corpses lingering here. Do they bury them or something? Can a dragon carcass be burned?"

"Once the dragon is dead and the hide has been pierced, they decompose quickly, even their bones. Their bodies can be preserved, obviously, or we'd never be able to use them. But left to their own, they turn to ash and dust in a moons' cycle."

"That's incredible! I had no idea."

"Another secret. Scholars know it, everyone in this village knows it, but the knowledge is guarded. Until recently, no one knew what happened when a dragon died away from the influence of humans. It was common practice to cure the body and use its pieces, either as spoils of war when the dragon was killed in battle, or as a trade deal."

"I remember reading that some merchants used to make deals with dragons to use various parts of them after their deaths. That's how Nanny got a beautiful cloak for my mother."

Spark paused, remembering the one time she got to see that magnificent expanse of amethyst dragon skin. She didn't know where it was now, didn't know where any of her mother's things had ended up. If it was in the house in Pasdale, it would be gone. Destroyed with her family, or property of Loch.

"That practice ended when that magistrate in Pasdale started stealing dragons to drive industry. Dragons lost trust for all humans after that. They barely tolerate the people here, and this camp is full of the staunchest supporters they have. Dozens of people were here when the city fell; they refused to leave. Others have been coming and going since the early days when it was just Ondias and a tent or two out here."

Spark watched the city as the last of the dragons disappeared into it.

"So what are they doing up there?"

"Likely saying goodbye."

"What will they do with him once he dies? Will they leave him in the city?"

Ember shook her head and turned Spark to look north. Near the mountain that was half washed away and since rebuilt by terramancers under Nandara's guidance, stood a particularly impressive peak, one always capped with snow, even in the height of summer.

"Once this one dies, they'll bring him up there. Only dragons can reach the summit, and he'll be safe."

Spark let out a low whistle. "They really don't trust even us, do they?"

"Sadly not."

Spark understood some of the sadness Nanny carried around. Had the dragons continued to trust Nanny? Was that why Abyss lingered in the valley? Abyss was only one dragon, but one was all it took to turn the tide. Spark glanced up at the city. There had to be a way to mend the rift.

CHAPTER TWELVE

Despite Nandara's quiet entry, Spark noticed her arrival and watched her sit quietly at the work table. It had been a couple of days since they'd done any spellwork, but Nandara insisted they try something completely new today. Watching her, Spark wondered if she had second thoughts.

"Ondias doesn't think you're ready to learn this, but it can't be helped. It's a delicate subject and one you're going to have to use with caution. One you're not going to tell anyone about—not Stone, not Ember. No one."

Given the secrets Spark already kept about her power, she didn't think that would be too difficult. She sat across from Nandara, her leg twitching while she waited for more.

"You're going to need to learn to make certain tools. Partly to work with the dragon skin you have, but also to make certain other tools. Chains. Things that can harm or bind a dragon."

Spark's mouth fell open. "Why would I want to do that?"

"Because it's only a matter of time before Loch finds out you're here. It's only a matter of time before he comes for us all. We can run again, but the dragons cannot. He already has these kinds of tools, and more. It's time to prepare."

Spark's skin tingled. "Prepare? Are we in danger?"

"I have no doubts that we will be. Loch remembers that he failed to destroy this city the first time. He will find other aquamancers and come back. They have taken dragons from our friends, have stolen dragons from the wild, have stolen eggs and raised hatchlings into slavery. They are even managing to breed some dragons. He says it's for the mills, but I know it's more than that."

Spark went cold, gripping her hands together to stop the trembling. Her thoughts jumped to the night she'd lost her family, tried to imagine it on a grander scale. And there was that half-demon aquamancer Nandara had mentioned. Would they join Loch? Could Spark stop something like that? Spark focused on Nandara.

"He wants an army of dragons under his control to wipe out the last of the free dragons. And not just the dragons."

"Oh, tears of the moon," Spark whispered. "Me and Mamma. Do they know she's alive?"

"Who can say? But they will stop anyone who stands between them and their goal. They will wipe out the wild dragons and their supporters so they can keep using captive dragons for industry. I don't know what kind of man Loch is, but I know what kind of man Draxli was. I know he's passed on all of his worst traits to Loch."

Spark sank into her chair. "So this is all temporary. This home."

"I hope not. I hope this can be permanent. I don't know if negotiation is possible, but I believe that if we start preparing now, we can be ready. Perhaps we can put an end to this."

"You want me to build weapons against dragons."

"Yes. Obviously, you wouldn't be using them against our friends. But they're nervous still. They don't trust us. If they knew what you were learning, they would not be pleased. Some of them might be furious. You will have to be careful about the things you build."

Spark shook her head and stared into the middle of the room. Nandara was asking her for the impossible. And asking her to betray the dragons, no matter that it was in their best interest. She was right that they wouldn't see it that way if they found out.

"There's got to be another way."

"There are many ways," Nandara said. "We need to be as prepared as we can be. Ondias and I are still working with the Guild. There are pockets of resistance to the king and to Loch's kind of thinking, there are allies in other lands, and we're trying to help them organize more. Maybe they can free some of the dragons, and we can be there to collect them, help them rehabilitate. But we still need to do this."

Nandara took her pack and sat on the ground in front of the forge where the fire burned gently. Spark never let it burn out, for both comfort and necessity.

"It's careful work and you must retain full concentration," Nandara said. She held a simple needle, bigger than the ones Ember used.

"I'm going to show you how to call demons."

Spark stopped halfway out of her chair and stared at the back of Nandara's head.

"This is not a possession. You're going to call them, and you need a good source of the element you wish to call upon. You need to work with earth and fire demons, in tandem, in order to imbue a simple object like this needle. It will pierce dragon skin and you will be able to sew with it."

Spark swallowed, her throat feeling dry and the room too small. She moved carefully and sat next to Nandara.

"You bring the demons into their respective elements and ask for their assistance. It's a command phrased as a question. You hold your will over them until they do your bidding. Then you release them back to their realm. I will show you first, then I will teach you the intricacies of the theory. It will take some time, but then you will be able to do this on your own."

Spark shuffled to the edge of the forge where she could see what Nandara was doing while staying thoroughly out of the way. Nandara had a clay pot filled with earth. Would the pot itself be enough to call an earth demon? It contained uniformly black earth, with no twigs or stones. It was pure soil, like the fire in the forge was pure fire.

Nandara intoned in a language Spark didn't fully understand, a language she was only just learning. Nandara had been teaching it to her over the last week without telling her what it was for. It was the language of demons, and it had to be pitched differently for each element. Soft whispers for air, hissing demands for fire, burbling inquiries for water, low grumbling for earth.

Speaking quietly, Nandara started with the low grumbling of earth before weaving in the hiss of fire. She first alternated her sentences, then her words. Spark leaned forward. The fire grew brighter, slowly taking shape like a burning body. The flames seemed to solidify. It didn't move and the words Nandara spoke in flame were different than those she spoke in dirt.

It took much longer for the dirt in her pot to stir. Even longer for it to take form into something that looked like a dirty pixie.

Then her words for dirt and flame were the same. She held out her palm with the needle in it and let it float on a current of magic, suspended between the two demons. The demons moved as her words changed, flitting and swirling around the little pin. It took nearly an hour before Nandara snatched the needle and set it aside, her focus always intent on the demons. Her words changed and the demons thrashed. But they retreated to their respective elements.

Nandara was slow getting to her feet. Spark followed her to the work table, and Nandara set the needle in front of her.

"Did you see what I did?" she asked, her voice weak, her body slumped.

"You exhausted yourself for a needle."

"Normally, I would do this under different circumstances, in the middle of the day when I'm well rested. But secrecy requires us to use our evenings. You must get a proper door and windows before you begin trying this for yourself."

"Yes. Clearly I need to make privacy a priority."

Nandara nodded and then sat quietly, watching Spark. She'd asked a question Spark hadn't really answered.

"You called them. You held them. I noticed you change your words when the fire demon came before the earth demon."

Her smile was weak but genuine, and she gestured for Spark to continue.

"You held them both, sometimes giving them different commands at once. Are you sure I'm ready for this?"

"You are definitely not, not yet."

Spark let out a pent up breath and nodded, relieved by the honesty and that she wasn't expected to do anything like what Nandara just did. It was the exact thing everyone had been warning her against since she was old enough to know what elemental demons were.

"You got them to imbue that little needle with their power, and then you told them to go away."

"Yes. And that last part is where I failed your mother," Nandara said, her voice angry and sad. She bunched her hands into fists around the straps of her pack. "I performed similar tasks in her presence, while I thought she was busy with her studies. It would seem that I was her study. She learned to call the demons from watching me, learned to take them into her and strengthen her power and allow her to wield them. But she never properly learned to send them away."

"Is that what you're going to teach me first?"

"I am going to teach you all of the commands. I am going to teach you everything that can go wrong. And then I will teach you to send them away. I will call them and keep them under control, but you will send them away."

Spark looked hesitantly toward the forge.

"You're going to do this eventually, I know that," Nandara said. "You know enough, from what you know of your mother, not to plunge in unprepared. I trust you're going to wait until I've given you all the pieces before you do anything."

"So teach me to send them away first, if that's the most important step."

Nandara shook her head. "All of the steps are important." She watched Spark until she was certain her words had set in.

"Yes, okay. What about taking them into me?" Spark asked. "I know it's dangerous, but if I can learn to send them away, wouldn't it make possession safer?"

"We are not going to even consider this right now, Spark. Please, promise me you won't try this on your own. It is horrifically dangerous. And not just the risk of possession. If the demon breaks free of your control, it could possess you, yes, but it could also choose to run free in our realm. A loose fire demon, any demon, can wreak such havoc in a short time. Your mother used demons against Loch's floods and it worked, but the demons were more than she could control. They burned so much of the city. It was the demons that drew Lady Zyx out and left her vulnerable to the water."

Spark closed her eyes, a lump growing in her throat.

"Control with demon possession is even more fleeting," Nandara continued. "Your mother was lucky more than anything, right up to the end. And even then she's lucky Dionelle was there. I don't know the full story, Dionelle would never say, not even in her letters, but I believe she forced the demon out of your mother and back to its realm. I believe that the demon held tight to your mother's essence when it went. And I believe that's the true reason why your grandmother blamed herself above all for what happened to Neesha."

"Was she really so hard on herself?"

"She never explained why she refused to leave Pasdale, even when the danger became clear, but I suspect it was the guilt that held her there. In a way, I think she saw remaining there as penance for failing your mother. But she also wanted to convince them they were wrong about her and the dragons. She wanted to prove to everyone that Neesha had been a hero."

Spark grit her teeth against the bitter comments rising to her lips and helped Nandara clean up.

Nandara left not long afterward, just as Shadow came in for the night. Spark let the fire burn low and curled up in bed with the dog on her feet, Nandara's words echoing in her mind. The dire warnings clashed against the urgency of embracing her heritage, her terrifying lineage as fireborn. The necessity of it dropped ice into her guts, and the thought of the dragons learning what Nandara planned made her tremble.

It was so much pressure. Was this what her mother had gone through?

Spark held a small blade in the palm of her hand. It looked inconsequential, especially when she hadn't affixed it to a handle yet. It was so small for something worth so much risk. But Nandara insisted on something small, much like the needle she'd used in her first demonstration. The larger the item, the longer Spark would have to hold the demons in control.

After weeks of instruction and training and sleepless nights, Spark helped Nandara work with demons across three of four elements. Nandara didn't think Spark should ever work with water, especially not in the dragon city, given the history. Working with air was refreshing and always left her feeling light. But Spark hated working with earth. It was cold and gritty, like being immersed in grains of unmelting ice. She always felt sluggish and itchy afterward.

Nandara had her work with fire the least, but Spark naturally liked that element best. Could Nandara tell she liked it a little too much? The rare occasions Nandara let her work with fire demons, she was left energized and gooey warm. She understood why her mother took the insane step to full possession. And how it had consumed her. Spark was curious to learn more but not curious enough to carry it out, not with her mother's empty body looking down on the valley.

"Are you ready?" Nandara pulled the tarps tight across the windows and latched the new door.

Spark released a long, slow breath and nodded. She slid the pot of dirt into place near the forge while Nandara pulled up a stool and gathered her robes around her. Spark took another deep breath, looked to Nandara, who she was pleased to see was relaxed but alert. She focused on the two elements in front of her.

Knowing the earth demons moved slowly, Spark called to them first, then waited, counting in her head and forcing herself to keep breathing in a slow, regular pace. But she couldn't wait too long. Timing was everything. She had to finish summoning the fire demon before the earth demon appeared or she wouldn't have the focus to control it.

Once she felt the chill at the base of her neck that signalled the building presence, she called the fire demon. One appeared immediately. It was like they were always listening to her, waiting for the chance to come through between realms. The one she had now was eager, flickering toward her. It waited patiently when she told it to, but leaned forward, awaiting more commands.

The earth demon built itself in the pot, lingering drowsily next to her. Its presence felt gritty, but with the fire demon's power washing over her, the sensation was warm, like lying in sand at midsummer. It made it easier for her to focus. She gave them both instructions, starting with the earth demon, getting it started on hardening the metal in precise ways.

With both demons in front of her, it was easier to work, a counterintuitive fact she embraced as she moved fluidly between their languages. The demons worked in tandem, transforming the quality of the blade into something that could pierce dragon skin.

This was the easy part, requiring much care and focus but little energy. Spark felt detached from the magic as she repeated the commands over and over, not giving either demon an opening to run free.

Spark sensed when the blade was ready—it made a gentle ringing sound in the circle of spellcraft buoying it. She released the earth demon, gently pushing it back into its cool, dark realm. It was harder with the fire demon because she *wanted* it to stay. The tingling warmth washing over her melted away tension and made her feel giddy. It was intoxicating. But Nandara was vigilant, and she would force it back into its realm herself if Spark was too slow. But when Spark applied her will, the fire demon went even more easily than the earth demon had.

With the task complete, Spark didn't feel tired, not the way Nandara always was after summoning demons. Her mind was sluggish, but her body burst with energy. So she asked Nandara about it.

"Those demons are kin to you, and they want you in their realm. They will do anything they can to lure you there and keep you with them as they did to your grandmother and your mother."

"They kept Mamma?"

"They were trying, even after Dionelle went to fetch her. It was you that prodded her to leave. Your impending arrival pushed pain through their trickery and brought her home."

"And that's why I feel drained by the other elements but replenished by fire."

"Yes. Dionelle survived in their realm for months. The parts of you that are fire demon thrive on contact with that realm."

"I like it—the way it feels." Her cheeks grew hot.

"You'll need to be careful when you're doing this. Maybe you should have someone you trust around, even if it's not me. No matter how well I knew Dionelle and Neesha, you still offer me surprises when it comes to your power. Caution is needed."

Nandara inspected the blade, running her fingers lightly over the surface and tracing wisps of spell over it, testing. She nodded and smiled as she did.

"Flawless," she said. "Well done, Spark."

Spark grinned, some of the brain sludge oozing away as she felt warmer from the praise.

"Perfect, and on the first try!" Spark tried not to be too pleased with herself, knowing that without weeks of over-preparation and all the warnings, she wouldn't have had nearly as much success.

And when Nandara left her to her work for the evening, Spark wondered even more at her success. Had the preparation been the difference between her and her mother? There was only one way to tell for sure, but Spark immediately retreated from any thoughts of demon possession or fire portals. Demons had gotten away from her during their first two sessions, and Nandara had had to wrangle them. As well as she'd done tonight, she didn't have the control she needed.

She focused on finishing her blade, on setting it to the smooth stone handle she'd crafted for it. It didn't take long before she pulled out the swatch of dragon skin and used the newly enchanted tool to make a cut. She grinned when it worked. Spark set to cutting along the pattern for a pair of gloves and a hood Ember had traced out with a soot pen.

Spark woke earlier than she would have liked. These days, it took so long for sleep to come, and then it was quick to leave once it did. She'd been dreaming of darkness, cold and gritty like being buried in the earth, the film of an earth demon's presence. There had been a menacing quality to the darkness, like some great beast lurking in the deepest shadows, biding its time. Waiting to pounce.

So she woke up groggier than when she went to bed, with her thoughts sluggish like crystalizing honey. Was it residue from working with the demons the night before?

The morning was cold and Spark begrudged sleep for abandoning her to it. Hoping to drive away the chill, she stoked up the fire to a proper blaze before stripping down and climbing into it. She couldn't stand to be immersed in water at the best of times, but when the weather was cold she couldn't tolerate it at all. She bathed in near-boiling water to chase away the cold, but the combination of fire and water affected her badly. The resulting steam always felt suffocating. Bathing by fire suited her fine.

Delicious heat burned away the grime and obliterated the cold. Tired and tempted, Spark extended her senses, prodding into the fire, trying to see where the boundaries between realms were.

She knew better than to call the fire demons without anyone around to supervise, but she did so anyway. One instantly joined her in the blaze, its shape brighter than the flames surrounding her. It was so close it brushed against her when it appeared. Its touch made her skin buzz and her head swim.

Out in the middle of the room, Shadow whined.

The demon wanted in, to possess her. Worse, she wanted to let it. Its tingling touch across her skin weakened her resolve. She trembled. But the buzz of energy she got in the brief span of contact cleared her thoughts and replenished the energy stolen by nightmares. All at once she saw what a bad idea this was.

Panicking, Spark flailed backward and smacked her head into the side of the forge. The sudden pain gave her focus, so she could do as Nandara taught her, forcing the demon back into its realm.

Massaging the back of her head, Spark climbed out of the fire. She grabbed a damp cloth from her basin to wipe off all the soot. Once dressed, she broke a piece of bread from a loaf in her stores and nibbled away at it. She didn't feel hungry but couldn't remember the last time she'd eaten.

She ate the bread in random bites while working at the dragon skin. She laid out the pieces for the gloves and the hood in front of her, at a loss for what to do next. She could use Nandara's demonstration needle to sew the pieces, but she didn't have any dragon twine that would effectively hold it all together. Normal thread would be good practice but would burn away the first time anyone used the gloves.

Making dragon twine was beyond her skill, and she didn't know who to ask for help with it. She couldn't risk word getting around of what she was doing.

A hard thud from her front door startled her enough that she dropped her bread onto the floor and then stepped on it while trying to retrieve it. She let out a particularly blasphemous oath, booted the ruined snack over to Shadow who was too happy to gobble it up, and then went to the door. Spark was startled to see Abyss peeking in, the cool late-autumn air wafting in around her. The dragoness had been gone for days on a hunt, and Spark hadn't heard the hunting party's return. Maybe their racket was what contributed to the morning's nightmare.

"Mistress! It's excellent to see you again."

Abyss looked past Spark, and Spark realized all at once that the dragoness had seen what was on the work table.

"Oh. I've been learning to build new tools from Nandara..." Abyss's gaze pinned Spark to the ground. "I needed something to practice on. Someone traded the skin a while ago, said it was sanctioned. From before, when your kind still did that. They weren't lying to me, were they?" Spark's eyes widened.

Abyss gave her head a fractional shake but narrowed her eyes at Spark.

"Oh. I didn't realize it would be a problem for me to work on something old like this. I had no use for it otherwise, and it seems wrong to just cast it aside."

Abyss shot a precision blast right into Spark's face. Shadow barked in alarm and darted out the door, squeezing between dragon and jamb. The force of the flame knocked Spark into the middle of the room where she promptly fell on her ass. She was on her feet in a hurry.

"I'm sorry, Mistress, I meant no offence." Spark rubbed her forehead, confused. There had to be a way to make things right. "The gloves will help—I'll be able to start apprenticing someone else. I'll learn to make things that can help the dragons."

Her expression didn't change.

"Just this one skin. It's sanctioned. I would never ask for others. When I'm done making these items, we can bring what's left to the mountaintop. I'll remove the cured properties so it disintegrates like it should."

Abyss raised her brows and tilted her head.

"I know it's possible to do that. I'll find out how from the scholars. Then we'll give what's left a sky burial. Would that be all right?"

The dragoness was still for a moment, watching Spark. Gentle rumbling echoed from deep inside her, almost like a mountain-sized cat was purring. She gave Spark a quick, terse nod and stood up, disappearing into the sky.

Spark tried to call her back, left wondering what she'd wanted in the first place.

She closed her door and looked at the items on her table. It was a good reminder, if nothing else, that she must do a better job keeping her work hidden.

CHAPTER THIRTEEN

Spark returned home from an emergency stovepipe repair, wondering what the hell the villagers did in their ten years without a blacksmith, and stopped short when she spotted a tall, dark figure leaning against the wall outside her door. She wasn't familiar with everyone in town yet but then the mop of hair registered in her mind.

"Back for another earful?" she said before Jatt noticed her return.

He stood up straight at the sound of her voice and faced her. When he opened his mouth to answer her, she bustled past him and shut her door. It struck her only once she was inside that being rude to her mentor's kin was probably not the best life choice. So when he knocked, she didn't ignore it.

"Yes?" She kept her voice clipped and business-like.

He looked down at his feet and not at her, but he held something out. Two small knives, their blades snapped. He waggled a large package he had under his arm.

"I've come to barter."

"Ah, now you need a blacksmith, and suddenly I'm not so terrible."

"Gran went up one side of me and down the other."

"So you're here because of her again?" Her tone rose, sharp as dragon talons.

"No. Yes, well in a way." He glanced up at her before finding something interesting on the ground. "Can you fix my knives? They're canvas knives, I broke one last year and my spare halfway through work yesterday."

Spark took the knives and had a quick look at them. She'd have to remove the handles but they'd be easy enough, even if she didn't use magic.

"I don't work for free."

He held out the package. She took it and stepped in, jerking her head to motion him inside. She waved her hand at the stool near her worktable, indicating he could sit, and set the knives and package down. The package itself was weird, a large flat rectangle with a bulge in the middle. She pulled back the old sackcloth keeping it together and found a bundle of dried meat, enough for a week if she ate little else.

Her eyebrows went up, but she kept her back to Jatt as she unwrapped the rest. It was a painting. It showed a view of the dragon city from the sky, looking at it straight on the way it looked to the dragons, or to a human lucky enough to have flown with them. But it was more than the little base Spark had been to recently. This was a tall, spiralling tower of obsidian and diamond reaching into the sky like a frozen fire.

"Is this what it looked like before it fell?" Her voice was hushed, her breath caught in her chest.

"Near enough." His quiet voice sounded embarrassed. "I've never seen it, of course. I was a toddler when the city fell. But one of the dragons brought me up to see the new base and Gran has spoken endlessly about what it used to look like. Even Ondias, in her sad way, gave me some insight."

Something about the gently muted tones contrasting the bright spiral of the tower gave the painting a touch of sadness. A hint of longing for things lost forever.

"Yes," she said abruptly, folding the sackcloth back over the painting and setting it aside in one quick motion. "I can fix your knives. This is far more than you needed for a simple repair."

"I didn't think the repair was quite that simple." He held her gaze.

Spark nodded and picked up the knives, grabbing the tools she'd need to remove the handles. She regretted shouting at him.

"You can sit and wait if you want. It won't take me long. Unless your master is waiting for you?"

Jatt took a seat on the stool. "I've got today for personal study."

"I'll have you back at it in a few minutes." She got the handles off and put the first two pieces into the forge. "What in the name of the moons did Nandara even say to you?"

"Nothing you didn't," he said, finding interest in his feet. "I'm sure you understand how hard it was for us, for me here without any family, hearing all this awful news and worrying about Gran and Gramps."

"Yes."

The silence stretched out for a while.

"Worrying about my family is a luxury I have and you don't," he said. "Gran put it a little more, um, eloquently than you did. But she made her point. I didn't realize what had happened. I thought your family was safe too."

Spark removed the blades from the fire and, unlike Tueben—who had now left for the winter—Jatt didn't flail about at the sight of her handling molten metal. She hammered away in silence, setting up joints for the scarf weld, pounding them together, back into the fire, hammer some more. She focused on the work, hammering the blade flat to finish it up, pretending Jatt wasn't there. After she quenched the first blade and went to reattach the handle, Jatt spoke again.

"I was especially unkind before, and I'm sorry."

Spark looked straight ahead at the wall. "Yes, thank you. You've earned a truce."

He stood at the edge of the work table and watched her as she put the pieces of the second knife into the fire.

"Are you all right?" he asked.

"I'm still here."

"But that's not the same."

She leaned on the anvil and crossed her arms. He said the right words, seemed properly contrite, but she remained angry with him. She could be civil, but he seemed interested in more than civility. Did he expect her to welcome his company as she did Nandara's?

"I try not to think about how I am," she said. "I'm still here and that's got to be enough for now. My family was everything."

Jatt looked at his feet. He certainly understood, at any rate. Hopefully next time he would go a longer pace toward understanding a situation before blasting his opinions.

"Gran's told me about how bad things were in Pasdale. You didn't have friends at school?"

"Everyone hated me. Hated all of us. Did she tell you how we were dragged before the magistrate?"

"Yes."

Spark turned back to the work, but he continued talking.

"It's different here," he said. "No one hates you."

"There's River."

"He hates everyone." She heard the smile in his voice.

"Everyone here thinks I'm some living parlour trick."

"Well, no one else here, except the dragons, can pick up a molten blade with nothing but their skin. You're as close to the dragons as some of them get."

She stopped with her hammer poised to strike and looked at him.

"You haven't noticed? Your black dragoness is one of the few who bother with the valley floor at all. And most of the ones who will talk to humans will only speak to Ondias. She's the dragon whisperer here, and that's their way with humans. This village is full of people who love dragons and want to learn about them, but even here they still have to do it second-hand through Ondias. And you know what she's like."

"So it's not just me?"

Jatt smirked. "She's testy with everyone." He sighed. "Can't blame her a whole lot, she's had a difficult time. Travelling to talk about dragons was all she had for so long. Now she gets only the people who seek her out."

"She's still intolerable, even if she's got a halfway good reason for it."

"Yeah, well. You're a spell more tolerable than she is, so people want to talk to you. They see you talking to the dragoness, know you've been up to the city even though you just got here. Shitting moons, I was here two years before Ondias got me a ride up to see the city, and even then it was more a favour to my gran than for me. So people here want to see what they can learn from you."

"I don't know what the dragons intend to keep secret and what they don't. No one's going to get much from me."

"Just watching you can tell a lot. Tueben was mesmerized and you barely used pyromancy. I have a vague notion of what Gran is teaching you."

"Then you probably know I'm not going to say a word about that."

"Yeah, yeah. But everyone is here to learn about dragons, and here you are like a little white dragon in our midst."

"That doesn't help."

He sighed. "It will take some time, but people other than Stone and Ember will start to seek you out for you."

"Which are you here for?"

Jatt sputtered out a cough before answering. "The blacksmith."

She smiled, looking at him askance.

"And I don't particularly enjoy the company of any of the other apprentices. I always take note when new people arrive."

She finished off the second knife and returned it. "You'll have to sharpen it yourself. I haven't bartered for a whetting stone yet."

He nodded in thanks and then regarded her a moment.

"You've never been out to the pub hall, have you?" he asked.

"I don't even know what that is."

"It's that big tent, the biggest one, on the northwest corner of the marketplace. The apprentices go there in the evenings, if they go much of anywhere. The, uh, proper adults use the big wooden building on the east side of town. You should go to the apprentice hall sometime, if you're lonely."

"I haven't had time to be properly lonely yet," she said. "There's still a lot I've got to do if I hope to stay in this building through the winter. I really don't want to have to move back into Ondias's trash heap."

Jatt chuckled. "Why don't you talk to Gran? She and Gramps put their house together with an extra room. Well, two extra rooms, but it was a given I would live with them once they got here. I'm sure she'd be happy to have you."

"Thanks, I'll keep that in mind."

Spark cleared some space along the wall and then leaned the painting on the back of her work table. She would find some time later to make a hook to hang it.

"You know, I met your gran," he said. "It was a long time ago, but I still remember."

"Nanny never had any art of the city. Or the dragons. I guess she thought she could come see it whenever she wanted."

"She did come all the time," he said, laying a long hand on her shoulder. "Until about ten years ago when things got worse with the magistrate. Ondias always used to make it sound like your gran was here to see her, but she spent more time up the mountainside with your ma than down here with anyone else."

Spark smiled at him despite the hot lump in her throat. She hoped he wouldn't notice the way she trembled.

"Anyway, I'm glad you like the painting. I'll see you around."

Spark waited until he was out the door before sinking into a heap on the ground and sobbing.

CHAPTER FOURTEEN

S park pulled the drapes closed and bolted the door, startling Jatt, who had been staring intensely at the canvas with his face resting in his hand, brush between his fingers. He jolted at the sound, smearing black paint across his cheek.

From the corner of her eye, Spark saw him wiping away the paint and watching her go to one of her storage cupboards, a recent trade for her work. She planned on making a lock for the cupboard door, but for now it was enough to hide things in the back. She rummaged around in the back of it, pulled out a jar of yellowy gel, and carefully scooped some of it into the lantern she'd finished.

"Is that...?" he asked.

"Yes. I stole it from Ondias. I'll sneak it back into her stacks soon. Not a word."

Jatt shrugged. "Hurry up and find out how she gets it in the first place."

He'd come to the implicit understanding with Spark that if he kept silent about what he saw her doing, she'd let him keep coming around. He was an extra set of hands when she needed it, and she didn't mind the company. Mostly he sat in the corner she'd cleared for him, his easel set up as permanent fixture, and worked on his art.

And he was competent in crafting things, his artist's eye not limited to paint on canvas. He was useful, even if only to hold two broken pieces together while she fused them. He was the only one who knew how she did it. She hadn't even told Ember. She wanted to, but sometimes Ember talked too much when she was being playful. She'd say things she shouldn't, even if she didn't mean to.

Jatt found most of the other apprentices using the shared studio to be brutish blowhards who were completely intolerable when they drank—and it seemed they drank quite a lot. So he spent most of his personal study and spare time in the corner across from Spark's forge. The whole day could pass with them saying little more to each other than to ask for an extra pair of hands or for an opinion on colours.

He enjoyed the dark ambience, the deep contrast between the red glow of the forge and the dark corners of the room, particularly after dark or when Spark pulled the drapes to work on something secret. He worked on something secret of his own, some dark painting suited to the surroundings. Of course, everything he worked on was a secret until he was finished.

Jatt was usually around when Nandara mentored Spark, keeping quiet but adding to the quality of the silence. Spark had gone with him to take a couple of meals with Nandara and Riz, appreciating the family time, even if it wasn't with her own family. It lent warmth and depth to her days but highlighted what she'd lost. She knew Nandara would take her in if she truly needed it, but she hoped she never did.

Her little space began to feel like a home, especially with Jatt there so often and Ember coming and going regularly. Jatt's painting of the city hung on the wall above the bed, next to the forge. The work table still doubled as a dining table when Jatt or Ember ate with her, otherwise she used the anvil when she was alone. It was all she needed.

Having finished making clothes for Spark, enough that Spark had to trade for a proper wardrobe she'd tucked in behind Jatt's workspace, Ember was working on making Spark proper bedding. Spark traded work for a nice quilt, finally able to return the borrowed bedding to Ondias, and Ember made her more blankets and a decent mattress cover.

A knock came at the door and Spark fumbled the lid back on the jar of dragon venom.

"Spark?"

It was Ember and Spark relaxed, hiding the venom behind her toolbox while Ember let herself in. She came in with a pillow and a grin, holding it out and showing it off. But the instant she spotted Jatt in the corner, she slugged him with it.

"Hey!"

Ember chuckled and tossed the new pillow onto the bed. Jatt scowled at her. He always stiffened, sat straighter or stood taller, more vigilant, whenever Ember was around.

"I'll just have to make another and you can use it to defend yourself."

"Yeah, great." He stood up and headed for the door. "I need some more pigment."

Once the door closed, Spark stashed the jar of venom back in its hiding spot in the cupboard before anyone else barged in, then slid the lantern to the back of the worktable to get to her next task. She was working on a mold to make grommets.

"No offence, but this place doesn't seem that inspirational," Ember said.

"He says he wants to paint something dark."

"Oh. Well, then yes." Ember grinned. "How's the glass coming?"

"I think it's finally working." Spark gestured to the pan of water on the floor where the most recent panes cooled. "I'm not going to be able to make any decent size panels in here, but it's a start. Maybe once other people are done building, I can get some help putting together a workshop for glass. With the dragon venom to melt the sand, I think anyone can do this if they're careful."

"You know, Spark, I'm really surprised at how much things have changed since you got here. It's like a proper village now. Well, there's still the apprentice district, but they seem to wear their scummy tents like a badge of honour."

"Except Jatt."

"He's not like an apprentice at all. He's been here for a few years, and I don't think it's just because his master is. He likes the dragons nearly as much as Ondias does. And now that his family is here, I don't think he'll ever leave."

"Really? He seems so engrossed in his work, I thought he'd be eager to get out into the world and share it."

"Does he ever share his work? I've never seen any of it."

Spark nodded to the painting of the city before going back to the mold. "He only shares things that are done. Done and worthy. I don't have much of an eye for art, but I've seen him scrapping things that look just fine to me. He's set his standards pretty high."

Ember shrugged and sat on the stool to watch Spark work.

"Good for him if he does get out and travel a bit," Ember said. "We've been here most of my life. Ondias has been here since the dawn of time. She acts like she invented the place."

Spark's chuckle evaporated into a wince when River called from outside the door.

"This place can get buried by water again!" He shoved through the door and came in. "We're going to end up rotting here."

He stalked straight up to them and swiped a stack of repair work off the table. Spark's quick reflexes were the only thing that kept a broken axe blade from landing on the glass panes. Ember did little more than lean out of his way. Spark wondered if she could ignore him like that because she'd lived with it for so long.

Spark didn't give him the satisfaction of watching her pick up any of what he'd knocked down, but she got between him and the glass, knowing he'd break it if she didn't intervene. She'd worked too hard on it to let it go to one of his idiotic tantrums. River was a large man, but Spark was not tiny. And she held her chisel in one hand and swiped up her hammer in the other as she stood.

He didn't normally stay long, and Spark hoped this time wouldn't be any different.

"Why don't you leave then?" Spark asked. "You could go with the traders and end up anywhere you wanted."

"You'd like that, wouldn't you?"

"I think we all would." Spark stood her ground, stayed in his face.

"What do you know anyway, you godsdamned freak. We've never had a proper education, not even apprenticeships with trades. Stuck here in lands forsaken by gods and demons alike, cobbling together knowledge from a steady parade of new scholars. It's no way to live."

"You could work security on the caravans. The traders always need muscle to keep them safe. You could keep doing farm work through the lands. You're only anchored here because you anchor yourself, though I can't fathom why."

"Shut up. You don't know what the world is like."

Spark raised an eyebrow, but didn't state the obvious—that she just came from the world and had seen plenty more than he guessed.

"I'll make you a fine sword, or a battle-axe. To help you on your way with the traders."

"Just shut up."

"River, come on, let it go," Ember said. "You're the one who came in here. What do you want?"

"Pa needs you. You going to spend all day here? Why don't you move in?"

"Not a bad idea," she said flippantly, and Spark warmed at the very thought. "I'll be there in a few minutes."

River stormed out and Spark let out a long breath, setting her tool-weapons back on the work table. Once his shadow passed by the window and his footfalls receded, Spark gathered up the things he'd knocked down.

"I really don't know what I've done to him."

"He's a petulant child most of the time," Ember said. "You'd think he was the younger one. Hard to believe he's twenty." She helped Spark pick up the last of her things.

"Hi, River," Jatt's voice called with false cheeriness. "Off to disembowel kittens?"

Spark jammed her hands against her mouth to keep from laughing out loud. River's voice was distant, but the vulgar oath he hurled at Jatt was plenty loud enough for half the village to hear. Spark squeezed her eyes shut and held her breath against the laughter. Next to her, Ember had her arms tightly wrapped around her middle, biting her lips. Her body shook with a fit of giggles trying to escape. At last, they both got it together.

"He hates it here, but you're right, he should go." Ember wiped tears from her eyes. "He's a man now, but he seems to forget that. I could leave too, if I wanted, but it's so beautiful here and I'd miss Pa. He's really all that I've got."

"I really will make him some weapons to get him out of here."

Ember smiled, but with only one side of her mouth. "I'm sorry he's so hard on you. He's just a fool. Pa brought us here to be near your mamma after our gran died. We didn't get much choice in that, we were so young. But it's not as if you're the one who sent your ma here or made Pa follow.

He's here because he wants to be, like I am, even if for different reasons. River can leave if he wants. Something holds him here, but he won't say what. I couldn't even guess."

Jatt returned with a small packet that seemed tiny in his long, slender hands. He stiffened when he saw Ember, but came straight in all the same, plunking himself down into his corner without a word. Ember had started to leave, probably to keep River from returning to fetch her. Spark put a hand on her elbow to halt her.

"You are welcome to come here any time you want. If you've got a table to spare, you can set one up to do your sewing. I hope to get another work table of my own in here."

"Spark, really! This is your home. You're going to have no room to live in here if you fill the space with work."

"We're all busy." She gestured to Jatt working silently. "But there's room enough for you to come work with me. Home was like this too, all of us working together at different projects."

"I might. But I should get going for now before he comes back."

Jatt winced. If Ember unnerved him, River set him completely on edge. Spark continued scraping out the mold while Jatt stayed in his corner, scowling at his work with his shoulders bunched up around his ears even once Ember was gone. She could see River having that sort of effect on Jatt, but Ember was harmless.

"Why don't you like her?" Spark asked.

"I don't really know much about her, but her brother's got quite the reputation. Miserable thing, isn't he?"

"Oh, it's not just me?"

"Afraid not."

"I thought he was always so rude because of my mother."

"Ah, yes. That's the convoluted logic he's using to give himself an excuse for being so rude. I don't know how someone with manners like that hasn't been eaten by a dragon. To think he's lived here nearly his entire life!"

"Well, the dragons are fond of Stone. Maybe they're not eating River out of courtesy to him?"

"They're both so unpredictable," he said. "It'd be easier if they were more like their father."

"They've been stuck here so long with him and so little outside influence. They need to set themselves apart. And it sounds like they take after their mother, who was probably a lot like my mother, from what I understand."

"Then you must take after your father," he said.

Spark stilled. She didn't know how much everyone else knew about her family, about her mother and the ignoble things she'd done.

"Sorry," he said quickly. "I didn't mean..." He coughed. "Um, I know. Because of Gran. I don't think anyone else does. Not that half of them will care."

Spark kept her back to him, worried what he might see in her expression.

"It doesn't matter," he said. "It shouldn't, anyway. It's ridiculous that people get their ass in a bunch over something like that. Like you could have any control over what your mother did before you were even born."

Spark forced her hands to remain steady by continuing to chisel bits out of the mold. Jatt knew enough not to say anything else, and the comfortable silence settled over both of them.

Spark set aside the mold, having a hard time focusing on it, and went to inspect the pane of glass on the floor. It was ready to cut into shape for the iron frame she'd made for it. If she didn't break anything in the process, she'd have proper windows by the time she went to sleep. She took a few measurements and then got to work. Pressing her index finger along the top of it, she concentrated, letting the heat whoosh through her body and out her hand. She cut the glass with a line of pure fire, white hot.

Ondias abruptly pushed in, the door swinging around to bang against the wall. Spark jumped and got control of the magic in enough time not to destroy her work. Ondias marched straight toward Spark, her mouth open to say something, but then she spotted Jatt. She skewered him with her gaze, and he shrivelled deeper into the corner.

"Go," she snapped.

Jatt paused for only a moment, sass flickering through his expression before he looked away from Ondias and sprang from his seat. He didn't bother to collect his things, just plucked his cloak from the hook by the door and left without stopping to put it on.

Ondias slammed the door behind him.

Spark bunched her hands into fists and moved away from the glass. Her voice was full of fire when she spoke.

"What—"

"Dionelle is still alive." She bit off the words so they came out like little jabs.

Needling cold flushed through Spark's body while her mind tried to make sense of the words. She hadn't let herself hold on to hope—it had been clear what those dragons had been sent for. But she hadn't seen them actually kill Nanny. As the words truly sank in, Spark wondered why she wasn't overjoyed to hear them.

"How do you know?"

"A contact from the Guild was in Pasdale, heard rumours and caught a glimpse of her. They're holding her underground where it's difficult for dragons to reach her. They likely know you escaped."

"She wouldn't have told them."

"They may not have given her much choice. Especially after all this time, I'm quite sure they'd have broken her."

"Wouldn't she be dead then? If she's told them what she knows?"

"They might not be asking the right questions. As far as anyone knows, you died in the wilderness. But they're going to search. Traders have seen you. The truth will find Loch eventually."

Spark bit her lips and stared into the forge.

"What in the name of the moons are you doing bothering with glass?"

"I can't spend the whole winter with the windows boarded up or bricked off."

"You don't have time for luxuries. You need to focus on your safety."

"How am I going to get any safer than I am here?"

"They'll come. I know Nandara has hinted at that already. Loch will come with his dragons." She crossed her arms, staring at the glass with a troubled expression. Her gaze shifted to the lantern Spark had just finished.

"So that's where my dragon venom ended up!"

Spark's face flushed and she dug the jar out of her cupboard. Ondias ripped it from her hands.

"I was going to put it back tonight."

"You need to stop stealing from me and start asking."

"Fine. Will you show me how to collect dragon venom or teach me the right way to ask a dragon for it? Or whatever?"

Ondias clenched her jaw and turned to leave.

"Can we save Nanny? Now that we know she's alive and where she is…?"

"I know you're still just a girl," she said, her tone trying to soften, not quite making it. "But it's time for you to grow up."

Hot fury gripped Spark's chest so that she couldn't draw the breath she needed to scream at Ondias. When Ondias opened the door, Shadow slunk in and darted under the work table. Ondias slammed the door on her way out. The anger fizzled out of Spark, her limbs growing heavy as mountains. She drew in a deep breath and let it out slowly, turning to Shadow. He sat with his ears raised.

"She's horrible, isn't she?" Spark asked. "But Nanny is alive, boy. Maybe we can save her. What do you think? I think I should talk to Abyss. Abyss loves Nanny most of all. If anyone will help, it'll be her."

Shadow whined, leaning his shoulder into her thigh. Spark scratched his ears and let out another long sigh. Spark pressed her other hand over Nanny's pendant, feeling the hard lump of it under her shirt, but she didn't take it out. She went back to the glass, wanting her windows done, needing the task to focus on and stop her swirling thoughts.

The wind rattled the new lattice windows. It had been doing this all night. *All night*. Spark had grown accustomed to the prairie winds on the open fields of Pasdale, but this was something entirely different. It was colder. Persistent. It got into her bones. There had been a few nights where she stripped down and slept in the burning forge, just to feel warm.

It was no wonder people like Tueben—nearly half the village—cleared out for the winter. Returning home to their families, safe and warm, until spring.

These nights were the hardest. This night especially made her wish she could disappear into the fire. She could technically do it, but she also knew what it would mean. Her mother and grandmother had both done it, but they'd both had people to come for them when it went wrong. Who did Spark have?

Abyss was fond of her, but she'd been to the fire realm once already and couldn't risk going back. Spark didn't understand why; Ondias was vague on the point.

The cursed, howling wind was all Spark thought about. How alone she was. Nanny was alive, but she couldn't take any comfort in that. They weren't keeping her alive for anything good. And they certainly wouldn't keep her alive once they found Spark.

She tried not to think about Loch returning to the dragon city, about the damage he could do. But her mind kept turning to what could happen. To the dragons and to her. She wondered if he'd kill her or try to make her do horrible things. Did Loch recognize the value of her skill? Or was he purely afraid of her?

There had to be something she could do about it. She lay awake wondering where she could go if she left. Abyss would take her if she asked the right way. But if she left, where could she go? Finding her uncles would only endanger them. If Loch could track her to the dragon city, was there anywhere he *couldn't* track her?

She ran once already. If she was lucky, it would take until spring for Loch to find her. That gave her the whole winter to prepare, as Nandara suggested weeks ago.

Shadow startled her with a low warning bark, a soft little woof, an instant before someone knocked on the door. Spark thought about ignoring it but didn't want someone banging on her door all night. But if it was Ondias, Spark was going to cut her down with fire.

Grumbling, she pulled herself out of bed and shuffled across the cold slabs of her floor. She cracked the door open, blocking it with her body in case it was Ondias thinking she could push in. Spark's eyes widened and she threw the door open when she saw that it was Ember wrapped in her thick fur robe.

"It's late, what are you doing here?"

"I heard about your gran." Ember eased passed her. "I thought I should come check on you."

"In the middle of the night?"

"Had to wait till River went to sleep. He'd have followed me here. That wouldn't go well for anyone."

Spark waved a hand at the fire, bringing the flame up for more light and warmth and padded toward the work table to sit, as was their custom. Ember ushered Spark back to bed, guiding her with her hands on Spark's waist. Still wrapped in her warm robe, Ember sat on the edge of Spark's bed and pulled the blankets up around her. Spark warmed, like she'd melted.

"Are you all right?"

"It's good to know about Nanny. But I think it would be easier if she was dead. Is that bad?"

Ember looked at a spot on the wall under Jatt's painting. She breathed so shallowly that Spark could barely tell she was breathing at all.

"I think it makes sense," she said slowly. "I don't think it's bad to wish she was dead because she's suffering now."

"Yes, that's part of it. I know they must be hurting her. Or they're going to hurt her. They're going to use her to hurt us."

Ember lay on her side, wrapping her arm around Spark. It brought more warmth than Spark expected, but her stomach roiled as Nanny's peril consumed her thoughts.

"I want to go save her. Next time I see Abyss, I'm going to ask if she'll help me. There's got to be a way to get her back."

Ember didn't say anything else but gave Spark a squeeze and then stayed with her, a warm, quiet presence. Even the wind seemed quieter. Shadow hopped up onto the bed, lying across their feet.

Spark awoke in the morning, disoriented and groggy, not remembering having fallen asleep. Ember lay next to her, wrapped in her winter robes and sound asleep. Spark stretched, unravelling like a waking dragon, and began the careful process of untucking herself from blankets pinned down by Ember and Shadow. The motion woke the dog, who hopped off the bed and woke Ember as a result.

She sat up and smiled at Spark. Spark kept her eyes focused in front of her as she climbed over Ember to let Shadow out.

"I've probably got a little while before anyone notices I'm out of the house," Ember said. "I can stick around for a bit?"

Spark smiled at her but couldn't meet her gaze. Having Ember around made the difficulties ahead easier to face and solidified the notion that Spark had to stay where she was. She had to take a stand.

"Yeah, I'd like that. Can you help me with that hood? I tried working on it last night to take my mind off of Nanny and..."

Spark went into her cupboard and pulled out the hood, showing Ember where she'd accidently introduced a fold to the fabric and sewn it to the seam.

"I don't know how to get the twine back out without cutting it. I haven't got much of it left."

"You've bungled this properly," Ember said, grinning and playfully pushing Spark's shoulder. "I think we can save it."

Spark put more wood on the fire and fished out some bread and cheese from the pantry. Ember shrugged out of her robe and hung it on one of the hooks by the door. They both nibbled breakfast while Ember showed Spark how to get things going, carefully pulling the stitches out until the two of them worked in tandem.

Spark's fingers constantly brushed against Ember's, making her tingle all the way up her arms. Ember leaned in close, their faces only inches apart, so they could both see what they were doing. Spark kept stealing glances up at her, entranced by Ember's fierce concentration and the way she pursed her lips. Any time they made eye contact, Ember would grin, and Spark would blush and immediately turn back to their work.

When the last of the twine came free, Spark moved away from the table, but Ember took her hands to hold her in place. All Spark saw were Ember's dark eyes. She gave Ember's hands a squeeze before pulling away to store their breakfast leftovers.

Ember followed Spark to the little pantry, but bumped into one of Spark's storage crates while trying to keep out of Spark's way. The crate clattered to the floor, its contents glittering across the stone, tinkling like glass.

"Oh, damn, I'm sorry!"

She bent to put it all back, but Spark was frozen, her heart stilled.

"Are these arrowheads?"

"Yes." The words strangled out of her. "I'm experimenting."

But they were all uniform, all the same. Dozens of them. Ember wasn't buying it and stared at Spark.

"I was learning to use a bow back home." It wasn't a total lie. "Thought it couldn't hurt to take it up again. Maybe I can learn to hunt."

Spark didn't want to say that these were meant to be bolts for crossbows, and she definitely wouldn't reveal that she'd used elemental spellcraft on all of them. Like Spark's needle and knife, these could pierce dragon skin. Not that she wanted to put them to use. It had been mostly practice with only a little of Nandara's earlier warnings as a guide. Now she was glad for it. She would make more, and bigger. She'd gotten good at it.

She should start making chains, too, but didn't have the resources for chains big enough to contain a dragon. She'd need a bigger forge, more storage space, and probably a team of workers. Not to mention an endless supply of metal. How to do any of that secretly was beyond her.

She'd started work on a large crossbow, the design sketched out and hidden amongst the clutter at the back of her cupboard. It was meant to be something with enough power to get an arrow, or perhaps a spear, up into the sky. Something that could take down a dragon. Not that there was any way to test it.

Ember marvelled over the pile of arrowheads as she gathered them back into the crate.

"When do you find the time for this?"

"Plenty of hours in the day. Metal work is really all I do, especially in this weather."

Ember shrugged and continued cleaning up. She rarely left her own house, except to visit Spark or to occasionally visit the scholars when they'd been at her father's wine and were more spirited than usual. Spark went with her once and had fun, but it was far louder than she liked. She preferred to go when it was quieter and she could actually talk to whoever was there. They'd taught her an unfathomable amount, always pleased, if amused, to answer her questions.

With the arrowheads cleaned up, Ember returned to the work table and laid out the pieces of hood, carefully folded together.

"There, now you don't have to move anything before you start again. Be mindful this time and try to move it as little as possible until you get the hang of it. And if it gives you anymore trouble, I can do it for you."

"I should learn this."

Ember smiled. "I'll have to come back and supervise then."

Spark's face grew warm. "I'd like that. I meant it about you setting up a table in here."

"I might take you up on the offer yet." She stepped closer, standing right in front of Spark.

"You sure you're all right?" she asked.

"I'll see it through. It'll be a tough go, but maybe Abyss will have some ideas."

"I can stay."

Spark smiled shyly. "I'd like it if you did, but you don't have to. I know you have work. I do feel better now. I'm glad you came by."

Ember smiled and touched her palm to the side of Spark's cheek. Tingling warmth cascaded through Spark's body. Then Ember pulled on her robe, hood up, and slipped out the door.

As much as metal work had been calling to Spark all morning, she was intent on finishing the dragon skin hood. She had her cheek pressed against the worktable, tongue poking out while she concentrated on sewing the seam without moving the fabric from where Ember had set it. Working sideways was awkward, but she was mostly finished.

Something scraped at her door and she jabbed her finger with the needle.

"Damnit!"

Carefully as she could, she collected everything up and stuffed it into the cupboard before unlatching the door. Abyss was there waiting for her. When Spark opened the door, the dragoness pointed her chin up toward the dragon city.

"Do you want me to come help with the rebuilding?"

She nodded.

"Have you heard the news about Nanny?"

Her expression drooped.

"I need something to eat. Can you wait a few minutes? Or come back?"

Abyss dipped her head and went to wait in a wider space between buildings. She sat on her haunches, her tail curled around in front of her while she focused on Spark's home. Spark slipped inside to slice off a bit of hard bread and grab a handful of salted pork strips. She headed out to meet Abyss, eating as she went.

Spark ate in Abyss's hand, while the rush of the ground dropping away made her giddy. She'd tried talking Abyss into taking her for flights around the valley, just for fun and not for work, but no luck so far.

She was done eating by the time they reached the main room. The room was full of diamond and obsidian boulders, many of them larger than Spark although they looked like pebbles next to the massive dragons. The largest pieces littered the northern part of the valley floor, but anything worthwhile for the dragons and small enough for humans to carry off had been hidden away in the mountains, beyond human reach.

The dragons constantly carted pieces up to the city to continue the large, spiralling towers that used to exist. Spark was learning to fuse the diamond, but there was little spare material for her to experiment with. But she'd long mastered fusing the obsidian, and the dragons found her especially handy when it came to tight spaces.

Abyss picked out a large piece of obsidian and Spark climbed on top of it. The dragoness picked it up with Spark still on it and flew out to the top of the city. The wind howled, biting Spark's skin. She clung to the slick rock as best she could and put the dizzying height out of her mind. Abyss would catch her if she fell.

Spark climbed down and helped her fit the chunk into a good spot. Spark did the fusing while Abyss hung at the edge, watching. Once Spark had it fused, she climbed out of the way and let Abyss shape it. They repeated the process a few times while other dragons worked on the two diamond sections, slowly spinning them up into the sky.

The quiet work and close companionship let Spark consider what she really wanted to do before working up the courage to talk to Abyss. When the other dragons went down into the city for more stones, Spark paused. She peeked over the boulder at Abyss.

"I want to go free Nanny." She took a steadying breath. "I can't do it on my own. Will you help?"

Abyss clung motionless to the edge of the city, scrutinizing Spark with a gaze like a blade. Dragons came and went as the two watched each other in silence. Once they were alone, Abyss opened her mouth.

"This is a risk I will take."

Her voice was rich and deep, like words sculpted from thunder, but so gentle they were like a summer breeze. Spark blinked and went motionless as the stone around them.

"You must have a plan," Abyss said. "And you cannot rely on others of my kin."

Spark leapt across the space between them to embrace the end of Abyss's muzzle, planting a kiss on the tip of her snout. Abyss tolerated it for a moment, her black eyes glittering like starlight, before she huffed, blowing Spark back to her place. Trying not to weep while grinning like a fool, Spark continued rebuilding.

Spark kept nattering away at Abyss, but Abyss didn't say anything else. In the early afternoon she brought Spark home.

"I'll figure something out. I'll see if Nandara will help. If we're going to be successful, it's probably going to take us a long time to be ready for it. I hope we've got the time we'll need."

Abyss nodded, smiling, and headed up to the city. Spark watched her until she disappeared against a section of obsidian. Shadow was still out prowling the valley, and she'd be surprised to see him again before dark. She wasn't sure if she'd see Jatt or anymore of Ember, but she welcomed a bit of solitude.

Spark couldn't rely on other dragons, but she wasn't sure how to succeed without more help. She'd try to come up with some kind of stealth trip back to Pasdale. Maybe Jatt could help her with that. But she liked her chances more if she could convince other dragons.

So far, she'd been using most her skills for herself and the human settlement, but there had to be more to offer the dragons than a bit of fusing on the city. Instead of building weapons to harm dragons, she should come up with something they could use.

CHAPTER FIFTEEN

T he howling wind made Spark shudder, even though her little house held the warmth of the forge well enough. She hadn't seen as much work in recent weeks with everyone staying in their homes or out of the valley through the worst of the season. Spark wasn't worried—she'd amassed supplies galore, with the cupboards in the corner near the front door full of everything she'd need for at least a moon cycle.

Cupboards encroached on the corner where Jatt liked to work. He was with Spark now, working on the dark painting he refused to show anyone. He kept putting it aside and working on other things, including a portrait of Abyss in mid-flight that Spark had thought well done. But the dark painting was something he only worked on in Spark's home, and only when he was in the right frame of mind.

As they pushed into full winter, Jatt came most days to make art while Spark worked metal. She gave up on weapons to combat dragons and was trying to figure out how to make armour for them instead. She was also working on weapons dragons could use. But she couldn't see what a dragon would need for something like a crossbow. The best she could think would be to affix them with some kind of reinforced metal spikes, though they were certainly covered in enough spikes of their own already.

She'd started working on other things, like the little dragon venom lantern. She'd made some more and was adapting one of them into a clockwork. It was full of gears and springs, delicate work that took nearly a fortnight of near constant adjusting to get down to an art. It wasn't a clock even if it was crafted around the same principles. She'd built it on a small well of dragon venom, and the heat generated pressure to make the gears turn. The top of it spun like a carousel without the creatures.

Jatt had a low opinion of it since it was ugly with no obvious function. Ondias hated it because it reminded her too much of the mills in Pasdale. At least she wasn't around these days, off on one of her rare travels far to the south where people still wanted to learn about dragons.

Spark was focused on her clockwork and the page of designs spread out next to it, trying to daydream it into something that would help fight Loch. Jatt looked over at her work, studying the lantern on the tabletop next to the clockwork.

"You finally get the glass to stop cracking?"

"Yes, I've learned how to make tempered glass."

"Spending more time with the scholars in their dining hall?"

"Well, they don't mind me stopping in. I helped them build it, after all."

Spark wasn't sure why she'd been the catalyst to get the whole village going, but she'd helped turn the place into a proper little town. She was almost as popular as Ondias, who was like her own little queen in a tiny kingdom.

"They're generous with their information once they've had a bit of wine," Spark said.

"It's amazing what Stone has been able to do with that plot of land he's got."

Jatt didn't know about Stone's secret, which surprised Spark since he seemed so adept at knowing everyone's business. There weren't any livestock Stone and the other farmers could use to fertilize their fields. Instead, he used dragon droppings every autumn since they were primarily ash. It was one of the village's better kept secrets, and Spark wasn't sure how Stone had arranged it in the first place.

From what Spark understood, Stone always had a knack for farming. The only time she'd heard Ondias say anything positive about him it was to compliment the fine produce he'd grown. In Pasdale, he'd stood out in a community known for its farming and thrived out in the dragon valley despite other setbacks.

But the soil was rich and had only recently been cultivated for the first time. Back when it had mostly been Ondias and Nanny camping out in the valley, they learned what they could forage from the lush surrounding forests. Now, a couple of hunters and several farms provided the village with the necessities and familiar foods, along with some comforts.

"He does well for himself," Spark said absently. "And we're all lucky for it. Especially me. That wine they make of his grapes has a way of loosening tongues. Of course, the more they teach me, the more it helps everyone else. I've got regular and tempered glass now, and I can start making it large scale soon. Especially if I can get some help with a workshop for it."

"That's true, but I don't know that many of them are altruistic. It is nice to work with properly functioning tools."

"That's lucky for me because there's not much else I'm any good at that the dragons can't just do themselves."

"I'm pretty sure you've got more power than a lot of the dragons." Jatt gave her a pointed look.

Spark wondered about that. She didn't know how to use a lot of her power, though Nandara was accelerating her training. It did seem that she had more than her fair share of it.

"Have you broached it with your gran to help me with the workshop?" she asked. "It only took her a day to get her house up. She could erect my workshop in an afternoon."

Spark had picked a site and everything. The things she had planned, particularly if she started making weapons for the dragons and mass producing tools and windows, would need far more space than her little home forge could make. A cleared area in the eastern part of the valley, just across the river, would do nicely. It was out of the way, so she could have some outdoor space too, and perhaps use that to work more closely with dragons.

"I'll ask her tonight," he said.

Spark had just pushed a new cupboard against the wall of the new workshop when dragons cried out in the city. It was their hunting call. Spark dashed out into the large field to watch the sky, trying to spot Abyss, who was set to go out with the next hunting party. The dragoness swooped to land near Spark's workshop.

"Are you leaving right now?"

Abyss watched Spark with eyes like ebony bonfires. Spark knew Abyss knew what Spark wanted—Spark had harassed her about it for a fortnight—but Abyss was going to make her ask. It was maddening, but the prospect of it was too much for Spark to worry much about her pride.

"I want to fly. Take me with you on your hunt."

One scaly eyebrow went up, the corners of her mouth curled. Spark was certain the dragon was smirking at her.

"Right, you're hunting. There's got to be a way to make it easier for you to bring me—something to free up your hands so you can carry me and whatever you hunt. It would make it easier for you all the time."

She tilted her head, her expression more serious, the smirk vanishing. She nodded toward the old wagon fitted with a large metal handle.

"But you still need to carry it, and I'm really not riding in that thing with a dead stag. Or several."

Abyss looked around, pausing when her gaze reached Hextir and his mule pulling a cart of supplies toward the workshop. She whipped around to look at Spark, her eyes narrowing a moment before she knocked Spark down with a quick line of flame.

"I wasn't suggesting I ride you like some mule." Spark brushed herself off, not wanting to admit that was exactly what she was thinking. But you don't argue with angry dragons.

She turned away from Spark and shook out her wings.

"Wait!" Spark ran in front of her. "Just give me a few minutes to study you—your shape and size. I'll see if I can come up with something while you're gone. Something you won't find insulting."

A pause. She leaned her massive head down to look at Spark, eyes narrowed. Spark fought to keep her thoughts from how much easier it would be if Abyss would let her sit in between those massive horns on her head, or let Spark tuck in between her wings. She wouldn't need to build anything at all, just climb up and hold on.

Abyss crouched down, her belly on the ground, and gestured with her head for Spark to climb her foreleg. As Spark scrambled up her foot—which was as big as a horse—Abyss tucked her wings in along her side rather than folding them onto her back. She did nothing to make things easier for Spark while she climbed.

It was like standing on a mountain, a sawtooth range, and Spark never realized how spiny Abyss was. Still, Spark could sit in troughs between the ridges of her back if Abyss wasn't so difficult. But then Spark noticed there were troughs lined up with the top of her wings and the base of her wings. Spark could put straps through them and around her so that they wouldn't interfere with the movement of her wings or legs.

"I've got to walk. Just to make sure I get your size right."

Spark edged her way up near Abyss's shoulders and had to be careful, holding onto the ridges and spikes that were nearly as tall as Spark was, and count her steps as she walked, putting the heel of one foot against the toes of the other. When she got to twenty steps and hadn't reached the other side of Abyss's wings, she paused, seeing how much farther she had to go. Not too much farther, but it made her turn and look the long way back to Abyss's head and then out the other way to the end of her tail. From tip to tip Spark wouldn't be surprised if Abyss was three hundred paces long.

"Demons blow me down," Spark whispered, retracing the journey down the dragoness's leg. "I've got to see underneath you. Will you stand? On all four."

Abyss stood, watching Spark curiously, and crouched when she realized how far her belly was above Spark. Despite being bigger than a house, Abyss walked between the houses rather than over.

Spark wished she'd had the foresight to bring out some parchment to sketch with. She'd have to make do with mental sketches for now. The dragons were gathering and Abyss wouldn't linger much longer.

"Thank you, Mistress. I hope the hunt is bountiful. I'll try to have something done when you return. Blessed winds."

Abyss narrowed her eyes, not liking the way Spark condensed the farewell, but then she snorted playfully and headed skyward. Spark barely kept upright at the sudden gale. She stood where she was, watching Abyss join the others until they were out of sight. She hoped to join them next time.

She ran into the new workshop and pulled out her fresh pile of parchment she'd brought in, immediately getting started on sketches for a harness Abyss could wear. Spark was so engrossed in her work that she didn't notice Ember until her face was over Spark's shoulder. Ember's breath on her cheek startled Spark so badly she jumped, dragging a streak of charcoal across the page.

"Shit on the moons, Ember, are you trying to kill me?"

"I'm so sorry! How didn't you hear me coming in?" Ember started carefully smudging out the sloppy line. She took up the page where Spark had a basic sketch of Abyss and her dimensions scribbled on the side.

"What the devil are you up to?"

"I'm going to go flying with her next time. I'm going to make it easier."

"Easier for her to carry you? You'll need warmer clothes, won't you? I can only guess the winds are murderous at the speeds she flies."

"And it's cold high up to begin with. But I'll worry about that later. Need something to get flying with first."

Ember put the parchment down and pulled a fresh loaf, still warm, from the satchel hanging under her robes. "A little lunch?"

It was early, but Spark smiled all the same and the two of them sat at the long work table.

"Are you still busy?" Spark asked.

"It's getting quieter. Back to normal repairs, for the most part. You getting lonely?"

Spark's cheeks grew hot and she looked down at the chunk of bread in her hands.

"There's no way I can do all the work in here by myself. And I always enjoy your company."

Spark picked up the charcoal and kept sketching while the two of them ate in silence. Ember finished first and came to stand next to Spark, reading Abyss's dimensions over Spark's shoulder.

Ember whistled softly. "That's a lot of material," she said.

"I've got my work cut out for me—for us."

Spark doubted it would be possible. It would take forever. The length of straps she would need to get it all around Abyss was mind-boggling. But Ember set her outdoor robes aside, folding them on the far corner of the workbench. She went through Spark's supplies, pulled out what leather Spark had, and started taking measurements of her own, taking a spare piece of parchment and jotting some notes on it.

"I'll be back in a few minutes." Ember folded herself into her robes. "We've got plenty at home, ropes and some old leather just taking up space in the barn. Pa keeps it all. Ondias has the biggest mountain of trash, but no one here throws out much."

True to her word, Ember returned quickly with Stone hauling a hand-wagon full of supplies. He smiled at the two of them but didn't stay long. Ember spread her things out on the table, her nimble fingers moving swiftly, cutting and sewing. Working together, it took the two of them the day to stitch up a Spark-sized leather bag. A pocket for a dragon.

Spark hadn't realized how much time had gone by until Jatt came in, interrupting her conversation with Ember as they debated how to attach straps. Jatt bristled when he saw Ember, but came over to the table anyway, looking at the sketches. He inspected the sack.

"Run the straps through the back of it," he said. "Reinforced slits. You can do those, right?"

"Grommets, yes. Good idea!"

Jatt moved in seamlessly, cutting out what they needed while Ember stitched it up and Spark got to work on the metal pieces she'd need. Ember and Jatt were silent, only ever speaking to Spark and never to each other, except out of necessity.

Spark started planning reinforcements of her little travel sack where she could add pockets to store any supplies she might need on a longer trip. Jatt suggested an internal harness to keep her in the sack.

"You should have a way to close the pockets too," he said.

And so the days passed, Ember and Jatt working the leather and rope while Spark made all the grommets and buckles and secured them into place. And they'd spread the harness out in the snow-covered field to better visualize where everything needed to be, all the supports and extra bracing it would need.

Spark could only do so much without Abyss around. One afternoon, when it was just her and Ember, she announced they'd done all they could.

"This is going to be incredible if it works!" Ember said.

The two of them coiled all of the straps and ropes into the sling Spark would ride in, all of it piled into a corner of the workshop. Once they finished coiling the last bit of rope, Ember took a step back to stretch. She had her hands pressed into the small of her back, arching deeply. Spark watched her, forgetting what she was supposed to be doing. She waited for Ember to topple backward, but she kept arching gracefully so that her hair nearly touched the floor. The curved line of her body was so smooth it took Spark's breath away.

Spark only realized she'd been staring as Ember straightened. Spark jerked away, tidying the stacks of parchment designs on the table.

"I should get home for dinner," Ember said.

Only then did Spark realize how dark the workshop had grown. Big windows and a big sliding door stretched along most of one wall, keeping the place brightly lit as long as there was sunlight. The sun had dipped behind the mountains.

"I could come back later, give you a hand with other projects," Ember said.

Spark swallowed, tried to remember if Jatt was supposed to be around, tried to parse Ember's words, but her mind came up blank. Ember headed out the door, not waiting for a reply, leaving Spark with nothing but the warm, empty feeling of yearning.

Shivering in the pale dawn light, Spark burrowed deeper into her blankets and stared vacantly into the centre of the room. Cold in ways the deepest winter could never touch. Nightmares. Again. Full of ash and flame and the finality of Pappy's screams being cut short.

Spark was too tired for tears. Barely had the energy to breathe.

Shadow pawed her leg, but she was too tired to notice the warm comfort of him on her feet. She didn't take note of the low whines from the dog until dragon cries rang out from the city above. After a brief span of silence, Spark heard the distant cries they were answering.

"The hunting party!" Spark sat up, new warmth in her limbs, and flicked back a corner of her curtain. She couldn't see anything, but the cries were getting louder.

Spark pulled on clothes and stuffed her feet into her boots, spilling out her front door and into the laneway beyond. She sprinted into the market square and stood with her face tilted skyward. The main blaze of dragons was going out to meet the returning party.

"Spark! They're back!" Ember called, running up to join her.

Spark's shoulders sank away from her ears, and she let out a long breath when she spotted the black shard of Abyss among the rest of the colourful blaze. The hunting parties rarely faced danger, but anything could happen.

"It will be a while until she's rested enough to come down to see me," Spark said. "But will you help me bring the harness out to the field?"

"You don't need my help." Ember smiled.

With coils of rope slung over their shoulders and Spark clutching the folded sling, they went out to the field near the workshop. It was warmer than it had been in weeks, but midwinter was approaching and the snow crunched underfoot. Ember helped her spread out the harness as they had so many times with Jatt. This time, however, people looked on from the edge of town and a couple of dragons circled overhead, intent on what the two girls were up to.

It was obvious from the sheer size of the contraption what it was meant for, and under the scrutiny of other dragons, Spark had a moment of doubt, wondering if this crossed any lines.

But then Abyss herself dropped away from one of the city's obsidian panels and circled slowly overhead, just far enough away not to disturb the snow with her wing gusts. She studied Spark's invention and set down next to it.

"We've both been busy these past days," Spark said after the usual polite greeting.

Abyss remained still, watching Spark with an unreadable expression, an inky pool in the snow. Spark explained how the sling would work and was not immediately devoured or crushed.

"Do you consent to trying it on?"

Everything was stillness for a long moment, stretching out like Abyss's long sleek body. While Spark spoke aloud about wanting to fly for fun, she wondered if Abyss realized the usefulness this could have in rescuing Nanny.

Abyss whistled out a bit of steam and bent closer to Spark.

It was an awkward start getting the long straps over Abyss, like trying to put a sling around a mountain. With some trial and error, Spark was able to throw coiled ends over Abyss so they draped down the other side. Ember helped, and a couple of other townsfolk—a wizard and a couple of apprentices—joined in helping to secure the many buckles and untangle some of the supports.

Spark climbed up onto Abyss to position everything properly, out of the way of her wings and legs, making sure the ropes went between her spiny ridges. Already, Spark was making mental sketches of how she would have to adjust everything, where she could add more supports, where she should put some padding to protect dragon and harness from each other.

The straps slid and shifted, though Abyss was barely moving. Once it was all in place from above, Spark climbed down to make sure everything was tightened properly. While everyone stood around watching, Spark marked off the excess strap length with charcoal and then sent Ember to the workshop to get her designs and some blades.

"Mistress, if nothing is chafing you, shall we try it with me in the sling?"

Abyss reached out and carefully plucked Spark from the ground, holding her under the arms with thumb and forefinger and dropping her into the little pouch that looked ridiculously tiny against Abyss's vast chest. Spark struggled into the harness inside the sling.

When she called out she was ready, Abyss launched onto her hind legs and shook her body ferociously. Spark was flung around, but the harness did what it was meant to. Abyss stretched her wings out to their maximum reach and flicked them a couple of times, the people below bracing against the blizzard she churned up. Then she tilted forward and came gracefully down to the ground, crouching low so Spark could easily climb from the sling.

Once Spark was out and the contraption unbuckled, Abyss folded up her wings just so and straightened out on one side. Shaking gently, Abyss elegantly shrugged off the sling, then soundlessly sprang up into the air, scattering the onlookers with her wing-gale.

Spark's grin was mirrored on Ember's face. Seeing their hard work pay off made Spark's limbs twitch with the need to dance and whoop. But other dragons still circled, watching closely. She kept a lid on her excitement, gathering up the sling with all the dignity she could muster. Her thoughts spun and her heart raced to think of flight and all that she and Abyss could do if they could fly without Abyss worrying about Spark's safety. Surely, this was a necessary step in rescuing Nanny.

CHAPTER SIXTEEN

B iting wind lashed Spark's face, intruding through every fold and gap in her many scarves. It pulled the air from her lungs, leaving her gasping in sips. Prodded through her short frizz of hair like pins pricking her scalp. She gripped the bunched fabric under her chin, pulling scarves and hood tight, and clung to the edge of her sling, despite the harness holding her firm against Abyss. The harness would do far more to protect her than hanging on could. Spark held on anyway.

Snow pelted her like stinging sand. Through gaps in the clouds, the mountains slid past below. The vicious wind of storm and dragon-flight threatened to freeze Spark's eyes solid, but she squinted into the gale all the same. She couldn't look away.

Spark's pulse fluttered, terror icing her veins, but still she grinned into the searing cold, joyous freedom lighting a fire in her belly.

Abyss had flown most of the day, twisting and spiralling through the air to test what felt like ten leagues of rigging to fit around Abyss. Spark and Ember had finished adjusting it last night. Spark needed far warmer clothing, especially for winter flights, but so far the test was a delightful success.

The storm was unexpected, but Abyss was unconcerned, gliding at speed. Spark wanted to suggest they cut the trip short and head home—they were cutting it close to the Sky Fire Festival that neither wanted to miss—but the glittering red mountains were threaded with grey as they approached the end of the range. She was transfixed.

Something cracked. Abyss howled so loud it drove a spike of pain through Spark's ears. So loud it vibrated Spark's body, strapped firmly against the dragoness's chest. They lost altitude.

Another crack. Abyss's cries rose in pitch, ringing in Spark's ears. Girl and dragon tilted sideways, tumbling in the wind. Spark was buffeted against Abyss's body as the sling snapped loose on one side.

Spark screamed. It tore her throat but she heard nothing over the screeching dragon and roaring wind. Snow and cloud swirled past, an alternating spin of white storm and red-grey mountains. With a sickening flip of Abyss's giant body, Spark's sling came loose.

Abyss snagged her talons in the rigging and reeled Spark in as they plummeted, pressing Spark against her warm chest, covering Spark entirely, keeping her from flying away into the storm and to her death. But as the mountaintops drew nearer, Spark wondered if Abyss catching her only delayed the inevitable.

They jerked violently to the right, nearly flipped again. Abyss stabilized herself, but they were still falling. Spark peeked through Abyss's fingers. She had one wing extended fully, a black sail on some immense pirate ship.

The other wing was tangled in the rigging, wrapped with bits of rope and straps of leather.

Electric cold pulsated from between Spark's shoulders and through her body, constricting her chest.

"Blast the moons and sear the earth!" she wheezed.

If Spark knew how to properly work any other element at all, she could do something to stop their fall. Call a gale to set them down gently, control the water in the snow to make a cold path to safety, soften the earth before impact. But fire would do them no good.

Could she climb up to the straps and untangle her?

A glance at the ground was all the answer she needed.

Spark squeezed her eyes shut, clenching every last inch of herself. She couldn't die, not now, not when she'd only just settled in the dragon city, not after Nanny's sacrifice to keep her alive, not when she had friends after all these years, and Ember's soft smile and gifts of warm bread, and how could she think of Ember's bread at a time like this anyway, when she was about to die and hadn't done anything to help Nanny yet and—

Abyss roared and pitched. Spark screamed, peeked through one squinted eye. Abyss had clipped a mountain ridge, flipping. The dragoness gained enough momentum to ricochet from the ridge, over a valley and into the opposing mountainside.

When she hit the ground again, Abyss rolled, squeezing Spark tighter against her. Spark was certain she would be crushed.

The rolling stopped. Abyss skidded on her back, plowing through snow and shrubs and a few trees thicker through than Spark was. She finally came to a stop against a mound of boulders.

Spark trembled. If she'd had anything to eat since the morning, she'd have vomited. Hot tears froze on her cheeks while she gasped for air.

Abyss remained a warm presence against her back. But Abyss wasn't moving.

Slowly, with numbed fingers, Spark unbuckled the clasps of her harness and slid out of her sling. She held tight to the remaining strap and rappelled down the dragoness's side to the snow-covered ground.

Abyss lay on her back, one leg bent at wrong angles against the side of the mountain, her head pointing the way they'd come. A wide swath of crushed trees and gouged snow stretched on as far as Spark could see through the swirling snow.

Gritty snow squeaked under Spark's boots as she stumbled the length of Abyss's neck. Spark stopped near her snout, digging to find her friend's eyes. Abyss's breathing hissed and gurgled, a stream of icy water spreading out from her nostrils.

"Abyss?" Spark dug with nothing but her hands, painfully cold. The snow tumbled back into the hole as quickly as she scooped it out. The wind swirled it around her. She chose a few colourful curses.

Spark called a little blaze into the palm of her hand. The heat flickered through her, tingling through her fingers. The blaze in her hand billowed, twice again the size of Spark, before she pushed it all down into the snow beneath Abyss's head.

White-hot fire melted the snow and vaporized the water, steam roaring away in the wind, until Abyss's head flopped on its side. Only her horns had supported her head, and they skidded across the exposed bedrock until Abyss's cheek pressed against the ground.

A thundery rumble rolled from deep inside Abyss. A dragony groan. Her glittering black eye blinked open, seized on Spark.

"Abyss!" Spark threw her arms around Abyss's snout, hugging her like hugging a soft, warm wall.

Abyss huffed, blowing Spark back onto her bottom in the slush.

Spark tried looking over her friend, but couldn't see much of her from this vantage point.

"Are you hurt? Can you move? We need to get home."

Another stormcloud groan. Abyss pushed her massive forelegs against the snow, rolling at a glacier's pace. On her side, not quite all the way onto her stomach, Abyss stopped, the groan pitching into a screech. Abyss snapped her jaws at the air.

Spark didn't need to ask what it was. She saw the tattered hole in the membrane of Abyss's wing. The extra joint in her hind leg indicated a terrible break.

Couldn't walk. Couldn't fly. No one knew where they were.

Spark breathed out a desperate string of curses, lost on the wind. Abyss growled and snarled, likely a dragon version of Spark's blasphemy. Spark went closer to her, meaning to untangle her from the straps and ropes. Abyss clawed out her massive hand, raking it through the snow and narrowly missing Spark.

"Abyss! Stop, let me help you."

Abyss gnashed at Spark. Spark scrambled further back.

"Mistress, please, let me up on your back so I can help."

Abyss roared, snapped her teeth.

Spark pulsed a fireball into Abyss's face, a quick burst to get her attention. In the brief moment it had Abyss startled, Spark strode in closer, doing her best imitation of a commanding grown-up voice when she spoke.

"Mistress, that's enough. You'll harm yourself even more. You must be still if we hope to have any chance of getting off this mountain alive."

Abyss puffed fire at Spark, but it was a petulant, nearly playful act. Spark held still and the pair watched each other. Abyss snorted and lay her head down. Spark clambered up Abyss's back.

It took an eternity for Spark to pull the straps and ropes free. She discovered where the rigging had failed: some support rivets snapped, a buckle warped. She had enchanted every piece of the rigging to be dragon-proof, but not cold-proof. And it was those very enchantments that had enabled the buckle to tear through Abyss's flesh.

Abyss stretched her wing out before letting it drop into the slush. She breathed slowly, shallowly, and hadn't opened her eyes since calming down. Snowflakes pelted against her skin, sizzling as they melted.

"Abyss?" Spark slid down into the slush to stand before her friend. "Are you well enough to fly?"

A long groan was Abyss's answer.

Spark pressed her hands against her mouth and stared at the mountainside. She blinked, rested a hand on Abyss's snout.

"I'm so sorry. Oh, bleeding moons, Abyss, I'm sorry, this is all my fault."

Abyss only wheezed.

Don't cry, don't cry, crying won't help.

But Spark's throat was hot and tight, her eyes stinging. She sniffled, forced a deep breath.

"Okay." She inhaled deeply. Looked around. "Okay. I can... I can try summoning your mate?"

Abyss grunted.

"Or can you do that? Nandara only ever showed me how to summon you. And from my house. Is it different? It is, isn't it?"

Spark clenched her jaw against the urge to keep babbling and went to gather some of the snapped tinder in the field of destruction wrought by their crash landing. She dumped it in the drifting snow near Abyss's face, stacked it, and let fire bloom.

Holding an image of Abyss's bright blue mate in her mind, trying to focus on her surroundings, Spark went through the summoning spell Nandara had taught her. Her first attempt fizzled out in her face. The second sent a column skyward, slicing through the swirling snow for an instant, but it was a weak thing, not reaching the low clouds. Spark tried one more time with similar results.

Close. But not good enough. The hot sting of tears encroached. Spark blinked them away.

"Right. Okay. We're on our own. Do you need some rest before you can fly?"

Abyss's silence stretched between them like all the world's mountains. She opened her eyes and fixed her piercing black gaze, full of the darkest nights and deepest void, on Spark.

"We will freeze and die before I heal," Abyss said in her growling thunderstorm voice.

Spark held her breath. They were a full day's flight from the dragon city, in a storm, and had little provisions. The plan had been for Abyss to hunt what they needed. Now she was injured and could not hunt.

Abyss nosed the pile of straps and rope from the sling's rigging. "Patches."

Spark let the word roll like thunder through her mind, blinking at the pile of supplies.

"You want me to patch your wing?"

"And leg. Or we crash-land again."

Spark stared a long time, her gaze drifting between Abyss's injuries and the paltry supplies they had. Patches. She could probably use the undamaged rigging and the leather of her sling to cover the hole in Abyss's wing. But the leg...

Abyss always stood on her hind legs or jumped before catching air to fly. Even if she could get airborne with the leg as it was, another crash landing could kill her.

"But what can I do?" Her voice rose in panic. "I need to reform and reinforce the clasps and rivets. I haven't got a forge."

Abyss lifted her head around to face Spark, shooting a thin but intense line of fire at her. Spark saw it coming in enough time to shunt the flame around her.

"What was that?"

Abyss lay her head down, closed her eyes.

Spark stood, her limbs buzzing. She wanted to scream, run, never stop. Instead, she staggered forward and dropped onto the cool rock, leaning her back against Abyss's warm bulk. She listened to the dragoness wheeze each breath, to the wind howl, and to the snow swish around them.

Spark went through the exercise of figuring out how she could patch a wing and splint a leg thick as a wagon. How could she do it under ideal circumstances? The puzzle calmed her. She envisioned how to use the sling as a patch. If Abyss helped her drag some of the broken tree trunks over, she could use the excess strapping as a splint. It wouldn't be that difficult.

If she was in her workshop. Had an extra set of hands to help, especially as hers grew increasingly numb and useless.

Her mind seized on their paltry supplies. The rigging, the clothes Spark wore, half a day's worth of food and water for Spark, a couple of enchanted tools that could double as weapons in a moment of sheer desperation.

While her mind worked, her body shivered. When her teeth started clattering, she noticed how cold she was, even leaned against Abyss. Spark rested a hand against Abyss's midnight skin. It was warm, but not nearly as warm as before.

Snow pooled in the many troughs between spikes on Abyss's back and head. Snow covered most of her wings.

"Abyss?"

No response. Eyes closed, rasping shallow breaths.

Spark jumped to her feet and shoved her hands against Abyss's cheek, a poor attempt to shake the massive dragoness.

"Abyss!"

Spark had no idea when her friend had last eaten, and she'd pushed herself all day, flying hard to test the rigging.

Shrill panic gibbered at the edges of her mind. Spark forced herself to think rationally. Abyss needed to replenish spent reserves. Food was the best way. But Spark could not hunt, not even small animals, and never mind the kinds of large beasts Abyss would need.

But food was just energy. And fire energy sustained the dragons. Spark couldn't open a portal directly to the fire realm, but there were other ways to get that kind of fire energy.

Spark shivered, not only because of the cold. She piled more broken wood onto her little fire. Stoked it into a massive blaze with the barest thought. With a deep breath, she performed the demon summoning, focusing her fiery will and hissing in that strange language of the fire demons.

Dazzling white light in a vaguely humanoid shape erupted from Spark's fire. Still hissing the creature's language, swiftly asserting her will to keep the demon from running amok, Spark sent it to Abyss. Elemental demon possession was dangerous, often deadly for humans, but a fire demon was no problem for a dragon.

She watched the demon melt into Abyss, the dragoness heaving a great breath like the world's largest forge bellows. She sat with her back against Abyss, who was already warming, and sorted all the metal bits from the rigging.

Once that was complete, she needed to de-enchant the metal so it could be worked into new shapes. She needed demons for that. Even if she knew the terramancy involved, using that much elemental magic, especially pyromancy in a snowstorm, would probably freeze both her and Abyss solid before she got halfway through the task.

Demons could use their elemental magic without the side effects. They could draw directly from their realms. Spark glanced at the fire. Shrugged. She'd already called one demon.

She needed earth and fire demons to remove the dragon-proofing from her metal scraps. Nandara had always taught her terramancy with a pot of soil. Spark hoped it would work with the bedrock beneath her.

Nervously, and with no one to help if something went wrong, she set to work calling the demons. First the earth demon, because they were slow. Slow but powerful. It took forever, but pebbles coalesced on the rock slab next to the fire, sifting into the rocky shape of an earth demon.

Now the tricky part. Holding the earth demon with the slower, clunkier version of the demon language while using the snapping hisses that would call a fire demon. All while the snow drifted around her, clamouring for her attention.

She'd done this before.

Not in a blizzard.

Losing control of either demon would get her killed. Probably Abyss too. She needed to focus, to use the spellcraft Nandara taught her to hold the demons under her control.

She took a breath, focused half her attention on the earth demon, the other half on the fire, and called a fire demon. In an instant, the fire brightened. Weaving the two demon languages together, she compelled the demons to remove the enchantment from the metal pieces.

With her focus strained from the cold and worry, the demons worked slowly. The fire demon was especially irksome, tempting her with blissful heat, trying to break free of her control. She only realized she'd given it her full attention when she began sinking.

Spark barked a foul oath and barely kept her hold on the fire demon while she put the bulk of her attention back on the earth demon, which was trying to soften the ground beneath her. She held her focus after that.

When it was done, her limbs felt heavier, her mind packed with sludge.

As she stared at the metal before her, trying to figure out what to do with it, Abyss shifted. She'd been watching Spark the whole time. Now she grinned, baring her gleaming teeth. Tendrils of fire curled out between the gaps. Snowflakes sizzled as they met a fiery demise.

While the demon's energy could help restore Abyss, the demon would also be straining to use the dragoness to spread as much fire over the world as possible. It was their way. No danger to Spark, but a large conflagration was not what they needed.

Abyss held the demon in check. For now.

The longer Abyss had to rely on the demon for strength, the less of that strength would go to actually controlling the creature. As time went on, the demon would grow bored and start vying for control of Abyss's faculties.

Would the demon stay tamed if Spark used a bit of its power to reform the metal? She watched the fire curling from Abyss's mouth. Spark could do most anything a fire demon could. She was part fire demon, after all. She often wondered how much. A quarter fire demon? A third? Maybe even half.

"Blast it! I don't need a forge... I *am* a forge!"

Forgetting herself for a moment, she swatted Abyss on the snout, an exuberant, comradely gesture she normally used with Jatt. She flinched, worried for an instant that Abyss would take offence and eat her. But Abyss's ghastly grin only widened, her black eyes glittering in the firelight.

Night had fallen and the firelight was all they had.

"Right. Time to get to work."

With fist-sized rocks as hammer and the stone ground as anvil, Spark had a rudimentary workspace. She spread out the straps and ropes and heaped what metal she had into a pile. She examined Abyss more closely, forming a mental image of what she needed from her supplies.

Repairing the wing would be tricky. Spark had an idea, but Abyss wasn't going to like it.

"Mistress," she said formally, catching Abyss's attention. "I don't trust straps to be secure enough without impeding your ability to fly."

Abyss narrowed her eyes.

"I can apply the patch directly to your wing, but..."

Abyss rumbled a warning from deep in her chest.

"Hear me before you make up your mind." Spark watched the dragoness until she quieted, black eyes full of fire. Spark cautiously pulled a blade from the pack in her sling. "This blade has been enchanted, same as everything else. It will cut through the enchanted leather. It'll go through your skin. Through the flesh of your wing."

Abyss growled, teeth bared.

"To repair it. Nothing more. I can use the blade to make small holes, and then bolt the sling over the tear in your wing. Take it all out again as soon as we're home. It's far more secure than me trying to work straps around your wing. It leaves more straps to brace your leg."

Lips came back down over teeth, but Abyss rumbled, eyes narrowed. The growl faded. Snow swirled around them. With a petulant huff, Abyss fired another plume of flame at Spark. Spark harmlessly parted it like an oar through water. Abyss gave a nod and stretched her neck out, chin on the snowy stones, facing away.

But she stretched her injured wing out where Spark could easily reach. Spark emptied her riding sling, split its seams with the knife, and spread it over the hole in Abyss's wing. It was plenty big enough. She used some charcoal from her simmering fire to mark the injury and dotted where to insert rivets.

Then she set it all aside.

"Leg first. Sound good?"

Abyss was silent. Eyes closed. If not sleeping, then resting. Ignoring Spark.

Spark took the longest length of rope and used it to measure the circumference of Abyss's uninjured leg. Took splints into account. Working next to Abyss where the snow was melting rather than drifting, she refashioned the treated leather straps, cutting it to the lengths she needed, putting leftover scraps end to end so she could bolt them together later.

And all the while, she kept noticing the stitchwork in everything. Spark couldn't sew worth a damn. She easily spotted the clumsy attempts she had made on it. Most of the stitching was Ember's elegant work. As Spark cut the leather into the strips she needed, her thoughts drifted to how their fingers brushed together while they worked. The memory brought that same tingling warmth to her numb fingers.

Spark trembled. Tears pricked the backs of her eyes, and she took a deep breath. Tried not to think about never seeing Ember again. About not goofing off with Jatt or getting another lesson from Nandara. Not seeing the shining dragon city again.

She looked up, trying to centre herself. Ribbons of cloud raced overhead, hard starlight like diamonds sliced through the breaking storm. The snow eased, but the cold and the wind grew teeth and sank into her bones. She trembled and shivered.

Abyss huffed another plume of flame at her. This one was gentler, warm and welcoming, crackling comfort in her ears as it billowed around her like soft mist. Spark took another breath and turned back to her work. As she did, Abyss shuffled closer, the heat of her body radiating. She stretched the damaged wing out and curved it like a living tent to offer Spark shelter from the worst of the weather.

Spark worked, slow and careful with numb fingers. But every time she began shivering, Abyss blanketed her in a gentle wash of flame.

"Rest," Abyss said.

Spark blinked. Though the wind howled, the clouds had parted, revealing hard blue moonlight through the gap in Abyss's wing. It was late, but Spark had worked later than this to make the sling in the first place. Barely a wink of sleep for a week. She shook her head.

"I'll rest on the way home. I need to keep working. That demon in you will get bored eventually, I want to be off this mountain before it does."

She chewed on some jerky from her pack while she considered her work. It was time to reshape the metal. New buckles and rivets for the straps. Rivets for the wing.

She started with the rivets because they'd be easiest. Holding them in her hands, she concentrated, poured all of her will, all the pyromancy she could muster, into her hands, into the metal. Heat coursed through her, reviving her numb fingers. Despite the fire demon, the air around them grew crisper and frost formed on Abyss's side.

The metal gave in her hands, soft like putty. Holding the metal in her palm, she squeezed with fingers, pounded with the flat of her hand, forming it into a crude rivet.

Abyss continued pelting her with flame, keeping her warm and pushing back the cold effects of pyromancy, as Spark worked through the night, testing and tempering, pounding with stones when necessary. It took longer than she wanted, but she had everything she needed before the second moon had the chance to set.

The work with fire and earth demons to enchant her new rivets and buckles was more draining than anticipated. She'd been tempted to use untreated metal, but she couldn't risk another failure in the rigging. Working with fire demons wasn't an issue, but she needed more concentration to hold two demons under her will.

Finished at last, she leaned against Abyss, sinking into her friend's warmth. Her eyelids drooped, but she shook herself awake and sat upright. When she stood, Abyss tried to nudge her back down.

"No. You can't live on demon magic much longer. If I sleep now, I may never wake up."

Abyss nodded.

"Now you've got to help me. I can't brace your leg with straps alone. What do you think of those trees just there?" Spark pointed. "Can you reach them?"

Abyss stretched and snagged one broken trunk that looked like kindling in her hand, but she had to drag herself to grasp more trees. Spark focused her attention on the fire and not her friend's pain, knowing it would embarrass Abyss for anyone to see her crawl.

But it wasn't long before Abyss had a neat stack of trunks, all of them thrice the thickness of Spark.

"Now you've got to lift your broken leg. I need to arrange the straps."

Abyss growled.

"Fine, we can just die out here then." Spark waved a dismissive hand, too tired for dragon vanity. She wasn't surprised when a lance of fire knocked her on her ass.

Abyss snarled, but there was no menace in it. Just the typical warning over insolence. They were both tired.

Abyss tried to leverage her damaged limb, but the bones shifted an instant before the world exploded with fire. Something knocked Spark, like the whole mountain coming down on her. Abyss roared.

Spark tumbled from the blow, coming to a rest in a snowdrift far beyond the bedrock exposed by all the pyromancy and dragonflame. Trees were ablaze near Abyss's face. The brace trunks, though scattered, had at least been spared. But Abyss writhed, flame erupting from her mouth. Her tail thrashed. That must have been what hit Spark.

She was lucky it hadn't killed her. That she hadn't been impaled.

"Stop now or I'll take that demon straight out of you!" She wouldn't. They'd get nowhere without Abyss doing the heavy lifting to splint the leg. "You want to take off and land on a broken leg? Keep it up!"

Flame roared Spark's way. It lasted a moment longer than it needed to, but Abyss subsided.

"We have to try again. We have to splint your leg. You said so yourself."

Abyss used her tail this time, wrapping it around the leg, holding it steady with her hands and other foot. Spark worked quickly to get the straps into place. Abyss eased her leg down.

"Now the tricky part. Splints. You've got to hold them all until I get the straps tightened."

Abyss groaned, but set to work, Spark calling instructions. The second moon was long gone by the time Spark tightened the final strap, Abyss groaning all the while. Spark heard the bones grinding, the splint helping set the break, at least to an extent. Abyss didn't thrash anymore. That was a small miracle.

"Wing now," Spark said. It was everything she could do not to devolve into grunts. If they made it home, she intended to sleep for a whole week.

Abyss leaned on her side so the damaged wing spread out evenly against the ground while Spark gathered her dismantled sling, the rivets, stone, and her knife. She climbed onto the wing as gently as she could and spent more time than she wanted spreading everything out.

It had to be right.

"Ready?"

She waited until Abyss nodded. Spark pressed the tip of the blade against the fabric, worked it through.

"Okay. Now." She drove it through wing-flesh.

The world erupted in flame. Spark slid off the wing as Abyss moved. Just as she started pushing the fire away from her, a slice of night snapped at her.

Spark screamed. Barely dodged Abyss's teeth. She scrambled on hands and feet through slush and ash. Pulsed fire out around her to obscure where she was. Once she stood firmly at a safe distance, she pulled all the fire in, all of it swirling through her and away into nothing.

She tugged at the fire demon in Abyss. Spark hadn't done anything against Abyss's will, hadn't inflicted injury nearly as grievous as the leg. It had to be the fire demon setting Abyss off. It was getting bored—they were running out of time. Spark drew on it, pulling like she meant to pull it straight out. Abyss stilled.

"I don't need you conscious for this. You contain that demon now, or I will pull it out of you and leave you lying there like a small babe."

Abyss blew a fireball at her.

"Neither of us wants to see you that helpless." She softened her tone.

Spark sighed, picked everything up. Back to the wing. Line it all up with numb fingers in shrieking wind. Abyss had torn the hole in her wing wider during her tantrum, and Spark had to realign the patch. Despite Abyss blowing gentle flame to keep Spark warm, her hands trembled and her body shook.

The palest suggestion of light on the horizon indicated dawn wasn't far off. The wind howled, snow swirling around them, drifts starting to encroach on their little crash-camp.

Stay alive stay alive stay alive, the internal mantra was endless. The only focus point she had. *Stay alive stay alive press leather stay alive press flesh pound rivet stay alive...*

Her numb fingers could barely grip the stone, exhausted arms could barely lift it. But this was the last rivet. She pounded it in through sheer stubbornness.

She forced herself not to cry. Wouldn't let herself feel relief. Not yet. She slid off the wing.

"Try," she grunted, flapping her hands.

Abyss pushed up on three legs, towering over Spark like a black mountain, and unfurled her great wings, blotting out the sky. A sharp tremor rolled through them, a sheet snapped suddenly in the wind. All the while, Abyss watched the patch. Satisfied, she faced Spark and flapped her wings properly, gently. Everything held.

A warm tingle of hope blossomed in Spark's chest. She ignored it. Held her breath.

Abyss flapped vigorously, hard enough to scatter broken timber, stir up a small blizzard around her, and nearly send Spark tumbling off the mountainside. Spark wedged herself among some boulders to shelter against the wing-gale. And now she did allow herself relief. And tears.

Abyss's front legs lifted off the ground. She could fly. The patch held.

Spark laughed and cried, flinging victorious arms in the air.

Abyss wore a ghastly, toothy grin, watching Spark intently. She huffed more flame at the girl and chuckled like gurgling magma. Abyss leaned forward, nuzzled her massive snout against Spark.

"Not bad for an on-the-fly forge."

Abyss rolled her eyes and huffed Spark onto her arse.

"That was a good pun!" Spark protested, grinning.

Abyss held out her massive hand, palm up, in front of Spark. Spark climbed on and Abyss set her down between two spikes on the back of her neck, right behind her great head. Abyss dived forward, propelling herself on three legs, the splint holding while the fourth leg dragged along.

The cliff-edge drew near and Spark clung to Abyss, unable to look away. Abyss stretched her wings in the instant before they shot over the side of the mountain, into a long dive. The trees of the valley rushed at them. Too close for comfort.

"Please, please, please..." Spark whispered. She couldn't tear her gaze from approaching death.

The storm-winds caught them, filling Abyss's wings. She glided above the valley and angled herself into the darkness remaining in the west, putting the grey light at their back. Heading toward the dragon city. Heading home.

Once Abyss was above the mountaintops, her wings holding steady, she plucked Spark from her back and clutched her against the warm expanse of her body. Spark was too exhausted to sleep. Too exhausted to cry properly, weeping frosty tears as she settled against her friend for the long trip home.

CHAPTER SEVENTEEN

While Ember helped with adjustments, Spark got the sling buckled onto Abyss as they prepared for their fifth flight. But Ondias shouted from the edge of town.

"Demonshit, what is she on about now?" Ember asked.

Spark couldn't quite make out everything Ondias was shouting but got the gist of it. She pulsed out her power and a line of fire ten feet high and twenty feet across leapt up between them. Why couldn't the woman have stayed on her trip one more sodding day? When she hadn't made it back for the solstice festival over a fortnight ago, Spark had held out the hope she'd stay away until spring.

"Hurry. Maybe we can get out of here before she tries to interfere anymore," Spark said.

Spark was in the middle of dropping her bag of supplies into the sling when Abyss stood up, spilling Spark across the ground.

"Mistress?" Spark called.

Ember backed away entirely. Ondias had parted a gap in the wall of fire and stormed toward them. Spark sighed and withdrew the flame. She was really going to have to take better stock of what Ondias could do with magic. She pulled her winter robes tighter around her and crossed her arms, huddled next to the dragoness.

"This is madness," Ondias spat.

Spark rolled her eyes. Ondias went up one side of her and down the other as soon as word of the sling had made it to her. She called it rude and disrespectful. Spark tried pointing out Abyss would never have allowed five humans to buckle her into the thing in the first place if she didn't agree to the measure. Of course, their first test run had set a bad precedent, and Ondias was stubborn as a mule at the best of times. But this was not the best of times.

Spark was confident in the rigging now, Abyss's injuries were fully healed, and they had been double sure to check with weather scouts this time. Ondias wouldn't listen.

"She's not a pet, Mita. She's not some farm beast you can just hitch to a wagon."

"She carried you in a wagon," Spark shot back. "This is even less cumbersome."

Ondias was nearly in front of Spark, who thought their confrontation would get physical. Again. She'd had to forcibly remove Ondias from her house last night, pushing her out the door and locking it in her face. But Abyss intervened.

The dragoness leaned way down, glimmering in the early morning light with prisms from the city shining across her dark form, and nudged the tip of her nose between the two humans. She snorted a gust of warm air at Ondias, who gasped. Fury crept across her expression before she reined it in.

"Have you even bothered to ask Abyss what she thinks of this?" Spark asked.

"Stop calling her that!"

Abyss huffed, blowing more warm air in Ondias's face, this time forcefully enough to make her reel. She took a step back to keep her balance. Her mouth fell open for a moment before she snapped it shut and pulled a composed mask over her face.

"My apologies for making assumptions, Mistress," Ondias said with a contrite bow. "Mita has been reluctant to observe your ways. I wanted to be sure she wasn't using any familial ties to bully you."

Abyss snorted.

"A reflection not on you but on her," Ondias said quickly.

The dragoness shifted to easily see them both.

"You truly don't mind her calling you by a human name? Is Abyss your name in your language?"

"Near enough," Abyss rumbled in her deep thunderstorm voice.

Ondias blinked, her mouth an O of surprise. Spark looked up at Abyss and grinned, resting her pale hand on the side of the dragoness's endlessly black snout.

"This doesn't surprise you?" Ondias asked Spark. "Has she spoken to you before?"

"Yes," Spark said, giving Abyss a cautious glance.

Abyss nodded in her fractional way and stood up.

"Your power is affecting her," Ondias said.

"Is that good?"

"I'm not sure." She glanced at Abyss. "But she's always been different, this one. Even in a time when dragons were on much better terms with humans, she's always stood out."

Ondias sighed and backed away, though her eyes shone with anger. "Do try to be careful."

Spark sagged with relief at the woman's retreating back. She picked up the last of her supplies and waited as Abyss crouched toward her. Ember returned.

"That went better than I could have hoped," Ember said. She gave Abyss a careful look. "I heard they used to be able to talk. Never believed it."

"Nanny used to talk to them all the time, I heard. Nandara said the dragons all went quiet when Mamma... Well, when whatever's happened to her happened."

Ember looked up at Abyss, awe glittering in her brown eyes. "Your nan went quiet then too," Ember said.

"Mostly. She spoke to me once in my whole life, and it was just before the magistrate sent those dragons after us. She told me to trust the dragons. Not those ones. These ones, obviously."

Ember took her hand, squeezed it.

"I'll get your supplies into the sling. Why don't you give all the buckles a last check?" Ember said.

The check didn't take long and everything was ready when Spark came back to stand in front of Abyss. Ember took her hand, pulled her closer and hugged her quickly.

"Be safe this time. Come back soon."

Ember gave Spark a boost up into the sling and then backed away a safe distance, watching with a grin. Spark secured her harness and double checked all the pockets she had stuffed her supplies into, not wanting to leave anything to chance. No falling, no snapped rigging, no misadventure. A proper test flight that was planned to span a few days.

Her stomach fluttered.

She'd done two more fittings of the repaired harness on Abyss, making it as comfortable for the dragoness as possible. More stress tests and reinforcing straps and redesigning buckles. Three short test flights around the valley. Extra buckles and rivets in one of the storage pockets. And she'd made Nandara teach her how to do a proper dragon summoning in case they needed help. Now it was time to put it all to the test, properly. Somewhere far enough away that it would give the harness time to malfunction again.

They'd made it home in time for the Sky Fire Festival on the solstice, not that either of them had enjoyed the meteor shower and ensuing celebration. Abyss had slipped straight into the dragon city, her mate bringing Spark back to the village after she'd removed all the rigging. Spark slept through most of the festival, but Ember dragged her out of bed, insisting she couldn't miss it entirely. The way the sky glittered had been stunning, but Spark had been too exhausted to appreciate it, collapsing back into bed after a few minutes. And Abyss had spent over a week in the city, convalescing under the watchful eye of the Superiors and their healing magic.

Spark was certain she had accounted for everything this time. But she needed to be sure. Needed the harness to hold up when it really counted. When it was time to go back to Pasdale.

Abyss spread her great wings, shaking them out and flexing. She pushed off with her hind legs, a motion that always looked like a graceful little hop, but the full force of it slammed Spark to the bottom of the sling. Then they lifted away from the ground, Ember a speck in the snow. The city came and went, and they soared out over the ridge of mountains that shielded the valley.

The rush of wind was more intense than Spark remembered, biting in the depths of winter. The sparkling crimson mountains were all capped with bright white snow, all of it glittering. Spark blinked into the scoring wind, her eyeballs already feeling frozen, and cupped her hands around her face for shelter.

In the fallout of their first test flight, Spark forgot about the sting of the cold on her eyes, though she had warmer clothing to protect the rest of her. Goggles were immediately added to the top of her mental list of modifications. She couldn't see much of the harness around the vast curve of Abyss's body, but it all functioned properly.

Spark held her breath anyway. Suspected she'd hold her breath until they were back on solid ground. Not crash landing, either.

The world fell away below them, the Red Mountains spreading out forever to the north and west but giving way to plains in the south. East was lost in haze. Spark hunched deeper into her sling and settled in for the trip. She didn't know how long they'd been out in the sky when Abyss started flying manoeuvres to test the integrity of the harness and sling. She started with a simple loop. It was all sky, and then Spark caught a glimpse of the city sparkling on the distant upside down horizon. Then the mountains came plummeting back into view.

Abyss pulled out of the loop to dive hard, pressing Spark deep into the sling and against the dragoness's warm body. Spark squeezed her eyes shut, trying not to think about last time. Falling uncontrolled.

Everything held and Abyss angled them up into the sky, barely skimming the ridge of one mountain. Spark was certain if she reached out, she'd scrape her hand on stone.

Abyss angled them into a tight spiral. Spark scrunched her eyes closed and held her breath, gripping the straps of her harness so tightly her hands ached. Blood rushed to her head, her mind spinning out of sync with Abyss's roll.

And then they were level, everything where it should be. As the horizon levelled off, Abyss voiced a deep cry, this one unmistakably triumph. The dragoness was emboldened, but Spark was not quite ready to breathe easily.

Abyss did barrel rolls, flew evasively, swooped erratically.

Spark was thrown against her restraints and tossed around the sling when she wasn't jammed flat against Abyss. Spark worried that the waterskin she'd strapped to her back to keep it from freezing would burst under the pressure.

As they flew, Abyss normalizing her flight pattern, Spark considered all the ways she could keep from losing her breakfast every time Abyss went through a spiral. She would have to tighten the straps, but that would mean making the sling smaller. Maybe buckles around the outside to tighten it all down once she was inside?

They flew well into the afternoon before Abyss dived to the ground, skimming along a valley floor, and Spark caught sight of the dragoness's quarry—a bear, larger than any Spark had seen before. It was a shaggy white monster nearly invisible against the snow, evidently running at speed as the huge dragoness closed in on it with her talons extended. The bear cleared a ridge and suddenly two little tufts of white fur ran alongside it.

Abyss screeched and pulled out of her dive so abruptly Spark was certain her mind dropped into her toes. The screech sounded as close to a dragon cursing as Spark had ever heard. Abyss stopped on a cliff overlooking the family of bears, and Spark staggered from the sling, clutching some supplies against her heaving chest.

"This is going to take some getting used to." Spark sat and watched the bears disappear into the forest while Abyss swooped off over the next ridge.

Spark drank some of her water, pleased it hadn't frozen, that it was actually warm enough she wished she'd brought some tea. She didn't eat much of the dried meat she'd packed, her stomach still doing barrel rolls. It only clenched around the food, not sure what to do with it.

She was ready when Abyss returned, licking some gore off her talons before burning the rest away. Wherever she'd gone, she'd at least found a worthy meal. Spark checked all the straps and buckles to be sure everything was still in place before she climbed into her sling.

Abyss flew lower, just above the summits, weaving in and out of sawtooth peaks. Spark trusted Abyss to go where she wanted and bring them home safely. She imagined it must be a relief for the dragoness to roam freely, her blue mate staying in the city with the eggs.

Spark wasn't looking forward to sleeping on rocks or dragon but was confident she'd at least stay plenty warm nestled against Abyss. When the dragoness wasn't in flight, the air was only cold on Spark's exposed face. She wondered about making a full mask with goggles to help keep her face protected. The rest of her body was warm, despite the rush of wind.

Not more than an hour after taking off, judging by the angle of the sun, Abyss made another sudden dive and nearly crashed into the ridge of a mountainside, skidding along its surface as she came in too quickly. Spark called out, but her voice was lost over the chaotic sound. Abyss clung to the rock, hanging on the side of the mountain near the jagged summit.

Spark could barely see her with part of her face peering over the top. Abyss didn't seem to hear what Spark said. Moving carefully, Spark unharnessed herself and climbed out of the sling. She had nowhere to fall, pressed between dragon and mountain. So she climbed up to grip the stone and one of Abyss's spikes.

Abyss watched the summit of one of the taller mountains a few ridges over, but Spark couldn't see anything out of the ordinary. Just snow and slate. They'd gone far enough to meet the neighbouring range where red gave way to grey.

Spark studied the landscape below, devoid of vegetation, only gravel and a wide river shining silver in the late day sun. But movement from that tall summit caught her eye and she looked up, trying to make sense of what she saw. The summit itself and most of the glacier sitting atop it appeared to fold away from the rock and rise skyward.

It looked like the glacier had wings. Another glacier came out of the clouds above the first. Flying glaciers.

"What the—"

Abyss gripped her hard, so hard it squeezed the words from her mouth and the air from her lungs. Spark had a brief moment to fear she would be crushed right here on this mountaintop. Abyss stuffed her hastily into her sling and dropped away, falling toward the valley. It was not the controlled dive of earlier.

Whatever those glacier things were, Abyss was in a panic. Spark didn't want to consider anything that could frighten a dragon.

Pressed into the sling, she struggled into her harness and looked where they were going. Abyss flew low and fast. Spark couldn't properly open her eyes against the force of the wind, nor could she breathe without forcing a hand in front of her mouth to act as a windbreaker. It was slow, hard work, but she got her other hand up to shield her eyes.

She almost wished she hadn't. They flew so low that a massive tree loomed up and zipped past close enough Spark feared she would get a face full of pine. She certainly smelled the forest zipping past beneath them.

She doubted Abyss would hear her if she called out. And she couldn't risk hailing whatever had spooked the dragon.

Spark nodded off in the sling after sunset and didn't awake until Abyss cried out, startling her. A cold buzz tore down Spark's back, tightening her shoulders. She looked into the darkness around them for the danger. Then she heard the answering cries and saw the distant glitter of the city, a massive star on the horizon. Warmth rippled over Spark's skin as Abyss angled in for a hard landing.

As soon as they were on the ground near the workshop, Abyss plucked Spark from the sling and dropped her onto the ground, still crying out to the other dragons. She spread her wings.

"Wait! What's going on? What were those things?"

Abyss crouched down close, her black eyes large like planets in the dark.

"Ice dragons," Abyss whispered, her soft voice a teakettle hiss.

She turned and leapt, screeching into the air. Lights came on all over the village at the late-night racket.

On unsteady legs, numb and tired from hours of disuse, Spark shamble-ran into the village and straight to Ondias's house. At least she wouldn't have to wake the woman who was out on her porch looking skyward.

"Mita! What the devil? Who's raised the alarm?"

"This is their alarm cry?" Spark hadn't heard this one before.

"Why are you back already? What's happened?"

"Something spooked Abyss while we were out in the mountains. Strange glaciers. Then she just said something to me about ice dragons."

"What?" Ondias snapped out the word with such ferocity that Spark took a step back. "Mita, are you sure? She said *ice dragons*?"

"Yes, that's what she said. We saw something that looked like a flying glacier, then she rushed back so fast I thought we'd die."

Ondias cursed out something particularly filthy and stormed into her house, pacing and swearing and pulling books from her stacks seemingly at random.

"What does it mean?" Spark asked. "What's an ice dragon?"

"In that war your mother ended, Draxli had four traitor dragons helping him. The bargain was that if they helped him stop Neesha and Dionelle, he'd help them bring down this city and let them rule dragonkind. But then the fire demons realized what those four dragons had done and deserted them entirely. They became the absence of heat. From what I understand, Loch filled them with the only element he knows in order to save their lives, but it's turned them to ice."

"Then Loch's the one who's sent them." Spark bunched her hands into fists and paced along next to Ondias. It was pace or run screaming through the streets. She needed more information.

"Almost certainly." Ondias spoke through clenched teeth, flipping through one of her books as she went. "They're looking for you. Or scouting our actions."

"We have to stop them." Spark stopped and stared at Ondias. "We have to take a blaze of dragons and destroy those monsters before they can bring any information to Loch."

Ondias snapped the book shut and stopped. "Absolutely not. It's unlikely they'll bring him anything he doesn't already know. It's best to let them go and not draw attention to ourselves when we're unprepared to battle Loch's forces."

"We're not battling Loch's forces, just two dragons! What if they tell him I'm here?"

"If he doesn't know that already, how would he learn it now? Unless those ice dragons saw you on that foolish little adventure of yours. I knew that was a terrible idea. I should have stopped you going."

"How is it terrible that we discovered we're being spied upon? We need to stop them."

"He'll see it as an act of war if they don't return. He'll know it was us. Then what? He'll take it out on Dionelle. Or send a host after us. For heaven's sake, Mita, let this go."

"You're an insufferable coward!" Spark turned on her heel and stormed out of Ondias's house, stomping off into the night. She only half paid attention to where she went, intent only on going as swiftly as she could, driven forward by her pounding heart.

Spark cleared the edge of town, came out north of her workshop and skirted the village on her way to it. She heard terrible screeching from the city and stopped, looking in vain into the darkness. The stars were blotted out an instant before Abyss dropped into the snow mere inches from where Spark stood. A puff of snow flew up around the dragoness, spraying Spark with cold shards.

Abyss scraped the ground with her talons, roaring like nothing Spark had heard before, a terrifying gout of flame searing the darkness and leaving Spark blinded by it long afterward. She noticed, at least, that Abyss wore the sling, still packed with Spark's supplies.

"You didn't have any luck either? Well to hell with everyone here, let's get those bastards. We can melt them right out of the sky."

"Spark!" Ember called.

Spark tried settling Abyss enough that she could climb into the sling, but she stopped and waited as Ember came running out into the field.

"What's going on? I saw the fire, what's happening?"

Spark did her best to explain and then took Ember by the shoulders, looking her square in the eyes. "But we're going anyway. Just the two of us, we can do it."

Ember looked like she might argue, but Spark didn't give her the chance.

"If you see Ondias, let her know she can rot."

Then Spark was in the sling, and Abyss leapt skyward before Spark was buckled in.

CHAPTER EIGHTEEN

There was a hazy grey fleck on the horizon, the dawn getting its legs beneath it, and Spark realized the direction they were headed was much to their advantage. The sky would be dark at their back, concealing Abyss that much longer, as it had on their trip out of the city. There had been dragons circling around, of course, knowing what she'd do and planning to stop her, but Abyss silently shot straight up into the sky, skimming along one of the city's obsidian panels and into the nighttime nothingness.

A few dragons came close, but she'd evaded them. Some gave chase, knowing her target lay to the east, but none of them knew the exact location. She'd sunk into the inky shadows of the valley, perfectly camouflaged. Abyss flew higher, now that she'd lost them all, but continued skimming along the mountaintops.

Spark was vigilantly awake through it all, grateful she'd slept on the way back to the city. Even if shocks of adrenaline weren't coursing through her blood, she wouldn't have been able to sleep. Just after they'd evaded the last of the dragons from the city, a worrying thought crossed her mind.

What if there are more ice dragons?

They'd only seen two, but Ondias said there were four. Spark was confident in a battle against two, maybe three. But what if all four of them were nearby? What if they were together now? Surely Abyss had taken that into account. Hadn't she?

As the sky around them brightened, Abyss dropped down closer to the mountains. Spark saw something in the sky glinting off the rising sun up ahead.

It didn't take long for that glinting something to resolve into three somethings getting larger. Closer. Then the shrieks started, distant and barely audible over the rush of wind. Abyss remained silent and dipped farther into the valleys, moving south. Spark couldn't see the ice dragons anymore, but heard them. They were getting closer. All Spark could see was the gravel of the valley below.

Things went too quiet and Spark pulled a ball of flame into her cupped hands. She wanted to be ready to burst out with the full force of her power the instant she needed to.

Her wait wasn't long.

Abyss erupted skyward, spiralling as she did so. Spark barely saw anything, just rock and ice spinning past. She assumed the worst of the ice and lashed out with a white-hot lance of fire. She couldn't hurt Abyss or herself with it.

Shrieks rang out all around them.

Spark saw only ice and sky. Abyss burst straight up into the midst of the ice blaze. Spark's fire lance whipped one of them, and the dragon's cries intensified for an instant before it dropped away.

Abyss pulled out of the spiral and let herself drop. Below her flew two male ice dragons, with the third recovering from Spark's attack.

The air was already colder in the midst of these dragons, but Spark pulled flame from the air and poured molten fire down onto the one directly beneath Abyss. It struck the creature in the lower half of its body, most of its legs and tail melting away. It screamed like nothing ever had.

The leather sling creaked with the cold, though the burst of fire had been brief. Thankfully, the proximity to Abyss's warm body helped restore some of the heat in the air.

And just in time because the third dragon collided with Abyss, making everything so cold it took Spark's breath away, freezing her nose shut.

Abyss shrieked a battlecry through fiery breath, aiming it straight into her attacker's face. Both dragons clawed at each other. Abyss's talons found little purchase, scraping off shards of ice like a summer treat, but doing little damage to the dragon.

Fearing that overusing pyromancy would freeze both her and Abyss solid, Spark pulsed fire out in short, intense bursts aimed at the ice dragon's wings. One of Spark's blasts tore through the icy membrane of the dragon's wings, causing it to falter. Abyss seized on the opportunity, sinking her teeth into its neck and flinging it from the air.

Even as she did, she shrieked and clawed at her face. Most of Abyss's snout was covered in a thick rind of frost. A quick huff of hot air fixed the problem, but the air grew so cold it burned from the ice dragon's passing.

As soon as the ice dragon fell away, another streaked up to replace it.

Abyss looped backward, her tail slamming into the face of the approaching dragon. It floundered in the air, fighting to stay aloft, when she completed her arc and sliced back around underneath, firing a blast of heat into its wings. One wing melted away entirely, and the dragon careened out of the sky onto the icy peak below.

The other two ice dragons returned, recovering from previous attacks. Spark saw tendrils of hoarfrost knitting together the hole she had blasted through one of the dragon's wings and slung another fireball at the wing out of pure spite. She nicked the side and the dragon pitched but didn't fall.

Abyss went into a wild spiral, her tail whipping out below her and fire streaking out in all directions. Spark let a tendril of her fire lance snake out around them, lashing at the ice dragons. Fire hissed on ice but little of what she saw made sense.

An icy shard of dragon talon stabbed at Spark's face. She cried out and dodged, taking the hit to the shoulder instead. Burning cold pain made her flesh throb, blacking her vision and dropping a ball of ice into her stomach. She clenched against the pain. An empty stomach was the only thing keeping her from vomiting.

Blinking and forcing herself to take deep breaths, Spark sank deeper into the sling. She looked up, seeing a trail of ice-encrusted gashes all the way up Abyss's chest. Two ice dragons were on her, both of them snapping at her neck.

But Abyss was bigger and had the longer reach, keeping both at bay. Spark tried pulling herself higher in the sling to get a good shot at one of the dragons, but the agony from her wound threw her down in nauseated blindness. She took careful, shallow breaths and tried very hard not to move.

The sound of a third ice dragon rose up from below, and Spark's terrible wound numbed at the sound of it. She wasn't sure if the fourth had come to join the battle or if the one with the melted wing had recovered entirely, but Abyss could not fight three of them on her own. Spark had little energy for fire left, and certainly couldn't move to throw it.

She needed a wilful fire.

Without moving her damaged arm, she cupped a tiny bonfire in her hand, holding it above the lip of the sling. She pulsed it out as big as she dared, a ball slightly bigger than her head. It was a terrible idea, but dying was the alternative.

She hissed out the words Nandara taught her. As always, the result was instantaneous. Spark didn't have to give a single direction.

Ice dragon, meet fire demon.

As soon as the creature was fully out of its realm, it hissed furiously and launched itself at the nearest ice dragon. It hadn't even taken note of her.

Spark extinguished her fire and sank deeper into the sling, growing cold despite the heat of demon and dragon. With only her face poking out of the sling, she barely saw the one ice dragon disappear from sight, crashing out of the sky in a shriek of steam, the fire demon riding it all the way down.

That left Abyss with two ice dragons to fight on her own. Shivering, Spark tried to pull more fire from the air, tried to summon another demon. She managed little more than a candle flame for all her efforts.

There were more dragon cries from overhead, this time familiar. Spark looked blearily up. Had she more energy, she would have been startled by the sky falling from the sun onto one of the remaining ice dragons.

With her thoughts muddled by pain, it took her a moment to realize she was looking at Abyss's blue mate. If any dragon in the city could track Abyss, it would be him. And lucky for them.

The demon-riddled ice dragon was nowhere to be seen. Abyss's mate shredded one of the others. Abyss tore at the wings of the remaining dragon while spewing fire into its face, melting its teeth down to dull nubs and melting its eyes away entirely.

Spark's head throbbed against the change in pressure as Abyss dived toward her mate. He had already dispatched his foe, flinging it from the air to slam into the summit beneath them. The third ice dragon was not far behind. Chunks of ice and bits of slush spewed from the mountaintop like a freezing geyser.

The blue dragon was searching, but Abyss turned away, angling westward. Spark grinned and shook. Had they really just done that? The victory warmed her despite the pain and lingering cold. She glanced up to Abyss, but couldn't see her face. Only the gashes along her neck and down most of her chest. The heat of her body thawed the wounds and thick blood oozed from them, dripping scarlet down her onyx flesh.

Spark shuddered and looked out over the mountains, still grey. There was a wash of pink on the horizon, likely the Red Mountains, diluted with distance, but they were a long way from home. Spark wanted to ask Abyss if she'd be okay, but doubted she'd get a response even if Abyss heard her over the wind and the rush of her wings.

The blue dragon glided up from underneath Abyss, and the two of them hissed and snarled, conversing in their language. It was an angry sound. As the blue dragon frequently looked over Abyss's wounds, it became clear he was berating her.

Was that what they had to return to? There was no doubt they'd stopped some vital information from reaching Loch, but if Abyss's mate didn't support what they'd done, who would?

Spark's thoughts spun. What sort of greeting awaited them?

"Shit on them all," Spark grumbled. She would not be made to feel ashamed for doing the right thing.

She pulled her robe tighter around her, trying to huddle closer to Abyss for warmth. Her teeth chattered and her body vibrated. Blinking her eyes open, Spark fought to stay awake. It had been so long since she'd had proper rest, but she was alert to danger, despite the blue dragon so close to help them. Even so, her eyes kept drooping shut until they stayed that way and she went limp in her sling.

CHAPTER NINETEEN

Furious pain in her shoulder jolted Spark awake. Her pulse throbbed in her ears, and a rising urge to vomit stung the back of her throat. Someone pressed what felt like pure ice to her shoulder, but through the pain and the disorientation of sleep, Spark couldn't tell who.

"Easy now," Lina said.

Spark blinked and looked around, shocked to be back in her home, in her own bed. Hadn't she just been flying with Abyss?

"Abyss!" Spark tried to sit up but pain forced her back down. "Is she all right?"

"I assume so, she flew out early this morning," Lina said.

"Morning? It's morning still?"

"It's mid-afternoon, and it's been two days since you and that dragoness foolishly disappeared on us."

Spark groaned and lay back on her bed, watching as Lina applied a poultice to her shoulder.

"You're lucky you weren't killed," Lina said, her tone gentle but full of reproach.

"We stopped them."

"Mother isn't so certain of that. The blue dragon indicated they had all been taken out of the sky, but he found no evidence of them in the snow. A larger group is off to inspect."

Spark scowled up at the ceiling.

"I understand that you're frustrated, that you're scared," Lina said, taking a softer approach than Ondias ever had. "But you were nearly killed. Look at this wound."

Lina unwrapped the bandages and removed the poultice so Spark could swivel her head on a stiff neck and see the gash sealed up with ugly black stitches running in a jagged line along the edge of her collarbone toward her left shoulder.

"Your shirt and robes were soaked with blood. Gods only know how much more you lost in flight."

Spark closed her eyes and lay still while Lina bandaged the wound.

"You'll be lucky to have much use out of your arm for at least a moon. Maybe two. How are you going to work?"

Spark pretended to go back to sleep while thoughts swirled in her mind. Even with the ice dragons taken care of, it was reasonable to assume that if Loch didn't know where she was, he would find out soon enough. From traders if no one else. Word would spread. Maybe it would spread slowly, maybe the magistrate already knew.

That Spark would have to fight again was a certainty. She would need armour. And maybe she could make some armour for Abyss? And she would certainly need a proper helper. She was glad to have made the fireproof gloves and hood from the dragon skin. Hopefully Ember would be able to spare her hands. Spark could make do on some things with only one functioning arm, especially if she made some clamps. She'd need help with that, but it would get her started.

With her arm in a sling to protect the shoulder wound, Spark was clumsy at absolutely everything she did. Except bolt the door. She kept it bolted almost all the time so that Ondias had to give her angry sermons through the wood. It was easier than trying to throw the woman out with only one good arm. Lina warned her against doing any strenuous activity for at least a week lest she tear her stitches.

At the moment, there wasn't much to be strenuous over. She couldn't work yet, not even on anything small. Most of her metalwork had gone toward fighting Loch and his dragons anyway, and Spark needed to change her focus. With the ice dragons, she would need to focus on pyromancy. Armour for Abyss was also a priority. The challenge was in finding something light enough but large enough to cover vast swatches of the dragoness. She needed to be protected without being encumbered.

Spark was too furious to focus on much, though. Ondias's first angry sermon—delivered not long after Spark recovered enough to walk around a bit—let her know that Abyss had been sent away. Not excommunicated, but forcefully encouraged to leave the city for a time. A long time.

Ondias or Lina or Nandara always hovered around. Or River was shouting at someone from just beyond the walls. Spark tried going out to her workshop but had been sent home to bed. Jatt had been gone a week now—some family trip or something. Only Ember came to see her, but briefly. She'd brought some good news, letting Spark know that the sling she'd made to fly with Abyss remained intact and that Ember and Stone had cleaned it and stored it properly in the workshop.

Shadow was curled up in front of the fire for the night, and Spark sat at her work table, going through old sketches and plans. She had a spellbook open in front of her, lazily flipping through the pages for inspiration. Nandara wasn't holding back her education, at least.

Someone tapped at the door and Spark considered pretending she'd gone to bed. Lina had left only minutes before, and Spark wondered if she'd forgotten something. So she kept quiet. The knock came again, just as softly as before.

"Spark?" Ember whisper-called.

Spark sprang from her seat and unlatched the bolt, opening the door just enough for Ember to slip in. She pressed the door closed and threw the lock once more.

Ember clutched a large jar against her lovely chest and held it out, grinning. "Brought you some stew. Only way I could get out here to see you without River hovering over everything. No doubt he'll be here in a few minutes anyway."

They both glanced at the door, waiting for someone else to knock on it.

"I might have a way around that." Spark glanced at Ember and her mouth went dry, the words trying to evaporate before she could speak them. "I need help around here, with my recovery but also just with everything. I've got so much I need to work on. I need an extra set of hands."

Ember grinned. "Not tonight. But I'll get Pa to help me bring some of my sewing supplies here for tomorrow. I'll work here and help you when you need it. I can be healer and apprentice."

Ember's dark eyes shone and a dopey smile stretched Spark's face. She took the jar of stew over to her table before she embarrassed herself too much. Spark enjoyed the late-night meal Ember brought while Ember looked over Spark's notes.

"You're going to go right back out there as soon as Lina takes out your stitches, aren't you?"

"Near enough. Soon as I can use my arm properly again. I'm not going looking for trouble, but it's going to come looking for me. I need to be ready."

Ember nodded, her expression darkening. "You think the magistrate will come for you?"

"After what my mother did? And after what he did to the rest of my family?"

"And he'll want to see this city fall again. For good."

"So we have to be ready. I've been working on things..."

"Those arrowheads," Ember said, narrowing her eyes.

"And other things. Nandara has encouraged me to start, Ondias too, but not a word of this can get to the others. Not even the dragons. Especially not the dragons, they're too mistrustful right now. The Superiors would never see it as trying to help. We'll have to tell them what I'm doing eventually, but Nandara doesn't think they're ready to hear it yet."

"What's she think it will take?"

Spark shrugged. "For now I've got to keep working on things that will help if the city is attacked. Some pyromancy, but building things too. I'm going to figure out armour for the dragons. Dragon-proof dragon armour."

Ember chuckled.

"And Nandara is prepping for some huge spells. She's getting me ready to use fire demons. I think I'll need to figure out how to open portals to the fire realm."

Ember's eyes grew wide and she shook her head and stood tall in front of Spark.

"No way. Not after what it did to your ma."

Spark sighed. "I don't like it, to be sure. But there might not be another way. I let a demon loose on one of those ice dragons and we'd probably be dead if I hadn't."

"Spark! Isn't that risky?"

"Very. But the demon was so furious about the ice dragon it didn't even notice me. If I can get some good armour and not get hurt like this again, I'll have the concentration to use demons in battle the way I've been using them to make weapons."

Ember shook her head.

"I can't let Loch topple this city again. My power is stronger than Mamma's, and I've been learning things she never did. Nandara has been teaching me how to do it right, to be aware of the dangers. I wouldn't try opening a fire portal without someone around who could help. Wouldn't try demon possession on a whim. I won't use it at all unless I have no choice."

Ember let out a long breath and stared at the plans on Spark's table.

"You're going to learn to do it safely?" she asked.

"As safe as it can be done."

"This is madness."

"I wish there was another way. But no one has power like I do. I have to do this, or I'll have to run from Loch forever."

Ember stared at the plans for a long time, her jaw tight. "Your options are terrible. But I think it's right that you stand your ground."

Spark shovelled some more stew into her mouth to mask her relief. "But you need to keep it between us. Really. No one else needs to know."

"Needs to know what?" River's voice bellowed from the door a moment before he pounded on it.

Startled, Shadow yipped out a warning.

"No one needs to know how much she fancies your stupid face," Ember called, marching to the door. She threw the bolt and River shoved the door open so suddenly it nearly hit Ember and she stumbled away.

"Shut up!" he roared.

"What do you even want?" Ember asked.

"Freak needs her rest, you shouldn't bother her so much."

"How nice of you to take my needs into consideration." Spark rolled her eyes.

River snarled at her, curling his lip and baring his teeth like some kind of beast. Spark turned away from him altogether to finish the stew. Ember weathered her brother's storm with the same grace as always, shoving him off as soon as she could. It meant Ember going with him, though, collecting the now-empty jar from Spark on her way out.

The house was all the emptier without Ember around, and Spark lay on her back next to Shadow well into the night, staring up at the ceiling.

Ember had been there all day, arriving first thing in the morning to help Spark dress. She remained nearby to retrieve things, pick things up, clean things off, and help Spark build a large clamp and attach it to the anvil, all between working on her own projects. It was a lot like having Jatt around, but far more pleasurable.

Late in the evening, with Shadow in for the night and curled near the forge, Spark put all her tools on the work table and went to sit on the bed, sitting against the wall while she waited for Ember. When Ember joined her, she had a bundle of Spark's plans with her and spread them out on the bed.

"You going to solve the design flaws for me?" Spark asked, her voice light with amusement.

Ember laughed softly. "I haven't got a clue what I'm looking at. Does this even make sense to you?"

"It's magic," Spark said carefully. "You need to be a wizard to make sense of it."

"All right, then, tell me what I'm looking at?"

Spark pursed her lips and furrowed her brow while she went over her plans. She couldn't just talk about it, or it wouldn't make anymore sense to Ember than it already did. So she explained what Nandara taught her about calling elemental demons to do specific work. How Spark enchanted some of her tools and weapons.

"So you use a special demon language to ask the demons to help you with magic?"

"Yes. I'm trying to think of things I could ask them that will have different results. And maybe different combinations of elements. Earth and fire made weapons hard enough... or whatever... to pierce dragon skin."

"So, what are you thinking of? Earth and air or something?"

"I don't know. That's what I'm trying to work out."

"Okay, but what about this one?" Ember held up a new page. "This looks impossible."

"Dragon armour. Yes, I think it might be impossible, but we need it."

"Too heavy," Ember said.

"And no matter how thin I beat it out, I don't know where I'm going to find enough metal to cover a whole blaze of dragons, let alone just Abyss."

"Could you enchant the dragons themselves? They can enchant people, can't they? Surely the reverse must be possible."

Spark stared at Ember's back, increasingly grateful and relieved to have her around.

"You're a genius."

"Course I am." Ember flicked a grinning glance over her shoulder and shuffled through Spark's plans. She picked up the papers and sat next to Spark, stretching the plans out across their laps.

Spark would have to ask Nandara if it was possible to enchant a dragon.

But then Ember leaned the wrong way while tracing over one of Spark's sketches, bumping Spark's shoulder, and Spark sucked a sharp breath through gritted teeth.

Ember recoiled, then knelt near Spark and cautiously lifted the bandage to have a look. "No harm," she announced. "But maybe we need to get some armour for you first."

Ember drew back the blankets and helped Spark into bed.

"That's definitely a good idea," Spark said. "Armour for me will be easier."

"Good place to start. But tomorrow," Ember said with mock sternness, smiling. "You need rest now."

Ember tucked her in and turned out the lanterns before leaving. Spark wished Ember would stay. She leaned back in her bed, sleep eluding her as she bent all her thoughts toward making dragon armour.

CHAPTER TWENTY

S park gingerly picked up the cooled sheet of metal and brought it to the work table, Ember trailing hopefully behind her. But Spark didn't get more than a few steps when the metal folded under its own weight. She'd beat it too thin again, compromising the strength. She cursed loudly and dropped the sheet on the floor.

She plunked herself onto a stool and stared down at the latest failed experiment. Ember put a comforting hand on her shoulder, while Spark rifled through her papers, going over her calculations. She went back to the worthless bit of metal on the ground and measured its thickness. Checked it against her work. Swore again.

"It's too heavy. If I use enough metal to protect a dragon to any degree, they won't be able to even take off."

Ember looked over her shoulder at the calculations. She shook her head.

"They can carry a lot, Spark. You sure a little thicker won't be okay? I mean, you're just covering a few key parts, right? Neck and chest, maybe some underbelly?"

"Even at this thickness that much metal will slow them down. I checked with a couple of them, got them to carry things at equal weight." She growled. "They can carry it, sure, but for days? No. It's a five-day flight to Pasdale. And they need to have the energy to fight once they get there. And it would make them so heavy they wouldn't be able to outmanoeuvre other dragons in a fight."

"I still say you find a way to enchant the dragons," Ember said.

Spark gave her a smile she didn't really feel. "I ran it past Nandara. But even if I could amass the power for it—and it would take several wizards working together, more than we've actually got here—I'd only be able to do one dragon at a time."

"Okay, well how long does the enchantment last?"

"Until it's removed."

"That doesn't sound so bad." Ember tilted her head.

"That's not the problem. The problem is that this sort of protective enchantment only works properly for so long. Even if we could get enough wizards here to do it and slowly do one dragon at a time—apparently it would take nearly an hour per dragon—but once we had them all done, it changes after a few days."

Spark looked down at her pages.

"So when Ondias and Nanny first came here, they came with Pappy because he'd been enchanted to withstand fire. The dragons had made him like a fireborn. So he could go into the fire realm and get Nanny from the fire demons. And it worked, he saved her and they used a fire portal to get home. But then Pappy got sick. The enchantment almost killed him. They had to bring him here so the dragons could remove it again."

Ember sat heavily on the stool next to her. "So you could enchant all the dragons, but they'd start getting sick before we got to Pasdale."

"Yes. The armour is the only way."

"Is there something lighter you can use? What about large sheets of canvass enchanted properly?"

Spark shook her head. "If it's possible, I don't know how to do it yet. It's got to be something already fairly sturdy on its own."

"I'm sorry, Spark. I'm sure you'll come up with something. How's your own armour going?"

Spark dug into one of her crates and pulled out the breastplate she'd made.

"I still need to get the straps bolted on. I need to make the bolts first. But it's going well enough."

"Well, if I can help just ask."

"I think I will need your expertise for my flight hood. I want to make a fur lining for when I'm flying, but it's got to be removable so I can get a helmet over it to fight."

"That I can do. Are you still going to go with a metal mask, or do you want to try something else? Leather maybe?"

"I need to put more thought into it. Ask me again in a week."

Ember pulled off the dragon skin gloves she'd been wearing to help Spark with metalwork. She set them down on the table and then paused, staring at them. Spark stared at them too, excitement buzzing across her skin.

She and Ember shared a glance.

"It could work, couldn't it?" Ember asked.

"It's already the toughest substance I know, aside from a dragon's teeth and talons."

"But?"

"They wouldn't let me work on it. They're sensitive about it. They don't even want me building weapons for them."

"Then don't tell them and just do it. Bring them the armour once you get it right. And if they still don't want you working with their skins, to hell with them."

Spark wanted to, but knew what could happen. Relations with the dragons were tenuous at best.

"Just try it with a scrap from making these, just to see if you can," Ember urged. "And if it doesn't work, they don't have to know. And if it does, try to convince them."

"I can't spend too much more effort on this if it's a dead end," Spark said.

"Then don't. You've done all you can. So do this one last thing. What's the worst that could happen?"

Spark gave her a sidelong look. "They could raze our village and eat us all."

Ember waved a hand. "But what will they actually do?"

"Raze the village and eat us all."

"That's really that much a risk? Come on now."

"They could force me out. Or kill me. I'm the one trampling their customs and going against their wishes. So it's most likely I would face the consequences alone."

"Then the question is whether those risks are worth it to you."

Spark remembered the way Abyss's blood oozed from her wounds. How lucky she was to have made it back to the city. She couldn't fathom losing a dragon in battle to something she could prevent.

"I'll look through some of Nandara's spellbooks and see what I can come up with."

With her brow furrowed, Spark bent over the mask and dragged her index finger between the seams connecting it with the glass pieces she crafted the day before. Once the goggles were in, she attached the little hooks to the padding around the edges where the metal would make contact with her face. Ember made the padding for her, and she was excited about having it ready. Attaching straps to keep it on would come later.

Spark was at home today, not wanting to work on this late at night when she was more prone to being tired. She was getting good at using her fingers to direct beams of flame to weld the pieces together. It made fusing so much easier and far more precise.

But she kept as much of her power to herself as she could. This was easier now that her shoulder was healed, as Ember had no pretense for being around, aside from friendship, which grated River's nerves.

Jatt wasn't around either. He'd been gone more than a moon. Nandara hadn't mentioned where he went or what his business had been, but his master had been with him. Although they'd returned a few days ago, Jatt remained scarce.

Spark finished fusing the seam and inspected it. One eyepiece in, one to go. She was setting the next piece into place when there was a scrape at her door.

She tossed a few rags over her work and went to answer it. Blinking at the dizzying darkness beyond her door, she checked that she hadn't actually worked all day and deep into the night.

"Abyss! You're back!"

She'd caught sight of the dragoness a time or two over the last month, always coming or going from the valley. Nandara told her that Abyss came in regularly to check on her eggs and to take her place on hunting parties, which she was being sent on more often than usual. Her superiors forbade her from contact with humans in all that time.

"Are you allowed to be here?" Spark drew in her enthusiasm.

Abyss nodded.

"That's wonderful! Are you back for good?"

The dragoness growled, a rumble deep in her chest like an approaching earth tremor.

"Well, it's good that at least some of the restrictions have been lifted. I've missed you terribly, and I'm sorry for what happened. Have your wounds healed?"

Abyss stood, extending her neck to show Spark the unbroken expanse of her black skin. She crouched down with her face near the doorway and tapped at Spark's shoulder with her claw, being surprisingly gentle.

"It's better. Lina and Ember did well to get me back to health. Hurts a bit sometimes, but my strength is back. I've been at work. I'm trying to make dragon armour. And I'm working on a mask so my face isn't so frozen in flight. I could barely see! Maybe I'll be more use to you in a battle if the wind isn't freezing my eyeballs."

Abyss raised an eyebrow.

Spark retreated into her house and brought out the mask with its one empty eyehole. "I'm almost done. Ember has been helping me make warmer clothing too."

Abyss nuzzled Spark with her soft nose before backing away.

"Are you leaving already?"

Abyss nodded up toward the city.

"Do you want more help with rebuilding?"

Abyss shook her head.

"You just came to say hello? ...But you don't want to push your luck?"

She nodded.

"That's probably for the best. I'm so pleased you're back. I hope I can see you again soon."

Abyss grinned one of her awful toothy grins before leaping into the air, her wings like great bellows fanning the whole of the village. Spark watched until Abyss disappeared into the city then returned to her work, looking guiltily at the other project she was making progress on, hidden under a stack of spellbooks.

Spark was in the workshop far later than she'd ever been, with her guilt project tucked into a crate full of leather scraps and seldom-used tools. She took it out, just one little swatch, and left it lying in the middle of the cleared table. She wasn't entirely certain about the protocol on this sort of thing, but if she couldn't at least get Abyss's approval, there was no point in continuing with it.

She would have liked to ask Ondias about it, but this wasn't anything she could tell Ondias. It would go over as well as bringing it straight to the Dragoness Superior. So she had to proceed as carefully as she could.

Spark heard a scrape at the door and went to answer it, pleased to see Abyss. She greeted the dragoness formally and slid the large door open.

"It honours me that you would take the time to join me, I know you have so much else to do."

Abyss narrowed her eyes at Spark.

"I have been hard at work at many things in your absence. And some of that work has gone against the wishes of your kind, but I have done so with the sole purpose of benefiting you and your kin. It wounded me more to see your blood spilled than my own. Loch will bring his fight to us one day, and I want to be certain we're ready."

Abyss snorted, her eyes narrowed.

"I know that what I've done is offending, but I want you to know my reason before you move to fury. And if you are truly displeased with what I've done, I will undo my work. But first, I want you to see exactly what I've accomplished."

Scowling, Abyss at least tilted her head.

Spark retrieved the swatch of dragon skin and brought it over, holding it in her hands for Abyss to see. The low grumbling growl trembled deep in Abyss's chest, so low it was more a vibration in the ground than something Spark heard.

"I'm treading in dangerous territory, I know. But I want you to try to tear this. Use a claw and try to puncture it."

Spark gripped the edges of the little bit of dragon skin and held it up and out where it would be easy for Abyss to reach, and where, if Spark's enchantment failed, the talon would not easily tear through and cut Spark.

"I combined the elements wind and fire, using demons, and it has repelled some of the tools I've made to work with dragon skin. Now I want to see if it truly holds up to its purpose."

Abyss growled louder, her teeth bared.

"I know, and I'm sorry. But this is the only spare bit that I worked on, and we can still remove the enchantment and give it a proper sky burial, like I promised. But right now, please, just try."

Abyss was quick, far quicker than Spark would have expected, and she nearly wasn't ready. But her talon stabbed into the centre of the swatch, stretching it. Abyss pressed harder but only sent Spark sliding backward across the stone floor. She picked at it, trying to tear it that way, then stabbed once more, nearly knocking Spark down.

Spark fought to keep the grin back, biting her lips and focusing on her breathing and watching Abyss closely.

"It repels you. It will repel others."

Spark's world erupted with heat and light, searing brightness like being dropped into the centre of a new, angry sun. She slammed onto the floor, realized what Abyss was doing, and pushed back to suppress the flame. Her clothes were already largely incinerated and she internally cursed herself. She hadn't thought to put on her firecloak, though that probably would have been even more insulting.

Abyss's flame ebbed and Spark stood taller, not caring that she wore only her slightly charred boots. She knew the story of how Abyss had done this very thing to Nanny the first time they'd met, when Nanny had been stuck between good manners and terrible nobles and made one misstep too many.

Spark clenched her jaw and stared down the angry dragoness, standing tall and defiant. She held Abyss's eye for a moment, and then went to retrieve her cloak.

"I'm putting it on for the warmth."

Abyss kept growling.

"You've had your say. But think about this. I can keep you safe in battle! It's this or I have resort to more demon-work and maybe opening fire portals. Just give it some thought. Wait until you are no longer furious, and then let me know if you still wish for me to stop my work. I will still honour my word of sky burial for these remnants, either way."

Abyss watched her for a beat, stopped growling and huffed. Then she disappeared into the night.

CHAPTER TWENTY-ONE

Spark furrowed her brow, focused on the straps and not buckling anything too tight or too loose. Working with an unfamiliar dragon, even if it was Abyss's blue mate, had her on edge. Everything had to go right. She needed to win over someone other than Abyss, and this was the best place to start. She'd refrained from trying to give him a name. Well, at least out loud. She'd initially wanted to call him Heaven, even if it was on the nose. But now she quietly thought of him as Zephyr.

"There, that should do it. How does it feel?"

He stood up and trotted a circle around the workshop's exterior before giving his great body a shake. Nothing came loose and he settled down near Spark.

"May I climb into the sling to test it?"

He leaned forward to make it easier for her. Once she was in the harness, he stood and flapped his wings experimentally for a moment, before springing into the air to do a lap around the valley. He went only part of the way at a leisurely pace, and then zipped at his top speed, far greater than Abyss's. The smaller males were generally much faster.

She could barely breathe even before he started spiralling at top speed. He did one loop, slowing slightly for it, before settling down on the ground near her workshop.

Spark wobbled her way out of the sling and started removing it.

"Well done. Thank you."

She had only one buckle left to unclasp when Abyss swooped down to stand next to Zephyr. She'd been in a meeting with the Superiors, and Spark stopped what she was doing to look hopefully at the dragoness. Abyss shook her head. Spark cursed and helped Zephyr out of the sling, which she coiled up and stored inside. Zephyr was gone when she came back out, but Abyss was still there.

"They really don't want the benefit of extra armour when battle comes our way again?"

Abyss shook her head. Spark felt heavy, tried not to let the despair show.

"They don't think it will, do they?"

Abyss narrowed her eyes.

"Or do they plan to bring the battle to Pasdale first?"

Abyss didn't move, didn't blink.

"Ah, so they are, but I'm not to know about it." She glanced up at the city. "Tell me, if it were up to you, would you let me use dragon skin to make armour for war?"

Abyss snorted, but remained still.

"Fine, have it your way. I've removed the enchantment from that bit of skin I have left. Would you like to do the sky burial today?"

Abyss shook her head and looked up to the city.

"Repair day?"

Abyss nodded.

"If you give me a few minutes to tidy up the shop, I will join you."

Nandara was teaching Spark about the other elements and how to wield earth and air. While Nandara could manipulate water as well as the other elements, she only did so when she absolutely had to and wasn't showing Spark how to work that element. But Spark had done well with both elements she was learning, including how to work the cursed, gritty earth. She helped Nandara pull earth and stone from the ground to build into walls for new homes in the settlement. There weren't many scrappy tents left. And she had become exceptional at fusing the diamond and obsidian in the city.

Spark had such a command over fire and earth together that she could fuse intricate patterns into the city. All of the dragons could, but none of them could get into the smaller spaces like Spark, and none of them could fuse with the fine detail she could. Despite wariness over her use of dragon skin, they brought her up more and more frequently to help with rebuilding.

It was late afternoon when Abyss brought Spark home, the sun already disappeared behind the mountains.

"Should we do the sky burial tomorrow then?"

Abyss shook her head and looked east, over the mountains.

"Are you leaving again? Already?"

Abyss stood tall and shook out her wings.

"Will you be long?"

Abyss stretched out her hands, most of her talons extended.

"Eight days this time? Are they making you go, or is this your choice?"

Abyss narrowed her eyes, but leaned forward to nuzzle Spark briefly. Then she stood tall and pushed her wings out across the sky. Spark held her doorframe to brace against the wing-gale and watched until Abyss disappeared over the mountains.

Spark had all of the dragon skin she'd been gifted, including the gloves and hood, set aside. Now that she could enchant any fabric with fireproofing, she didn't need these items at all and planned to bury them with the rest, whenever Abyss decided it was time to do so.

Spark had plenty to do in the meantime. The likelihood of making armour had all but vanished, so it was time to shift her focus. She ate quickly, questioning the wisdom of her plan, but there was nothing left to try.

With the shell of her mother haunting her, she secured the curtains and bolted the door.

The warm blissful feeling was so intense that Spark couldn't let her focus waver for an instant. It tried to wash over her, roll her under, claim her. She held it at a whisper in her ears and put her focus into the magic. It came so effortlessly that it was like the magic read her mind and simply performed what she wanted. She'd been testing this new ability on repairs and focused her attention on the broken spade on the stone in front of her.

She didn't have to direct the flame with her hands or anything. Just envision a repaired tool and let the fire do the rest. And the way it lit her up inside... Her head spun and every last inch of her tingled. That tingle ran cold up her spine as her mother's fate crept into her thoughts. It made her more aware of the addictive pull of all that warmth.

Her door rattled in its frame, something slamming against it as if trying to force through the bolt. The distraction jarred her focus and the bright wave reared up over her, ready to push her so far down into herself as to be lost. But she pushed back, pushed hard. She stuffed the wave down and out into the hearth and snapped a bright door closed behind it, even as Ondias shouted from the threshold.

"Let me in this instant or I swear by the moons I'll tear the whole wall out!"

"Yeah, yeah," Spark muttered, swaying to her feet. She had enough sense to scoop up the repaired spade and leave it on the anvil to cool, then she stumbled to the door, tripping over her feet—so full of energy her body didn't know where to put it, tried to put it everywhere at once.

As soon as Spark unlocked it, it swung inward and Ondias barged in, slamming the door behind her.

"Always with your damned work," she said, looking at the spade.

"What else am I supposed to do?" Spark asked, genuinely curious and too drunk on the power she'd been manipulating to care about winding Ondias up.

Ondias narrowed her eyes. "The way you hide in here. You can't keep burying the pain behind metalwork."

"What do you even know."

Ondias's tone softened a fraction. "Spark, you have lost everything. I know that agony, and hiding from it like this will not make it better."

"No one you love is dead!"

"There are different kinds of death." Ondias's jaw tightened. "They all cause the same kind of pain."

"Oh, yes, and no one has lost as much as you, no one knows pain quite like you do." Spark took a half step, beginning to turn away, done with Ondias already. But Ondias's hand shot out and gripped a fistful of the front of Spark's shirt, hauling her around so the two women were nearly nose to nose.

"Loch knows where you are." Each word dropped out through a jaw clenched so tight Spark waited for it to snap. Now that Ondias had her attention, she let her go but didn't lose any of her intensity. "Those ice dragons are all still alive too. I've just received word from a contact in Pasdale."

"Not much I can do about that. It was only a matter of time. What do you think I'm working on all this time? You think there are really that many spades in need of repair in this valley? How thick are you?"

Ondias grabbed for the front of her shirt, but Spark slapped her hands away and took a step back. She stumbled, regained her balance. Ondias watched it all closely.

"Oh weeping moons, what have you been doing?" The woman's voice was low and full of horror. Her power swept through the room. Ondias's gaze flickered to the blade on the anvil. "Oh, Mita, you reckless little fool."

Ondias moved quickly enough to take Spark by surprise. She grabbed Spark by the chin and pulled her face down, staring into her eyes. She shook her head as Spark pushed her off.

"Demon possession." She turned away, still shaking her head. "Why did I ever think you were somehow better than this? All those warnings, your mother's near-corpse looking down on you every day, and still you think letting a demon in is a good idea?"

"I have to do something!"

"Getting yourself killed won't help the dragons or this city."

"I have control."

"That's exactly what your mother thought!"

"I'm stronger than her."

"And you've got her inflated ego, I see. She thought she could control the demons too."

"She probably could have if she'd had more training. I do just fine with it, even with you trying to tear down my wall, shattering my concentration. Still kept it under control."

Ondias barked out ugly laughter. "You truly believe that holding control through the insignificant distraction of me knocking on your door means you can control a demon through anything?"

"Oh, and you're the expert on pyromancy?"

"I've watched demons nearly destroy Dionelle and completely overtake your mother. But you go ahead and tell yourself you know everything about them."

"I'm going to use them against Loch, just like Mamma did."

Ondias whirled on her, jabbing a finger at her. "The battle you anticipate is coming much sooner than you think. It was those ice dragons that saw you and brought the message of your whereabouts to Loch. So what, exactly, do you believe you've achieved, Mita? You've isolated yourself from the dragons, you've put the dragoness on thin ice with her peers, and you've tipped off the enemy to where you are. You've given them a big target and put us all in danger."

"It's the same danger you've been in all along! If you'd all stop being such cowards and help me—"

"Enough! This is enough. This is not a game. It's time for you to put your talents to sensible use. Do you hear me? If I hear or even sense that you're doing anything as foolish as demon possession again, I will bloody your face."

Spark bit against the angry words rising to her lips and took a step toward Ondias, ready to shove the woman out her door. But Ondias wasn't quite done with her yet.

"Put your ego aside before you end up in a pillar with your mother. The heavens know you're just as damned reckless as she ever was."

Furious heat erupted across her shoulders, and Spark's hands flew out so fast she had no hope of stopping them, not that she really wanted to. One slapped against Ondias's jaw while the other shoved at her shoulder. The woman's expression darkened, her shuddering fury rising, but then Spark's hands gripped her shoulder and the door and ejected Ondias out into the night.

"If you come back in here unannounced again I will reduce you to cinder where you stand and damn every last consequence!" Spark slammed the door and bolted it.

She heaved in a great trembling breath against the trapped scream and the hot prickle of oncoming tears. It was hard to tell if Ondias's sharp words about her mother bothered her more than the insistence she stop practicing the only thing she could think of to keep any of them safe. Did Ondias truly believe Spark *wanted* to do any of this?

Shaking and gulping air to keep from screaming, Spark gathered up her tools and threw them onto the worktable, trying to keep her hands busy and her mind calm.

There was a scrape at the door, and Spark briefly wondered if Ondias really was that stupid until she heard Shadow whimpering from outside. Spark cracked the door open, just to be sure it was only the dog. She let him in but slipped out into the night, quiet and cool and empty, shutting the door behind her.

She pulled Nanny's pendant out from under her shirt and watched the warm light swirl.

With flame called to her hand for guidance, she picked her way westward between the buildings to the narrow footpath Stone had first shown her. Spark hadn't made a habit of going up the mountain, but knew the way all the same.

Caught in winter's fierce grip, the cool night air was crisp, and with neither moon out yet, the stars shone extra bright. In their cold light, her mother's entombment seemed to glow against the darkness.

When Spark reached the glittering column rising out of the mountainside, she sat down on the ruby rocks, black in the lack of light. It was cold, but she kept herself cloaked in flame for warmth. She gave her mother a fleeting glance, never able to really look at her, and then looked out over the valley. A few lights sparkled down in the village as people slowly found their way to bed.

"So what would you do?"

Of course she knew what Neesha would do. She was being sustained in that diamond column exactly because of what she would do, what she *had* done. But everything Neesha did had been to keep Spark safe.

"So what should *I* do?"

She knew what she wanted to do, but was it worth risking herself as Neesha had? Was she reducing her mother's heroics if she ended up being entombed alive right alongside her?

"Nanny couldn't stop you. Doesn't sound like she really tried. Would you try to stop me now?"

Spark stood and looked at her mother, serene in her endless slumber. She wouldn't let herself shudder.

"You'd help me, wouldn't you?"

Spark clenched her jaw and hissed a breath through her teeth, fighting against the prickle in her eyes.

"I wish you were here."

Two powerful fireborn women working together. That would be something. It dredged up memories of the brief moment Spark spent fighting alongside Nanny. Her stomach clenched. She'd have to do it again, and she'd have to do it better this time.

And she'd have to do it alone.

No matter what Ondias or anyone else said, there wasn't much choice in the matter. Loch would come for them—for *her*—and she had to be ready.

Gritting her teeth, Spark turned away, heading down the mountainside.

CHAPTER
TWENTY-TWO

Dinner hour came and went with Spark frequently peering over at Jatt as he worked in the corner, wondering when he was going to head out for the day. She hadn't seen much of him since he got back, but today he'd been around since the morning. She was hungry and wanted to eat, wasn't sure if he planned on staying and expected her to feed him. She had work she didn't want anyone seeing and wanted him to go, but she had gone so long without any proper company that she couldn't bring herself to ask him to leave.

She stood in the middle of the room and cleared her throat so he looked up.

"I'm going to make some dinner now..."

He blinked and looked around, glanced out the window.

"Oh. I didn't realize how late it was." He waved a hand. "Don't let me keep you." He rooted around in his bag, which was stuffed to overflowing, and pulled out some crockery with the lid firmly sealed on, wrapped in twine. He picked off the wrappings and then lifted the pot. "Mind if I leave this by your fire to warm up?"

"You moving in or something?"

"Um... Could I?"

Spark watched him without blinking.

Jatt scratched the back of his head and stared down at the pot. "Had a fight with Gramps. Probably should have stayed in the south a bit longer."

He shrugged. "Nothing for it, but I'd rather not go back there for a couple of days if I can help it."

Spark took his little pot from him and set it next to the flames. She couldn't find it in herself to turn him away.

"I've got a sleeping mat." He nudged at his bag with the toe of his boot.

Spark nodded slowly. "As long as it's only for a couple of days."

"If Gran doesn't get it smoothed over by then, she never will."

"You could have your own place. You did before they came here, didn't you?"

"Well, yeah, but it was awful. Turns out I can clean up anything as long as it isn't my own."

Spark chuckled. Bren had been much the same. The ping of grief stabbed into her gut, and she turned away from Jatt, busying herself with food. She ate without tasting and swept it all back into the pantry without much thought before settling into her work making armour.

Long after Jatt finished whatever was in the little pot of his, he sat at the table nearby and watched Spark work.

"Do you think you could show me how to do that properly?" he asked. "So that I could work up to working metal on my own?"

Spark looked up at him. "You think I need competition or something?"

He grinned. "Nah. You don't leave anything left over to compete for! I'd like to try metal art, see what I can do with it."

Spark sucked on her bottom lip.

"I know you use a lot of pyromancy," he said. "But there's plenty I could do without magic."

"Sure. I can talk out what I'm doing when I work, if you think that will help you learn some of it."

"Whatever you think is best to start."

So she went through it all while she worked, telling him why she needed certain metals at certain colours before she worked them, what the different hammer strokes were for, how to temper the metal and how to mend it. She talked herself hoarse, drinking far more water than she normally would.

"Do you plan on stopping?" he asked out of nowhere. "Do you sleep at all? Or is the bed for show?"

Spark stared at him, trying to parse his meaning, until she saw the long blue light of the moons slanting through the window.

"There's not much for me to do most nights except keep working on all this." She gestured. "There's a lot I want to finish as soon as I can, so it doesn't seem right to waste time. I don't sleep well if I try before I'm properly tired. You're welcome to turn in if you're ready. Don't let my routine dictate yours."

Jatt stabbed the air with his shoulders and went to dig around in his bag, pulling out a thin straw mat. When he looked around the floor for somewhere to put it, Spark felt guilty.

"Don't worry about that. Bed's plenty big enough for two." She forced herself to not think of Ember. "I can't abide you sleeping on the cold floor."

Jatt watched Spark for a lot longer than she thought was necessary. Had she said something wrong? One of his shoulders twitched at the air, and he stuffed the mat into his bag. When he pulled out his bedclothes to change, Spark turned to her work. Jatt bid her good night, but she only waved to him without turning, listening to the sound of him getting comfortable.

When she looked his way, he lay on his side, facing the wall, with Shadow curled up behind him. Spark drew the tarps across the windows and willed the fire down low. She only needed the lamp on the table to see by.

After her internal clock told her it had been hours and she heard the slow, steady orchestra of sleep-breathing from Jatt and Shadow, Spark wondered if it was safe. She stood in the middle of the room and whispered Jatt's name. Shadow's ears twitched but neither of them so much as paused mid-breath.

"Jatt? Can I tell you something?"

She kept her voice to a whisper, as loud as she intended to be while she worked. It didn't reach him. She knelt at the fire, keeping it at a smoulder. It didn't need to be very big for her purpose anyway. She whisper-hissed the summoning that had become so familiar and waited, squinting as the fire flared.

This demon's energy was familiar. The call of its magic something she'd experienced before, and she wondered if she had previously summoned this same demon. She'd never asked if that was possible and wasn't sure if it was a good idea to start asking now, even though she was sure that Nandara had learned what she was up to. Maybe Nandara understood better than Ondias that this was their only hope.

But Spark couldn't wonder about it long, not right now. She had to focus. She let the demon in but kept her will clamped around it. It didn't like the restraints, thrashed against them, but was powerless so long as she maintained her focus. The heat of it tingled through her body until she felt like she buzzed and floated—a fiery bee, giddy with power.

Tonight Spark didn't have any metal to work, at least none that required this kind of extreme power. Tonight she wanted to test her control and nothing else. So she set to cleaning up for the night, focusing a fraction of her attention on normal tasks with the demon trapped inside her. Ondias had hit on something about distraction, and the whole point in trying possession in the first place was so Spark could be battle-ready.

She could still only assume that practice was the difference between her possible success and her mother's failure. She tried not to think too hard about Neesha but had accepted she might be wrong. If she could save her friends, even for a time, the risk was worth it.

She found herself constantly turning toward Jatt, wishing he would go home and sort out his problems—leave her out of it. Give her peace and privacy. His slow breathing was the only reminder of his presence, but he could wake any second and interrupt her at a critical moment. Unless she did something about it. Make sure he didn't wake up. It wouldn't take much, not with this wild and furious power at her command, to reduce him to ash.

Could she do it before he screamed?

Did she have the precision to incinerate him without harming Shadow or scorching her bed?

Spark gasped and wrenched her gaze away, gripped the broom and set to sweeping the floor. She kept her back to Jatt.

The demon drove these thoughts, of course, and she kept pushing it further down into her and returning to her work. But it was intent on Jatt.

When it couldn't get her to think of Jatt, her thoughts would turn to going out into the town. Maybe go see what Ondias was doing. Reduce her home to rubble.

She certainly had much to learn about the demons and possession before she could use their power anywhere outside the controlled environment of her forge. Before she could use them around other people.

She went to the forge and surged her will behind the demon's desire to escape her, easily pushing it out. Pushing it out and stuffing it deep down into the flames, deep into another realm. Once it was gone, she was more tired than she had been in ages. Tired and hollow, like her skin was made of lead with nothing at all inside.

Barely the energy to change, she managed, and shooed the dog out of her bed before dropping in next to Jatt, the two of them sleeping back to back.

Jatt left for the day to work with his master, and Spark set aside her armour, worried about its adequacy. She wondered if she should head over to the workshop to see if the workers needed any help with the fresh round of armour testing. That the workshop got so much use delighted her, but it was still hers—she had built it. She also wanted to make sure no one was mucking things up.

She was making enchanted tools for the others to use. She couldn't work with dragon skin and hadn't yet made metal light and sturdy enough for armour, but she wouldn't give up on it yet. There were other materials she could use. Basic leather could be enchanted, much as she had done with the swatch of dragon skin Abyss got so furious over. It wasn't as strong, but it was better than nothing.

There were village members curious about learning to blacksmith, others who'd always been competent at it but never truly used the skill, who spent more time at the workshop where she could guide them and they could support each other. They were helping her build the leather dragon armour for practice as much as anything. Spark enchanted her harness and sling for Abyss so that it would hold up to an attack. She wanted the same for other dragons.

She'd just pulled her robe off its hook by the door when Ember pushed through, her smile filling Spark with fire. She had a package in her hands, something small, and she went straight to the worktable to unwrap it.

"A little treat," she said. "I haven't seen you in so long."

"It's been a hard winter." Spark leaned forward to see what Ember had brought. She smelled the warm, yeasty scent of the bread before Ember got all the wrappings off.

"New recipe." Ember's grin widened. "Best bread I've ever made. I just had to share. A little breakfast, maybe?"

Ember broke off a piece for her, and it was sweeter than Spark expected, with buttery undertones. It dissolved in her mouth. She closed her eyes and let it.

Ember cleared her throat like she meant to say something but jammed a piece of bread into her mouth instead.

"Are you still busy?" Spark asked.

"You getting lonely?"

Spark's cheeks warmed and she crammed bread into her mouth and looked out the window, getting an excellent view of the stone house across the lane, ruby mountains dotted with clan towers jutting over it in the distance, all of it glittering with dappled light from the city. Around the mouthful of bread, she mumbled something about Jatt keeping her company.

"Oh, what good is he," Ember said with unexpected vitriol. "Just skulking in that corner not saying a word. He's like a slug."

Spark gave her side-eye. "Be kind, he's all right. He talks plenty."

"I don't think I've heard a dozen words out of him in all this time you've been here."

"Maybe you could try being kinder to him."

Ember huffed as if Spark suggested she strip naked and run through the streets. She crossed her arms and looked around the room, her gaze lingering on Jatt's extra things scattered in his little corner before making a slow journey over the still-rumpled bed to where Jatt's bed robe was draped over the pillow he'd been using. She turned far too quickly to look at Spark, eyes narrowed, chin jutting out.

Spark read the anger clear as day, but her mind struggled to catch up on what set it off. Then it clicked.

"He's staying here for a few days." She rushed to explain about the fight and their arrangement, words tumbling out all at once.

"You can't share your bed like that with a man! Steal the moon, Spark, you're so daft sometimes! Did your family never tell you about being proper?"

"Proper? For what?"

Ember grinned. "Oh, Spark. You're like a wee babe sometimes."

Despite the momentary anger lurking in Ember's dark eyes, Spark didn't detect any malice in the statement. What was she being so naïve about then?

"It's not a big deal," Spark said.

"The whole village will talk."

"They never shut up. What are they going to talk about? He can stay here. You did."

"That's different. I'm a woman."

"I don't see what that's got to do with anything."

"Don't you?"

Anger again. Spark blinked.

"Ember, really. It's my home and I can do what I want with it."

"Is that honestly what you think?"

"Steal the moons, Ember, have I got to consult with you on every little thing I do here? Would you like to know what I've got stocked in my cupboards?"

"Is it another man? How many of them are you keeping around?"

Ember's voice rose in pitch. She stood stalk straight in front of Spark with her hands balled into fists, her dark eyes black as ink. Spark inched further away, wary of the ground she tread.

"I don't understand." She tried keeping her voice as calm and even as she could. "This isn't a big deal."

"Yes. Well. Fine."

Ember was nearly hysterical, shoving the bread into the wrapping in jerky motions, her eyes glittering with tears. She pushed Spark out of her way and stormed out the door. Spark watched after her, blinking stupidly.

"What the blazing moons was *that*?"

She shook her head and grabbed her robe, heading to the workshop with the odd conversation playing over in her mind. It ceaselessly repeated through clumsy interactions with the two men working in the shop that day. And it played out in every piece of metal or leather she tried to work until it was dinnertime and she could take a break.

Jatt was already back at her house, at the corner of the forge she used as a kitchen, preparing something in a larger pot than he'd had before. It was her pot.

"Hope you don't mind," he said. "I picked up some extras in the square as thanks for giving me somewhere to camp out."

Spark shrugged and dropped her things onto the worktable. She'd hoped making dinner would take her mind off of what happened.

"Can I ask you something?" she said. "It kind of has to do with you, and I'm really confused."

He nodded for her to continue, and she did, haltingly at first.

"Ember was by this morning..." And she gave him the full script, as much as she could remember. He was silent for a long moment, and she had the feeling she'd said something wrong. Again.

At last, he took a deep breath and closed his eyes.

"She's right. You're like a wee babe." He shook his head and looked at her. "I don't even know where to begin."

"Why is she angry at me?"

"Spark, do you know anything about having a lover?"

"There's a lot of kissing. And something about nakedness?"

Jatt squeezed his eyes shut, then looked into the fire. He went back to making dinner, but kept talking, his voice in hushed tones as he did.

"Yes, there's definitely something about nakedness, but it's what you do with it that counts." He went on to explain to her exactly what lovers did with their nakedness. Spark felt cold and was no longer interested in her meal.

"Gross..." she whispered.

"I know. But that's only for a man and a woman. I don't know much about what you and Ember would get up to."

She swallowed a couple of times to clear the dryness from her throat. "Me and Ember? Up to...? I don't... What...?"

"Come on, Spark, I see the way you look at each other."

"We do?"

Jatt stared. "You mean she's not your lover?"

Spark had no idea how someone could choke on dryness, but she near enough managed it.

Jatt's dark skin flushed, and he turned to his pot, all the while fiddling with his dark mop of hair. He muttered a curse under his breath, took the pot off the flame and looked at her.

"The two of you have been making eyes at each other since you got here. She clearly fancies you."

"What, like she wants me in lace and frills?" Spark blinked at him, wished anything at all would make the barest sliver of sense.

Jatt slapped his hands over his face and sucked in a long deep breath.

"Do you want to kiss her?" he asked.

The heat rose to her cheeks.

"I'll take that as a yes." He leaned closer, whispering forcefully. "She *wants* you to kiss her."

Spark coughed and turned away from him to lean on the worktable. Her legs wobbled under the lightheadedness, and her pulse skipped along merrily. Her thoughts swirled like a firestorm. She couldn't pin a single one down.

"After all the time she's spent here, making eyes at you, the way she stayed with you after those ice dragons tore you up... I really thought... You're really just friends?"

Spark glared at him. He held up his hands in a placating gesture.

"Look, fine, you're just friends. But Ember would clearly like you to take a deeper interest in her. And now she thinks you're taking a deeper interest in me."

It all clicked and a glacier dropped into Spark's stomach.

"Shit on the moons, Ember's jealous?"

"Jealous of nothing, but yes." He sighed. "She's been here forever and doesn't even know..." He shook his head. "So much for rumours."

"So... So Ember wants..." Spark coughed. "She wants me to be... um. Her lover." She squeaked out the last word. "But she thinks you are?"

"You're not the only daft one." Jatt smirked.

Spark looked at him blankly. How had she missed out on such obvious things? Not having friends was an impediment, of course, and Nanny didn't speak, but there had never been so much as a hint about any of it. Maybe because her mother had been so foolish about lovers?

"So... I should go tell her the truth?" Spark ventured. "And then kiss her?"

"It might be better if I have a word with her first. You're so daft you'll just muck it up even more."

Spark glared at him. He grinned and continued making dinner.

"But that's okay? For me to kiss her?"

"If that's what she wants."

Spark blinked. "But... In Pasdale. There was a girl. Janny. But..."

"Everyone hated you in Pasdale."

"But I thought marriage was supposed to be a man and a woman..."

"Oh, marriage, yeah. But no one cares about who your lovers are. Even if you're married. It's fine." He waved a dismissive hand.

"But why's being married any different?"

His shoulders stabbed at the air. "Mostly, it's got to do with babies. Or at least it did to start." His face contorted, full of disgust but other things too. "Marriage is always about a man and a woman, right? Because that's the recipe you need for a baby. That's what everyone's end goal in life is supposed to be, right?" He did nothing to hide the sour note in his voice.

"Well that doesn't matter then. I'm never having babies."

He looked around at her, setting down the spoon he'd been using to stir the pot.

She crossed her arms. "It's hardly a good idea, is it? I mean, I'm barely human as it is."

"What, because you're fireborn?" He turned back to the pot.

"I got it from my mamma and she got it from Nanny. No way I'd have a baby that wasn't fireborn too. Or maybe just pure flame or an actual demon."

"Come on, don't be so hard on yourself."

Spark stared at the back of his head. "Look at me." She left no room for negotiation in her tone. When he was too slow to turn, she flared the fire beside him.

"Hey! All right, fine." He turned. "Yes. I see you. What?"

"Your gran is about as pale as normal people come, yes?"

He nodded reluctantly, giving her a sullen, hooded look.

"And I make her look as dark as Abyss. People aren't supposed to be this colour, Jatt."

Jatt wave her off, started to turn around. She took a quick step toward him and grabbed his arm.

"Listen to me," she snapped. "Look at me. Look, damn you. Look at my eyes."

"They're orange." He sounded annoyed.

"Not just orange. *Fire* coloured. The exact colour of fire, Jatt. And not just the colour. *Look* at them."

So he leaned forward, that infuriatingly bored look on his face. But it blanched away in a hurry and his own eyes widened.

"Wait…" He stood straight, looked behind him to the fire in the forge, back at her. "No, it's got to be…" He took her shoulders, turned her away from the fire, ensuring it couldn't be a reflection. Still holding her shoulders, he leaned close.

Now he was looking.

And she knew what he'd see. Even turned away from the fire, even if there wasn't a fire left in the world he'd see this same thing, the strange fire-flicker motion in the amber of her eyes. He leaned closer, their faces inches apart.

"That's—"

The door burst open, both of them startling and standing straight to face the visitor. Ember. Her hand gripped the door handle so tightly her knuckles were almost as white as Spark's. Her jaw was jutting out the way it had that morning, and Spark was quite certain Ember was trying to murder them both with her eyes.

"Right," Ember said. "Sorry to interrupt."

She slammed the door so hard the entire house shook. No small feat given the amount of magic that went into building it.

"Ember, wait!" Spark called, moving toward the door.

Jatt gripped her shoulder.

"There's nothing you can say to her right now that will make it any better. Given what she thinks I'm doing here, what do you think that looked like to her?"

Spark gasped, her chest tightening.

"Is she really that foolish?" Spark asked.

"Romance clouds the mind. It's why I've never had much use for it."

"But what should I do? She's wrong, why can't I just tell her?"

"She won't believe you. I'll try to talk to her, once she's had some time to cool off. No guarantees though, she's never liked me much."

Spark sat heavily at the worktable, staring into the fire.

"It's probably for the best," he said, his tone gentle. "These sorts of rumours won't hurt any of us."

"What do you mean?"

"Some people—a few bumpkins from certain backwaters, and River—react dangerously toward people who don't fit in the way they think everyone should. No harm in feeding everyone a little lie that we're exactly what they think we should be."

"What's so odd about you?"

"They all think I'm like you, but the other way. That I like men the way you like women. Ember's probably confused out of her head after all this time knowing me." His smirk returned, but it was bitter, his expression dark. "I'm not interested in men. Not women, either. They'd probably think that's even worse if they knew."

"But why does anyone even care?"

"Backward bumpkin busybodies." He tried to make it a joke, but his expression darkened even more. "Anyway, most people here don't care. And there are places in the world where no one cares. Where getting married doesn't matter and having kids doesn't matter and who your lovers are don't matter."

"Just not Pasdale."

"Entire kingdom full of bumpkins."

Spark's thoughts were restlessly sluggish the rest of the evening, barely tasting the meal Jatt made. She liked it better when she hadn't known the truth, hated her family for not letting her know sooner. Felt guilty for hating them when they were all dead or worse.

Spark lay awake for hours, sleeping fitfully once she managed sleep at all. The morning dawned cool and gloomy, Spark's thoughts buzzing like a nest of angry wasps. The only thought that stood clear was how tenuous her friendships had become. She'd had such grand hopes of convincing Jatt and Ember to stop sniping at each other, but now Ember wasn't going to talk to either of them. And Jatt had been quieter than usual since their dinnertime conversation. He left to his apprenticeship without so much as a word to her.

Jatt let Shadow out when he left, while Spark lay listlessly on her back, staring up at the ceiling. Cold gloom prickled across her usually hot skin, and she shivered against it despite burrowing deeper into the blankets.

Wallow in misery or do... what?

She tossed off the blankets and pushed out of bed to pull the curtain all the way closed and throw the lock behind Jatt. It would be hours before anyone bothered her, and she had techniques to master. She went to the forge and called another demon.

CHAPTER TWENTY-THREE

J att slung his bag over his shoulder and went to the door, while Spark stood near the forge with mixed feelings. She'd be able to stretch out in her bed, no more rumours to worry about. But it would be far too quiet. He would make a point of not talking to her for a few days, perhaps as much as a week. Feed the rumours. Lovers' quarrel. Then he'd be friendly again.

Neither of them had spoken to Ember, and Jatt thought staging a fight would help in that regard.

That left a lot of empty days ahead of her, nothing but Nandara's lessons to fill the silence. There were plenty of people in the village she was friendly with, but no one she really much trusted.

She wondered if she should be more forthright with Nandara. Until coming to this valley, she'd been more trusting with her mentor. Befriending Jatt had changed the dynamic in subtle ways.

So Jatt stormed out, heading home after repairing things with his granddad, peace that was likely brokered by Nandara. Spark bent over the worktable, spreading out a couple of spellbooks and her notes.

Her head ached and her stomach was sour and grumbly when Nandara came in for her evening lesson. Spark blinked into the evening gloom and wondered where the day had gone. Had she fallen asleep? She couldn't remember getting through much work.

"Everything okay?" Nandara asked.

Spark shrugged. It was most definitely not okay, but she scarcely knew where to begin. Hadn't thought to ask Jatt where his grandmother stood on all these new problems Spark suddenly had.

"I know Jatt was here quite a bit and... Did something happen?"

Spark opened her mouth to go with the rehearsed story Jatt came up with. She closed it, scowled at the worktable. Nandara deserved better. And if Spark couldn't trust her, then who could she trust?

Spark shook her head. "Nothing happened. I'm just tired. He wants people to think something happened to feed gossip. You know how he loves his gossip, even if it's about him."

Nandara smiled and nodded, but Spark noted how the smile didn't reach her eyes. Somehow she'd given the wrong answer. So she asked about the day's lesson. Nandara pulled a book out of her bag and started going over it, something about terramancy. Spark sagged.

"All right," Nandara said. "Let's talk about the demons. About possession." She set the book aside.

Spark sat up straighter and opened her mouth to respond but Nandara kept going.

"We're repeating the same mistakes all over again, and I'm not watching you vanish into yourself the way your mother did. I'm not failing you the way I failed her."

Spark snapped her mouth shut and blinked.

"I'm not sure you can do it safely, Mita. In the end, it's what brought your mother her doom. That said, our overcaution drove Neesha to practicing dangerous things unsupervised. I don't know if I can help you, but I can at least be here to keep you safe." She tapped her fingers against her spellbook before meeting Spark's eyes. "I haven't told Ondias that I'll help you. I know she still thinks you shouldn't explore this. I know you will regardless."

"So... You'll help me?"

Nandara sighed. "I don't know how much help I can be, but I'll do what I can. We can talk about what your mother tried, how she practiced. I'd like it if you stopped using demon possession when you're alone. And I know you think it's your last option, but I strongly encourage you to rethink it."

"But Mamma stopped the flood."

"She did. But look at all that's happened since. There was a hope of keeping Pasdale from turning on the dragons if your mother had been awake to tell her story and demonstrate without question what she could do. But the demons she called wrought havoc and that was all anyone remembered."

"She was unprepared and not exactly in the best health. Trying to fight that battle hours after I was born couldn't have helped."

"Mita, you're not listening." Nandara's tone sharpened. "You've only seen demons under controlled circumstances, but they are horrifyingly dangerous. When your mother released them into flooded Pasdale, they burned away the water, yes. But that's not all they burned. Whole neighbourhoods burned. People were incinerated where they stood. Or half incinerated, dying in agony with parts of them reduced to ash, sometimes from the inside out."

Spark's mouth went dry.

"I know you want to protect those you love, just as Neesha did. But you must understand the risks. And not just the risk to yourself."

Spark nodded slowly. "Demons truly need to be my last resort. What of fire portals? And can you advise the safest way to use demons, if that's what it comes to?"

Nandara was quiet for a long time. "There's one thing I want to see, before I agree to anything else, all right? Before we go any further, I want to be sure I can push a demon out of you safely and back into the fire realm without harm to you."

"You want me to do a demon possession now?"

Nandara sighed. She got up and stood near the forge, Spark joining her.

"I've mentioned before that I think Dionelle forced Neesha out of herself right along with that demon at the end, so I want to do this slowly and carefully. I want to force the demon out first and make sure you're still you before I send it away."

Spark was suddenly more hesitant to call a demon than she'd ever been. And also deeply relieved to have Nandara here and on her side. She nodded slowly and summoned a demon, familiar again.

"Is it possible to keep calling the same demon every time?" Spark glanced at Nandara.

Nandara didn't take her eyes off the demon when answering. "I've never heard of it, but your power is unprecedented so we can't rule it out."

"Do you think it's more or less dangerous if I've worked with this demon before?"

Nandara bit her lips. "My instinct is that it's more dangerous. It could be testing your weaknesses, looking for a way to gain control. If you think you've done a possession with this one before, then call another while I hold this one."

"Okay, I'll call another."

Nandara took over, hissing fiery commands at the first demon while Spark called another. This one's energy felt different, new. And as soon as it was out of the flame, Nandara stuffed the first one back into its realm.

"Are you ready?" Spark asked.

"I'm not sure I ever will be, but go ahead."

Spark invited the demon in, holding fast against the euphoric heat threatening to undo her. Nandara's horrified expression helped keep her focused.

"I'm okay, I've got it."

"I'm going to push it out of you now."

Spark didn't have time to react, pain erupted inside her like she was being torn to pieces, like her mind was being seared. She couldn't even scream.

And then it was over. Spark pitched forward, hands braced on her knees and breathing heavily while the demon struggled against Nandara's spellcraft.

"Mita?"

"I'm okay."

"What are the names of your uncles in Baymouth Shores?"

Panting, Spark bent her head to meet Nandara's gaze, momentarily forgetting she still had uncles. She blinked. Nandara went pale.

"Cusec and Bly," Spark said, and Nandara's colour returned. The demon immediately vanished back into its realm.

"All right, Mita. If you're up to it, I'd like to try that again, but this time I want you to let the demon take control. We'll have to time it closely so that—"

"No." Spark shook her head vehemently, thinking of the searing, ripping sensation. She relayed it to Nandara and her expression fell.

"I'm going to bring this to the Grand Chancellor, all right? And we do need to practice it with the demon in control if you're to successfully use this in battle, but I want to do it with more high level elementals present."

"Not Ondias."

Nandara gave her a reproachful look. "Ondias is a competent wizard, and she cares for you even if she's forgotten the best ways to express that care. But I think I'd like to find some higher level elementals. Maybe pyromancers specifically. Maybe even Abyss to help with it. You've given me a lot to think about. For the remainder of tonight, your normal lessons." She opened her spellbook.

Spark huffed and bent over the work, only half paying attention to Nandara's lecture on different terramantic strategies based on the element's consistency. The memories of cold grit on her soul weren't enough to drive out echoes of the sundering pain of the recent possession, how certain it made her that Nanny had accidently ripped Neesha out of herself. Was there any way to keep the same thing from happening to her? Would she have to give up on possession? But then there was the possibility they could find out how to safely separate her from the demon. And if they could do that, maybe they could help Neesha?

After Nandara left, Spark went back to her notes, trying to make sense of what she'd done through the day. But the evening's revelations hadn't done anything to help with her inability to concentrate. Her focus shifted to making weapons people could use from inside dragon slings. She had some basic ideas for launching venom and was trying to work out how to make a crossbow that could be fired from a moving dragon with enough power to damage enemy dragons.

It was well into the night by the time Spark had some workable diagrams. When so much of what she was doing needed to be done in secret, she was left trying to work from models, rather than making any full-sized weapons. But she might have an answer to the crossbow problem.

Spark twitched back one of her curtains to see that one of the moons had already set and the other would soon dip behind the mountains. It was later than she thought. She dimmed the fire and put out her lanterns. As she pulled on her bed robes, a scrape came at the door.

Shadow was asleep by her bed.

Spark launched herself to the door and threw it open. In the dim light, it didn't look like anyone was there. She had to strain to see Abyss at all.

"Secrecy," the dragoness grumbled, her words coming out in a whispery gust of wind, skipping the pleasantries. Ondias was right, Spark was wearing off on her.

"Mistress?"

Abyss stuffed something large and soft through the front door, piling it at Spark's feet, the great bulk of it pushing her back into the room. Spark gasped.

"Truly?"

"Secrecy," Abyss repeated.

"Bleeding moons, this is a full hide!" Spark struggled to keep her voice as conspiratorially quiet as Abyss's.

Spark didn't know how she'd keep it out of sight, but she pulled it deeper into her home, running her hands over the soft expanse as she did. She allowed a little more firelight to see by, stunned by the beautiful quality of the skin. The dragon it belonged to had been silvery grey with large black spots. Judging by the endless swatch of it threatening to fill her whole house, it was likely from a dragoness.

"You've spirited this off from somewhere. So I assume your superiors don't know."

Abyss remained silent and still. It was answer enough.

"Did the dragoness this belonged to consent to this sort of thing?"

"Long ago."

"Well, yes. It's been ages since anyone has cured dragon skin. I don't even want to know where you got this."

Abyss grinned her horrible gleaming grin.

"So, just to be clear, you are giving me permission to use this one skin, of a comrade of yours with that comrade's permission but not the permission of your superiors?"

Abyss nodded.

"And you want me to make dragon armour with it."

Another fractional nod.

"And then what? What are we going to do with it? A demonstration for your superiors to show them their folly?"

Abyss tilted her head and waited. Spark was close. But she hated these guessing games.

"You don't mean to go after those ice dragons again, do you?"

Abyss snorted and bared that awful grin again.

"We'll need more than just armour. I'll need at least a week. Are there any others coming with us?"

A fractional shake of the head.

"I'll make armour for both you and your mate, just in case. I assume if you have any ally at all, it will be him."

Abyss pressed her nose into the doorway to nuzzle Spark.

"Once I have everything I think we'll need, I will summon you in the night."

Without another word, Abyss melted into the darkness beyond Spark's door. Spark tried not to be giddy with relief, but couldn't stop thinking how she wouldn't have to risk it all like her mother had—especially now that she had a better idea of exactly what that meant. To keep her mind busy, she immediately went to work shaping the skin into smaller pieces she could more easily hide, stashing most of it under her bed and folding the rest into crates and cupboards. If only she could use the workshop, where she had the space. But she couldn't deny Abyss's request for secrecy.

When Jatt appeared at her door with his easel and paints at the end of an exhausting week, Spark was not nearly as pleased to see him as she should have been. It was morning, for starters, and she'd been sound asleep when he knocked, having only fallen asleep two hours before.

"You've taken this a little too far." He grinned. "Shutting yourself away from everyone was genius, but for the whole week? Come on now, no one believes you're that fragile."

"Can you come back after lunch?" she asked.

"You don't want to know how it went? The performance was spot on! Gran had new rumours for me every single day! People have mostly lost interest now. Ember's been weird, even for Ember. She's getting all the attention at the moment."

"Weird?" Spark stood straighter.

Jatt pressed his lips together and pushed into her house, closing the door behind him.

"Sorry, I guess I shouldn't have brought it up, considering…"

"What?"

"She's been getting drunk in the apprentice pub every night the last four. Flirting with everyone. Like some girl with her vapours running hot."

Spark closed her eyes and held a deep breath for a moment before letting it out slowly.

"So… she's trying to make *me* jealous now?"

"Seems like it."

"I thought you were going to talk to her."

"I tried," he said. "She tried to hit me with one of her father's big jugs of wine the instant I got too close. Didn't even get any words out."

Spark swore.

"I'm sorry. I'll keep trying, once she's had more time to calm down."

Spark crawled into bed without another word.

"What's going on with you?" he asked.

"Busy. Tired."

She pulled the blankets around herself and fell asleep almost instantly. Jatt was still there when she woke up, having taken up residence in his little corner near the foot of her bed, busy working on some painting. He'd opened the curtains on the other side of the room, and the low angle of the light told her it was late afternoon.

She gave him side-eye. "You stayed here all day while I slept?"

"Why not? You didn't ask me to leave."

Spark carefully pulled some bread out of the pantry, not wanting any of the bits of dragon armour in there to tumble out. It was not going to go well with him there. She'd been working later and later into the night, sleeping through the day and starting work in the evening. With him around until nearly a normal bedtime hour, she'd have that much less time to work. Her work time ended in the dead of night, out in the field near the workshop as she fitted Abyss in utter darkness.

Spark had finished the armour for Abyss and now worked on some for Zephyr. It was fumbling and difficult in the cramped space, working in the dark, and without Ember's expertise to guide her. This armour was a seamstress's work, not that of a blacksmith.

It worked out that Spark had been able to use all of the black pieces from the skin and only a few of the silver to make the armour for Abyss. It wouldn't do much to affect her stealth. The remaining pieces were all varying degrees of silver and grey, and that was what Spark would use for Zephyr. It would help him blend in to cloudier skies, and she was saving the palest pieces to cover his chest.

There would be plenty left over, enough for Spark to make some new armour for herself. A suit she could fly in, one with a removable lining to keep her warmer. That bit of dragon skin was stuffed in her pantry with the bread and other sundries. There was so much work left before she could finish anything with enchantments. It was that, or make new tools, and she didn't have the time to test for that.

Abyss's armour, the only thing she'd finished, was stored in a lockbox in the workshop.

But working on it with Jatt around would be tricky. She wished he'd stayed away longer.

"So you're going to barge in here like nothing's happened?" she asked.

"That was the plan. Because nothing *has* happened."

"But that's not what everyone thinks. It makes it weird."

"I told you, Spark, they don't care anymore. Long mouths and short memories. You trying to get rid of me?"

She almost said yes. But she missed having an extra set of hands around, and there were plenty of components of the armour he could help her with that wouldn't lead to him seeing the dragon skin itself—as long as he didn't peek under her bed.

"No, it's just weird. And I've been doing most of my work through the night."

"So I've heard. What are you up to?"

Spark gave him a warning look. He held his hands up in surrender.

Once he turned his full attention to his work, Spark got dressed and pulled out the crate of weapons she'd been working on. She was focusing on things for battle, including a compact crossbow with dragon-piercing bolts. She'd have to aim for key places for it to do any good—eyes and wings, mostly. It was better than nothing. And she'd enchanted her battle-axe too.

Those two weapons were all she could think of that would be any good against a normal dragon. Against the ice dragons, fire was the best weapon, and she had no problems with that. She'd been working less with demons, although she called one into her when she went to work with Abyss two nights ago, despite her promise to Nandara. The dragoness had been watchful, but it had helped Spark learn more control of the creature.

Spark got back to work, Jatt doing the same, both of them working in the same bubble of comfortable silence she'd missed. He didn't pay any attention to her work until she asked him for some help. Then he had a glance at her plans.

"It's getting real, isn't it?" he asked.

"Loch knows I'm here. It won't be long until they bring the fight to us."

"And that's what you're up all night working on? Weapons?"

"And more armour."

"You really think the leather will hold up?"

"The enchantment is strong. It'll have to do."

Just like that, he was only minimally interested, back to helping her where she asked for it and staying engrossed in his own work otherwise. Spark let her guard down enough that two days later she worked on her dragon skin suit while he was around. Fed him a line about it being old burlap that went strange when she experimented on it with the same enchantment as the leather armour. He'd stabbed his shoulders into a shrug and gone back to his mound of clay.

Jatt was packing up for the evening, and Spark slipped her pieces of dragon skin into the pantry, meaning to follow him out for some fresh air before she settled in for a long night of work. The early spring air held the right amount of chill to wake her up without being uncomfortable.

She'd just shut the pantry door when he came up next to her.

"I'm not a fool, Spark," he whispered. "You should keep it for the middle of the night, just in case."

She tried to cut him to pieces with her glare.

"Hey, I assume you got it from Abyss, and she must know what she's doing." He held his hands up. "I'm not going to tell anyone what you're up to. I assume you've got a plan?"

She nodded slowly.

"Good. It'll be grand. I look forward to the results."

He continued packing up while Spark watched him, searching through his words for any sign of treachery. He liked gossip, sure, but only to a point. If anyone around her was going to be a problem when it came to her secret projects, it was Ember.

Spark pulled the pieces of a new sword closer to her and assessed the quality, planning her evening's work. Jatt was right, the dragon skin had to wait until the village slept.

When someone started pounding on the door, Jatt nearly dropped his supplies. Spark's sword clattered down onto the tabletop. Having just been thinking of Ember, Spark wondered if the girl had decided to come shout at Spark some more.

But it was not a furious Ember barging into the room when Spark unlocked the door.

"What madness are you getting into now?" Ondias snapped, going straight to the worktable to rifle through the pieces.

"Weapons," Spark said immediately. No point lying when Ondias held pieces that weren't a secret. "Things people can use against the ice dragons."

"Oh, you should see this one." Jatt pushed between the two women to pull a long tube from the clutter at the back of the table. "I helped her put it together. It's a marvel!"

Before Ondias could snipe at them, Jatt loaded in one of the little glass orbs Spark filled with water. He took aim at the blaze in the forge and then fired the little weapon. The ball of water zoomed into the forge and exploded against the brick, the water inside hissing as it evaporated.

"In a battle, it'll be filled with dragon venom," Jatt went on. "The tube's got a little spring in it, we've got to calibrate it for more—"

"Enough!" Ondias snatched the pipe from his hands. She looked down at it, shaking her head. "More toys?"

"The venom burns for a long time," Spark said. "Against the ice dragons—"

Ondias shook her head. "You don't have time for this nonsense. My contact in Pasdale just sent a message. The ice dragons have left. It's time. At best we have five days."

Jatt and Spark fell silent and exchanged a troubled glance.

"I don't know what foolishness you've been up to in the dead of night, with the dragoness flying off just before dawn, but you must take this seriously."

Spark swallowed and nodded, for once unable to argue with Ondias, even if her accusations were baseless. She'd have to be more careful. Abyss wouldn't be around tonight, and Spark wouldn't need her again until it was time to set out. That would have to be soon, regardless of what Ondias said.

CHAPTER TWENTY-FOUR

Spark methodically went through her gear while she had a rare moment alone in the workshop. She'd got a half-normal night's sleep and was out through the day, but had to be ready. She'd summon Abyss after midnight and needed to be sure she had everything. And in case others wanted to join them, she was going to leave Zephyr's armour and sling, both finished and properly enchanted.

But she couldn't let anyone know what she was up to, so she kept pausing to look over her shoulder, making sure she was alone.

"Okay, I've got a blanket and waterskin. But how much food?"

It was two days' flight to the ocean, and she and Abyss agreed that they wouldn't fly beyond the shore, wouldn't go past the desert as they awaited the ice dragons' approach. Maybe she should bring only water and let Abyss help her hunt in the wild?

A great cry rose up from the east. The dragons had been active for nearly two days since Ondias had come with her dark tidings. Spark had seen bolstered patrols heading east in rounds all day, each one noisier than the last.

She ignored it and set weapons out on the long workbench between two forges. These would be for others to use. She hoped they never needed them. After stuffing her gear and the armour into the lockbox, Spark turned to the little glass balls full of flint and dragon venom that Abyss had been volunteering. Spark had emptied three jars' worth on making the little weapons but still had two more jars at home. The launchers had been easy enough, once she got the hang of them. The trick was in the springs.

Since Ondias's warning of an impending attack, Spark had made over a dozen launchers, which she lined up along the worktable with the other weapons. There were carefully packed crates full of the venom balls. These were not a secret. Spark had shown a few of the villagers how they worked and left instructions with them, just in case. Everyone expected she'd be with the dragons when the battle came, and Nandara commented on her foresight in making sure others could use her weapons.

It was true Spark would be with the dragons, but not the way they all anticipated.

She pulled out the final crate of venom balls when Jatt burst in.

"Spark! You've got to come!"

He was breathing hard, a thin sheen of sweat on his face. He must have run the whole way. She set the crate aside and dashed after him, the cacophony of dragon cries worse than anything she'd ever heard. It was mournful, like the death cry, and dangerous and angry like when Abyss fought those dragons upon first bringing Spark to the valley. Spark's legs went rubbery. It was like she was back in Pasdale about to lose everything all over again.

"What the bleeding moons is going on?" she gasped, trying to change her focus.

"Gran thought the battle was here, but I heard Ondias say something about it not being the right kind of cry."

Spark stopped and looked up at the dragon city, glimmering orange in the light of the setting sun, where a colossal blaze of dragons was headed inside. The innermost dragons of the group supported a dazzling white dragoness.

"Come on!" Jatt called.

She chased after him, following him all the way to Nandara's where Ondias had gone. Spark headed inside, but Jatt caught her arm on the doorstep.

"They forced me out," he whispered and motioned for her to follow him around the side of the house. A window stood open on the warm spring day, voices whispering out on the breeze. He leaned against the wall next to it, and Spark did the same, each of them on either side.

"Mortally wounded, are you certain?" Nandara said.

"I can't see why they would lie," Ondias said, defensive as always. "And I told you it wasn't a battle cry. It's more. She's dying."

"So what happens? Surely they have contingencies."

"You know how arrogant they are. They have no emergency plans for the death of the Dragoness Superior. Even if the other six can decide on which of the three minor Superiors will replace her, it takes them weeks to choose from their second tier for the new dragoness to fill out the seventh role. If they're divided at all, they need that final Superior in order to make any decisions."

The silence that followed drew on forever, and Spark tried to make sense of the words.

"So there will be a power struggle, now, with enemy dragons on our doorstep," Nandara said.

Spark and Jatt looked across the span of the window at each other, both with eyes wide as moons. He ducked under the window and took her hand, pulling her away, all the way back to her house.

"Whatever you've got planned, you better get to it," he said.

"I was supposed to go with Abyss tonight, under cover of darkness. We were going to go out and meet the ice dragons head on. Not scouting, but to fight them to the end."

"Ondias was right, that is madness." But he was smiling. "Doesn't look like anyone will stop you if you go now."

Spark nodded slowly. "But should I take Abyss away from this? I don't know enough about their tiers, but I know she's mistress superior of the fourth rank and maybe she can help restore order?"

"Guess it doesn't hurt to ask her."

Dragons swirled around the city, a kaleidoscope of awe. As she headed out to the field, Spark spotted the bright blue speck of Zephyr, but there was no dark shard of Abyss. She could be biding her time against one of the obsidian columns, waiting and watching as she so often did.

"I'll have to summon her then."

"She's not there," Nandara said softly, coming from between two buildings.

"How can you tell?"

Nandara came closer and laid a hand on Spark's shoulder. Her face was pinched up, like she was in pain.

"Ondias was just in contact with an emissary from the city," Nandara said, her voice hollow. "The Dragoness Superior has died, succumbed to injuries she suffered on patrol. She was able to tell them what happened before they lost her. She was in a patrol blaze with Abyss and others. Two other dragons were injured, one fallen at the site of battle and they're uncertain if he'll survive. Abyss was taken by the ice dragons."

Spark was running before she realized it, blazing toward the field where Ondias took counsel with the dragons. Her thoughts spiralled. Her heart slammed icy blood through her veins. Her stomach plummeted with the weight and cold of a glacier. Spark thought she'd vomit ice at any moment. The emissary, a bright teal and amethyst male, scratched with one claw in the bare earth that covered the patch of field where Ondias conversed with the dragons. A shorthand the creatures devised to communicate with the woman.

"We have to get her back!" Spark shouted the instant she spotted Ondias. "We can't let them bring her to Pasdale, they'll kill her!"

She barely reached the edge of the field when the emissary, enraged by the interruption, speared Spark with a blast of fire. But she shunted it around her, parting it like she had the wheat in Pappy's fields as a child. She was barely aware of doing it and kept moving forward.

"Mita, now is not the time to get yourself killed."

"We have to stop them! We have to get Abyss back."

Ondias seethed, but there was sadness and fear in her eyes, softening her tone, ever so slightly, when she spoke. "We have bigger worries right now."

"It doesn't take all of them to pick a new Superior." Spark didn't know much about their hierarchy, but she remembered that much from Ondias's lessons. "I just need a blaze, no more than ten. The blue one, her mate, he can carry me. All males to catch up to them, and we can get her back."

"We've had enough loss," Ondias said tersely.

"You know I never stopped practicing with demons. I can melt those ice dragons right out of the sky."

"There are more than just ice dragons."

"And I've made armour for the dragons. Not just the leathers that will blunt most strikes. There's armour made of dragon skin. Abyss brought it to me to work, anticipating this day."

The emissary had been tolerating the interruption to this point, but he snarled and ducked his head forward, teeth snapping at Spark. Her stomach dropped into her feet and she fell out of the way, while Ondias shouted something incomprehensible and got between girl and dragon. Spark scrambled to her feet and further away.

"Enough, Mita. You've done more than enough for one day. How could you be so foolish? Go now, and mourn the loss, then prepare for the battle to come. No more insults, not today. They've got too much work to do to worry about your trivialities."

Spark bit back her angry response when the emissary glared at her. She whirled away and stormed home, hot tears snaking down her cheeks. Her whole body shook as she went to the fire and performed the summoning, a bright column of fire and magic whooshing up the chimney, like Nandara taught her, but calling for Zephyr. He was already dropping away from the city toward her house when she went outside.

Spark ground her teeth together, trying to collect her thoughts as Zephyr approached. He didn't have quite the disregard for the usual formalities that Abyss had, and Spark would have to watch what she said. She greeted him accordingly.

"I apologize for taking you away from your kin in this time of need." She bowed her head. "I grieve with you. Not just the loss to your kind, but the loss to you personally."

He bowed his head forward, nuzzling her with his soft snout.

"I believe I can help her," Spark said. "I have been working with demons. I can wield their power, just as my mother did in the battle of Pasdale. I just need a dragon willing to carry me after them."

He shook his head immediately.

"She's your mate!" Spark snapped.

He nudged her with his snout, this time unkindly. He extended one talon, drawing an oval in the dirt at her feet. He looked from the drawing, to her, to the city in the sky. Had he meant to draw an egg?

"Your young?"

He nodded. Then he looked from her to the east and back before dashing out the image he'd drawn. Spark closed her eyes and forced air into her tightening chest.

"I think I understand. Do what you must."

She managed to wait until he'd flown off before she started sobbing. Staggering inside, she could barely breathe through the tears and collapsed into her bed. Shadow returned and curled up against her legs, but she barely took note. Her door clicked shut, and only then did she claw out of the void of despair, lifting her head. Jatt had come in, his arms folded across his bony chest.

"You left it open," he said, sheepish. He sat next to Shadow and rested a hand on Spark's side. "I'm sorry. I wish there was something I could do."

"If I could open a portal to the fire realm, maybe I could follow them."

"You'd really go after her on your own, wouldn't you?"

Spark shifted to look at him.

"Right," he muttered.

"I can't do nothing. I can't. I did nothing when they came for my family. I won't go through that again."

"But what can you do?"

Spark shook her head and lay on her bed. Silently, she turned to face the wall and pretended to fall asleep until Jatt left. After the door clicked shut again and the crunch of his footfalls retreated, she swung her legs off the bed and pushed to standing. She packed a few provisions and left them by the door. She changed into her new dragon skin flight suit and got back into bed, for real this time. It was dark, but only just. She would take a few fitful hours of sleep, with no idea when she'd rest again.

Spark gobbled down her meal, barely tasting it, before strapping on her chestplate and picking up her bag. She took off Nanny's pendant and held it in her hand—it felt heavier than normal, the light dimmer somehow. She sighed and set it on the workbench. Shadow was curled up at the foot of her bed and watched her curiously, but didn't get up as she left. The door was unlocked, so someone would find him in the morning—there'd be no shortage of people to barge in.

There were a few lights on in windows, but most people had gone to sleep, so it was easy for Spark to slink through the shadows and out to the workshop. She strapped on her waterskin, wearing it on her front. She would bring only water and what food would fit in her pockets. The rest of her strength would be devoted to carrying the massive pack formed by Abyss's armour. She had it bound up in her sling, which was turned inside out so she could strap herself into the harness and carry it all on her back.

Her journey would be precarious, but this was the only way. If she could somehow reach Abyss and the ice dragons, there was no doubt they would have to fight their way out. She would not leave the armour behind.

Spark leaned into the large pack and got her arms into the harness. The door to the workshop clicked shut, and she squirmed out of the pack and spun toward the sound.

"I knew you were up to something," Ember said. "Working straight through all those nights and then changing your schedule all over again today." Her tone was triumphant.

"You've been watching me?"

"Noticing." Ember tried to be indifferent. "I've had plenty to keep me busy through the night too." This she aimed at Spark like a dart.

"Ember, I know what you think—"

"Oh, I'm sure Jatt's been keeping you up to speed."

Spark sighed. "I don't have time for this."

"No, I suppose not. When did I become so unimportant?"

"You've never been unimportant. Ember, you said it yourself: I was foolish and I didn't see. I do now, and we have so much to talk about. But right now Abyss's life is in danger. That trumps everything. If you're not going to help me with this sling, please just go home."

Ember strode right up to Spark, holding up her lantern. Spark smelled the wine on her.

"Demon's fury, you've been working with dragon skin." This was an accusation. "And you've done some sloppy work."

A smile flickered across Spark's face. "You can criticize my needlework all you want when my best friend's life isn't in jeopardy."

Spark tried to turn away but Ember caught her shoulder.

"That's unsanctioned work!"

"More than you know. I've enchanted it to withstand a dragon strike. I mean to come back, and when I do, we'll do all the shouting you want. But I need to go."

"No way. Does Ondias know about this? Shall I fetch her?"

"Ember, you've had too much drink. You're only hurting yourself with this. And there's no point in trying to talk about anything when you don't want to listen. Go home, sleep it off. Tell Ondias all you want in the morning."

"Oh, I don't think so." Ember raised her voice.

Spark worried someone would hear her and come snooping. She needed to get away cleanly.

"I'd hate for Ondias to find out about your work," Ember shouted, her head turned toward the village.

Spark didn't think about what she was doing. When Ember turned, still shouting about Ondias, Spark grabbed a tube from the worktable, like the other launchers, but smaller and with a reservoir instead of loaded glass balls. She leaned closer and Ember paused, head tilted and lips parted, watching her. Spark aimed the launcher right in her face. It sprayed a diluted solution of dragon venom all over her, some of it getting in her open mouth. It was too diluted to burn but potent enough to incapacitate.

"I'm so sorry," Spark whispered as Ember's dark eyes grew wide.

Spark dropped the launcher onto the table and rushed forward to catch the lantern as it fell from Ember's hand, then Ember herself. Bracing the other girl, Spark set the lantern down on the floor and then got both arms around Ember, carefully bringing her over to where the soft armour meant for Zephyr was heaped. Spark lowered Ember onto it.

"You'll be all right," she said. "This is temporary. It's frozen you, you'll fall asleep soon, but it won't hurt you. When you wake up in the morning, tell Ondias all you like. Tell her I've got to get Abyss. If I don't come back, then I want you to know how sorry I am about all of this, how much I care for you."

Spark leaned forward and kissed Ember's cheek. Ember glared at her, but already her eyes were going unfocused and glassy. Spark draped all the forge aprons over Ember to help keep her warm through the cool spring night.

Then she struggled into the harness and left, heading into the forest and toward the southern pass. She had to get out of the valley and east.

CHAPTER TWENTY-FIVE

Mid-afternoon and partway through the pass, Spark began to understand the gravity of her error as sweat poured over her brow and her back ached. Still, she was helpless against the need to keep going, to find Abyss. She could see out into the rest of the mountains from where she was, and understood why so few humans chose to make the journey by foot. There was no road, but anyone brave (or stupid) enough could hike into the valley. The trail was nothing more than a narrow footpath over rock, often winding along cliff edges and gullies.

Normally, there were sentries near the pass, but when Spark looked back she saw them all around the city and the clan towers along the edges of the valley. Still in turmoil, still unprepared for impending attack. But out to the east there was, at least for now, no sign of other dragons. Of enemy dragons.

To keep her concentration, Spark counted through all the ways this was foolishness, suicide. From the absurdly large pack, which grew impossibly heavy, to the lack of climbing gear, she was ill-prepared to survive a trek through the mountains. The large pack she wore affected her balance as badly as the lack of sleep and food. She drank sparingly, knowing it would be some time before she reached the riverside to refill her skin. And how long would it take her to get even as far as the end of the Red Mountains? A week? A month?

She tried not to look at the river far below, silvery in the light, nothing more than a ribbon at the bottom of the canyon it carved between mountains over the aeons. It was pure good fortune that Spark hadn't reached the pass until daybreak. She would have certainly died trying to navigate it in the dark.

Going through the forest toward the southern pass, Spark had used flame to guide her, but little more than a candle's worth. Just enough to keep from tripping over anything. Now that she was on the mountainside, she realized how far ahead she needed to see to plan a careful route in the places where she was doing more climbing than hiking.

Feeling suddenly dizzy, Spark halted and leaned the pack into the rockface beside her. She popped the end off her waterskin and drank deeper than she had since starting this foolish trek. She waited for the dizziness to pass, but her knees buckled and she lurched forward.

Spark pinwheeled her arms, desperate to regain her balance, but the pack pressed her down. She staggered, trying to compensate, and her feet hit some gravel over the stone. She slid. Landed on her ass hard enough for her teeth to click together. Then she careened right over the edge.

And stopped. Dangling by the harness from the pack. Her feet hung out over nothing, a fatal drop to the river far, far below. She twisted to see how she was still alive at all, but couldn't see much for the pack. She assumed it snagged on something.

Spark grit her teeth.

"Come on, you fool, there's got to be a way out of this."

Craning her neck, Spark tried to see what her predicament was. But she had to be cautious, not wanting to shift the only thing keeping her alive. If she was careful, she might be able to unhook herself from the harness and climb the pack to safety. Of course, she was more likely to unhook herself and plummet to her death. The cliff wall was uneven, so she was sure she'd slam off the rocks and bounce around a good bit before what was left of her ever made it to the water.

But what else could she do? It could be days before the dragons re-established old routines and any sentries came out this way. If she hadn't fallen to her death, the elements were sure to take her in that time.

"What have I gotten myself into?" The urge to laugh rose up behind the words, and she held her breath until it passed. She swallowed a scream and breathed carefully through encroaching tears until that too had passed.

It was too soon for despair and panic. There had to be a way out.

If she could fly, she wouldn't be having this issue. Even if there was something remotely safe for her to drop down onto and climb back up, that would be a vast improvement. If there was a raging inferno instead of a river beneath her, that would also improve her chances. Especially if she could open a fire portal.

She could make her own fire, of course, but wasn't sure she had the energy to pull a fire out of the air *and* open a portal in it. Getting the portal right on the first try would be a miracle. From the fire realm, she could open a portal to any fire anywhere. She could go back to the village, or straight to Abyss. Or even back to Pasdale.

She'd have to practice. But was there time? She held still, but how long would she remain snagged?

Nandara hadn't had the time to talk to Spark more about where Neesha had gone wrong. Spark was even more hesitant to use demons, but there were more possibilities in fire portals.

So she called a small blaze into the palm of her hand and focused her will. She'd summoned so many fire demons it had become routine. In that time, she'd noticed a similar sensation of hot energy flaring right before each appeared. She concentrated on that, on recreating that in her hand.

On going deep into the fire and finding its true source.

The fire in her hand flared, each attempt doing *something*. Nothing she tried actually opened a portal. She growled in frustration and rubbed her hands over her face.

Something above her snapped and she dropped a fraction. She gasped in a breath and squeezed her eyes shut, desperate to stop the way the motion had caused her legs to swing out over nothing.

Over the rush of her pulse in her ears, she didn't hear wings beating the air or notice a shadow fall over her. At least she took notice when her pack moved and she was jerked upward by the harness. The pack was too big to see around, but a flash of cerulean wing in the periphery put her at ease.

"It's about time!"

"Honestly, Spark, how have they not eaten you yet?" Nandara called from above her.

The knot in Spark's chest unravelled, and she breathed easier for the first time since learning Abyss had been taken. In a few moments, Zephyr lowered her to the valley floor on the other side of the pass, a journey that would have taken her until dark on her own (assuming she'd survived). He wore the armour she'd left out, with Nandara tucked into the sling. The woman was bundled up well, including a pair of goggles and a scarf wrapped around her face. Spark burst into a grin.

There were five other dragons with them: one crimson, one orange, one grey, one green with black markings, and one spotted fuchsia and white. They were all male, and two carried humans in the leather slings Spark had crafted. Jatt flew with the grey dragon, and the orange one carried Stone.

If it was possible for Spark to pale anymore, she would have. What on earth could Stone possibly be doing here after what Spark had done to Ember? And seeing Jatt was a surprise too. He hadn't seemed especially keen on being part of the danger. But there was no time for questions. Spark unlatched her harness and quickly secured her pack between the sling and Zephyr's body, then pulled on her mask and squeezed into the sling with Nandara.

The dragons wasted no time getting back into the air and resuming their pursuit.

As they rushed after the ice dragons, Nandara filled Spark in on everything she'd missed, how this blaze of dragons coming to her aid had been possible. Ember made plenty of noise upon waking before dawn, going straight to Ondias, just as she'd threatened. By then Spark was far enough out they couldn't easily pursue, and all of Spark's plans had been uncovered.

It took most of the day to convince the Superiors that Spark couldn't be left on her own, and that Abyss must be rescued. In the end, one of the lower-ranking Superiors, the deep crimson dragon, volunteered to come along so that in his absence the dragon council would have odd numbers. Decisions had been made quickly after that. Some dragons had been appointed, others, like Zephyr volunteered, and each dragon willing to wear a sling had been strapped in. The dragons carrying humans were formerly from the Pasdale blaze.

"But why bring Jatt?" Spark asked. "Ondias could have come instead."

"Ondias needs to stay in the city. She's the best person to work with the dragons. These dragons are going to do as they like without consulting us. We're just here for the ride."

"Can we catch the ice dragons in time?" Spark asked.

"We think so. The ice dragons have a head start by a full day, but they'll be dragging Abyss, and she will do everything she can to slow them down. We hope to catch them before they reach the ocean, but it means flying at top speed with little rest."

Little rest for the dragons, but Spark welcomed the opportunity to nap. She shook, and not from the cold. The fall had taken a lot out of her, but so had her failed efforts to open a fire portal. But despite her exhaustion, Spark found it difficult to calm her mind enough to sleep much. She couldn't stop thinking about Abyss.

Long after dark, the dragons descended into a valley, led by the Superior. Once the dragons were unstrapped from the slings, the humans gathered in a loose circle between Zephyr and the Superior. Spark took the opportunity to thank them properly for saving her and for coming on the rescue mission.

"What of your young?" she asked Zephyr.

He glanced at the Superior. All of the dragons remained still.

"He's convinced one of the remaining Dragoness Superiors to treat them as her own until we return," Nandara said. She looked up at the red Superior. "It was a generous act and will be greatly appreciated. I know that your interactions with us have been quite limited, and I suggest, for simplicity, that perhaps your blue companion act as your emissary and converse with Spark as ours. They are already familiar with each other."

Spark hadn't considered the necessity of it. She hadn't ever interacted with the Superiors before. She was so used to freely interacting with Abyss and Zephyr that she didn't even think of any kind of hierarchy.

The dragons were all silent. A tense moment stretched out before them. The dragons glanced at each other. There were some low grumblings—not quite words, not quite growling. The red Superior stretched his wings and flew up into the surrounding mountains. The other dragons followed, leaving only Zephyr with the humans.

"What just happened?" Spark asked.

"They've agreed to let him act as their voice," Nandara said. "We'll leave you to it." Nandara took Jatt and Stone to the edge of the field they were in, spreading out what supplies they had to take some rest.

Zephyr settled in with his chin on the ground, and his glittering black eyes fixed on Spark.

"I wish they hadn't come," she said quietly, looking the way the other humans went. "I appreciate the company, but I worry for their safety. We need to do what we can to keep them safe."

Zephyr snorted in agreement.

"Tomorrow, I'll ride with you and Nandara again. Tomorrow and for as many days as it takes to catch up to the ice dragons. I'm sure you and your kin already have battle plans. I think it best we stay out of the way until we get to Abyss. Then I want you to get as close to her as you can. Whatever they're doing to restrain her, I'll go in and get her free and give her the armour I brought. I'm glad the Superiors have let you wear some too. I'll use fire on the ice dragons. I might be able to open a fire portal, and I'll use demons if I have to."

Zephyr had been watching her closely as she spoke, not moving, but he tilted his head.

"I think I almost had it today before you plucked me from the mountainside. I'll try it again if it looks like we need it."

He gave a slight nod.

"All right, I'll take stock of what they've got and advise them, but we'll keep out of your way. Do you know what we're dealing with? Have the Superiors sent scouts ahead of us?"

Zephyr nodded.

"Good. So it's a matter of waiting now. How awful."

Zephyr grinned, his rows of teeth gleaming in the moons' light. He curled in on himself and tucked his wings in.

Spark left him and approached the three humans, who were hunkered down around the little fire.

"Everything in order?" Nandara asked.

"Yes. Really, we need to stay out of their way until we get to Abyss. I'll do what I can to set her free, if it's more complicated than one of our dragons just swooping in and scattering her captors. Once we get her free and into the armour I brought, she'll help even the odds plenty."

"How long have you been planning this, then?" Stone asked her.

"What are you even doing here?" she blurted.

He chuckled. "I promised your mother."

"I froze your daughter."

"Aye, and she was plenty cross with you, let me tell you." His eyes twinkled in the low firelight. "But no harm done, and she was being plenty foolish herself."

Spark's cheeks warmed. "I've been planning this since the winter. Not this specifically, but something similar. The last week has been frantic, since Abyss brought me dragon skin I could make armour out of."

"It had better work, or she might be better off with whatever fate awaits her in Pasdale," Nandara said. "The Superiors aren't pleased that she went against their wishes."

"But they're using it."

"Practicality. They'll use it for now. But they are angry."

Spark looked at the scant gear they had with them. A waterskin each, some food, a bedroll and some of Spark's weapons.

"The launchers are going to be your best bet if we get into battle with the dragons," Spark said. "But you'll need to concentrate your shots. Have you tested them?"

"Yes, quite clever." Nandara smiled.

"Normal dragons, shoot for the eyes or mouth. If you get them in the eyes, it will temporarily blind them. If you can get enough in their mouths, well, it'll have the same effect it had on Ember."

"And for ice dragons we should do the same?" Stone asked. "Or wings if we can hit them?"

"Yes. If you get enough venom fires going on their wings, it will melt them off and they'll fall out of battle. It's not much, but every bit helps." Spark stood and yawned. "Now I'm going to go join him," she nodded toward Zephyr, "and get some rest."

Spark's body thrummed with anticipation. She was ashamed of what she'd done to Ember and didn't really want to be around Stone. She leaned against Zephyr, under one of his wings, and he didn't even stir to acknowledge her presence. But he was like lying against a blast furnace, and she welcomed the warmth after the cold air of flight.

She'd settled in, pulling some of the dragon skin armour loose from the pack and tucking it around her, when Jatt sat beside her. He brought his small pack with him and sat next to her, leaning against Zephyr too. Nandara watched them, a look of approval on her face.

"You and Stone are about the last people I'd expect to be here."

"Gran made me come, said it's my punishment for keeping your plans to myself," Jatt said. "And of course, since I've helped you so much, I know more about your weapons than the others. I dunno, though. I think Gran's taking those stupid rumours to heart."

Spark glanced at him. "Does she know about what you told me before?"

"Yeah. She thinks I'll grow out of it, I guess. And she doesn't know about you at all."

"Oh."

Jatt stabbed the air with his shoulders. "Get some rest. We're going to need it."

CHAPTER TWENTY-SIX

Despite her mask, Spark could barely see the landscape rushing past far below. Next to her, Nandara strained against the harness, trying to press herself down into the bottom of the sling where it was warmer and the rush of air more tolerable. The desert rushing past baked like a forge, but not a trace of its heat reached them where they flew.

The red Superior flew ahead of them, gliding closer to the sand where he would blend in better. The other dragons were behind them, also flying lower. Zephyr was higher than he needed to be, using the sky's camouflage to its maximum effect.

It was how he helped Spark and Abyss against the ice dragons the first time. An eternity ago.

Spark didn't like how the land kept disappearing beneath them without any sign of their quarry. The desert was vast but would give way to plains before long, then the marshes, then the ocean. Loch had the water demons on his side, and Spark knew the dangers of trying to follow his ice dragons across the ocean. So she kept her gaze fixed on the horizon, watching and worrying, waiting for the line of shimmering blue to appear.

But long before they reached the marshes, something else appeared. Two dark blotches, solid against the heat shimmer in the distance.

"Scouts," Nandara said. "Theirs."

They closed in enough to see the markings of the dragons. They were dull coloured, dirty—slave dragons from Pasdale. They didn't appear to notice they were being pursued. The Superior closed in on them, and Zephyr raced to match pace.

Spark pulled out her battle-axe. But Nandara pressed the weapon down into the sling.

"We mustn't harm those dragons. Ondias has convinced the Superiors they be kept alive to see if we can heal them, make them free and wild again."

Spark looked out ahead of them. These dragons, or ones like them, helped kill the Dragoness Superior and took Abyss. She didn't think sparing them would lead to anything good.

"If we don't at least try, what's the point in liberating Pasdale?" Nandara continued. "They have to know if it can be done."

Spark grumbled wordlessly but secured the weapon. She pulled up one of the spare launchers Nandara packed and watched as the two scout dragons drew nearer. One of them spotted the blaze bearing down on them, igniting a cacophony of dragon cries.

The two scouts veered off in opposite directions.

The Superior and half the blaze seamlessly broke off to the north, while Zephyr and the other two peeled south after the second scout.

The other two dragons, the green-black one and Stone's orange one, swooped to flank the scout, while Zephyr sliced into a ferocious dive, attacking straight on. Spark felt like her stomach had been thrust up into her head as the rest of her went cold. She struggled to breathe against the tightness in her chest.

The dusty green scout stopped snarling and snapping at the green-black and orange dragons, and rolled in mid-flight to receive Zephyr's attack, talons extended. Nandara screamed and shrank deeper into the sling while Spark pulled her mask secure and gripped her launcher. The scout's talons scrabbled at Zephyr's underbelly. Spark dodged them before Zephyr's sweeping attack drew onward.

With her stomach firmly back where it belonged, Spark took a deep breath and got ready. The scout's face came into view, snapping toward the sling. Spark fired the launcher. A venom ball smashed and ignited against the scout's chin. Flames rose into his eyes, startling him. He fell away as Zephyr pitched skyward into a flip to come around for a second attack.

Spark turned against the forces of flight in order to get a good look at Zephyr. A long, shallow gash in his side ended where the silvery armour began.

Nandara looked too. She glanced at Spark and nodded.

Zephyr pulled out of the loop and the scout came into view, spiralling toward the ground with the other two dragons latched on to either side. They banked out of the spiral, leaving the scout to plunge into the dunes below, a great plume of red dust billowing around the impact.

Zephyr followed him down, crashing onto the scout and letting the fallen dragon take the brunt of the dive.

As the red dust settled, Spark saw they were in a nest of talons and cried out as talons ripped toward them. Screaming, Nandara ducked into the sling. Spark wasn't quick enough, taking a hit to the chest. The world exploded in pain and searing white light. A loud buzz drowned out the sound of dragon battle as Zephyr banked away.

When the blinding pain eased enough for Spark to see, she ran her hands over the tender spot on her torso, below her right breast where her metal armour over the dragon skin was dented. She expected blood and bone, but found soft silk covering her.

Nandara's hands worked quickly, pulling away armour and dragon skin and the shirt Spark wore beneath. An ugly purple bruise already welled up around the injury. But no gash.

"You'll have broken bones."

Spark struggled for each ragged breath. Speaking hurt far too much for Spark to agree. Zephyr had landed, and the green-black male held down the little green scout. The other two examined Zephyr's superficial wounds. They had some of their own, with scrapes on their leathers, but no real injuries.

The red Superior returned with the fuchsia dragon. Jatt returned with the grey dragon, who dragged the dusty white and yellow-spotted scout. Both scouts had numerous lashes bleeding into the drifting sand. Nothing looked even as bad as the wounds Abyss previously survived. Once they were all on the ground, Spark stumbled in the sand while Nandara helped her. Jubilant, Jatt and Stone rushed over wearing smiles that fell when they saw Spark's state.

"She okay?" Jatt asked.

"We need to get her to Lina." Nandara pressed her lips into a tight line.

"No!" Spark wheezed. "Get Abyss."

"If your ribs aren't broken, I'll eat my own house," Nandara said.

"Aye," Stone agreed. "They're broken, sure enough. How much does it hurt?"

Spark told him while he ran his fingers over the bruise.

"Wrap some cloth tight around her middle," Stone said to Nandara. "Come on, boy."

Stone took Jatt and Spark's warped chestplate and disappeared over a ridge. Nandara bound strips she cut from her bedroll around Spark's ribs. This made it harder to breathe but kept the pain constant, making it easier to bear the stabbing agony ripping through her.

When Stone returned, the dent in her armour had been crudely beaten out. She'd need to work on a better job tempering it if they survived this.

"You won't take another direct hit like that," he warned. "You certain you don't want to turn back?"

Spark scowled.

"Stone, don't encourage this," Nandara snapped. "It's Neesha all over again."

"Aye, it is. She's every bit as stubborn as any Joasera woman ever was. You try to make her go back, she'll walk this desert on her own. Tell me I'm wrong."

"Abyss." Spark left no room for argument. She struggled into her armour, metal and dragon skin alike, and lurched toward Zephyr while Nandara and Stone shouted at each other.

Jatt jogged up to her side. "You sure about this? Getting killed isn't going to help Abyss."

"Hurt isn't dead. We go."

Zephyr and the other dragons loomed over the injured scouts. They were also arguing with each other, judging by all the hissing and snapping. She cleared her throat as loudly as she could, and Zephyr came away and leaned down to her.

"Prisoners need guards," he said, his voice the sound of lava rumbling through a vent.

Spark blinked. "You talk now too?"

Zephyr narrowed his eyes.

"Guards?" she asked. "How many?"

"Two."

"Leaves us four on four, or worse. Bad odds."

"Um…" Jatt stepped closer. "We came this far, seems wrong to turn back." He nodded toward the injured dragons, who had been bound in makeshift restraints from bits of chain and strapping. More of Spark's handiwork, but not much of it.

"Those dragons aren't going far on their own, even if they're not bound. Why not leave just one guard with them?" he asked. "We can get them on our way back. We can't be more than half a day behind. And if we're successful, we've got Abyss to help us with them."

Zephyr tilted his head.

Jatt and Spark exchanged a glance. "We go," she insisted.

"Spark's hurt, but not too hurt for magic, and that's what we need her for," Jatt said. "The four of us," he gestured to the humans, "are close enough to equal another dragon. If I hadn't got the venom in that yellow one's face, the battle wouldn't have been over nearly so quick. We can help. If we leave one dragon here with the scouts, we have good odds still, even if the ice dragons have more help."

Spark nodded, glad Jatt understood what she wanted but was too injured to say.

Zephyr returned to the other dragons. Another hissing argument ensued, and the Superior glared at Spark for long enough she was certain he was going to come eat her where she stood. But then he growled at the fuchsia dragon, one of the two not wearing a sling. That dragon nudged the yellow scout closer to the green, and then perched menacingly on top of them both.

Nandara and Stone joined the group, Nandara fussing over Spark but clearly swayed by something Stone had said to her. They all helped get Spark into the sling. Then they were back in pursuit, one battle behind them and one ahead.

CHAPTER
TWENTY-SEVEN

The plan was simple. Zephyr would get in close—with his armour he had the best chance—and he and Spark would free Abyss. If they could get Abyss into armour safely, they would, and Spark would fly with her. In any case, once they freed her, they would have that much more power in the fight. Then they would destroy the ice dragons.

As they flew over the marshes and the blaze of ice dragons came into view, Spark wished they'd had some backup plans. There were four ice dragons, one of them a large dragoness, with two more slave dragons with them. The male ice dragons carried Abyss in something that sparkled in the late day sun. The ice dragoness flew between them and the approaching blaze from the dragon city.

Zephyr was far above, granted some measure of camouflage by the bright sky, but the fast approaching sunset would soon put an end to it. The nearer they got to the enemy dragons, the more Zephyr angled them farther into the sky. Nandara pressed her lips together. The three of them had a dragon's-eye view of the unfolding battle.

The Superior was a crimson blot against the shimmering green marshland, and the ice dragons were nearly lost against the reflection off the patches of glassy water. But Abyss stood out like a dark shard. Zephyr circled above as the ice dragons turned to meet the attack. None of them looked overhead. Zephyr circled twice more, all the dragons clashing together in flashes of fire, except for the ice dragoness, who remained with Abyss, circling above her.

Spark heard the cries of battle even from their great distance.

Zephyr angled in, his wide circle tightening into a spiral as he picked up speed. Nandara crouched deeper into the sling, trying to protect herself against the crush of wind. Spark pulled down her mask and pressed against Zephyr, letting the air wash over her.

Zephyr gained speed and straightened his dive, shooting silently out of the sky like a dart.

Spark's heart vibrated in her chest as the rush of wind stole the air from her lungs despite the mask. The ground raced up to meet them. Adrenaline thrummed hot through her veins. She wanted to scream. Nandara had her eyes squeezed shut and her hands crammed against her mouth, suppressing a scream of her own.

When they were an instant away from colliding with the ice dragoness, Zephyr gave voice to a mighty roar and rained fire upon her. Steam billowed where fire met ice. Shrieking, the dragoness twisted to meet Zephyr's attack.

Spark couldn't see what happened for all the steam, but they suddenly fell away from the pair of dragonesses and spun wildly.

Zephyr, unable to control the fall, flipped in midair and the change of force pulled Spark, who was not strapped in, out of the sling. Nandara caught one of her legs as she went.

"I've got you!"

Nandara slowed Spark enough she could grab hold of some of the sling's rigging. The sudden movement slammed a spike of agony through Spark's ribs. She nearly let go, but Nandara still held her. Spark managed enough shallow breathing to compose herself, but Zephyr remained out of control.

His wing was encased in solid ice.

Trying to ignore the stomach-flipping spin of marsh-sky-marsh-sky, Spark concentrated on the wing and with shaking hands sent a pulse of fire toward it. It was larger than she intended, vaporizing the ice immediately. Zephyr arched both wings out, catching the air like a sheet on a line, stabilizing the fall. Spark was torn from the rigging, but Zephyr snatched her out of the air as he pulled them skyward.

They'd come close enough to crashing that Spark smelled the stagnant water. As they came up and around the edge of battle, the orange dragon carrying Stone sloshed up out of the muck, blasting ice off one of his wing tips.

"They must breathe ice the way our dragons breathe fire," Nandara said. "And they know what they're doing. We can't get close enough for fire to work on them. Look!"

The Superior was knocked from his course by ice to the wings. He melted it before he fell far, but it was enough to disrupt his attack.

"We can put up fire screens," Spark said. "Use fire from our dragons, use pyromancy to drive it beyond its normal range. You focus on our dragon, I'll focus on the Superior. Maybe we can get them close enough."

Spark called her plan to Zephyr. He banked closer to the Superior. Spark poured all of her will into drawing out the Superior's fire, flaring it beyond reason, ballooning it to shroud one of the ice dragons. Nandara did the same. Spark pushed the dragonfire out further and further, fragmenting it in different directions to lash any bit of ice that came into view.

It looked like it might work.

But the slave dragons moved in from either side to attack Zephyr and the Superior. Their diving attacks broke Nandara's concentration. The Superior stopped breathing flame to battle the dragon who could not be harmed by it.

Before either Spark or Nandara could use launchers to help Zephyr, the slave dragon dropped away from him.

These dragons fought more ferociously than the scouts they'd faced earlier. And they didn't have to win, merely disrupt the attacks.

Spark called up to Zephyr to make another run for Abyss. He angled upward, circling to find an opening. But now that the ice dragoness knew he was there, she remained between him and Abyss. He would dive and spiral, but couldn't get close enough for a successful attack. She was waiting with gouts of ice.

"Jatt!" Nandara screamed.

Spark followed her gaze to see Jatt's grey dragon mostly encased in ice. It plummeted earthward. Jatt was lost beneath the thick film of frost.

Spark's blood ran cold, like glaciers creeped through her veins. She called fire to her hands, used a precision cut of fire, like she would to meld two pieces of metal. She lanced it straight for the grey dragon, a touch to the right of where Jatt was imprisoned in the sling.

The ice erupted into a plume of steam. Dragon and rider disappeared into the marsh. Spark couldn't tell if she'd successfully blasted away the ice.

Nandara whimpered, watching the point where Jatt and the dragon disappeared in the water. Spark placed a shaking hand on her shoulder but noticed frost on the woman's eyelashes and in the hair that poked out of the scarf around her face. The sling and most of Spark's clothing were covered in hoarfrost.

The grey dragon hadn't reappeared, and the Superior was recovering from another iced wing. None of them got close enough to do any real damage to the ice dragons. Spark couldn't use any significant pyromancy without endangering Nandara.

They couldn't keep this up much longer.

The grey dragon crawled from the muck, but his wing hung at a bad angle. It was unclear if Jatt was okay.

The green-black dragon plunged into the water, encased in ice. And an ice dragon got close enough to put Zephyr back in a spin that Spark had to frantically contain, melting his wing free.

She gasped, each breath burning agony. Her damaged ribs wouldn't allow anything deeper. There didn't seem to be enough air anymore.

As Zephyr climbed above the battle, Spark caught sight of Abyss. Her aching chest tightened. The two of them held each other's gaze for a moment before Zephyr carried Spark out of range.

Whatever the ice dragons were using to restrain Abyss, they had it wrapped around her snout so she couldn't use fire. Spark bunched her hands into fists and her rage flared hotter than her pain.

"Get me over Abyss! Close as you can!"

Zephyr circled above, high enough to be out of range of the ice being shot at them. Spark, very carefully, climbed out of the sling, gripping it from the outside. She had one arm twined in a strap so she could put less focus on falling to her doom. When Zephyr plunged toward the pair of dragonesses, Nandara clasped hold of Spark's arms, helping to keep her from flying away.

"Don't let me fall."

She needed to call fire, just enough. After weeks of practice, she knew exactly the minimum amount of fire she could use. And she did it now.

"Spark, no!"

But Spark had control of the demon she'd called, keeping its attention on her and not Nandara. She only needed to hold it a moment longer. When the ice dragoness came up to meet Zephyr's attack, Spark directed it her way.

The hissing fire demon erupted into the sky, expanding like a scorching storm to control its descent, a blinding inferno. It engulfed the ice dragoness's face like a shroud. She screamed and fell away, leaving trails of steam.

Two ice dragons held the tethers restraining Abyss. A third dived toward Zephyr. But Spark held that little flame in her hand. She called another demon, watched it stretch toward the dragons, hissing, but still tethered to the blaze in her palm.

Letting go of the sling, she flung herself out over Abyss an instant before Zephyr swooped past her. With her heart pounding, each beat a stab to her ribs, Spark held the air, suspended for a moment, the demon with her like she gripped a flaming bouquet.

Then she dropped.

Holding her breath and braced for it, Spark slammed feet first into Abyss's back, above her wing. Her legs absorbed most of the impact, but searing pain jolted through her broken ribs. She stumbled, listing to the left, facing the murky water far, far below. Cold buzzed across her skin and in her ears. Abyss twisted in her restraints, Spark listed the other way, her right hand gripping for purchase.

It closed around a tether, only to draw back in pain. A vast net made of ice held Abyss. Pure ice so cold it burned.

The new demon she'd called broke loose on landing, but remained behind her, its fires pulsing toward each swooping dragon. The ice dragon closed in on them, and Spark hissed a crackling command, drawing the demon's attention to it. The demon took care of the rest.

The ice dragon had no time to cry out. Flame devoured it in an instant, raining water and gushing steam

Stars danced across Spark's vision. Her ears buzzed like all the world's bees clouded around her head. It hurt even more to breathe.

She had to free Abyss. It had to be now.

She pulled one more fire out of the air—the size didn't matter—just concentrating on the flame. Remembering the agony of Nandara forcing the demon out of her in practice—and not having the chance to try with the demon in control—Spark couldn't rely on possession. She began calling a demon and stopped, following the path they normally took when they came to her.

The fire in her hands grew. Its intensity burned her eyes even as she averted her gaze. She'd never seen fire like this before.

"I've got you!" she called to Abyss.

She ripped more heat from the blaze, it coursed through her. The heat numbed her aching ribs. Digging deep into the light, she let more and more flow through her until she saw nothing else.

Abyss flexed beneath her, air rushing past, but Spark kept drawing fire. It was bottomless. She would unleash it all, evaporate the whole of the marshes if it meant ending the ice dragons.

The whole world became nothing but heat and light. Like Spark had fallen into the sun. Exhilarating as it was, Spark couldn't remember ever feeling so tired before. She fell deeper into that light. Part of her panicking mind thought of Neesha and urged Spark to fight, that it was enough fire, that she needed to stop. Falling was bad.

But she was so tired.

And then a slice of midnight pierced through the blazing light. This—this felt right. Darkness was for rest and sleep. She plunged into it.

CHAPTER TWENTY-EIGHT

It was the pain that woke Spark up and let her know she was still alive. She tried to talk but it felt like her mouth was full of wool and sand. Opening her eyes was like dragging hot metal shavings over her pupils. So she kept them closed and groaned. It seemed like the best plan.

"Hush now, everything's all right," Lina crooned.

That was a good start. Either Lina had found the courage to fly in a dragon sling, or Spark was home. Lina went on to report all of Spark's injuries, the severest of which was the broken ribs. But she had burns on her hands, presumably from the ice net she'd clung to in order to keep from slipping off Abyss.

"Once you think you can open your eyes and talk to me about what you're feeling, I'll have a better idea of how you're doing."

Spark groaned more.

Lina cradled Spark's head with one arm, sending a throb of agony through Spark's head, and then tipped some water into her dry, woolly mouth.

"Is that better?"

Spark croaked out something meant to be a no.

Lina chuckled and patted her arm. "You just need more rest."

Spark heard the smile in her voice. Rest sounded like an excellent idea.

When she woke again, she was pretty sure it would stick this time and got her eyes open enough to see that she was at home and in her bed, Shadow curled up at her feet. Lina was there, sitting at the work table.

"What happened?" Spark managed.

"I think my mother is waiting to tell you that." Spark didn't like the sound of that. "But without giving you any details, I can say that everyone made it home safely."

"Jatt?" she wheezed. "Abyss?"

"Yes. Everyone."

Spark burst into tears.

Ondias trailed along behind Spark, rattling off all the ways Spark had been foolish, careless, reckless. Spark didn't care. Ondias had already rattled off the list of ways Spark had been successful. For now, that was all that mattered.

Spark, or more accurately the demons she unleashed and that Nandara had been left to drive away, had badly wounded the ice dragoness and outright killed one of the ice dragons. Whatever madness of fire Spark summoned to melt away Abyss's restraints had been plenty successful and had wounded the other two ice dragons.

Between their injuries and Abyss free to wreak havoc, the ice dragons swiftly retreated. Zephyr had scooped unconscious Spark from Abyss and rushed her back to the dragon city.

That was nearly a week ago.

Jatt, Nandara and Stone returned days later, after more dragons were dispatched to help with the four captive dragons and the injured grey dragon. The slave dragons had been liberated and sent to the plains in the south to be healed with the captured scouts.

Spark was well enough to walk, and she marched out to the field between the edge of the village and her workshop. Hearing the words was one thing, but Spark had to see with her own eyes. She stood in the field, a beacon of white against the green, and craned her stiff neck up toward the sky. She picked out the shard of obsidian as it broke away from the blaze of dragons circling the city and landed in front of her.

Ondias called warnings from the edge of the field. Spark ignored her and darted to Abyss. As the dragoness lay her chin on the ground, Spark leapt at her and threw her arms across her friend's snout. Spark wept, her tears evaporating quickly against the dragoness's hot skin.

"You're going to break another rib or puncture a lung if you don't get more rest," Ondias called.

It was Abyss who answered, huffing a gust of hot air at the woman, knocking her back a step. Spark buried her face against Abyss's smooth, soft skin and listened to Ondias's retreating footsteps. Something warm rubbed soothingly against Spark's back, and she glanced over her shoulder to see Abyss had raised one careful talon in a delicate embrace.

Spark wept more.

"You saved me, didn't you?" she asked. "From that light. I don't know what it was, but it wanted to eat me. It was you that pulled me out."

Abyss pressed Spark tighter against her. It was all the answer she needed.

"Spark," Nandara said softly from somewhere near the edge of the field.

Spark patted Abyss on the tip of her nose before going to Nandara. Abyss came forward as well, leaning her chin on the ground next to the pair of tiny humans.

"That light," Nandara said. "You really don't know what it was?"

Spark shook her head.

"You did well out there."

"You wouldn't know it to hear Ondias talk."

"Ondias wasn't there to see what I saw or feel what I felt of your power. What you did with the demons was a foolish risk, but you held it all in check. Right until the end. That light... I think you opened a fire portal. It's been so long since I last saw it done—since your mother did it. I wasn't sure. I'm still not sure."

Nandara looked to Abyss.

"Yes." The dragoness's voice was soft and deep like a gentle tremor in the earth.

"Then you're lucky," Nandara said.

"I don't even know what I did. I was so angry about them keeping Abyss in those burning cold nets."

"Rage and desperation helped Neesha open a fire portal for the first time."

"And then she learned to control it, right?"

"Yes." Nandara watched Spark thoughtfully. "Trying to keep your mother from her full potential didn't do us any good, and keeping you from yours is certainly not helping anything."

"Are... you going to keep teaching me to use this safely?"

"I'm going to explore if there *is* a safe way first, but I think it's time we stop being afraid of how your power might go wrong and start preparing for how it can go right." Nandara turned to Abyss. "What do you think, old friend? If Spark agrees to stop practicing dangerous magic in secret, we'll guide her in it not-so-secretly?"

Abyss grinned her dreadful grin and Spark hugged her snout again.

Nandara let out a long breath. "Did Ondias give you the good news?"

"About Jatt and the others?"

"There's more. But I'm sure she'd want to leave that out until she was done lecturing you." Nandara smiled fondly. "That armour of yours really made a difference. The dragons in leathers fared the worst. One's armour was shredded completely, but he would have been killed without it. And the dragon skin the blue dragon wore saved him a dozen times over. He was able to take incalculable risks."

"I knew it would work. We tested a patch of it before I started for real." Spark glanced at Abyss, whose mouth was upturned.

"Yes, well, that part still has plenty of dragons feeling sour. But there's no denying the effectiveness. A new Dragoness Superior still needs to be elected, but once she has been, it looks like you will be granted sanction to work with dragon skin. For the purpose of armour only, you understand."

Spark stood taller and let out a low whistle. "That's incredible!"

"You both knew that testing it would help sway them."

"They could accept the armour and still choose to punish us."

"Yes, that's true. But there won't be any punishment for this, foolish as your actions were. Since you were successful, you're now considered innovative. Ondias hates that part."

Spark chuckled.

"But there's also talk, once there's a new Dragoness Superior, of Abyss being elevated to the third rank. She'd be the first dragoness admitted to that rank without live hatchlings."

Spark looked to Abyss. The dragoness was still, but her bottomless eyes glittered.

"Maybe they should just elect you Dragoness Superior now and get it over with."

Abyss snorted and Spark laughed.

"This will set Loch back, but it won't deter him," Nandara said, caution in her tone.

"It gives us more time to prepare. More armour to be made. Maybe even train some people in using those launchers and flying in the slings."

Nandara smiled. "But maybe first you can take a bit more rest?"

Jatt stopped by briefly, and it pained Spark to see him go, especially with his arm in a sling. As much a deterrent as it would be to his art in the short term, at least he still had his life. Spark regretted she hadn't done more to ensure that no one had come home injured. He'd been quick to remind her that at least everyone came home. It didn't stop her from feeling guilty.

Spark didn't mind having her place to herself, though she enjoyed Jatt's company. Lina wasn't coming in to check on her anymore, as long as she wasn't out getting into trouble. But for now, Spark was content taking all that rest everyone insisted she needed. She left her door ajar to invite visitors along with the warm spring air. So far, she had received the expected guests: Stone and Jatt and Nandara. Abyss peeked in through the windows and door a time or two.

She'd fallen asleep sprawled out on her back and awoke at the sound of the door clicking shut. Groggy and slow, she lifted her head and sat up quickly when Ember threw the lock. Fumbling, Spark pushed herself to sitting and swung her feet to the stone floor. Her chest hummed and she couldn't quite tell if it was fear or excitement. And why pick one anyway?

"Ember..." But what else could she say? Every thought that presented itself sounded stupid. She wanted to apologize, but she'd done nothing wrong. She wanted to be angry, but Ember's actions were based on misunderstanding. And really, she was just happy to see Ember—as long as she didn't start shouting.

Ember sat at the worktable but looked sideways at the smouldering fire in the forge.

"I talked to Jatt. Had a long conversation that made me want to break his other damned arm." Ember scowled at Spark. "I mean, how was I supposed to know how cursedly naïve you are?"

Spark cleared her throat to speak but didn't have a sodding clue what to say.

"I'm sorry I froze you with venom," she blurted.

One side of Ember's mouth pulled up out of the scowl.

"I guess I deserved that. I know how much you love Abyss, and I never should have tried to stop you. I was just..."

"You were hurt."

Ember cocked her head on one side and gave her a look. "I was still acting like a child."

"Once Jatt explained it all to me, I understood why."

Ember's voice was soft, breaking with tears glistening in her eyes. "Everything's a mess."

"It doesn't have to be."

Spark closed her eyes, tilting her head back. She breathed deep, no idea where to go from here. Ember looked at the forge, rivulets of tears coursing down her cheeks. Spark stood in front of Ember and took her hands, rubbing her thumbs over Ember's knuckles.

"Am I to understand you wish for me to be your lover?" Spark asked quietly, her tight throat trying to strangle the words.

"Yes." Ember's response was immediate, spoken in a breathless whisper. A slow smile spread across Ember's face, sunshine pushing through a long rainstorm.

Spark's pulse raced and her stomach fluttered. She traced her fingers up Ember's arm and over her shoulder, her gaze taking in the soft lines and smooth curves. Gently, Spark pressed her fingertips to Ember's jawline and drew her face in close.

Ember's gentle lips met Spark's briefly. They were hot like fire and dry like parchment but soft like nothing Spark had ever felt before. It stirred

Spark's stomach to fluttering and sent a tingling thrill down her body, like when the fire demons touched her. She could barely breathe.

Ember wrapped her arms around Spark's shoulders. Spark relished the soft, green scent of her, the silky feel of her hair, the warm pressure of their bodies pressed together. She pulled back and looked into Ember's dark eyes. Spark touched Ember's cheek and ran her fingers through her dark hair.

Maybe it would be all right after all.

"You sure you don't want to come with us?" Spark asked Jatt.

"I definitely want to keep my feet on the ground until all my parts work properly again," he said.

He picked up his paintbrush, holding it awkwardly, lips pursed together. He practiced brushstrokes on a piece of parchment on the easel in his little corner of her home. A worktable for Ember crowded into the corner on the other side of the room.

Ember leaned closer to his painting and sniffed. "You're improving. It's worthy of a nursery now."

Jatt brandished the paint brush at her and she hopped away. He'd painted a green streak across her face the last time she'd commented on his left-handed attempts. Of course, that time she'd said it was worthy of fire-starter. Her laugh was light, like music.

"We'll probably be gone an hour or so," Spark said. "Will you still be here when we get back?"

He stabbed at the air with his shoulders. "I don't know where else I'd be."

"See you later, then."

Ember skipped along and gripped Spark's hand, practically running out to the workshop. They both took up the rigging of Abyss's sling and brought it to the field, spreading it out in the grass. Abyss wasn't long in joining them, drifting lightly down to the ground. The pair got the dragoness buckled into the straps. Spark helped Ember into the harness, squeezing in beside her, like she had with Nandara.

This would be a much different flight.

"We're ready," Spark called to Abyss.

Ember shrieked in delight as Abyss pumped her wings and the ground fell away. Abyss flew lazily, but the air rushed around them, rustling their clothes and whipping Ember's hair around her face. The dragoness flew around the outside of the city, taking them up close and climbing skyward around its exterior. Ember's eyes shone like the diamond columns they passed, though she couldn't stop giggling nervously.

"How have I lived here all my life and never seen it like this?" Ember's voice was barely a whisper as she took in the glittering Red Mountains and the village as a small dot on the valley floor stretching out far below.

Spark took her hand and nestled in closer. It didn't matter how many times Abyss brought her up into the sky, Spark always felt the same sense of wonder that Ember felt now. But as Abyss glided past Neesha's diamond resting place, Spark's stomach tightened. She pressed one hand over her chest, Nanny's pendant against her palm.

Ember squeezed her other hand.

"You'll figure it out," Ember said. "Your ma and your nan. There's time yet."

Spark wasn't so certain, not after the battle with the ice dragons. There hadn't been any word from Ondias's sources in Pasdale, but no doubt there would be retaliation. Spark worried for Nanny and missed her all the more, ached for the mother she'd never known.

But then Ember nudged her nose against Spark's cheek and kissed her jaw. The cold ache eased and Spark smiled. She had family again, though it looked like nothing she'd ever imagined, with Abyss and Ember, Jatt and Nandara, and even Ondias in her abrasive but loving way.

There was always room for more. She glanced down at Neesha one last time before letting Abyss carry them out over the mountains.

Scan here or visit thodestool.ca/news to learn more about Vanessa's work or to sign up for her newsletter.

FIREBOUND: FIREBORN SERIES BOOK FOUR

A SNEAK PEEK

PROLOGUE

I t was the perfect day to go flying—bright and clear with strong thermals—so Void Behind the Stars struggled to hold her patience as the small human spidered across her shoulders to check the new handholds on that side. She supposed Spark wasn't actually small as far as humans went but didn't know how else to think of her when she easily fit in Void Behind the Stars' hand.

The carrier's rigging grew more elaborate with the girl's desperation. And she'd already checked the handholds once today and likely a dozen times before getting all of the straps around Void Behind the Stars. It always felt excessive and also like no amount of checking could be enough. They'd come to the unspoken agreement that the accident would remain unspoken. It was certainly the worst humiliation Void Behind the Stars had suffered, left in the nursery with her eggs afterward through her recovery like some misbegotten hatchling.

Spark growled. "This just isn't working."

Void Behind the Stars turned her attention away from the dazzling light display of sunshine off the city to watch Spark fiddle with the tiny apparatus on the end of the tether meant to keep Spark from falling to her doom. The contraption appeared to work perfectly. The tether was securely attached to the handholds, unlike her last attempt—a simple hook that had cast her out into the skies the first time Void Behind the Stars had changed course during flight.

"It's too slow." Spark got it detached and tossed it, a long arc to the grass below. She rubbed her hands over her face. "I might as well not leave the sling at all."

While Void Behind the Stars was not used to the sensation of being crawled on—and the other dragons believed she was debasing herself by submitting to the girl's machinations (fools, the whole lot of them)—she conceded that it would be a clear benefit for Spark to have freedom of movement during a battle. There were other dragons, four blazes in total, with close relationships with humans like Void Behind the Stars had with the fireborn women. The dragons and humans fought together as one with similar rigging that enhanced their battle prowess. Void Behind the Stars and Merciless Winter Sky worked seamlessly together, rarely leaving the other exposed, but they had been outnumbered as of late. The girl's sharp eyes and sharper spells filled the gaps.

It would, of course, be lovely if it didn't matter whether the girl had sharp eyes and sharp spells, that there was no impending threat, no stolen dragon eggs, no imprisoned family and friends. Long years of many troubles left most dragons with little time to fly for pleasure—for the enjoyment of the cold wind over scales and a warm lift under wings, the wisp of clouds and the hard light of the sun.

It was worse now. Loch knew with certainty that Spark was alive and a threat. She had embarrassed him.

The Superiors agreed that the attack would come and very likely before the snows closed the passes and froze the water he loved to menace them with. So every last dragon in the valley not busy caring for young was out scouting or hunting. Void Behind the Stars and Merciless Winter Sky got a small measure of reprieve by being favoured by the fireborn girl. Their success with the armour meant Void Behind the Stars and her mate had more time to remain in the valley to assist her.

And when they did leave, they did as much scavenging as scouting or hunting, clawing through abandoned human settlements searching for scraps of metal for Spark to build new weapons and more rigging. Void Behind the Stars ferried Spark in the supply wagon every time a new caravan came to the plains in the south to trade for metal.

The girl had tentatively asked Void Behind the Stars one day about a moon cycle ago whether the sparkling red mountains surrounding them had ore that might be suitable to her needs. Void Behind the Stars had held her anger then, and wished someone who knew the depth of the girl's offense had been around to see it.

"These mountains are sacred," she had said gravely.

Spark had not brought it up again.

Though with distance and time Void Behind the Stars saw that ore from these mountains would make the most dazzling weaponry. Cursed and blasphemous weaponry, but dazzling all the same.

It was bad enough wearing her dear friend Winter Storm's skin as armour. Even worse that she was now helping the Superiors convince others to donate their flesh after they returned to the starbursts in the sky on their deaths.

"Would it be okay…" Spark began and hesitated, standing on Void Behind the Stars' shoulder near the base of her neck. "Would it be okay if I stand on your head?"

Void Behind the Stars once again begged for an understanding witness to her patience. She did not immediately flick the insolent little beast off her shoulder. In fact, she didn't respond at all. Void Behind the Stars had already abandoned all sense of dignity by agreeing to the carrier, and so she continued to stare at the city arching overhead, its supports spanning the valley, casting pinpricks of light across the drab human residences and the glittering mountains alike.

"Thank you, Mistress," Spark whispered.

While Spark was still terrible at anticipating when she was about to ask something unbearably rude, she was at least getting better at realizing when she'd done so.

While the girl's clambering about Void Behind the Stars' back tickled and itched, her journey up Void Behind the Stars' neck to the spot between her vast horns—more than twice the girl's height—was particularly disconcerting. Spark stood there for only a moment before Void Behind the Stars looked up, inadvertently tilting her head to one side as if that would give her a better view.

Spark shrieked as she fell away, arms pinwheeling to catch onto something.

Void Behind the Stars easily caught her and set her back on one shoulder. Spark muttered her thanks and continued her checks, a little spider-puppy crawling around and dangling off Void Behind the Stars' side to check more of her work. Up and down the handholds, hanging her entire weight off of each one and swinging to truly test their stability.

Like most humans, Spark had such clever little hands to go with her sharp spells and sharp eyes. And it was a true failing of so many of the other dragons to not see that about humans. To not envision the opportunity there. They saw humanity's capacity for art, of course, but there were less frivolous reasons to keep the species around.

Many of Spark's tools were foolish, but some of them had already saved dragon lives.

Spark walked the length of Void Behind the Stars' back and turned around, muttering to herself, asking questions she didn't expect Void Behind the Stars to answer and thinking out loud. Calculations for expanding the rigging, it sounded like. She nattered frequently—nearly constantly—and the grief driving it was what stayed Void Behind the Stars' frustration with the girl.

Void Behind the Stars knew what Spark had lost. What they'd both lost.

Void Behind the Stars' gaze shifted to the glimmering diamond support column in the west where Neesha dreamed and didn't age, sustained by magic Void Behind the Stars was still learning.

Dionelle hadn't spoken in so many years, and Spark was used to working in silences filled only by her own voice. Void Behind the Stars wondered for not the first time what the family would have looked like whole. What banter and arguments and brilliance had the world lost?

It was hard not to dwell on what three fireborn women working together could accomplish and all the good they could do. It would be simple for them to assist the dragons in storming Pasdale and liberating their kin. Rescuing the stolen eggs, like the one Void Behind the Stars missed so acutely.

Spark asked something she'd evidently expected an answer to because she repeated herself.

"Abyss? How much can you carry? Easily, I mean?"

Void Behind the Stars turned her head to face the girl where she stood between her wings.

"Void Behind the Stars."

Spark stopped staring at Void Behind the Stars' back and doing whatever mental calculations she'd been doing and stood up, blinking a lot and staring.

"I'm sorry, what?"

"That is my dragon name. You asked for it once."

"Oh." Spark continued to blink at her. "Would you like me to call you that instead?"

"Abyss is acceptable. A nickname."

Spark gave an amused snort, walking toward Void Behind the Stars' front. "Would you tell Ondias that?"

"Ondias has not asked."

Spark looked at her so fast she nearly slipped. "Wait, gossip queen and control freak Ondias, greatest dragon scholar of all time, has never asked you your name?"

"Scholars believe our names are sacred, not to be shared."

"Wait, are they?" Spark's eyes widened the way they had after she'd asked about mining the Red Mountains.

"No. Humans never ask."

Spark narrowed her eyes. "You could just tell her."

"Then what secrets would we keep?"

Spark laughed and tossed a playful fireball at Void Behind the Stars' face before undoing the buckles and clasps on the rigging, freeing Void Behind the Stars from her duty for the moment, though preparations never truly ceased. Battle would find them soon.

ACKNOWLEDGEMENTS

It's a little weird trying to put together the acknowledgements for books in a series. Do I get repetitive and thank the same people this time as last (because everyone who helped make Dragon Whisperer and Trueflame a reality also played a role in Fireborn getting out into the world). Once again, hat tip to my spouse and kid, my writer pals in KW Writers Alliance, Write Club and By the Potted Plant, and to everyone who supported the Kickstarter. Thanks to my editors Kris and Una for helping make the words a little clearer and the story so much stronger.

But also, many thanks to Kelley Armstrong, who gives so much back to the SFF community. She's an absolute treasure. One of Kelley's talks inspired me to try to write a series in this world in the first place, and her feedback on this book's opening gave me a lot of much needed confidence in Spark and in my ability to tell her story. Kelley's feedback also helped me find a stronger place for this book to begin. And a final shoutout to everyone in Kelley's 2017 Thrills and Chills writing class. It was a wild week but workshopping with all of you helped me grow so much as a writer.

And thank you, dear reader, for coming along with me. I hope you'll stick around, because I'm just getting started.

ABOUT THE AUTHOR

photo by Mike Thode

Vanessa is a word sorceress and Nebula Award-winning fantasy author whose life seldom strays from the world of books, especially during winter hibernation. Even her volunteer work revolves around the literary world, currently as co-founder and events director of KW Writers Alliance and as coordinator for the SFWA volunteer team.

When she's not being bookish, she's into astronomy, hiking, gardening, and has a personal goal to visit all the national parks. Don't ask her about her love of trees unless you've got some time. She loves Halloween and hates to be cold. Vanessa lives in Waterloo (no, the other one) with her spouse, daughter, and dogs, where she can be found in her butterfly garden, achieving her final form as a garden witch.

To learn more, visit thodestool.ca or follow her on social media @VRicciThode

www.ingramcontent.com/pod-product-compliance
Lightning Source LLC
Chambersburg PA
CBHW051128190726
48290CB00006B/1746

9781738845040